"Let's get this part out of the way," she suggested. "You call me Naomi and I'll call you Casey. We can't pretend all this formality. Not after what we shared."

He stroked his chin as if considering her offer. "All right, Naomi."

"Drive safely."

She reached for her door.

"I'm not going anywhere."

"Why? I have a security detail. Is it really necessary to have two right outside my door?"

He considered the deputy in the cruiser then turned back to her. "I don't really care for motels. I'm more at home in my SUV. I'll be fine."

He started down the steps.

"No."

He looked back. "No?"

She shook her head. "You don't have anyone to relieve you. You can stay on my couch. Get some sleep, like you said. If anyone tries to get to me, you'll be right there *on the couch*."

"As long as you're okay with the arrangement, ma'am."

"Naomi," she reminded him as she unlocked and opened the door.

"Naomi," he amended.

THE BONE ROOM

USA TODAY Bestselling Author
DEBRA WEBB

HARLEQUIN
INTRIGUE

This book is dedicated to my readers! I adore you! Thank you
for following the journey of my characters through nearly eighty
Harlequin Intrigue novels!

ISBN-13: 978-1-335-48914-2

Recycling programs
for this product may
not exist in your area.

The Bone Room

Copyright © 2021 by Debra Webb

This edition published by arrangement with Harlequin Books S.A.

For questions and comments about the quality of this book,
please contact us at CustomerService@Harlequin.com.

Harlequin Enterprises ULC
22 Adelaide St. West, 40th Floor
Toronto, Ontario M5H 4E3, Canada
www.Harlequin.com

Printed in U.S.A.

Debra Webb is the award-winning *USA TODAY* bestselling author of more than one hundred novels, including those in reader-favorite series Faces of Evil, the Colby Agency and Shades of Death. With more than four million books sold in numerous languages and countries, Debra has a love of storytelling that goes back to her childhood on a farm in Alabama. Visit Debra at debrawebb.com.

Books by Debra Webb

Harlequin Intrigue

A Winchester, Tennessee Thriller

In Self Defense
The Dark Woods
The Stranger Next Door
The Safest Lies
Witness Protection Widow
Before He Vanished
The Bone Room

Colby Agency: Sexi-ER

Finding the Edge
Sin and Bone
Body of Evidence

Faces of Evil

Dark Whispers
Still Waters

Visit the Author Profile page at Harlequin.com.

CAST OF CHARACTERS

Naomi Honea—She left the hills of Tennessee to pursue her dream in Hollywood. When her father passed away and she returned home to take care of the family farm, she never expected to end up playing the most important role of her life.

Special Agent Casey Duncan—Casey's never forgotten the young girl who stole his heart almost twenty years ago. He can't allow his memories of her to get in the way of a homicide investigation with multiple victims.

Arlene Beck—She's been the trusted agronomist for Honea Organic Farms for more than two decades, but when bodies start turning up, she's suddenly missing.

Elmer Cotton—Though he seems like a harmless hermit, he's hiding something more than the motive for his most recent conspiracy theory.

Donnie Brooks—He's Naomi's uncle but can't seem to remember any truly useful information.

Rowan Dupont Brannigan—Also known as the undertaker's daughter, Rowan is now the county coroner.

Chapter One

Thirty.

Thirty.

It sounded old.

She looked old.

Naomi Honea stared at her reflection and grimaced at the beginnings of crow's-feet around her eyes.

"Too much time in the sun without a hat," she muttered. She knew better. It was the curse of pale skin.

It was true. But there was nothing she could do to prevent spending time outdoors. She was a farmer now, after all. Just like her dad. At least she had been for the past year. She reached up and bundled her wild red hair into a sleek ponytail, then looped a band around it. Had the calluses on her hands like he'd had, as well. She searched the blue eyes she had gotten from her mom—the eyes, the hair and the freckled pale skin she'd inherited from the woman who had taught her about being strong and stubborn and utterly independent.

Naomi sighed and turned away from the mirror.

It was her birthday. The first one she'd spent entirely alone.

That was the thing about being an only child. When the parents were gone, there was no one else.

Well, there was her mother's brother, Donnie, but he wasn't exactly known for keeping in touch. At seventy, he still considered himself a sort of playboy. She could count on seeing him at funerals and the occasional holiday. But hearing from him on her birthday? Highly unlikely.

It wasn't entirely his fault. She'd been gone for all of a decade. He and everyone else she'd once known around town had gone on with their lives. Her reappearance was scarcely a blip on their radar.

She walked into the kitchen in search of her boots. Found them by the back door. The neighbors and a few of her old school friends made an effort in the beginning when she first moved back. But everyone was busy these days. Besides, she really didn't *know* anyone her age around town anymore. Plenty of acquaintances but no true friends. Too much time and distance. No fault but her own. Her mother had warned her about scurrying off to California to follow her dreams.

You'll be all alone, Naomi. You won't know a soul.

Until her nineteenth birthday she'd never been farther out of the state of Tennessee than LA—lower Alabama. Growing up her family had taken vacations to Gulf Shores, Alabama. At the ripe old age of eleven she'd met a boy on their annual trip to the beach who turned her world upside down. He wasn't just any boy, mind you. A boy from the *real* LA. His mother was the lead in a movie being filmed in Fair Hope. Naomi had soaked up his every word about living in California and having an actress for a mom. She'd even been allowed to visit the set and watch a scene filmed—four different times. Who knew that acting was such difficult work? The actors carried out a scene over and over until the director was happy. Her new friend's mother said that some directors simply could not be pleased. Many years later, Naomi learned this firsthand. The hard way. The acting gig was not the romanticized life she'd grown up believing it would be. It turned out to be terrifying and frustrating and unforgiving. But when things occasionally went right, there was immense joy and fierce satisfaction. Like the high of an intensely addictive drug, the wannabes struggled over and over to find and hang on to that moment again.

For several months after that sultry couple of weeks on the sand when she was eleven, this incredibly interesting boy and she wrote to each other. Eventually he'd lost interest and the emails had stopped coming. Or maybe he had moved. Who knew? Regardless, she had been smitten with the life he had described so vividly. The life she had witnessed ever so briefly that one summer. She could hardly wait for the years to pass. Living in Winchester was the most boring thing in the world, and she wished the time away.

She was going to be an actress and live in LA and maybe find her old pen pal and live happily ever after.

Well, she had lived in LA rightly enough. After a brief attempt to be a good daughter and go to college first, she'd dropped out—to her parents' dismay—and driven away from home in her ancient convertible (the one she'd inherited from her daddy's sister after she passed). She'd found a room to rent over a garage and snagged a job as a stand-in dog walker and part-time waitress. Her story was cliché at best, but it was hers and she was determined to live it to the fullest. She'd spent the next ten years struggling to find her big break in the world of television and movies. There had been a good many commercials, even a few appearances on a reasonably popular sitcom and one dramedy. Enough to keep her hopes alive.

Six years into her adventure her mom had died suddenly. She'd come home for a month to help her dad. Not only had she learned that he'd been keeping her mom's terminal illness from her, he also begged her to stay, but she couldn't. At twenty-five she still believed that her dream could come true, and on some level she felt betrayed by him and her mom—both of whom had made the decision to hide the truth from her. It had taken some time, but she'd forgiven her dad. A brief visit here and there had mended the hurt and Naomi had thrown herself fully back into the struggling actor role. The rejections continued to far outweigh the callbacks. She was too Southern-sounding (despite having worked so hard to lose her Tennessee drawl). She was a redhead who refused to go blond. Too thin. Too this. Too that.

Then only four years later her dad had died. This time it was truly unexpected. No one had known his heart was failing him. By that time her dream had dimmed, and the loss of her dad had finished breaking her heart. She'd come home to prepare her parents' beloved organic farm to be sold, but somehow, she hadn't been able to bring herself to follow through.

This was the home where she'd grown up. The house where she'd been born, since her mom had waited too late to say she thought the baby was coming. Naomi had gone to school in Winchester, had her first taste of acting in a middle school play and lost her virginity in the back seat of the class president's car during a high school football game.

For all its ordinariness, this *was* home.

Her parents had poured their lives into this farm and she owed it to them to carry on that legacy. Owed it to herself, too. After ten years of struggle it was fairly clear that she wasn't actress material. She simply didn't have that special something the casting directors were looking for.

But she had no regrets for trying.

As her grandmother once told her: if she hadn't gone after her dream, she would still be wanting to.

Maybe this was her way of hiding from failure. That wasn't true. But she hadn't exactly come home with her tail between her legs. She'd survived in Hollywood. Paid the rent and other necessities. So she hadn't exactly failed, she just hadn't soared as she had hoped.

Not the end of the world, just the end of that goal. Now she had a new goal. Take this organic farm to the next level.

She pulled on her boots and walked out the back door to start her morning chores. Now she was more popular than she'd ever been back in high school or in Hollywood, for that matter. With the help of Arlene Beck, the agronomist, who had begun working with her parents before Naomi was born, the two of them had turned the struggling farm into a thriving enterprise. The CSA—community supported agriculture—deliveries had boomed. They made deliveries all over the county and many more folks had signed up for next year. Watching the growth was exhilarating. It wasn't like the high of acting but it was amazing in its own way.

If the growth continued Naomi would need to hire more full-time hands. The two full-time employees along with the part-timers she employed now would never be enough at this rate of expansion. Her parents would be thrilled. She certainly was. It was the oddest thing. She'd wanted so badly to be far away from Winchester and now she was so grateful to be back and to carry on with the dream her parents had worked so hard to do.

It was far more satisfying than she'd expected. Her only regret was that it had taken her so long to see that ultimately this was where she belonged. She'd missed the final years of her parents' lives and that made her sad when she allowed herself to dwell on the thought.

The work was physically demanding but it was unexpectedly fulfilling. Now she understood what her mother loved so about the soil. While Naomi was growing up her dad had tried charming her with the planting of seeds and nurturing of the tiny sprouts. But she'd only had eyes for the stars. Back then she hadn't been afraid of anything. She'd wandered all over this farm alone, daydreaming.

There was little time for daydreaming these days.

The air was cool this morning. She shivered, wishing she'd pulled on her sweater. The rain had kept them out of the fields for the past four days. As soon as the soil had dried out enough it would be time to get back to work. There was a good bit to be done this time of year. They'd finished a second greenhouse for growing the salad mixes folks typically picked up at the supermarket this late in the year. In fact, the variety they offered was the envy of the local supermarkets. For now, they focused solely on selling to families who signed up for the program. In time, the goal was to open up a new revenue stream through local supermarkets. Keeping the product top-notch quality was the most important aspect of their forward momentum. Expansion and all else had to be secondary.

A cow lifted her head and watched as Naomi passed.

"Morning, Gertie." She couldn't help smiling. Naomi only had a few head of cattle so far. By spring she hoped to offer designer cheeses as part of their biweekly delivery. She passed the goat pen. As the herd grew that pen would need to be expanded. The goats and the cows kept her on her toes. But it was the chickens that soothed her soul. Honea Farm was very close to needing a second chicken house. One small local restaurant, the Good Earth, was already buying eggs from the farm.

The CSA subscribers loved the fresh eggs. She'd decided to move forward with the second chicken house over the winter when certain other work was slower. Sean Riley and Joe Jones, her only two year-round, full-time employees, would do much of the construction on the new chicken house. The concrete work and metal roofing would be subbed out.

By spring she hoped to be ready to add to the flock. She already had her eye on new Rhode Island Reds, leghorns and Sussex chickens. When she really thought about it, it was strange how she'd moved so far beyond the glitz and glitter of the west coast world. The best laying hens and spring planting were her primary obsessions now. She headed for the place she and Arlene called "the lab." It was where Arlene performed all her soil and plant testing with new foods and organic fertilizers.

Besides the lab, there were two barns, a hay shed and her dad's old workshop. She hadn't been in the workshop in ages. The last time she'd walked in she'd inhaled the scent of wood and oils, grease and gasoline. It had reminded her so much of him that it literally hurt. Her right boot suddenly sank into the mud.

"Well, hell." She made a face at the sucking sound as she pulled her boot free of the dirt. This is what she got for journeying into the past rather than paying attention to where she was stepping. She swiped her boot, one side, then the other, against the nearest fence post.

With the worst of the clumped soil gone, she unlocked the door and walked in. A flip of a switch had light filling the dark space. The smell of organic fertilizer concoctions and clean soil made her smile. Arlene was quite the chef when it came to creating organic enhancements for the crops. Naomi's mom had spoken of Arlene as if she were a goddess of science. Naomi's dad had, as well. The three of them had been more like a family than coworkers. The farm had gone through some rough times after Naomi's mother passed away. She wasn't sure of all the details as to how things went so far downhill, but Arlene had been instrumental in helping Naomi's dad pull it back together and into forward momentum once more.

In the lab, Arlene had a setup not unlike a high school chemistry lab. She gathered organic materials from all over the country—occasionally the world—to create the finest foods (aka fertilizer) for their plants. She also worked hand in hand with the veterinarian to ensure the animals received no hormones or other unnecessary substances. She truly was a bit of a magician in all things natural.

In truth Naomi felt a bit guilty for invading Arlene's territory without her this morning. This really was the older woman's domain and she was more than a little territorial, but Naomi needed the invoices for yesterday's delivery. Generally, Arlene dropped off the invoices on her way home each evening. But she hadn't last night and Naomi hadn't heard from her this morning. At any given time there was far too much going on to allow the paperwork to get behind. Naomi stayed on top of it. The others called her overly picky, but she had her way and they had theirs. Truth was, the lack of control she'd had over anything during her California days had kind of turned her into a bit of a control freak. She was working on relaxing and going with the flow. Easier said than done.

She surveyed the tabletops and file cabinets. No invoices.

As she circled the room once more the small flashing red light on one of the freezers snagged her attention. She frowned as she moved closer and leaned down to check the temperature status on the control panel. Forty degrees Fahrenheit.

Her frown deepened. The temp was too high. Had Arlene somehow bumped the panel and caused the discrepancy? Naomi tapped the necessary keys until she'd lowered the desired temperature to a more appropriate setting. Since she couldn't be sure how long the temperature had been that way, she opted to open the lid and check the contents. Again, this was Arlene's territory and she hated to invade but this was necessary. If there were items already thawed, to refreeze them would not be a good thing.

One touch of the first package she encountered,

and Naomi knew they were in trouble. It wasn't that the item was completely thawed but it was far softer than it should be.

Not good.

She needed to call Arlene and hurry her up. If there was anything in this freezer of particular importance there could be a serious issue. A bag, not a plastic garbage bag—something cloth—drew her attention deeper into the stack of frozen items. She tugged it from the mass, pressed one of the lumps in the bag and felt a little squish.

Definitely not good.

How in the world had this happened?

She opened the drawstring on the bag she now recognized as muslin and peered inside. What appeared to be the tip of a nose…definitely nostrils… dragged her attention to one package in particular.

She shook her head and looked again, expecting to find a mask left in the freezer to freak her out. Arlene was quite the prankster when the mood struck. Halloween was coming up. She probably had plans to give Sean or Joe a little payback for all the times they had pulled one on her.

"Arlene, you are one sneaky old lady."

In truth, the woman's sense of humor kept things from ever being boring around here. Winchester was a small, quiet town. Peaceful. Trouble rarely happened. Before Naomi came back there was a bit of a stir with the undertaker's daughter. Her dad had told her about Rowan DuPont Brannigan and the bizarre goings-on at the local funeral home. But that trouble was a rarity. Not much happened around Winchester. Weddings and funerals were the biggest social events besides church on Sundays.

Naomi reached for the package containing what appeared to be a nose. If this was Arlene's or maybe Sean's or Joe's idea of a joke, all she could say was payback was a devil.

Like the first package she touched, this one was slightly soft. She studied the fake nose that was actually part of a fake face. A mask. With Halloween coming up maybe Arlene was making something creepy for a friend. Seemed a little odd since Arlene was like Naomi. She didn't do a lot of socializing.

Naomi stilled. Damn. This mask certainly looked realistic. A shudder quaked through her and she sat the bag on the counter behind her to study it more closely under the light. Blood pounded in her ears as her pulse rate picked up. Naomi couldn't be sure what drove her at that point—perhaps some instinct hovering way down, deep inside. Whatever it was, it compelled her to turn back to the freezer. She dug beyond the packages scattered around the top of the pile.

Ear.

Her stomach clenched as her brain assimilated what her eyes saw. Ear. *Two* ears. Her hand shook as she reached for the clear plastic bag. The same sort of bag her mom might have placed ears of corn in for stocking the freezer. Only this was certainly not corn. Another poke into the pile of packages revealed a wad of dark…something. *Hair*, she realized as she clutched the clear plastic bag.

Wait. Wait. Wait.

Her heart pounded harder and the air seemed to trap inside her chest.

This wasn't some mask to be used for a prank. This was…

No. No. Impossible.

Even as she shook her head at her own thoughts and warned herself the idea was totally crazy, she started to dig once more. *Skin.*

Hand skin…it looked as if it had been peeled from the bone like a natural glove.

Fingers trembling, Naomi reached into her back pocket and tugged out her phone. Whatever this was, it was time to call the sheriff.

Sheriff Colton Tanner needed to see this…whatever it was.

"Arlene," she muttered, "if this is some sort of joke…"

Every instinct Naomi possessed warned that this was not a joke.

It was the start of a nightmare.

Chapter Two

Honea Farm, 11:00 a.m.

Sheriff Colt Tanner and several of his deputies were scattered over the farm. Two of Winchester's new forensics technicians were going through the farm's lab. The sheriff had confirmed Naomi's potential nightmare.

The remains were human. Real human. Not silicone masks. Not a Halloween prank.

Naomi reminded herself to breathe. She grabbed hold of the nearest fence post and steadied herself. There was a dead person in her freezer. Or at least part of a dead person.

Holy moly, as her dad would have said. How the devil did this happen? Arlene, Sean and Joe were the only people who had access to the lab. Besides Naomi, of course. There was no sign of a break-in. She shook off the silly thought. Who would break in and leave human remains?

Sheriff Tanner had asked her to wait outside the fenced area that surrounded the lab. She didn't mind. The more distance between her and the remains, the better. She'd called Arlene's cell phone three times, but the call had gone to voice mail on each attempt. Maybe Arlene was on her way and had forgotten her cell. She could have been in an accident. A heart attack? She was seventy-two or -three.

"Stop it," Naomi muttered. She was making herself crazy.

"Naomi."

She shifted her attention to the man striding her way. "Did you find anything else?"

Sheriff Tanner was the quintessential cowboy—boots, hat and all. He stopped a few feet away, propped his hands on his hips and glanced around as if he was unsure where to begin with what he had to say. Not a good sign.

"Any luck reaching Ms. Beck?" he asked.

"My calls keep going to voice mail. I'm hoping she'll show up anytime." This was so unlike her. Arlene was as dependable as the sun rising in the morning. Naomi's parents had always complimented the woman's loyalty and dependability. Not showing up or calling was very much out of character.

The sheriff's brow furrowed with concern. "How many employees you have this time of year?"

"Just two. Sean Riley and Joe Jones. They both

have the day off today. The only person who was supposed to come in today was Arlene." Naomi stared pensively at the long drive that wound through the front fields connecting the road to the house. Having Arlene show up and explain everything away would be so good about now.

"Well, I'll send one of my deputies out to her house to see if she's had any trouble this morning. Maybe she broke down somewhere between her house and here. She drives that old VW Bus and the thing has been on its last legs for a while now."

"I appreciate that." Naomi had thought of going but she wasn't sure of the protocol. Was she supposed to stay put during this search? It was official police business. He was right: that old Bus of Arlene's was like something from the flower-child days. Although the era was right for Arlene's age, Naomi couldn't see her as the hippie flower-child type. Then again she had seen a photo of her mom and dad looking like hippies. Not so odd considering her dad was a farmer but a little strange given that her mother had been somewhat of an uptight physician. She'd operated a clinic in town until just before her death.

"Why don't you see if you can get Sean and Joe to come in? Don't mention the reason. If either one of them knows anything about those remains, I don't want him taking off or developing a cover story."

Naomi nodded, then shook her head. "I will, but

I really can't imagine either of them doing something like this." It was totally over the top. She'd known these two men for years. They had worked for her dad.

"I agree," Sheriff Tanner said, "but one of them may have allowed someone not employed at the farm to use the freezer. Maybe one or the other stored something for a friend. Probably had no idea what was in the bags."

Made a sort of sense, she supposed. "Okay. I'll call them." She tugged her phone from her hip pocket.

"Meanwhile," Sheriff Tanner went on, "I've put in a call to Dr. Brannigan. She's coming by to help us out."

Dr. Brannigan was Rowan DuPont Brannigan. Everyone knew the undertaker's daughter. She was also the county coroner. "Thank you."

Naomi wasn't sure what she was supposed to say but "thank you" seemed adequate.

"You don't have to wait around out here," he offered. "If you have something else to do, feel free to do whatever it is. We'll be here for a while."

If she went to the house, she would only walk the floors. She might as well stand around and keep an eye on how this situation unfolded. The idea that she might still make it in Hollywood with a film about an organic farmer who skinned people and froze their body parts almost made her laugh out loud.

She was delirious. Obviously.

"I'm fine," she said, forcing a stiff smile. "I don't think I could wait inside knowing all this was going on out here."

He nodded. "I understand." The sound of a car engine drew his attention toward the long drive. "We'll see what Dr. Brannigan has to say."

Rowan DuPont Brannigan was a gorgeous woman. Tall, thin, with blond hair. She was also smart. A psychologist, she had worked with Nashville's Metro Police Department for years before returning to take over the family funeral home after her father's death. Nowadays someone else ran the funeral home and Rowan served as the county coroner. Made sense. She had quite the reputation in solving crime and she certainly had a firm grasp on the ins and outs of the dead. In addition, she was married to Chief of Police William "Billie" Brannigan. Even though he was more than a decade older than her, Naomi remembered him from her high school days. Billie was a local hero. Hometown boy made good. Everybody loved Billie Brannigan.

"Good morning, Sheriff," Rowan said as she approached. She turned to Naomi. "Ms. Honea."

Naomi nodded. "I hope you can figure out our mystery. I'm completely at a loss."

Dr. Brannigan smiled. "I can promise you this—if I cannot, I will call in someone who can."

The woman's confidence made Naomi feel far better.

Sheriff Tanner and Dr. Brannigan headed for the lab and Naomi made the calls to Sean and Joe. Keeping the events of the morning to herself wasn't easy. Both men liked their time off, and since they'd had to work all weekend, the call wasn't one either had wanted to receive. While Naomi waited for the guys to arrive, she watched the deputies move about the area, checking for any little thing out of place. Footprints, etc. They would find plenty of hers where she'd stepped in the mud.

Unable to wait any longer, she walked to the house and used the bathroom. Brushed her teeth to rid her mouth of the taste of stale coffee. It was lunchtime and food had been the last thing on her mind. A cold glass of water settled her stomach and helped her feel slightly more steady.

Human.

There were human remains in the freezer on her property.

How in the world had this happened?

She watched for Sean's and Joe's arrivals as she sipped her water. These were people she had known for years. Good grief, her parents had known Arlene for decades! There had to be some reasonable explanation. Human remains hadn't just appeared in that bag in the freezer. Someone had put them there and, unless Dr. Brannigan said differently, they were real.

Who was she kidding?

They were real. *This* was real.

Naomi tried Arlene's number again. Same as before. Voice mail. "Arlene, please call me as soon as you get this message. It's really important."

Sliding her phone back into her pocket she spotted Sean's blue pickup sailing down the drive. Joe's white truck followed close on his tail.

Maybe one of them would be able to provide some insight into this insanity. Naomi started for the door, but Sheriff Tanner was already approaching the guys. She might as well hang back and let him give the news. It wasn't something she was looking forward to doing herself.

She should probably make a fresh pot of coffee. Distracted by the stunning find on her property she hadn't thought to offer water or coffee to the sheriff and his deputies. She had to get her head back on straight. Preparing coffee was the least she could do.

Ten minutes later with the carafe in one hand and a stack of disposable coffee cups in the other, she walked outside and caught up with the deputies one at a time. She thanked each one and was just pouring the last cup when Sheriff Tanner waved her over to the lab.

"I just ran out of coffee," she said when she

reached the door where the sheriff waited. "I can make another pot."

"That's a good idea," he said, to her surprise. "I'll give you a hand."

"Sure." He ushered her to the back door of her house rather than into the lab, which was yet another surprise. She wasn't sure whether to be worried about what he'd learned from Sean and Joe or if there was some other more horrifying update about this morning's find.

"Takes just a few minutes," she said as she prepared the grounds and refilled the water reservoir.

Sheriff Tanner removed his hat and sat down at her table. "Naomi, my deputy couldn't get anyone to the door at Arlene's house. Her vehicle is in the driveway so I gave him the go-ahead to use force to get inside. At this point we have to assume there's something wrong."

Naomi's chest tightened. No. No. No. She'd lost both her parents in the past few years. She didn't want to lose anyone else. In spite of the worry choking her she managed to give a nod. "Of course. I understand."

"Arlene was not at home, and based on what she's found so far, Dr. Brannigan believes we're looking at the remains of possibly three people."

The news slammed into Naomi like a load of bricks falling from the sky. "Three people?" She squeezed her eyes shut and shook her head. "How in the world?"

"Sean and Joe seem to be as surprised by all this as you." He shrugged. "For now, I'm reasonably confident they're telling the truth."

Of course they were. Which left Arlene.

"Why would Arlene do something like this?" The concept made no sense whatsoever. The woman was kind, caring. A little quirky. She wouldn't hurt a fly much less a person. It just wasn't possible.

"Both Sean and Joe said basically the same thing."

At least she wasn't the only one who hadn't noticed anything off. Surely one of them would have picked up on something off-kilter.

"Have you found…" How did she say this? "The rest of the parts?"

"No bones. No organs. Just…tissue."

"So the flesh and…muscle were literally filleted from the bone."

"It looks that way."

Deep breath. "I think the coffee's ready." She walked slowly to the coffeepot, struggling to maintain her composure. Someone had filleted three people and left the remains on her property.

Who were these people?

Who in the world—her world—would have done such a thing?

For the love of God, she was almost always here. Right here on the farm. How had this happened?

She managed to pour the sheriff a cup without spilling it. "Cream or sugar?"

"Black is fine."

She carried the mug to the table and placed it in front of him. "Can you use fingerprints or DNA to identify the…the victims?"

"We're going to try. Even if we're successful it might take some time."

Her head was swimming with possibilities. "Surely they've been reported missing?" With ubiquitous devices, people noticed when a friend or family member disappeared. Even those separated by geography stayed in touch via cell phone or social media.

But that wasn't always the case. There were people who had no family. Homeless folks. The ones society often ignored.

Her hand went to her stomach as acid burned there. "What else can I do?" She felt totally helpless under the circumstances.

"Right now," he said, "you're doing all you can, and we appreciate your cooperation." He sipped his coffee.

What she would give to have her dad here to work this out. He had never been one to operate on emotion. Sadly, Naomi seemed to have inherited the propensity for emotional unsteadiness. Her mom had been sure it was from her own mother's side of the family. On the other hand, her dad had insisted it was his only sibling, sister Trina—the one who left Naomi the car.

"What happens next?" She had an awful, awful feeling that this was not going away any time soon.

There were parts of no less than three people out there—of course it wasn't going away quickly.

"I've put in a call to the FBI office in Nashville. They're going to send a team to have a look around. Their crime scene investigators have far more experience and far more state-of-the-art equipment. If there's anything to be found they'll find it."

The FBI.

The ability to breathe escaped her for a moment.

The sheriff held up a hand. "Don't get unnerved by the federal authority becoming involved. I know the agent they're sending, Casey Duncan. He's a good guy and he knows his stuff. The case will be in good hands with him."

"But why the FBI? Why not the Tennessee Bureau of Investigations?" Seemed far more logical to her but then she knew little about police work beyond what she saw on television shows and in movies.

"Considering we have three victims," he explained, "there's a possibility we're looking at a repeat offender."

He didn't say the words, but she knew what he meant. *Serial* killer.

The queasiness returned with a second wind. "Serial killer?"

He gave a noncommittal nod. "Possibly. This is nothing we want going public, but we have to consider all possibilities. Whatever happened here, it happened more than once to more than one person."

She managed to swallow back the bile rising in her throat. "Should I be concerned for my safety?"

"I can't say for sure at this stage, but I'd feel better assigning a security detail. Just as a precaution."

She nodded, the movement so stiff she felt her neck would snap if she so much as tilted.

"We've focused our attention on the building where the remains were discovered and the immediate area surrounding it. The FBI will want to search your home. Your office. Basically, everything on the property. It would be best for all concerned if you agreed to all their requests. A warrant would be easy to obtain under the circumstances."

"Of course. Whatever they need to do." She had no reason not to cooperate. No reason at all.

"Good. I'll pass that along to Duncan."

Duncan. The name sounded familiar, but she couldn't place it. "He'll be here today?"

"He will. Might be three or four later this afternoon or early evening, but he will be here today."

"Thank you."

The sooner they figured out what in the world had happened, the sooner life could get back to normal.

She pushed away the idea that *normal* might just be wishful thinking.

How did you move on from something like this?

They were talking about *murder*.

Chapter Three

From her kitchen window Naomi watched the man called Casey Duncan. There was something so familiar about him. About his name. She'd heard it before…maybe seen him before. And yet she couldn't place him.

Maybe she was mistaken.

He didn't look like she had imagined he would— for an FBI agent. No suit. No shiny black leather shoes. Nothing like the ones in the movies and crime shows. He wore jeans, a flannel shirt in blocks of tan and brown that matched his eyes. His blondish brown hair was a little longer than she'd expected, touching the collar of his lightweight leather jacket at the nape of his neck. The well-worn jacket covered the weapon she'd gotten a glimpse of strapped to his side via a shoulder holster.

The strangest part of all was the cowboy boots.

The boots were the preferred footwear of locals, but he was FBI from Nashville. Judging by his Southern drawl he was definitely born and raised somewhere in the south.

Sheriff Tanner had introduced him, and Duncan had given her a nod. Hardly anyone shook hands anymore with concerns of the virus after last year's pandemic making the moment whenever she met a new acquaintance feel awkward. Not following the urge to reach out in that familiar social exchange seemed wrong somehow. In this case, however, she was grateful for the societal change. Whatever it was about this man—and she couldn't quite pinpoint the origin of the feeling—it disquieted her on some level.

Two forensics technicians, also from the FBI, had arrived at the same time as Agent Duncan. Their vehicle, the expected black SUV, appeared to be loaded with the tools of their trade. She'd watched them go back and forth to and from the lab loaded with a number of cases.

Dr. Brannigan had left with a new arrival, who'd wheeled what looked like a massive cooler in and then out of the lab. Naomi suspected the remains were taken for further examination. To the coroner's office, probably. She was surprised the FBI hadn't wanted to take them to their own lab. She had no idea of the protocols. No one had updated her since

Agent Duncan's arrival. The sheriff had his hands full so she didn't actually feel slighted, just anxious.

Sean and Joe had been allowed to go home. They hadn't come to her door and spoken with her. Just left with their heads hung as if they'd been given a stern talking-to. Probably a forceful interrogation. Completely unnecessary in her opinion.

Naomi wasn't sure when her crew could return to work. At this point she wasn't sure of anything. Still no word from Arlene. The deputy who'd dropped by her house hadn't gotten an answer, so he'd gone inside. Nothing appeared amiss. She simply wasn't there. But her VW was in the driveway, which was odd. Arlene preferred driving her vintage VW Bus to riding with anyone else. Naomi had racked her brain trying to think of someone Arlene might have needed to visit or some emergency contact who may have heard from her, but really there was no one. Sean and Joe hadn't heard from her and had no idea who to contact, either. Arlene was a bit of a loner as far as they knew. If she had any relatives, local or otherwise, Naomi certainly wasn't aware.

Naomi pressed her fisted fingers to her lips. This wasn't right. Arlene wouldn't just disappear like this. Naomi kept expecting to wake up from a nightmare. For the dozenth time she asked herself how this could have happened.

The answer was the same: she had no clue.

The fact that Arlene was MIA was surely a co-incidence. Maybe Naomi should go to her house and have another look around. Knowing Arlene as she did, Naomi might notice something the deputy hadn't.

She grabbed her keys and was turning for the door when a light knock stopped her in her tracks.

She moved closer and peeked beyond the curtain. *Agent Duncan.*

She drew back. Maybe there was news. She tossed her keys on the counter, unlocked the door and opened it. "Have you found something else?" Her breath stalled in her lungs as she waited for more bad news while mentally crossing her fingers in hopes that things couldn't possibly get worse.

The whole idea still felt utterly surreal.

There were human remains on her property. She had been so shocked by the discovery she hadn't actually taken the time to evaluate what this meant or how far-reaching the effects might be.

Who would want to buy from an organic farm where human remains had been found?

Good grief. She held more tightly to the door to keep herself steady. This was so, so bad.

"May I come in?"

His voice was the one trait that didn't seem familiar. "Sure." She backed up and held the door open wider.

He walked inside—swaggered actually. He had

the kind of saunter that spoke of a cockiness only found in the male species. She closed the door. "Have a seat." She gestured to the kitchen table. "I'm anxious to hear whatever news you have." She sighed. Gave her head a little shake. "No, what I'm anxious about is for some explanation of how this…" She searched for the right word, but it eluded her. "This…"

"Homicide," he provided.

She flinched. Couldn't help herself. "Yes. How this all happened." No point arguing or denying the reality. People were dead. What else could it be called other than homicide?

"I don't have any concrete answers for you just yet," he explained.

He stood at the table but hadn't taken a seat. She suddenly realized he was waiting for her to do so first.

She pulled out a chair and sat. He followed suit.

"What do you have?" she asked, cautiously hopeful that there was at least some measure of forward movement. Some form of law enforcement had been combing the lab and the area around it all day. Surely they'd discovered some clue to explain how this… homicide happened.

She didn't know any killers.

Sean, Joe and Arlene were good people. Certainly not killers.

The niggling idea that Arlene remained out of

touch tugged at her, but Naomi ignored the ridiculous possibility. Arlene wouldn't hurt anyone or anything.

"I ran background checks on Riley, Jones and Beck." Agent Duncan removed a pocket-size notepad and flipped over a page. "Jones and Riley are clean."

Naomi could have told him as much. "I wouldn't have expected otherwise."

"And Beck," he said, "how long have you known her?"

A frown tugged at Naomi's brow. "Are you suggesting you found something in Arlene's background?" The very notion was ludicrous.

When he didn't immediately respond, she said, "She has worked on this farm for more than three decades. My parents considered her part of the family."

"I understand," he said, not taken aback the slightest by her statement. "Do you know where she lived before moving to Winchester?"

He'd completely ignored her question and moved right on to another one of his own. This annoyed her far too much. What was it about this guy that got under her skin? "I don't recall, but I'm sure my parents or Arlene spoke of her life before. I simply can't remember anything specific. Exactly what are you implying, Agent Duncan?"

He shook his head. "Nothing. I'm only wondering why we can't find anything on a seventy-something-year-old woman beyond the time she has lived here, working for your family."

"There must be some mistake. Maybe Beck is a married name." Arlene had spoken of a brother. Where was it she mentioned having grown up? The answer just wouldn't surface through the fog of confusion revolving around today's events. Or maybe she hadn't mentioned her past at all. Naomi just couldn't say.

"I thought you'd like to take a ride with me to her home. Have a look around and see if you notice anything out of the ordinary."

The offer startled her. She'd just been thinking of doing exactly that. Only she'd intended to go alone. "Sheriff Tanner said she's not home."

"She wasn't when his deputy called on her and most likely she's not now. Tanner assigned a surveillance detail to her house and no vehicles have stopped by. No sign of Ms. Beck."

Naomi got it now. "You want me to go into her home when she's not there?" Naomi wasn't sure how comfortable she was with invading Arlene's privacy. This felt completely wrong. All of it. Crazy wrong.

"Ms. Honea," Agent Duncan said as he rested his forearms on the table and leaned in, putting him a little closer to her. "If whoever did this is somehow connected to or watching Ms. Beck, she could be in trouble. It's imperative that we do everything possible to find her and any connection she may have to this situation."

When he put it that way, Naomi couldn't exactly deny the logic.

"All right." Naomi stood, pushed in her chair. "But I warn you, you're barking up the wrong tree."

Beck Home, 5:20 p.m.

ARLENE'S HOME ON Pleasant Ridge was deep in the woods. A prepper's dream. The old cabin had a homey charm despite the No Trespassing and warning signs. The VW in the classic dove-blue color sat in the post-and-beam carport.

"Put these on."

Naomi turned to the driver, who offered her a pair of latex gloves. She'd kept her attention focused on the passing landscape on the drive over. He hadn't spoken and she hadn't, either. But the smell of his aftershave had made her very uncomfortable. It wasn't that the scent was overwhelming or unpleasant. In fact, it was so subtle she wondered if it was nothing more than him. Soap, maybe. Either way, it made her uneasy.

She took the gloves and tugged them on. He donned a pair, as well. When he opened his door, she did the same. Rather than go straight to the front door of the cabin, he stopped at the VW and tried the driver's side door. Locked.

He peered through the windows, moving from one to the next. Curiosity getting the better of her, Naomi mimicked his moves. Arlene's emergency bag was in the back floorboard. The older woman insisted that being prepared was the key to survival. In case of a breakdown of some sort, she carried bottled water, protein snacks, a blanket and some handy survival tools. Her shopping bags were in the back. She outright refused to touch a plastic or paper bag. Too wasteful, she insisted.

Naomi's mom had once said that Arlene was an old hippie. Until she was older, Naomi hadn't understood what her mom meant. Then she'd watched a documentary on Woodstock. Oh, yes, a hippie was right. Arlene wore the jeans and tees and had the long braided hair with the occasional flower tucked in when she felt the urge. Never mind that her hair had long since gone gray and that her weathered skin was now wrinkled, she wore the clothes and the confidence of her youth like a badge of honor.

"Anything jump out at you?"

Agent Duncan's voice made Naomi jump. She cursed herself and gave a shake of her head. "No."

She should pay closer attention rather than getting lost in thought.

"Let's have a look around inside her home and then we'll check the yard and outbuildings."

Naomi followed him up the steps and across the

porch. Arlene's rocking chair sat empty save for the hand-crocheted throw and a cotton pillow that were always there. The flowers in the scattering of pots looked healthy. No sign of neglect. Obviously the thriving plants had been watered recently. Arlene couldn't have gone far or for long.

The door opened without the knob being turned. The wood around the knob and lock was split from the deputy having had to enter the property by force. Naomi would need to have the damage repaired or, at the very least, the door secured until Arlene was back. Her home couldn't be left in this condition. Before following Agent Duncan inside Naomi glanced over her shoulder at the Franklin County cruiser stationed in the driveway. She supposed as long as the house was being watched securing the door wasn't a pressing need.

Inside the home appeared to be in order. Arlene's taste ran toward the very rustic. The walls were sawmill-grade wood. The one other time Naomi had been here the older woman had explained that the cabin had been built using salvaged wood from old barns. Inside, the floors and walls were created from the same vintage wood. The ceilings were vintage tin, complete with a little rust here and there.

There were only four rooms. Living room and kitchen were one big space. Two bedrooms with a single bathroom tucked into the corner of the larger

one. The second bedroom was set up as a home office. Agent Duncan lingered in that room sifting
through the contents of drawers and file cabinets.
Naomi wandered around the kitchen, checking inside
cabinets and drawers. There was yogurt and cheese
and a handful of grapes in the refrigerator. A mostly
empty carton of almond milk. She moved on to the
bedroom and looked around. Arlene wasn't one for
fancy clothes or jewelry. Jeans, tees and sweatshirts
were the mainstay of her wardrobe. Sneakers and
rubber boots were her chosen footwear. There was
one pair of well-worn sandals.

On the secondhand dresser was a single framed
photograph. Arlene was much younger in the photo.
Maybe late forties, early fifties. A man who appeared
to be several years younger held her in an affection-
ate embrace.

Her brother?

Naomi took the photo from the frame and checked
the back. As she'd expected there was a date but no
name as she'd hoped. Since she hadn't found anything else unexpected or suspicious, she took the
photo to Agent Duncan.

"This could be the brother I recall her mentioning."

He accepted the photo and studied it a moment.

"There's a date on the back but no name."

He turned over the photo and confirmed. Then he

snapped a pic of both sides with his cell and passed the photo back to her.

"Thanks," he said.

Naomi stood in the home office for a moment. The notes on the bulletin board about different fertilizer methods for the farm made her gut clench. For the first time since she found those remains in the freezer the possibility that something bad had happened to Arlene started to seep into her, tying her belly into knots and making her chest ache with worry.

"I think I'll have a look around outside," she said, desperately needing to get out of this house. Arlene's home. Away from this man who seemed to already know what Naomi still wanted to deny.

People had been murdered…dissected like biology specimens and stored on her farm—in the lab over which the missing Arlene ruled.

"I'll be right behind you."

Naomi managed a tight nod. She took the photo back to Arlene's room and placed it in the frame once more, hands shaking so hard she could barely accomplish the task.

Outside, she drew in a deep breath and reached for calm. What she needed more than anything was to keep her wits about her. This was not the time to come undone.

Arlene would be back soon and explain everything. Naomi was sure of it.

Pushing aside the fear that had her doubting that end, she took a peek in the well house. Nothing unexpected. There was an old smokehouse and a barn that had been a part of the original homeplace. Arlene had built her cabin on the same footprint as the previous home.

The smokehouse served as a toolshed. Naomi checked the bigger toolboxes. The sight of the chest-type freezer in the far back corner made her heart start to pound. She walked slowly in that direction. Naomi felt reasonably sure she would never be able to look at a chest-style freezer the same way ever again.

A strange laugh sputtered from her. This was exactly like being in one of those cheesy horror flicks she laughed at as a teenager. Then she'd ended up taking a part in one just for the movie credit. It was impossible to get a SAG card without those credits. Why in the world would she think of that at this bizarre moment?

Perhaps because of the sheer absurdity of this situation? Things like this didn't happen to her. She was a farmer now. In a small town where everyone knew everyone else.

"Where the hell are you, Arlene?"

Deep breath. She covered the final steps to the

freezer. Arlene would show up and there would be a perfectly logical explanation for all of this.

For a long moment Naomi stood very still, one hand on the lid. This freezer was an old one. Much older than the one at the lab. Made complete sense that Arlene would keep specimens here, as well. There was most likely all sorts of experimental plants and fertilizers around here. The woman loved her work.

Naomi moistened her lips and swallowed.

"Just do it," she muttered.

"Why don't you let me do that?"

She barely suppressed a yelp as her hands fell away from the lid. Naomi turned to Agent Duncan. "Thank you. Yes."

He moved up next to her and reached for the lid.

Naomi held her breath.

As he hefted the lid open, her gaze settled on the contents of the vintage freezer.

Gray…skin and hair.

Arlene.

The woman was clad in a long white flannel gown and curled in the fetal position.

A scream shattered the still silence.

Chapter Four

Naomi stared into the darkness beyond the living room window. The county cruiser sat in the driveway next to her vintage pickup. It had been her dad's truck. He'd had the Honea Farm logo painted on the doors. Naomi blinked. Arlene was dead.

Sheriff Tanner had insisted that a security detail was necessary just in case whoever murdered Arlene was still around and wasn't finished yet.

More murder. Body frozen. Naomi closed her eyes for a moment to block the horrible image. How could this be happening? Again she thought of that one horror flick in which she'd managed a small non-speaking part. Only this was real.

Arlene had been murdered. At least three other people had been, as well.

Naomi shuddered and pulled the curtains together, then hugged her arms around herself. Based on Dr.

Brannigan's preliminary exam, Arlene had been strangled and then stuffed into her own freezer. It must have been early when she was attacked since she had still been wearing her nightgown. If she'd been snatched from her bed, the killer had taken the time to make the bed.

What kind of killer made the bed?

Naomi had wanted to rush out of the house and wait in Agent Duncan's SUV until someone could take her home, but he'd insisted he needed her in the house with him. For her own protection. His request had made no sense at all. Primarily because she needed to be away from the horror of what she'd found. It wasn't until she'd collapsed in a kitchen chair at Arlene's small table for two that she'd grasped his reasoning for not allowing her to escape.

Whoever had murdered at least four people was out there somewhere. Maybe watching every step taken in the past twelve or so hours. Waiting for the opportunity to complete some other part of his demented plan. The idea felt surreal. Like a bad script that simply couldn't be salvaged.

Who would murder Arlene? It was true that she didn't have very many friends, but she had no enemies that Naomi knew of. She worked all the time. It was the story of farm life. You worked, you slept. If you were really lucky you made a living.

Eventually one of Sheriff Tanner's deputies had

brought Naomi home. She didn't recall his name. He was older and said that he knew her father. Not surprising. Everyone in town and around the county had known her parents. The move to organic had made the Honea farm the first of its kind in the area. Her mom's medical clinic had been highly respected and always busy. The deputy had assured her he would stay parked outside her home until the next shift took over. Somehow, she'd dredged up a smile and thanked him.

After walking the floors for a while, she had forced down a few crackers and a little water. Eating had been the last thing on her mind today. She turned away from the window and started pacing again. She'd done a lot of that today. If she kept moving, she wouldn't have to dwell on the shocking things she'd seen today. No matter, the haunting thoughts hovered at the edges of her mind.

Going to bed wasn't an option. There was no way she could sleep. No way she could stop the bizarre images from flashing through her mind.

Somehow the discoveries had leaked to the media. Another deputy was stationed at the end of her driveway keeping reporters off the property. She felt like a rare animal caged at a zoo. Everyone wanted a glimpse of the near extinct species trapped in its new habitat. She needed something to do until she heard from the sheriff or Agent Duncan again. Anything to keep her mind occupied.

She went to the study that had served as her parents' office. Amid the books on the wall of shelves were the family photo albums. She piled the albums on the floor and settled next to them. One by one she sifted through the decades of memories. Arlene had always been there in the background for as long as Naomi could remember. A blurred image in the backdrop or the one behind the camera.

Naomi frowned as she moved from photo to photo. Surely a clear image of the woman was in at least one photograph. Naomi remembered her being present at every birthday party…every holiday. She really hadn't liked having her picture taken, but she was in a great many.

One by one she flipped through the photo albums and found nothing. Not a single image where Arlene was looking directly at the camera. She was in plenty but never looking at the camera or in focus. How odd was that?

Quite, she decided, and for the first time since she discovered those remains this morning, Naomi understood that this, whatever it was, wouldn't be a simple case of mistaken identity or wrong place. This had something to do with Arlene. Maybe with her distant past. Naomi certainly couldn't think of one thing in her present life that would have made Arlene a target.

With the last album shoved back onto the shelf, she searched the bedroom her parents had shared. The idea was a ridiculous one but at this point she was beyond merely desperate.

According to Agent Duncan there was no documented history of Arlene's existence before she came to work for Naomi's parents. There had to be a mistake or some explanation. Her parents would never have hired anyone with a suspicious background, much less drawn that person into the family.

The bedroom search yielded exactly what Naomi had expected. Nothing.

She moved back to the study and prowled through the old files. Sean's and Joe's employment records as well as those of numerous other part-timers were all there but nothing on Arlene. Why had she never noticed this?

Because there had never been any reason to suspect, much less look for an anomaly. Omission actually. The only documentation related to Arlene Beck was a W-2 form. Naomi stared at the social security number and then the name.

"Who the hell were you?" she muttered.

Naomi closed the final file drawer and stood. She surveyed the room, her gaze roving over framed business licenses and milestones depicting her parents' journey from the purchase of the land to the official designation as an organic farm. Her mom's medical diploma and awards from various civic and community organizations.

Knocking on the front door drew her from the study. She glanced at the grandfather clock in the hall. Half past ten. Dread filled her belly. She'd just about had her fill of bad news today. At this hour, what else could she expect?

She made her way to the front door, took a breath and opened it.

Not surprisingly Agent Duncan stood on her porch.

He executed one of those single nods that men use so often to acknowledge someone or something. "Ms. Honea, I'm sorry to bother you so late."

Why not? Today had been one big, long bad day. "Come in."

He followed her inside, closing the door behind himself.

"Can I offer you something? Water? Coffee?" she asked. Personally, right about now she would prefer a stiff drink. And a vacation. She'd intended to take one this year. She'd been far too busy last year. But she and Arlene had gotten the books back in the black and the new aspects of the business in working order. The vacations would come later, she'd told herself.

She'd always wanted to go to Italy. Relax and enjoy for a couple of weeks. Nothing over the top. Just an out of the way villa in a quaint little town with lots of wine and books. Fat chance that would be happening anytime soon.

"No, thanks," he said, snatching her back from the fantasy that today's events had shattered. "Just a few moments of your time."

She nodded and gestured to the sofa. "All right. Sure."

They settled, her into the chair that had always been her mom's favorite and him on the sofa. She braced herself.

"Have you recalled anything else about Ms. Beck?"

"Nothing beyond what I've already told you." That wasn't entirely true, but she wasn't sure if what she'd noticed in the photo albums was relevant or just her imagination running away with her. It was late and she was mentally and physically exhausted.

He executed another of those nods that neither confirmed nor refuted his acceptance of her statement. Somehow this made her feel guilty of something. Maybe it was better to just tell him about the photographs whether it was relevant or not. She didn't like feeling deceptive on any level.

"I thought about how Arlene has always been a part of the family so I looked back through the family photo albums." She paused to gather her thoughts.

"She's just always been there. I never stopped to consider or to wonder why or how. But as I looked through the albums, I couldn't find a single photo of her that fully showed her face. She's either not in the frame, or her image is blurry or she's looking away. It's probably nothing but it feels strange." Like this entire day. There was always the chance she was reading too much into the notion. Could be nothing more than a touch of paranoia.

"Do you mind if I have a look?"

"Please do." She stood and led the way. No one wanted this mystery solved more than her. Even if the ending shattered all that she had thought she knew about the person closest to her parents.

Naomi lingered in the doorway while Agent Duncan reviewed the family albums. Using his phone, he snapped pics of several photographs. When he'd prepared to take the first one, he'd glanced up and asked if she minded. Of course she'd said she didn't mind. Saying she did wasn't exactly an option. A shaky breath filled her lungs and suddenly she felt more tired than she had since those first few months after her return to the farm…after her dad's death.

When he'd finished, Agent Duncan put the last of the albums back on the shelf. "Again, I realize it's late, but do you mind answering a question or two?"

Yes, it was late and she was exhausted but in the interest of getting this done she nodded. "Sure."

He was walking toward the door before she had
the presence of mind to back out of the way. She
headed for the living room and took her usual seat.
She should have made coffee whether he wanted any
or not. She had a feeling this was not going to be a
one-and-done sort of Q and A session. Some part of
her understood that simplicity had gone out the window hours ago. The situation happening here was
complicated and sordid and way, way over her head.

He settled on the sofa, making the white slip-
covered piece of furniture look far smaller. Naomi
placed her hands on the arms of the chair to prevent
clasping them in her lap in anticipation. She ordered
herself to relax. After this she was going to run a
very warm bath and soak while consuming the better part of a chilled bottle of white wine. She would
sleep tonight, she decided, one way or the other.

"You don't recall ever seeing or overhearing anything regarding Ms. Beck that concerned you in any
way? No comment by one of your parents that suggested some sort of concern?"

"No. Never." Hadn't she answered that question
before? Whatever had happened, her parents had
nothing to do with it. She needed to make that very
clear right now. The sheriff knew Naomi's parents.
This man did not. "My parents were above reproach,
Agent Duncan. I have no idea how this happened or

why, but I can guarantee you they were not involved
in any way."

Absolutely not. No way. No how.

When he remained silent for five or so seconds,
she asked, "Is it possible Arlene was in witness protection or something like that? Maybe that explains
the missing information about her and her apparent
need to avoid being photographed."

The idea certainly explained how she apparently
appeared in their lives out of nowhere since the agent
had already said she seemed to come into existence
when she began working on the farm. There had to
be a mistake or some explanation like witness protection—as far-fetched as that seemed. Arlene had been
in her late thirties when she began at Honea Farm.

Still, he said nothing. But he did study her.
Closely. This unnerved her completely. She shifted
in her chair. Forced her hands to stay put and not start
fidgeting. Told herself to relax. *Impossible.*

"I'm looking into the possibility," he finally said
in answer to her question—the one it felt like she'd
asked half an hour ago, though it had only been a
minute, maybe two.

"Good." It was the only answer that came to mind.

"Tell me about your parents."

He stated this with such a casualness, almost as if
he only wanted to fill the time and that the request
was not even relevant. Deep down Naomi recognized

this was no insouciant suggestion. This nontypical federal agent was feeling out scenarios. Searching for pieces that completed the puzzle he suspected as the most likely.

"My mother died five years ago. She was a medical doctor. The clinic closed after she became ill." Naomi smiled as she recalled how incredibly dedicated her mother had been to helping others. "In whatever spare time she had, she joined my father in his work on the farm. She felt strongly about what he was striving toward. She believed organic food is the best way to help the world take better care of itself. She started wellness sessions at her clinic and helped Arlene and my dad to develop the perfect crop plans for supporting the community with good, healthy foods. She was very passionate about helping others be healthier. She's the one who actually brought Arlene on board to help with the best ways to nurture the crops in a completely organic way. She firmly believed that totally organic was the way to go."

"And your father?"

"Bottom line? He wanted whatever made Mom happy. He wasn't quite so passionate about the organic path, but he would have done anything she wanted. He did feel strongly about not being wasteful and producing good food. He felt our throw-away, cancel culture goes against the natural order of things. He liked reusing and repurposing."

She couldn't help but smile as she thought of how her father would buy a certain candy bar whenever he was in town. If he and Naomi went to town together, there were always secret treats. *Don't tell Mommy,* he'd say. It was their little secret. He fully supported her mom's concept of healthy eating but he loved his Snickers bars.

Out of the blue a disturbing idea slid into her thoughts. *Was that the only secret her dad had kept?*

"Did your parents have out-of-town guests often?"

His question drew her from the worrisome thought. "No." She shook her head, then frowned. "When I was in high school there was an influx of visitors to the farm. I'm not sure where they came from or who they were. I probably wasn't interested enough to pay real attention. I think my dad mentioned something about the people being interested in how he and Mom had developed the farm. Something like that."

"Businessmen? Businesswomen? Suits? Casual wear?"

What in the world did it matter what the people wore? She shrugged. "I really don't recall."

"Casual wear, then," he suggested.

When her frown deepened, he added, "If there had been strangers visiting who wore suits or some other professional wear, you would have wondered about it. Maybe even asked. And you'd likely remember."

Made sense. "I guess so."

"Did you meet any of these people?"

She had to think about the answer for a moment. "I don't recall being introduced to any of them, but I did see some of the visitors. If it was the weekend or after school hours, I was generally here. I'm sure I met several."

"You may have heard one or more speak," he suggested.

She tried to recall an instance when she was home and overheard a conversation or walked into a meeting of some sort during that time. "I'm sure I did."

"But you don't recall," he pressed.

As if he'd given her a shake, a memory tumbled loose. "There was once when I overheard my dad talking about soil properties to this one man. I remember thinking that the way he talked reminded me of a friend from California I once knew. Not really an accent, more a nonaccent. TV talk. The nonspecific voice."

The usual nod. "California?"

Naomi couldn't pinpoint exactly what it was but something about Agent Duncan shifted just then. The way he looked at her…the sound of his voice. It was like a defense mechanism but not. Perhaps it was a guardedness that slipped into his bearing. She couldn't fathom why. Didn't try. She was way too tired.

"Yes, I met a boy on our annual vacation once. To Gulf Shores, on the coast in Alabama. He was from California. His mother was an actress." The memory relaxed some of her anxiety. Whoever Arlene Beck was and whatever had happened on this farm because of her, Naomi could truly say that her childhood had been a good one. A happy one.

Agent Duncan stood. "Thanks for your time. I'll keep you posted as we dig deeper into the case."

He was halfway to the door before she could make the transition from the past to the present. She shot to her feet and followed.

There were at least a dozen questions she wanted to ask but none would allow her to pull them out of the fog that suddenly swaddled her brain.

Door open, the man turned back to her and gave another of those nods. "Good night, Ms. Honea."

It was that moment, that single instant when his deep brown eyes collided with hers, that she felt the overwhelming sensation that she had met him or knew him somehow. Her mouth opened and, "Do I know you from somewhere?" popped out before her brain could override the reaction. Her cheeks turning warm with embarrassment, she stammered, "It—it feels like we've met before."

"I don't think so."

And then he was gone.

He was probably right. It was likely just one of those odd and unexpected feelings of familiarity.

But it sure felt real.

Chapter Five

"We have nothing," Assistant Special Agent in Charge Preston Wagner of the Nashville field office stated unconditionally.

Casey hadn't expected anything else. He'd hoped possibly there was information about Arlene Beck in some top-secret file to which he had no access. But that wasn't the case. Beck simply didn't exist anywhere on paper prior to her arrival in Winchester.

"Thanks, sir. I'll be in touch when I have more." Casey ended the conference call and surveyed the other two men at the table. Chief of Police William Brannigan and Sheriff Colt Tanner. Both appeared to have something on their minds, and it didn't take a psychic to figure out what.

"When something like this happens involving a well-known family," he offered, "it can sometimes be more than a little surprising. We all form opinions and have certain expectations for the people we know, especially those we know well."

The two local lawmen exchanged a look. Now he'd annoyed them. There was nothing for it. He had a job to do whether they liked what they were hearing or not. Whatever happened on the Honea farm, it was not accidental. It was murder. Likely it was somehow tied into something bigger.

"I've known the Honea family my whole life," Brannigan said. "Fine people. Whatever happened on that farm, it wasn't their doing. I'm confident."

This was the response Casey had expected. "I appreciate your confidence, Chief, but things are not always what they seem. This, unfortunately, is one of those times."

Since Chief Brannigan had about a decade on Casey age-wise and far more experience, he understood he'd likely failed to articulate this adequately. Brannigan had no doubt been faced with circumstances like this more than once. To suggest otherwise would be seen as an insult. But these were the sorts of investigations Casey worked every day. He imagined the two men rarely ran into a situation like this one.

Before Brannigan could respond, Tanner piped up. "We both know this family. There is no way—

no way—they were or are involved in criminal activity. You can take that to the bank."

"Agent Duncan," Brannigan said, his tone casual but his expression warned he didn't intend to budge on his stance. "I'm well aware that people can wear two faces, can be good and bad. But what you need to comprehend is the fact that Muriel and Nolan Honea were good people who supported their community. You'll be hard-pressed to find a soul in this county who didn't like them or have the utmost respect for them."

"We appreciate the need for us to keep open minds," Tanner offered to support what Brannigan was saying. "But understand that we expect you to tread lightly where Naomi is concerned. She's been through a lot the past year. You won't find a harder worker and more dedicated member of the community."

It was possible Tanner had a point. Casey didn't doubt his assessment. The question was whether either of these men could see beyond what they wanted to see. What they'd always seen. It was human nature. Think the best of those who've given you no reason to do otherwise. You see what your mind tells you to see.

"I want to share something with you." Casey opened the file folder lying on the desk in front of him and removed Honea Farm's bank statements for the past five years. "Have a look and tell me what you see."

While the two studied the statements, Casey considered Naomi Honea. He hadn't thought of her in years until he saw her in that offbeat horror flick. But it wasn't until the body lotion commercial that he was certain it was her. He'd spotted the half-moon-shaped birth mark on her left shoulder. Had to be her. How many blue-eyed redheads had a half-moon birthmark in exactly that spot on their left shoulder?

Not that many, he'd figured, so he'd done a little digging. This was early in his days with the Bureau. He'd just gone from flying a desk to fieldwork. Sure enough, he was right. The actress in the sexy body lotion commercial was Naomi Honea from Winchester, Tennessee.

Small world.

"Have you asked Naomi about these deposits?" Tanner asked.

Casey dragged his attention back to the present. "I intend to do that today."

"I can see how this looks suspicious," Brannigan admitted, "but there may be a perfectly reasonable explanation. He may have sold equipment or an acre of land here or there. Land prices have skyrocketed the past few years."

"Possibly," Casey agreed. Although in his experience, reasonable and logical weren't always the same thing. When a person was desperate, many things could be deemed reasonable. Logic rarely played into it. The survival instinct kicked in and all else was banished for the duration.

"I get the feeling," Tanner said, his gaze narrowing, "you're not being completely open with us. Seems like there may be more we should know."

Both were topnotch lawmen. He hadn't expected to pull anything over either man. "I've given you all I'm able to confirm." This was true. The rest of what he suspected was pure speculation. No need to stir that pot until something conclusive made it worth the trouble.

Brannigan leaned forward, braced his forearms on the conference table. "What parts have you not been able to confirm?"

This was where things got tricky. He really didn't want to go there just now but he might not have a choice. Tanner and Brannigan were accustomed to being in charge.

"I'm sure you've heard of the green burial concept." This wasn't really a question. Most people had at least heard of the method.

"My wife's father was an undertaker," Brannigan confirmed. "There's little in the field I haven't heard about."

"I'm vaguely aware of the concept," Tanner said.

"Green burials are an effort," Casey explained to ensure they were on the same page, "to eliminate as many chemicals as possible in the process of internment. Biodegradable products are used in the process. The end goal is to protect the environment. Bring life and death into balance, environmentally speaking."

"Last I checked," Brannigan said, "we don't have any cemeteries that meet the criteria in Franklin County."

"We have a *Green* cemetery," Tanner pointed out. "But not a green burial cemetery."

Casey had already checked and there were none in Franklin County. "Another method of dealing with the remains of the dead in a more environmentally friendly way is human composting."

He had their attention now. Both men sat a little straighter and peered a little more intently at him. "Also known as natural organic reductions. The first legal operations turn the remains of deceased loved ones into mulch or soil, to put it simply."

"I see where you're going with this," Brannigan said, his tone a warning. "I would encourage you to proceed with caution. I don't want this family's reputation damaged unnecessarily."

"You have my word, Chief," Casey assured him. "This is just one of my working theories based on what we've found so far."

"Maybe I'm not up to speed," Tanner said, "on the latest information but doesn't human composting include the bones? I haven't heard anything about the bones being separated from the rest of the body. Maybe I missed something."

No one appreciated a stranger coming to town and accusing a respected family of the latest craze in saving the earth. Casey got that but this scenario was at the top of his list. Maybe it was something else, but this was an option he intended to explore thoroughly.

"At this point, I have no working theory on that aspect of what we've found. The bones could be used in some other way or we just may not have found them yet. Whatever the case, the Bureau has tasked me with an in-depth search. Specialized equipment will be arriving later in the week. The Honea farm is a sizable one. Be aware this is going to take time."

"All right," Brannigan said, "we'll do all we can to support your efforts. Just keep in mind that we expect to be kept in the loop. *All* the way in."

Tanner offered a nod of agreement. "I'll keep one of my deputies on security detail at all times."

"I'll keep the media off your backs," Brannigan said.

"I appreciate the support, gentlemen." Casey gathered his file and stood. "We're good, then."

A few more minutes of conversation continued as they moved along the corridor toward the stairwell. Tanner agreed to have his chief deputy start interviews with friends of the Honea family. Brannigan and his wife, the coroner, would check through records to ensure all deaths over the past years were accounted for in terms of final arrangements. If any bodies couldn't be accounted for, they would go on a list for further investigation.

The remains found at Honea Farm had to come from somewhere. Could be local, could be from anywhere. But they had to start the search somewhere.

Honea Farm, 12:00 p.m.

CASEY HAD CHECKED in with his folks on the ground. Nothing new so far in the search. A call from Dr. Brannigan had given him an update on cause of death for Arlene Beck. *Homicide.* Not that he'd anticipated otherwise, but he'd been waiting for confirmation before interviewing Naomi again.

He climbed the steps to her porch and knocked on the front door. It opened instantly as if she'd been waiting on the other side. If she'd seen him arrive, she probably had been. She looked from him to the file folder he held and back. Uncertainty sparked in her blue eyes.

"You have a few minutes?" he asked.

Those blue eyes seemed to burn a hole into him. Judging by the dark circles beneath them she'd barely slept last night. She looked tired and resigned. And gorgeous. She'd always been a looker. Thirty really did look good on her. Yesterday had been her birthday and he'd wanted to say something, but he'd thought better of it. Hell, she didn't even remember him. She'd likely think he was a little off in the head for remembering her for all this time. Like he could forget. She'd damned sure made an impression that stuck with him. He'd fantasized about her way too often, especially after that body lotion commercial.

Unable to help himself, his gaze wandered to her shoulder. *Back off,* he warned. This was not the time to go stumbling down memory lane. He should have forgotten those memories long ago.

"Yes, of course," she said.

He followed her inside. She sounded tired, too. Frustrated and tired. Who wouldn't be? Her world had been turned upside down. Prior to just over a year ago, she had been away from Winchester for the better part of a decade. A lot could have happened back home on the farm during that time. A lot she didn't know about. Particularly after her mother's death. Her mother had appeared to be the one spearheading the operation to some extent. It was after her death that all the anomalies had started to show up.

Naomi sat in the same chair she chose every time and he lowered onto the couch. Over and over today he'd thought of last night when she'd asked him if they'd met before. He'd almost said yes. But muddying the waters at this point would be a mistake. Then again, it was possible she might trust him more if he told her. He'd play it by ear and wait for the right opportunity. Anything that impacted the investigation had to be handled with kid gloves.

"The coroner has listed Ms. Beck's death as a homicide. Cause of death was manual strangulation. Of course, that's just a preliminary. There's toxicology and such still to be done."

He allowed the news to sink in a moment before going on.

"As you can imagine," he continued, "this means we're looking for an active killer. One who perhaps needed to cover up something. Maybe someone who worked with Beck in some capacity."

Naomi cleared her throat delicately. "It sounds as if you've made up your mind about Arlene." She shrugged. "Maybe even my family and me."

There was an edge of anger in her voice. Nothing he hadn't expected. A shocking insanity had descended on her life. Before this was over she would experience a range of intense emotions. The survivors always did.

She wasn't a suspect in his opinion. Maybe that was a mistake but so be it.

For now.

"I don't believe you have anything to do with the remains you found or with Ms. Beck's death. Obviously, you wouldn't have called the authorities if you were somehow involved with the find in your freezer."

She blinked. Nodded. "At least there's that."

The tinge of anger lingered.

He placed the file folder on the coffee table between them and opened it, then he passed the bank statements to her. "Have a glance over these and tell me if you notice anything unusual."

She accepted the pages and with visible reluctance began a half-hearted perusal.

These weren't the full statements but the annual summary sheets of deposits and the subsequent balance after each for every month over the past five years. The report for five years ago showed little or no deposits. The balance from the previous year diminished quickly after that point. By midspring four years ago, the balance in the farm account was nearly gone. Then suddenly large deposits started to appear. The largest in more than a decade. His forensics accounting specialist was still reviewing records but what she had found so far couldn't be called anything other than suspicious.

He watched Naomi's face closely. The changing expressions that danced across her face told him she hadn't looked back as far as five years. Probably not beyond the past two. She'd come back just over a year ago to a hell of a mess and pulling it together had been top priority.

"Five years ago is when my mom died." She looked up from the pages. "It was a very difficult time. Obviously, Dad allowed the work to fall behind."

"If the work fell behind for better than a year, would he have been able to recover so quickly?"

Naomi righted the pages and offered them back to him. "It depends."

He resisted the impulse to ask on what. A miracle? Donations? He didn't have to ask. He already knew the answer. Sean Riley and Joe Jones had been employed by Mr. Honea for more than five years. Both had talked at length about how difficult things were for the year and a half surrounding Mrs. Honea's illness and death. Some weeks they'd only received half their pay. Others they weren't paid at all, but they hung in there to help the Honeas. Mr. Honea had made it right after things got better. Neither one could explain how things got better. Only that they did. New equipment, new plants, all sorts of new and improved items were brought to the farm.

"Your employees can't explain how the financial situation recovered."

"I wasn't here," she admitted, her voice sounding hollow. "I'm sure there was insurance money."

"No insurance." He'd already checked. Jones had explained the circumstances as a part of his statement regarding the "lean" years. He'd overheard the conversation between Beck and Naomi's father. "Ms. Beck loaned your father the money for your mother's final arrangements."

Shock claimed Naomi's face. "That can't be right. He would have told me." She stared at the pages lying on the coffee table. "He never said a word about things being so…difficult." Her gaze lifted to his once more. "The truth is he didn't tell me she was dying until she was gone. He said she wanted it that way."

Pain. The memory was still very painful. The people she loved and trusted the most had shut her out of something that may have landed them in deep trouble.

"Did he give you a reason why she didn't want you to know? The two of you were on good terms?"

"We were." She swiped at her eyes. "I had no idea she was ill. We talked every Sunday. To tell you the truth, when he died I still hadn't forgiven him for keeping the truth from me. Now I wish I had."

And there it was. Proof that her father could and would keep secrets from her. Her mother, too.

"Is it possible there were other things that were kept from you?"

"My dad wasn't a murderer," she snapped. She blinked back more tears. "My mom wasn't, either. I don't know how any of this happened, but I know— knew my parents. They would never harm anyone or anything."

Jones and Riley had said the same thing. The Honeas were above reproach. Except that the evidence said someone on this farm wasn't.

"Ms. Honea," he said, "our forensics technicians have found evidence of other remains on the farm."

"What?" She shook her head. "No. That can't be right."

"They've checked random locations on the property as well as various specimens Ms. Beck was working with in the lab."

"What the hell are you saying?" Naomi shot to her feet. "That can't be true. There must be a mistake."

"There's no mistake, Naomi."

Her attention arrowed to him, showing him the confusion and surprise in her eyes before she banished the reactions. "I'd like you to leave now. I need to think."

He pushed to his feet. "I really need your help. I'm not accusing you or your family of anything. I'm only trying to determine what happened here and who is responsible. Your parents may not have known exactly what was going on." He doubted this but he felt compelled to offer an out. He needed her to trust him.

She considered his words for a moment. "I can assure you they had no idea." She folded her arms over her chest. "You can make all the allegations you like but I am certain you will never be able to prove a single one."

"I'm not trying to prove anything, ma'am. I'm attempting to find the truth."

She flashed a fake smile but even the intensity of it jarred him. "It doesn't feel that way from here."

"I can imagine it's not a comfortable place to be," he offered, "but you are the one person who can speak for your mother and father. There's no one else. If you don't help me—for them—no one can."

Her angry face vanished, and hope glimmered in her eyes. "Tell me what I need to do to help."

"Work with me. Help me find something that will tell us what really happened here and who was responsible. There's always evidence. Always. It's just the finding it that can be an issue sometimes."

"I'll help you," she said. "Whatever you need me to do. I want the truth."

Unfortunately, what he needed her to do and what he wanted her to do were two entirely different things.

That problem was one he would have to work on. He never allowed personal feelings to interfere with an investigation. He wasn't going to start now.

Then again, maybe he already had.

Chapter Six

Naomi couldn't remember the last time she'd talked to her uncle Donnie. He had this habit of popping in and out of their lives, more out than in. When he showed up, he always had lots of adventures to share. He was the spotlight on the rare occasions he bothered to visit. But his mind remained as sharp as a tack and he loved talking about the past—especially his past. But he knew Naomi's mother better than anyone else. He had even helped out at the farm now and then ages ago.

She rang the bell and waited, hoping against hope he was home. Knowing her uncle he was out gallivanting around. That was what her mother always said. Donnie loved women. The problem was he couldn't love just one. Her mom would say he had the same problem with jobs. He never loved even one long enough to call it a career. Instead, he had floated around from one to the next, using his social security check as his main source of income. And the occasional donation from her mom—who'd sworn if he didn't do better she wouldn't help him the next time.

But she always did. Isn't that what mothers or rather sisters did?

To Naomi's surprise the door opened. Donnie wore ragged cutoff denim shorts and a sweatshirt, hood up. He'd kept his summer tan with the help of the ancient tanning bed he had in the second bedroom of this dinky apartment. Her mom had told her about the tanning bed. She'd laughed and said he refused to be pale like her. The O'Connor Scottish roots had given the three of them red hair, blue eyes and creamy pale skin. She smiled. Except that Uncle Donnie had spent so much time in the tanning bed that he looked perpetually sunburned. Redheads never tanned that nice golden brown the way other people did.

"Naomi!" He grabbed her for a hug, then drew back. "What brings you to my humble abode?"

He ushered her inside, closed the door and dropped the hood from his tangle of red hair. He obviously hadn't combed the thick mop today. This was something else they shared, very thick hair. Like a horse's mane, her mom had always said. Today Donnie's looked a little more horsey than usual.

Naomi sat on the sofa. Donnie dropped into a recliner that had apparently been his favorite for most of his adult life judging by the wear to the fabric and the indention in the padding that seemed to cradle him perfectly.

"Did you hear about Arlene?"

He scrunched up his face in a frown. "Arlene? No. I've been in a cleansing cycle. I'm not my best as you can see. I'm avoiding everyone and everything— except my favorite niece, of course—for two more days." His frown returned. "So what happened to Arlene? Don't tell me the old hag finally croaked."

Naomi winced. She knew he was kidding but he wouldn't find it funny when she told him. Donnie had loved sparring with Arlene. Naomi always thought he had a thing for her, but she always ignored him, which made him pretend to dislike her.

"She's dead. Murdered."

He leaned forward as if he wanted to ensure he was close enough to hear more clearly. "What did you say?"

"Dead. She's dead. Strangled and stuffed into her freezer."

He collapsed back into his chair. "Who in the world would want to kill Arlene?" He made a face, eyes shimmering with a new brightness. "Except for me on the rare occasion when she didn't tell Muriel or Nolan I'd called."

Her parents, Muriel and Nolan. Her chest ached.

"There's more. The remains of three people were found in the lab freezer."

He held up his hands. "Okay, wait a minute. You're blowing my mind here." He took a big breath, met her gaze and said, "Come at me again."

"Arlene is dead. Murdered. And the remains of at least three other people were found in the freezer at the lab. The FBI as well as the sheriff and the chief of police are investigating the farm. Me." Her hands went to her chest. "Mom and Dad. Everything. It's crazy…but, sadly, real."

She struggled to hold back the tears. Even after twenty-four hours and having discussed the situation repeatedly, it still felt shocking. Surreal. Like a nightmare that refused to end after she awakened.

"That's just ridiculous. My sister took an oath to help people. She wouldn't have hurt a fly, much less a person. And she loved everyone." He waved his arms magnanimously. "God knows Nolan couldn't possibly have hurt anyone. He was too kind for his own good. Trust me, I know. I took advantage of him way too many times when Muriel turned me down."

Naomi opted not to respond to the latter remark. "Do you remember when Arlene first came to Winchester? Where she lived before? Anything about her past before her life here?"

"I just remember coming back from a trip to Cancun with one of my old college buddies and there she was. She never liked me and I never liked her." He made a face. "God rest her soul."

"Why didn't you like each other?" Naomi knew the answer, but she might as well hear his side of things. She doubted it would make a difference.

"I had a thing for older women, and I guess I came on a little too strong and she never forgave me." He shrugged. "What can I say? I'm human and Arlene was a looker in her day."

"Just how strong are we talking?" This part she hadn't heard. Knowing her uncle, he made a pass or two.

"Let's just say I kissed her, and she didn't want to be kissed."

"So, you assaulted her," Naomi offered, horrified. Why was it that some men could never understand that no meant no even if it was just a simple kiss?

"It wasn't like that, Naomi. It was just a sloppy, drunken kiss on New Year's Eve. She overreacted. Anyway, Muriel held it against me for, like, forever. I think Arlene was pleased she'd put that wedge between Muriel and me. She had a mean streak like that."

Interesting. Naomi had never heard anyone mention Arlene having a mean streak. She'd have to ask Sean and Joe if they'd ever noticed Arlene being anything other than bossy. This was the one negative the two always said about the older woman. Moving on, she asked her uncle, "You really have no idea where she lived before?"

He shook his head. "Sorry. Muriel always said I drank so much the first fifty years of my life that I killed a lot of brain cells. I guess they were mostly memory cells."

Just Naomi's luck. "Was there anyone else Arlene was close to? I mean, I know she basically knew everyone in town, but she was always kind of a loner as far as I could tell." Almost standoffish, if Naomi was completely honest. A very private person.

"She didn't let anyone close. If she had any friends, you would never have known it." His eyebrows shot upward. "But there was one guy she seemed to have a thing with for a while." He rolled his eyes. "I don't know why when she turned me down flat."

"Who?" Naomi had never known Arlene to have a boyfriend. She figured the older woman was widowed and never got past the loss or just chose not to have a partner in order to remain independent.

"You remember that old hermit, something Cotton is his name. He lives over in Shake Rag. Last I heard he's still alive. A real strange one, though."

"Strange how?" If she was going to show up at someone's door in the middle of nowhere, she needed to understand what kind of strange she would be facing. Just eccentric or a killer?

"He was some sort of space engineer with NASA. Big top-secret stuff. He, like, kept his briefcase handcuffed to him, the rumor was. Wore dark glasses all the time. A real peculiar guy."

As strange as it was, he sounded exactly like Arlene. She had always been secretive and sort of odd. But she'd been kind and loyal. Naomi's parents had relied on her. More than once she remembered her mom calling Arlene a genius. Maybe some measure of odd came with being a genius.

This was likely the best she was going to get from Donnie. It wasn't much, beyond his personal recollections, but she intended to follow through. "You have more specific directions to this Mr. Cotton's home?"

"I don't, but if you ask anyone in the area, they're bound to know him."

"Please call me if you think of anything else, Uncle Donnie. I need to find the truth about Arlene—otherwise, Mom and Dad are going to end up looking like the ones who did something wrong." Agent Duncan had helped her to see that she was the only one who could or would be their voices in this.

Naomi couldn't help feeling guilty about making Arlene seem like the bad guy in this unholy mess. But what else was she supposed to think and do? The lab was Arlene's domain.

Donnie gave her a hug and promised to call if anything came to mind. Which was code for she likely wouldn't hear from him again unless she knocked on his door or he ran into financial trouble.

The drive to the community of Shake Rag didn't take long. She took Highway 64 from Winchester to Huntland and made a couple extra turns, and there she was in the middle of nowhere. Maybe she should have asked Agent Duncan to go with her. No, she needed to do this on her own. His job was to solve the case—hers was to clear her family name. The first house where she stopped, the owner had no idea who she was looking for, but house number two proved her uncle hadn't been completely wrong. The owner had given her directions to the "nutty as a fruitcake old hermit's house." Folks could be judgmental. Especially about things they didn't understand.

She followed the directions and ended up at a ramshackle old cabin tucked deep into the woods next to a creek. The place looked deserted. At least three of the four vehicles had weeds and small trees growing up through their decaying frames.

She held her breath all the way to the door, hoping there wasn't an aggressive dog running loose. The first step up to the porch had her drawing in a lungful of air. So far so good. A couple more steps and then half a dozen feet across the porch. The wood creaked with her every move. She grimaced, mentally crossing her fingers that she didn't fall through the old floorboards.

A rap on the door, then another. The place looked and sounded deserted. The occasional burst of breeze whispering through the trees and the distant trickle of the creek were the only sounds. As if to prove her wrong, a bird cawed from amid nearby tree branches. She started. Ordered herself to calm.

"What do you want?"

The harsh voice made her jump again.

It originated right in front of her on the other side of the still closed door.

Okay. Deep breath. Just do this. "Mr. Cotton?"

"I said, what do you want?" roared through the rickety wood door.

"I'm here about Arlene Beck."

The door opened a crack. One pale silvery eye peeked out at her. "What about her?"

"May I come in, Mr. Cotton?" She really didn't want to tell him the news on his porch. Plus she really wanted to get as much info from him as possible. Inside, she might have more luck. Out here it would be too easy for him to tell her to go and not respond once she answered the question asked.

The door opened wider. "Well, come on, then."

She stepped inside and when the door closed behind her the room was nearly dark. Her pulse reacted to a rush of adrenaline searing through her veins. Before she lost her nerve completely, a light flickered on. Fluorescent bulb, she decided. The lamp sat on a table next to a chair.

"Who are you?" he demanded.

"I'm Naomi Honea from Honea Farm."

"What's going on with Arlene?" His voice sounded rusty as if he rarely used it.

Rather than tell him, she asked, "You don't watch the news?"

The story had reached last evening's regional news. The Honea Farm sign over the front gate had flashed on the screen just before the headline: Murder in a Small Town. She worried that the headlines were only going to get worse and more targeted. The more sensationalized the news, the more viewers who tuned in.

God, she hated this sort of publicity.

"I don't watch the news," he said. "You can't trust anything they say. It's propaganda."

Deep breath. Just say it. "Sometime after she left work at the farm on Monday, Arlene was murdered."

On the drive here she had come up with a story to explain her questions. If Mr. Cotton was as strange as Donnie had suggested, he might have conspiracy issues, as well. For once she thought her uncle had been right. A quick glance around the room revealed boxes and boxes of what appeared to be files. They were stacked from floor to ceiling. The one part of the wall she could see was like a bulletin board with yellowed newspaper clippings pinned all over it. Most of the headlines appeared to be political in nature.

Very strange.

Maybe he was writing a book, she told herself. Some of the writers she had known in Hollywood created story or inspiration boards.

The man abruptly burst into sobs. The unexpected reaction rattled her. Should she say something? Do something?

"I'm so sorry, Mr. Cotton. This is a terrible tragedy. Do you know if she had any family? I just want to be sure anyone who should know what's happened is contacted."

His sobs stopped as abruptly as they'd started. He wiped his eyes with the sleeves of his khaki shirt. She noticed then that he wore khaki trousers, as well. Khaki socks. Like a uniform of beige.

"She had no family." He reached into his pocket, retrieved a handkerchief and blew his nose. "The farm and the people there were her family. She loved that farm."

Emotion burned Naomi's eyes. "She was family to us, yes," Naomi agreed. "She was like an aunt." Arlene had always been there. She had been a tremendous support since Naomi's dad died. Moving forward would be difficult without her.

"Do you know where she lived before she moved to Winchester? I'm so worried there might be someone we don't know about. A distant relative or close friend."

He stared at her for a long moment, his silvery eyes seeming to narrow as if he were assessing her motive for asking about the possibility of next of kin.

"What do you know about me?"

Oh, no! He was a conspiracy theorist and already paranoid that she was here spying on him. If there was a way out of this cabin besides the front door that she would have to get past him to reach, it wasn't visible beyond all the boxes. "I'm sorry, Mr. Cotton, I only know that you knew Arlene. I wanted to make sure you heard about what happened."

He nodded. "Good. Knowing anything about me is dangerous. More dangerous than you could possibly comprehend."

She suddenly wondered if she had misjudged the innocuousness of this man. Paranoia might not be his only issue. He could indeed be dangerous. "Is there anything you can tell me about Arlene and where she came from?"

He chuckled, an out of practice and oddly out of place sound. "They're on to what she was up to, I take it, and they've sent you here. That didn't take long."

"I don't know what you mean."

He stared at her, evaluating her motives, she imagined. Was she lying? After something only he possessed? Paranoia did that to a person.

"If you don't know now," he countered, "you'll know soon enough."

The man was very good at answering without actually telling her anything.

"I'm afraid I have no idea, Mr. Cotton."

"They'll keep looking until they know all the answers, trust me. It's what they do."

Well, that was as clear as mud. "Do you know of anyone else in town who might have known her or had a connection to her?"

"I can tell you that Arlene learned everything she knew from the master."

Now she was really confused. "I'm sorry, who is the master?"

He stared at her for a long, uncomfortable moment. "You should know the answer to that one. Everyone who ever studied history, however briefly, should know."

But she didn't. Before she could say as much, he lifted his hunched shoulders and let them fall in a careless shrug. "You could have a look around that house of hers. Perhaps you'll find what you're looking for there."

"I've already been to her house on Pleasant Ridge. I didn't find anything useful." At least nothing had been found as far as she'd been told. Now she was getting paranoid.

He shook his head. "Not that house. The one on High Street." He grinned, showing his stained teeth. "The one no one knew about."

"Arlene had another house?" She was absolutely certain this was a mistake. At some point in all these years she would have heard about that.

"She did." He gave her a knowing look. "It was a secret, but I knew. She didn't know I knew, but I did. I'm smarter than she wanted to believe."

Naomi's heart rate kicked into a faster rhythm. "Do you know the house number?"

He frowned. "I never noticed the number."

Naomi rephrased her question. "How will I know which house?"

"Oh, that's easy." He nodded adamantly. "Look for the cats. She loved cats."

Cats? How on earth could Naomi have known the lady all those years and not have been aware that she loved cats?

High Street, 5:30 p.m.

SHE DROVE SLOWLY along the street, craning her neck to visually search each yard and porch for cats. Cats. Who knew? Naomi wondered if her mom had known Arlene liked cats. Or that she had some sort of odd relationship with an even odder hermit living at Shake Rag?

Maybe Naomi just never paid attention. From the time she hit puberty she had been focused on one thing—getting off the farm. She only had eyes for the stars on the west coast. There were probably lots of things she had missed.

She thought again of Casey Duncan. He was so familiar to her. She must have met him before or something. He'd said no. Maybe he only reminded her of someone she'd run into eons ago.

Something darted out in front of her. She slammed on her brakes. Her heart launched into her throat. A cat pounced across the yard to her left. Close. Too close. She had to pay better attention.

She glanced in her rearview mirror, grateful no one was behind her. Then she checked the houses on either side of the street. This was the first cat she'd spotted.

On the right, a dozen or more cats lounged on the porch of the old bungalow that had seen far better days. This had to be it. Naomi backed up a few feet and turned into the driveway. As she emerged from her car, felines bounced off the porch and romped out to the driveway to greet her. She leaned down and stroked the sleek back of one and then the next. Dark velvety bodies twined around her legs, rubbing and purring.

By the time she reached the porch she had counted seventeen cats of all types and colors. Besides a rocking chair and a rickety table, three boxes waited on the porch. She checked the labels, didn't recognize the senders' addresses. The boxes were addressed to "occupant."

The squalling cats drew her attention. She realized they were probably hungry. If this house did belong to Arlene, she hadn't been around to feed them. An ache bloomed in Naomi's chest. She checked the door...locked.

"Okay, kitties. I can go to the store and get food." One of the cats trotted over to a large plastic container tucked behind the rocking chair and rubbed against it. Naomi wandered in the same direction. She had a look at the container, white plastic. With little effort she popped off the lid. "Aha."

The scent of cat food had the many felines crowding up against her. Since she didn't see any bowls she dropped handfuls all around that end of the porch. When she estimated she'd distributed enough, she closed the lid and went back to the boxes. Why would Arlene have things delivered to this house instead of her own? If intended for her, why wasn't her name on the boxes?

She cupped her hands on either side of her face and stared through the windows. The house looked empty. No furniture. Dark inside save for the tree-shaded light that filtered in through the windows.

Naomi moved down the steps and from one side of the house to the next and peered into each window. Every room she could see was the same: empty. Mostly dark.

When she reached the front porch again, she knelt down to examine the boxes more closely. Three typical cardboard shipping boxes, three different senders from three different addresses. California, New York and Idaho. She picked at the packaging tape across the top until she'd peeled it back far enough to open the box flaps of the first one. Inside was a white Styrofoam object.

Cooler? She shuddered at the thought of what she'd found in not one but two freezers.

This was just a cooler, she reminded herself. Not big enough for a body. She tried to pull it out of the box, but the fit was too tight to lift the cooler free. She turned the box upside down and shook it. It was heavier than she'd expected. Slowly but surely, her arms burning with the effort, the white cooler slid out of the box. The cooler was taped across the top, as well. More picking and tearing with her nails. She kept them cut short, so it took some time. Finally, the stubborn tape was all peeled back, pulling white dots of Styrofoam with it.

Briefly she considered she should probably call

Agent Duncan. He would want her to wear latex gloves for this. He would most likely want to check this out himself.

Too late. She'd already touched the packaging. She might as well finish what she started. Besides, her curiosity was killing her. She tugged at the lid until it came loose. A steamy fog rose from the container. She reared back.

Dry ice, she realized. Her mom had ordered holiday hams that came packed this way. The dry ice wasn't like regular ice. It was best not to touch it.

She waved away the fog and peered inside. She closed her eyes a second, shook her head and then looked again.

Eyes, wide open, peered back at her.

Face.

Dread expanded in her stomach.

A face. Female.

It was a face…a *head*.

A muffled cry tore from her throat. She fell back onto her butt, then scrambled away like a crab.

She clawed at her pocket for her cell phone.

She had to call Agent Duncan.

Chapter Seven

Casey tucked his cell phone back into his pocket and surveyed the ongoing work in the High Street house allegedly rented by Arlene Beck. The place had appeared vacant but had proven anything but empty.

As he watched, more of the paneling on the walls was removed. Two forensics techs had crawled around under the house checking between floor joists and in any other potential hiding place. So far, they'd found just under two million dollars. All in small bills and bundled neatly for storage in the wall cavities.

The call he'd just received had added another twist to this already bizarre case. Dental records had confirmed the identity of the woman whose head was in the box Naomi opened. The woman had been missing for more than a week. Her identity had changed everything.

This was no longer a mere homicide investigation. This thing had sprouted roots that went far and deep.

"Got more money in the back bedroom."

The words echoed through the house.

Casey walked through the rooms, each one lit like a photo studio with all the auxiliary lighting they'd brought in, until he reached the newest piece of evidence. More bundles of cash lined sporadic spaces in the wall cavities.

The tech glanced at Casey as he entered the room. "I'm guessing we have another million in here."

Earlier today Casey had decided on the most likely scenario for what Arlene Beck was up to. He'd suspected she was conducting illegal green burials. It was fairly easy to set up a professional-looking website and then to make the necessary arrangements. Once the body was turned over to Beck the family probably never inquired as to additional details or locations.

Beck was not simply burying the bodies free of chemicals and anything else that inhibited decomposition, she was using the bodies for her own purposes. Doubling her money so to speak.

With today's find he understood the business was far more sadistic.

Casey snapped more pics with his phone to use when he briefed Naomi. "Check them all," he said to the tech. "The attic, too. If there's anything else in this place I want to know about it."

Sheriff Tanner was outside briefing Brannigan, who'd already done a walk-through of the house. Casey joined them on the back porch. A crime scene perimeter had been set up around the yard, front and back. Already reporters had gathered on the street out front and shouted questions at any uniform or official-looking person who appeared. Brannigan had agreed to handle tonight's crowd at a ten o'clock press briefing. The three of them—Casey, Tanner and Brannigan—had put together a statement that really didn't state a lot. But it was all they were prepared to give at this time. Far too many unanswered questions remained at this point.

"The vic in the box has been ID'd," he told the chief and the sheriff as he approached their position on the porch. It was well past dark but the single bare bulb in the overhead light provided enough illumination for Casey to see the lines of worry on the other men's faces. No one wanted this kind of evil to visit their community.

But crime didn't pause at the borders of any town. It crossed lines of all kinds.

"Helen Radner. She vanished just over a week ago. Her abandoned car was only a few blocks from her home in Philadelphia. She had agreed to testify against Big Tom Richmond."

Brannigan gave a long, low whistle. "I heard something about that. The missing woman was the first witness who'd ever agreed to testify against him."

"She made the mistake of calling to say she was coming in. They were monitoring her phone and had her before she was out of her neighborhood." Casey shook his head. "I guess now we know where she ended up."

"Damn." Tanner pushed back his cowboy hat and rubbed at his forehead. "This will go national," he said, stating aloud what they all already knew. "I'll call in my reserve deputies. We'll have reporters from every major news outlet in the country descending on us."

"Good idea," Brannigan agreed. "I'll do the same." To Casey he said, "The lab in Nashville picked up the other remains found at the farm. Rowan will be forwarding her final report to you tomorrow."

"Thanks." This was officially the Bureau's case now. Brannigan and Tanner would continue to assist as needed, which would be immensely helpful since this was their territory. They knew the place and the people. "I should go break the news to Ms. Honea."

Casey made his way toward his vehicle. A local shelter had called in volunteers from all over the county to pick up the cats for safekeeping until they could be rehomed. Photos of each one would be posted on the city website in case anyone in the neighborhood had a cat missing. Cats liked to roam. Casey had never been a cat person but his older-by-two-years sister and only sibling had loved them.

"Agent Duncan!"

"Agent Duncan!"

Reporters shouted his name but officers prevented them from following Casey to his SUV. There would be a second official press conference tomorrow or the next day that he would conduct. Tonight Brannigan and Tanner would inform the citizens of their community about the ongoing investigation and give assurances as to their safety and the steps local authorities planned to take.

Driving along the country road in the darkness Casey considered how often he'd thought of Naomi over the years. She had been his first real crush. Of course she had no idea. She'd basically ignored him, but he hadn't been able to ignore her. Once he'd learned what became of her with that glimpse into her Hollywood life, he'd made an effort to keep up with her. Looking back, he decided his walk down memory lane after seeing that commercial must have been the result of a breakup. His relationships never lasted very long. Even when he put in the extra effort.

The situation only grew worse after he *found* Naomi again. He ended up unconsciously comparing every woman he dated with Naomi. It was totally ridiculous, he recognized. When the right person came along, he'd forget all about Naomi and ancient history.

The front porch light at the end of the long driveway to the Honea farmhouse had his pulse skittering like a guy about to go on his first date.

"Idiot," he grumbled.

He parked next to her vintage pickup and got out. The conversation to come wasn't one he looked forward to, but it was necessary. At this time, he had no reason to suspect she was involved in whatever Beck had going. The concept that he wasn't completely objective where Naomi was concerned wasn't lost on him.

He glanced up at the full moon hanging low in the night sky. Halloween coming up and the full moon seemed somehow fitting with this increasingly strange case. He glanced around the place. The big old white barn in the distance and the towering dark trees crowded around the white farmhouse spoke of peace and quiet. Solitude and contentment. But there was a lie behind that picturesque facade. The real questions were how did that lie start and how deep did it go?

Equally important, who started it?

The door opened as he climbed the steps to the porch. Naomi, her fiery red hair backlit by the light inside, waited for him to say something, he supposed.

It wasn't unseasonably cool tonight, but she had the afghan that usually hung on the back of the sofa draped around her shoulders.

"I know it's late," he offered, "but I hoped we could talk."

Almost eleven by now, he guessed. He was tired and she probably was, as well. This had been a hell of a two days.

"Would you like coffee?" She turned into the house, leaving him to follow.

"Coffee would be good. Thanks." He closed the door behind him, locked it before joining her in the kitchen.

The scent of coffee grounds filled the air as she scooped generous heaps into the brew basket. When she'd added water to the reservoir and hit the brew button, she faced him and said, "I watched the press conference. Chief Brannigan was very vague."

"Vague is the best we can do right now," he explained, hesitated, then went on. "We've identified the woman."

She pulled the afghan tighter. Waited. Said nothing.

"She was to be a witness against the head of an organized-crime syndicate in Philadelphia. She disappeared about a week ago."

Naomi's eyes closed for a moment as she absorbed the impact of his words. This was not the kind of news one wanted to hear about a longtime employee—a member of the family, really.

"Why…" She drew in a sharp breath as if what she had to say was almost too difficult to convey. "Why was her head mailed to Arlene?"

The brew process started its gurgling and hissing routine, ushering renewed smells of dark roast coffee into the air. "I can't answer that question with any measure of accuracy, but I can make an experienced guess based on the only other evidence found at the property."

She squared her shoulders, causing the afghan to drop from one side, revealing a pale length of skin between her shoulder and her throat. "I'm listening."

"Money. Bundles of cash hidden in the wall cavities. A lot of cash."

"But you can't be sure the money was Arlene's."

"We've confirmed the house was leased to her. The landlord stated she—Arlene—leased the property for immigrant workers at the farm." He knew this to be only a cover story. The employees of the farm were all locals who didn't need housing.

Naomi turned away, reached for a mug with a trembling hand. "Then you're telling me that Arlene was somehow connected to organized crime." She poured the mug full of steaming coffee and offered it to him.

He accepted, grateful for the caffeine-infused liquid. "I believe she was, yes." He sipped the coffee, winced at the burn of hot liquid, but at the moment he needed the fortification it promised.

She walked back to the living room and sat in her usual chair. After downing another swallow, he wandered back the same way. Took a seat on the sofa.

"You've decided my father was taking money from Arlene and most likely was helping her do…" She hesitated as if uncertain how to label the horrible thing lying cold and raw in front of her. "To cover up murders. Why would this Philadelphia mob bother sending a victim all the way to Tennessee? Why not just dispose of her there? Or someplace closer? This seems far-fetched at best."

"That is a piece of the puzzle I don't have yet. It doesn't add up strictly from a logistics standpoint. I can only assume there is—was—some sort of agreement between Arlene and the man in charge."

"This makes no sense at all. If she had an agreement, why is she dead?"

"Mob families have rules. They have territory. To cross the line is to make yourself a target. When a person makes the decision to go into business with these kinds of criminals, there is no going back and no room for error."

"Now you're saying she double-crossed the mob." Naomi held up a hand and the afghan fell to her elbows. "You've been here hardly more than twenty-four hours and already you've decided my family is involved with organized crime. What happened to innocent until proven guilty?"

Casey stared at the dark brew in his mug for a moment, took another swallow, a deeper one now that it had cooled. Then he sat the mug on the coffee table. "I'm speaking in general terms, ma'am. At this point, it's difficult to rule out Ms. Beck, with the mounting evidence that points to her involvement, but it's not my job to prove her guilt. My job is to find the evidence and solve the crime based on what I can actually prove, not on speculation. There are lawyers and judges who determine if the evidence I find is significant enough to prove the actors I allege to be involved are guilty."

NAOMI WATCHED THE movements of his hands, the way he inclined his head as he spoke. Somehow, she knew this man. "I'm sorry," she interrupted his monologue about the difference between what cops do and what lawyers do. "Are you certain we've never met? You said no before but I swear…" She shook her head. "There's something about you—maybe your eyes?— that seems so familiar."

Her timing was ridiculous, of course. There were far more pressing issues. But she needed to know or maybe she just needed a moment that wasn't about murder and bodies and mobsters.

He stared at her for so long she decided he wasn't going to respond. Then he finished off his coffee and leaned back on the sofa, his attention fully on her.

"I grew up in Mississippi. Meridian, Mississippi. Attended Ole Miss. My first assignment with the FBI was in Jackson. Then I ended up in Nashville."

"I don't recall ever having been to Meridian," she said. Why did he seem so intent on evading the real question? "I've been to Nashville a million times. Maybe we ran into each other there."

"Every summer my family spent a lot of time on the coast. Gulfport. Biloxi. But one summer we went to Mobile instead. Stayed at a resort in Gulf Shores."

Naomi's eyes locked with his and in that instant she remembered. "I was eleven that summer. You were thirteen. You had a dog… Jefferson. A chocolate Lab."

A smile tugged at the corners of his mouth. "Loved that dog. He died while I was in college. I still miss him."

Her heart pounded so hard she could scarcely breathe. "We played all the time. The first few days I was there we were inseparable." How could she have forgotten? The boy had grown into a very handsome man. "Why didn't you say something?"

"I wasn't sure myself at first."

"Wow." The memories flooded her, making her feel light somehow. "It really is a small world."

He leaned forward, braced his forearms on his thighs. "Actually, I wasn't completely honest with you. I did remember you. I saw you in a commercial and I thought, wow, that looks like the girl from that summer in Mobile. Later on I spotted your name in the cast of characters in a movie and I knew it was you. I sort of kept up with you after that. Your career, I mean."

She made a face. "The career that wasn't really a career." A sigh burst from her. "I wasn't cut out for showbiz, as they say. I was lucky to land a few parts and a decent number of commercials but I'm fairly certain things were never going to take off. When my dad died, I came back here to settle his affairs and ended up staying. It felt a lot safer, career-wise, than Hollywood." She laughed at the irony. "Good grief, just look how that worked out."

"Hey, you made it a hell of a lot farther than most. You were actually in a movie."

"Two," she corrected with a sad laugh. "The other one never made it beyond the cutting room floor."

"Lots of commercials." He nodded. "The body lotion one is my all-time favorite."

"I was so embarrassed when my dad mentioned that he'd seen the commercial." It wasn't that she hadn't been fully covered or that it was even remotely related to anything pornographic, but it was definitely suggestive. It really hadn't fit with the daddy's little girl image she'd always felt described her dad's view of her. Surprisingly he'd told her it was great. She was all grown up and had every reason to be proud of how beautiful she was.

Of course, daddies were supposed to say things like that. She'd never considered herself beautiful. More unique with all the freckles and the wild red hair. A sort of Nicole Kidman. Maybe that was stretching it, but a director had once made the same comparison.

"When did you decide to join the FBI?" The different paths their lives had taken fascinated her. "I don't remember you talking about cops and robbers or anything related that summer."

He shrugged. "I was thirteen. The only thing on my mind was girls." He chuckled, looked away. "But going into law enforcement was no surprise to my family."

"I'll bet your father is a cop, too." God, it was such a relief to relax just a little. The past forty or so hours had been brutal. She could use the respite.

"No, my mom was the influence. Captain Irene Duncan of the Meridian Police Department. She's planning to retire next year."

"Wow. What does your dad do?"

"Believe it or not, he's a defense attorney. The best one in town, most people believe. The crookedest one, according to my mom."

Naomi's jaw dropped. "How do they manage?"

"They don't. That summer at Gulf Shores is the last time we were a real family. They divorced. Mom got primary custody of me and my sister. My father found a new wife who appreciated his talent and started a new family."

No wonder he remembered that summer so vividly. He'd lost his father that year. His whole life had changed. "I'm so sorry. I'm sure it was a difficult time for you."

"It was the best and the worst summer of my life all wrapped into one."

Wow. She couldn't imagine having to bounce back and forth between parents. It was so unfair to the children. The opposites-attract thing, however, she had experienced firsthand.

"My parents were like that, very different. My mom was a medical doctor. My dad always said she was so studious she ignored a social life entirely. He, on the other hand, dated every single girl in Franklin County before they married, I think. I can't tell you how many locals I have run into over the years who explained how they'd dated my father pre-Muriel. His father was a farmer. There were no siblings, so he inherited the farm. He had a little run-in with a chain saw, cut his leg and had to go to the ER. Until the day he died, he swore that Mom bewitched him that day. She was the physician on call and stitched him up. Forced him to have a tetanus shot and anti-biotics, both of which he strongly insisted were un-necessary."

"How did they end up together?" Agent Duncan asked. "Did he break an arm for a return visit to the ER?"

Naomi laughed. Now there was something else she remembered about the handsome young boy from that summer—he had a wicked sense of humor. "No, he sent her flowers at her clinic. That same evening she showed up at the farm, the big vase of flowers in hand, and said she didn't accept gifts from patients. My father explained that he was not her patient. It wasn't his fault she was on call that day."

Casey laughed. *Casey.* How could she have forgotten his name? The idea that he had remembered hers and followed her career warmed her, maybe a little too much.

"Did she keep the flowers?" he asked, grinning.

"No. She left them on the porch. She did the same thing every day for a week. He kept sending flowers and she kept bringing them back. One night he had dinner prepared and suggested she join him. She was so exhausted from a long day at the ER she gave in and had dinner with him. There was no going back then. They were married a few months later but it was a while before I came along. I was a surprise. Mom thought she was too old to be having children. Not medically, of course, but just as a person. She was set in her ways. Had her routine. Dad insisted that he made her fall in love with me. After I was born, she started a clinic to better control her work hours. She didn't want to miss out on raising her child."

"I like your story way better than mine."

"Thanks, but it seems my story is all tangled up now." Reality rushed back in with a sharpness that almost took her breath.

"Sometimes great stories don't have a happy ending for reasons outside a person or persons' control."

Defeat kicked her in the stomach. "You're convinced my father was somehow involved."

"I can't ignore the sudden influx of large deposits. I know the farm started to thrive after you took over but that doesn't explain the years before. Show me where he sold property or other assets. Maybe there was an insurance policy of some sort you didn't know about." He turned his hands up. "Did your mother publish a paper that earned unexpected royalties? Find an explanation for the money and you have my word I will take him off the suspect list. Otherwise, I have to follow the evidence. There is a possibility that evidence will show that your father was completely innocent. We can't be sure what sort of private deals he made with Arlene. Did he or she mention his selling shares in the farm to her?"

Naomi hadn't considered that possibility. "No one mentioned any arrangements like that. There was nothing in the settling of the estate about any business shares belonging to anyone except my dad. Surely Arlene would have told me."

"It'll take time, but I will find the truth. With this latest development, there will be a whole team of agents working on this case. Between now and then, my primary job will be to ensure your safety."

She suddenly wondered who was supposed to ensure the safety of the woman from Philadelphia. Following that train of thought right now was not a good idea. She would only offend him if she verbalized her concerns, and she was too tired to deal with a deeper discussion on how federal agencies worked. She pushed aside the nightmare and forced a smile. Better to stick with something lighter. "I can't believe I didn't remember you. I remember that summer so well. It changed the course of my life."

"I think you only had eyes for one boy that summer."

"Slade," she said. "Slade Kenton. His mother was in Fair Hope filming a movie. He invited me to the set and from that day forward all I could think about was becoming an actress."

"A good old boy from Mississippi couldn't compete with what he offered."

As if the defeat in his tone had kicked a memory

loose from her brain, she instantly remembered her first kiss. Her *real* first kiss. The one this man—the boy version of him—had given her.

"Ah," she said, "but he didn't get to be the first boy I kissed."

For a moment they stared at each other. The tension was thick.

Then he stood, picked up his mug. "I'd forgotten about that kiss."

"Me, t-too," she said, feeling offended somehow. "Completely. It only j-just occurred to me." If only she hadn't stuttered and stammered and sounded like a complete liar, her story might have been believable.

"I wonder whatever happened to him?" Casey asked. "I don't think his career took off the way his mother's did. I guess celebritydom isn't meant for everyone."

With that profound statement he took his mug to the kitchen. As he passed back through on his way to the front door, he gave her one of those nods and said, "Good night, ma'am."

Chapter Eight

Ma'am.

For a few minutes Naomi had been certain the human part in Agent Casey Duncan had emerged. They'd had a personal connection that went back decades. On some level she had recognized him, but she hadn't been able to pull the memory from the gray matter that was so shaken by the events of the past two days.

Maybe if she'd run into him under different circumstances...

She stalked back to the kitchen. Glared at his cup, then tucked it away in the dishwasher. He'd acted almost annoyed that she had recalled how they first met. Was she not supposed to remember? Or was he somehow still miffed that she'd only had eyes for Slade instead of him, as he put it. She'd been eleven, for goodness' sake. She hadn't known what she wanted.

The notion that he would hold the actions of an eleven-year-old against her was ludicrous.

Her determined pace back into the living room slowed and her gaze narrowed. Maybe the fact that they'd met before was just coincidence, but he'd used it to take her off guard. Certainly she'd opened up more than she would have otherwise. But nothing she'd said had confirmed his conclusions about her dad or Arlene.

Though it was difficult to justify in any way whatever Arlene had been doing.

How could such a seemingly nice woman have been making bodies disappear? Not just any bodies at that, the bodies of murder victims. She fully expected that when the remains discovered in the lab were identified they would be those of homicide victims, as well.

What did you call someone who made bodies disappear? Not exactly a cleaner since they typically cleaned up an entire scene or situation. This was only body disposal.

At least as far as Naomi knew.

What if there were notes or files about the bodies hidden somewhere on the farm? Surely Arlene kept business records. It was a business, wasn't it? Based on what Agent Duncan—she refused to call him Casey since he'd behaved so strangely before leaving—said it appeared that Arlene was paid vast sums of money to get rid of human remains. Add to this information the evidence found in the lab and in other areas on the farm, it made sense that Arlene, as an agronomist, would have taken her work to the next level.

Human composting.

Fear snaked around Naomi's chest. If Arlene had composted human remains on the farm, using it as some sort of fertilizer, there would be endless lawsuits. Whether Naomi or her dad knew about it or not, they owned the farm. They signed up the subscribers for the CSA.

Holy cow, she was in serious trouble. She needed a really good lawyer.

She hesitated, one hand on her hip, the other on her chin as she tapped her cheek in hopes of prodding forth some revelation that would provide an out. Could a lawyer actually help if the question of who did what still remained? Or did it matter? Was she and her dad as well as her mother still culpable simply because they owned the property? "Of course you are, dummy."

She'd gone over the house fairly well and found nothing unexpected, certainly nothing that suggested there was some illegal operation on the farm.

What she needed was the opportunity to go through the lab and office.

Hurrying to the kitchen, she found her jacket,

tugged it and her boots on and found a flashlight. Before going out the door she confirmed that her keys and her cell were in her pocket.

Check.

Slipping out the back door she disappeared into the darkness, opting not to use the flashlight. She'd made the trip to the barn and lab a million times. She knew the way. Besides, in retrospect, if she turned on the flashlight her security detail would see. She needed some time alone in the lab to think and pick through the decades of papers documenting the work done on the farm.

The door to the lab was locked. Since the investigators would be returning tomorrow, they hadn't sealed the door with crime scene notices. No matter, she understood that what she was doing probably broke the law.

She entered the building, anyway. Now she would use the flashlight. If she turned on the overhead lights anyone outside would be able to see the glow cast through the skylights. Unless she directed the flashlight upward, that wasn't going to happen. First, she did a walk-around and assessed what the forensic investigators or technicians had been doing. Thankfully they put things back as they found them after completing their tasks on a given worktable. She'd expected lots of jumbling and fingerprint dust. Did they even use that stuff anymore?

The storage room was the same. The items on the shelves weren't exactly where she and Arlene had put them, but they were close. Arlene preferred everything in its exact place all the time. If you moved it, you'd better put it back precisely where you found it.

This was one of the traits her mom had loved about Arlene. Everything was always in its place. Her mom had been basically the same way. Even now Naomi found herself lining up the cereal boxes and cans in perfect order, arranged by product.

But Naomi was more like her dad. Not so picky about where things were. Perfection wasn't even an aspiration in her reality.

The familiar tables and small greenhouses were comforting somehow. Without the darkness to distract her she noted the humid scent of warm soil and rich green plants.

This was where Arlene tested her plant food. She never called it fertilizer. Food. Like humans, the plants needed food.

Naomi shuddered at the idea that the woman may have been feeding the plants humans.

Finally, she moved on to the office. The desk was hers, but she and Arlene had shared it, depending on who was doing what. No need to try cramming another desk into this little office. She sat down in the wheeled chair and began her search. The drawers first. Picking through each scrap of paper, business card and report, she moved from drawer to drawer. In the bottom right she found a piece of her favorite soft caramel candy. She peeled off the wrapper and popped it into her mouth.

"Hmm." Nice. On busy days those chewy delights were sometimes her lunch.

A thorough check of the credenza and she moved on to the row of file cabinets. These massive file cabinets were the primary reason there was no room for another desk in the room.

Not that she would need a second desk now.

She stilled. Arlene was dead. Her parents were dead. She was it now.

And everything had gone to hell.

Emotion burned in her eyes, but she blinked it away and focused on the task at hand. Now, finding the facts was the most important task she had to accomplish. Folder by folder she read the headings of each. Customer names. Each business from whom they purchased goods or sold goods had a file. Each individual who bought from the farm had one, as well. She knew them all personally.

She passed the Franklin County Lumber file but went back. Something stuck out of the folder. Arlene never left anything arranged in a sloppy manner. Maybe the forensics folks had bunched up some of the papers in this file.

Naomi removed it but it wasn't the lumber company's file that was the problem. It had gotten tucked into another folder. This one was unmarked.

Pulse thumping, she opened the file. Empty. Maybe it was just an extra file that stuck to the lumber company one. She scanned the front of the folder with her flashlight, then the back side.

The beam of light stilled midway across the back side of the brown folder.

Numbers.

She placed the folder down on the desk and went over it more carefully. There were dozens—no hundreds—of numbers written on it.

"What is this?" she muttered.

Holding her breath, she turned on the desk lamp and looked more closely. Numbers. Numbers. Lots and lots of numbers. She took a photo with her phone, then slid it back into her pocket.

Her first instinct was to call Agent Duncan.

"Nope."

She intended to look into this herself before handing it over to him. After turning off the desk light, she slipped the folder back into the drawer next to the one labeled Franklin County Lumber. Maybe the numbers were combinations to locks. But there were no locks with combinations that she knew of on the farm. They all had keys.

Something else she would need to look for.

Maybe it was time to take the UTV, a utility terrain vehicle, around the property. See if there was a building somewhere she had missed. She really couldn't say for sure that she had been over every acre of the property since she came back. Considering it wouldn't help to do it in the dark, tomorrow would have to be soon enough.

The air felt chillier as she left the lab or maybe it was just the idea that it was dark save for the moonlight. She paused and stared up at the low-slung full orb. There was no comparison when it came to country nights. It just wasn't the same in the city.

"You really shouldn't be out here in the dark."

Her scream came out more a squeak.

Fear slammed into Naomi like a fast-moving truck. *Casey.* Agent Duncan.

When she could breathe again, she said, "You scared the hell out of me."

"Spotting something moving in the dark didn't do anything for my serenity, either. Imagine me picking up movement between two trees. I am armed, Ms. Honea, as is the deputy on duty. This is a bad idea for everyone."

No matter that she knew he was right, anger overrode her good sense. "What are you doing here? I thought you left."

"I decided to hang around awhile."

"Why?" Her anger and frustration amped up a notch. "So you can come up with some other way to make me believe one or both of my parents was involved with whatever the hell is going on here?"

"Looks to me like you were the one searching for something. Maybe you could tell me what was so important that you had to go out in the middle of the night and enter an ongoing crime scene to find it?"

She didn't have to tell him anything. "I needed the latest invoices, but I couldn't find them. They must be in the house. I guess I overlooked them."

"Your invoices aren't on some app or software on your computer?"

"Good night, Agent Duncan."

She strode toward the house. The moonlight was plenty for her to see the way. Even if it hadn't been, she wouldn't have turned on the flashlight. Maybe he'd run into a tree. She rolled her eyes and mentally scolded herself for being petty.

At least she wasn't holding a nearly two-decade-old rejection against him. And it wasn't even really a rejection. It was nothing but two silly kids and hormones.

She stamped up onto the porch and still he followed right behind her. She wheeled around. "Why are you following me?"

"I intend to make sure your house is clear before you lock yourself in for the night."

She gestured to the county cruiser in the drive. "I have a security detail."

As she made the statement another car pulled up and the one that had been parked all evening backed up and drove away. Shift change, she supposed.

The driver's door opened and an older deputy, broad shouldered and round bellied, got out of the car and waved. "Evening. I'm Deputy Lawton. I'll be here for the night."

"Thank you," Naomi called back. "If you need anything please let me know."

He nodded and climbed back into his vehicle.

"Was there anything else you wanted to say?" she asked the man still towering over her. He looked almost as irritated as she felt.

"Whatever I said that ticked you off," he announced with an exaggerated sigh, "I apologize."

"You accused my dad of being a criminal. You even suggested I might be one. All because you have no idea who the criminal is in all this." Probably not entirely true but saying it felt good.

It gave her quite the bit of glee, in fact.

"You're right. I apologize for that, too."

Too. So, he did realize he'd been petty.

"Thank you." She turned to the door once more.

"Ms. Honea, I really need you to think long and hard about the difference between what you've always believed and what the evidence shows. This will go a whole lot more pleasantly and a lot more quickly if we work together."

He'd said she should help him prove her parents were innocent in all this. So maybe she was the one being petty. Maybe he was only doing his job and she was the one fighting the process.

"I looked through the files. There's an extra empty folder next to the Franklin County Lumber file. It's empty but it had numbers written all over it. Combinations or some other number sequences."

He nodded. "Thank you. I'll check it out."

He descended the steps, heading back to the lab.

She went after him. He glanced her way as she caught up with him. "It's late, Ms. Honea."

"I can't go in the house." She pressed onward, matching his long strides as closely as she could.

He cut a glance in her direction. "Why is that?"

"You said you had to make sure it was clear before I go in."

CASEY LAUGHED. "YOU'RE RIGHT. I did say that. I guess I owe you another apology."

She made a "who cares" sound and kept walking.

"You know you can't go back in the lab." Casey knew she would. That was something else he remembered about her. She was fearless. *Are you brave enough...?*

"Then I'll wait outside."

He unlocked the door and waited for her to go in before him.

This time she turned on the lights. He'd followed her here. He'd been doing a walk around her house when she'd exited through the back door. Years of experience weren't necessary to know where she was headed.

In the office he pulled the file she'd told him about. He propped against the desk and reviewed the numbers. Some were written in black ink, others in blue.

"Do you think the coloring of the ink is significant?"

A logical question. "Maybe." He glanced at her. "Maybe not."

She stared at the scribbled numbers. "There aren't any combination locks around here. We only use locks with keys."

"Passwords," he suggested.

She leaned closer and he stopped breathing.

"None of our computer passwords are number sequences. We use a combination of letters, numbers and special characters." She smiled up at him as if she fully understood he couldn't breathe. "The passwords are stronger that way."

When she drew back, he breathed again. "What about online accounts? Any of these resemble bank account numbers? Credit cards?"

Her brow lined as she studied the numbers again. "I don't think so, but I can check."

"We're here." He moved away from the desk. "Why not have a look now?"

Beyond the fact that it was the middle of the night and that she shouldn't be in here.

Naomi slid into the chair behind the desk and started clicking keys. Casey walked around the office, surveyed shelves and items he'd already inventoried two or three times. Never hurt to have another look. Mostly he just wanted to let her feel like she was accomplishing something. He'd played this all wrong. Bringing up the past and making her feel vulnerable was the incorrect tactic. He didn't usually make those kinds of elementary mistakes.

Maybe the truth was that he'd let that tiny slice of shared history rattle him just a little.

"Let me see the folder." She held out her hand and he placed the folder in her fingers.

He watched as she looked from the computer screen to the folder time and time again. Her pink lips were pursed, making him wish he could touch her there. A lock of red hair fell across her face and it took every ounce of strength he possessed not to reach out and tuck it aside.

Maybe that was why he'd asked for this case as soon as it came across the SAC's desk. He wanted to see her. To see if she remembered him. To help her find the truth. Or maybe to prove she was involved somehow.

But that third option was wrong. She wasn't involved. He knew this already. Could he clear her father's name? Maybe not. But he would find the truth and he would do what he could to prevent tearing her world any further apart.

"None of the accounts we have match any of those numbers." She logged out of the computer and shut it down. "Back to square one."

"It's late." Past midnight, he imagined. "We should call it a night and have a fresh look in the morning. I'll run it past our forensics accountant."

"At least we tried."

If having tried made her feel as if she were helping, he'd made the right choice. He really did need her cooperation.

He followed her out of the building, locked the door.

When they reached the house, he gave her a nod. "Good night, Ms. Honea."

"Why are you calling me that?"

He hesitated, looked at her. "It's your name."

"Let's get this part out of the way," she suggested. "You call me Naomi and I'll call you Casey. We can't pretend all this formality. Not after what we shared."

He stroked his chin as if considering her offer. "All right, Naomi."

"Drive safely."

She reached for her door.

"I'm not going anywhere."

Her attention swung back to him. "Why? I have a security detail. Is it really necessary to have two right outside my door?"

He considered the deputy in the cruiser, then turned back to her. "I don't really care for motels. I'm more at home in my SUV. I'll be fine."

He started down the steps.

"No."

He looked back. "No?"

She shook her head. "The deputies get to change up every eight hours. You don't have anyone to relieve you. You can stay on my couch. Get some sleep, like you said. If anyone tries to get to me, you'll be right there *on the couch*."

"As long as you're okay with the arrangement, ma'am."

"Naomi," she reminded as she unlocked and opened the door.

"Naomi," he amended.

She nodded to the open door. "I'll let you go first. Make sure it's safe for me to come inside."

He doubted she had anything to worry about in there and most likely she knew it. She was using his own words against him. In reality, the problem was right here. With him. Maybe she didn't understand or maybe she did.

Guess he'd find out.

Loyal Readers
FREE BOOKS Voucher

We're giving away **THOUSANDS** of **FREE** **BOOKS**

Suspense

Suspenseful Romance

Don't Miss Out! Send for Your Free Books Today!

Get up to 4
FREE FABULOUS BOOKS
You Love!

To thank you for being a loyal reader we'd like to send you up to 4 FREE BOOKS, absolutely free.

Just write "YES" on the Loyal Reader Voucher and we'll send you up to 4 Free Books and Free Mystery Gifts, altogether worth over $20, as a way of saying thank you for being a loyal reader.

Try **Harlequin® Romantic Suspense** books featuring heart-racing page-turners with unexpected plot twists and irresistible chemistry that will keep you guessing to the very end.

Try **Harlequin Intrigue® Larger-Print** books featuring action-packed stories that will keep you on the edge of your seat. Solve the crime and deliver justice at all costs.

Or **TRY BOTH!**

We are so glad you love the books as much as we do and can't wait to send you great new books.

So don't miss out, return your Loyal Reader Voucher Today!

Pam Powers

LOYAL READER
FREE BOOKS VOUCHER

YES! I Love Reading, please send me up to 4 FREE BOOKS and Free Mystery Gifts from the series I select.

Just write in "YES" on the dotted line below then return this card today and we'll send your free books & gifts asap!

➡ YES ⬅

Which do you prefer?

☐ **Harlequin® Romantic Suspense**
240/340 HDL GRHP

☐ **Harlequin Intrigue® Larger-Print**
199/399 HDL GRHP

☐ **BOTH**
240/340 & 199/399
HDL GRHZ

FIRST NAME

LAST NAME

ADDRESS

APT.#

CITY

STATE/PROV.

ZIP/POSTAL CODE

EMAIL ☐ Please check this box if you would like to receive newsletters and promotional emails from Harlequin Enterprises ULC and its affiliates. You can unsubscribe anytime.

HI/HRS-520-LR21

Chapter Nine

Casey's eyes opened to darkness.

He listened.

All quiet. But something woke him. He reached beneath the pillow Naomi had provided and found his cell. Checked the time: 3:00 a.m.

He tossed aside the blanket and sat up. The sofa, he had to admit, was far more comfortable than the bucket seat in his SUV. He pulled on his shirt as he stood, buttoned up while he searched for his boots. Tucked his weapon into his waistband. Then, running his fingers through his hair, he took a moment to allow his eyes to adjust to the darkness. Turning a light on would wake Naomi. No need for that.

Taking his time, he moved across the room to the stairs. The Honea home was a typical two-story

farmhouse. Bedrooms were upstairs. As best he recalled from the search of the home on Tuesday, there
were no squeaky steps on the staircase.

He moved up quickly, going straight to the room
on the right at the far end of the narrow hall. He had
known this was her room the moment he entered it.
Celebrity posters still covered the walls from when
she was a teenager living at home. The posters were
the right era, so he had assumed as much, anyway.
The walls were white, allowing the colorful posters and banners to stand out on a blank canvas. The
bed had been unmade. He had her figured for a girl
who didn't bother making the bed every morning.
He, too, was firmly rooted in the what-difference-
did-it-make camp. He was only going to climb back
in that night.

She'd left her door open. Good. At this point his
eyes had adjusted well to the lack of lighting. Her
form was easy to make out in the soft white covers.
He knew the covers were soft because he'd touched
them. Hadn't been able to help himself. Her red hair
was a dark cloud spread over the pillow. The sound
of her soft, steady breathing confirmed his estima-
tion that she was sleeping soundly.

Back downstairs, he pocketed the key she'd left
on the table near the door and grabbed his jacket. He
slipped out and stood for a moment on the porch as-

sessing the county cruiser parked in the driveway. The best he could tell the vehicle was empty.

Where was the deputy?

Maybe he'd needed to take a leak and the car door was what Casey had heard.

Palming his weapon just in case, he made his way down the steps and toward the cruiser. No one in the car. Next he looked through the windows of his own SUV, then looked under both vehicles. Naomi's truck was the same—empty.

From there he took a walk around the house. All quiet. No shadows moving through the moonlight.

Where the hell was that deputy?

Moving toward the lab a sound alerted his senses. Casey stilled. The snap of a twig, crunch of gravel. Then he spotted the movement. A dark form progressing through the night, only visible when it passed beneath a slip of moonlight that filtered between the branches of the trees.

The form moved closer to the house. Casey waited until he—presumably the deputy—was close enough to touch. He lifted his weapon to the form's head.

"Stop right there."

"Whoa!" Male voice. "I'm Deputy Lawton. Just had to do some private business, if you know what I mean."

Casey lowered his weapon. "Sorry about that, Lawton. Special Agent Casey Duncan. I thought I heard an intruder lurking about."

"You hear all sorts of sounds out here in the country, Agent Duncan. Owls, raccoons messing around the trash cans. It's not like in the city. Sometimes a sound we're not used to hearing will rouse us from a dead sleep."

"You're right." Casey tucked his weapon back into his waistband. "I'm more accustomed to the wail of sirens and the rush of moving vehicles."

"I had you figured for a city boy," Lawton said.

"How long have you been in the Winchester area?" Casey asked as they moved back toward the front of the house.

"Since I decided life in Birmingham was not for me. Every time I turned around it seemed one of my fellow officers was getting shot. I headed north, spent a night in Winchester and decided this was the place for me. Until I got on with the department, I used to help Mr. Honea out on the farm. Stayed on even after I was hired as an auxiliary deputy. Once I got on full-time, I had to give up the extra work. He was a good man. Always the first to help when the community needed him."

"Did you notice any changes in the way the farm

operated or in Mr. Honea's personality over the past few years?"

"Not that I can say." He paused next to his vehicle, shook his head. "It was tough when his wife was sick and for a while after she passed. But that's understandable. You won't find a finer family than the Honeas. Good folk. Never any trouble out here. Like I said, always helpful to their neighbors. Always the first ones to pitch in during a crisis. This awful business is a real shame."

Casey had gotten pretty much the same statement from everyone he'd interviewed.

"What about Arlene Beck? How well did you know her?"

"Well, now." He adjusted his belt as if his trousers were having difficulty staying up on his round shape. "Arlene was a different kind of bird. Definitely an odd one. Friendly enough most of the time. She wasn't one to socialize. Not too many friends as far as I could tell. There was that one old conspiracy fella she spent a good deal of time with."

"Conspiracy fella?" Casey asked.

"Elmer Cotton," Lawton said. "He used to work for the government. NASA, I think. Had to retire early. They say he lost his mind." He made a circling motion at the side of his head. "Went a little crazy. Anyway, he lives sort of off the grid over in Shake Rag."

"Shake Rag?"

"A little community near Huntland. I'd be happy to show you the way when the next deputy arrives if you'd like."

Casey skipped over the offer for now. "How was Beck involved with this Elmer Cotton?"

"Well, I can't say for sure. I just heard she spent a lot of time with him. Might've been just a rumor. But you know what they say, 'birds of a feather flock together,' and those two appeared to have a lot of *oddness* in common. Don't mean to speak ill of the dead, but she was a strange one."

"How well do you know Naomi?" Saying her name always caught Casey off guard. He'd thought about her plenty of times over the years, especially whenever he spotted her on television. But saying her name aloud was new.

Maybe at some point he had gone beyond curious about her. Maybe he was a little obsessed. Not a good look on an agent. Particularly under the circumstances.

"Not as well as I knew her daddy, Nolan," he admitted. "She was gone out to California for a good long while. After Nolan died, she came back and helped Arlene pull the farm back into shape. Things were pretty bad there for a while."

Strange, it certainly didn't look that way on paper. The farm dropped into the red after Naomi's mother died. But a year later it appeared—on paper—to have been thriving with more cash flow than ever before. The bank statements showed a drop-off the final year of Naomi's father's life. Another oddity. Why the drop in income with little or no drop in production? Jones and Riley had insisted that work had been steady for the past five years, and even an uptick since Naomi came home.

"Failing crops?" Casey asked. "Equipment issues?" Most of the farm equipment appeared to be fairly new.

"I can't say," Lawton confessed. "Nolan wasn't one to poor-mouth. I just know he looked like a man at his wit's end. There was this one time that he mentioned he just didn't know what he was going to do if things didn't turn around."

Naomi hadn't mentioned any discussions with her father about ongoing issues. "Did he ask Naomi for help?" Casey ventured. "Maybe she feels guilty for not coming home to help."

"I don't think he would have worried her with whatever problems he had. He wanted Naomi to be happy. Even if it meant her chasing after her dreams way out in California."

"Maybe he discussed his concerns with Arlene since they were partners."

Lawton chuckled. "I don't think he and Arlene got on so well after his wife, Muriel, died. She and Muriel were a team, but Nolan was kind of like a third wheel. I think that might have been a sticking point for Nolan and Muriel. But now, I have to tell you that part is just gossip. Nolan never spoke ill of anyone, least of all his Muriel. Arlene was a part of this farm and always here. I guess it was the three's-a-crowd thing."

"Thanks, Lawton." Casey gave him a nod. "I appreciate the information. You need anything out here? Water? Coffee?"

The older man shook his head. "I'm good. Got a thermos still half full of coffee and a couple more bottles of water.

"How well do *you* know Naomi?" Lawton asked when Casey would have turned to go back into the house.

"I don't know her," Casey said, which was basically true.

"Oh." Lawton shrugged. "I just thought the two of you were close."

This was the man's roundabout way of pointing out that he was aware Casey had been in the house all night while he was out here in his county cruiser.

"It's my job to make sure Ms. Honea stays safe. If sleeping on her couch makes that possible, then I can handle it."

"We do what we have to," the older man said with a chuckle.

Casey considered saying more but decided against it as he watched the deputy slide back behind the wheel of his vehicle. A small-town thing, he decided as he headed back into the house. When everyone knew everyone else, it was human nature to be curious about a change or disruption to the norm.

As he unlocked the door a light came on inside. "It's me, Casey Duncan," he said as he opened the door.

For all he knew Naomi could have her dad's shotgun. He'd seen one propped behind the door in the man's bedroom. He felt confident Naomi knew it was there even if she hadn't bothered moving it—or anything else in her parents' bedroom for that matter. The room was like a shrine to the late Honeas.

It was a big enough house, he supposed, no need to be in a rush to clear out or pack up their things.

Standing at the bottom of the stairs, Naomi pressed a hand to her chest. "You scared the hell out of me. I heard voices outside and I worried that something else had happened." She closed her eyes, shook her head before meeting his gaze once more. "Anyway, is everything okay?"

"Everything's fine," he assured her. He closed the door and locked it. "The voices you heard were Deputy Lawton and me. We had a look around outside."

"Why?" She moved toward the sofa.

He raised his eyebrows in question. "Why what?"

"Why were you looking outside at this hour of the morning?"

He should have known that question would be coming. "I heard a noise and went to check it out." He explained the circumstances. "No worries. It's all good."

She pushed her hair back from her face, glanced around. "Okay, well, I'll be back down in a bit. Feel free to get some more sleep or make coffee or whatever."

He tried his best to keep the smile from his face. He got it now. She'd just realized she was standing there in a nightshirt and with her hair a wild mass of curls.

He loved it.

She hurried back upstairs.

He glanced at the couch. More sleep was out of the question. He'd log into the server via his cell and have a look at the latest reports from forensics.

Keeping his mind off the woman upstairs would be best for both of them.

Honea Farm, 8:00 a.m.

NAOMI NIBBLED A slice of buttery toast and contemplated how she could possibly answer the multitude of emails and text messages from concerned CSA subscribers. There was no way she would be making this week's delivery. Chances were she wouldn't be able to make the one after that. Sean and Joe were being allowed to come back to work tomorrow but how could she do anything until she understood the situation more fully?

Any second now she expected to receive notification that all deliveries were to be halted until a health and agriculture department investigation could be done. The farm's certification was unquestionably in jeopardy.

This was a major catastrophe. Thinking beyond the fact that people had died had been difficult until now. But at this point she had to face the reality that maybe she should have sold the farm last year.

And she'd been so certain she was doing the right thing for her parents' legacy. For her future.

She tossed the remainder of the toast into the trash. She needed more coffee.

Casey had left the house half an hour ago to meet his team in the lab. He hadn't mentioned any new developments. No news so far on the remains from the freezer. The identification could take months or years.

She'd spent some time searching the internet about human composting. Her stomach seized at the thought. It was a tricky business. Bodies used had to be tested for certain issues that might be passed along in the soil and onto plants. It wasn't an "anything goes" sort of concept. There were rules and laws and licenses. Not unlike the many, many hoops to jump through for an organic certification. If the remains found here were tested and any issues discovered, the situation would grow exponentially worse for her farm.

For the first time since Casey had shown her those bank statements, she asked herself if there was even the remotest possibility her dad could have known what Arlene was doing. This was assuming Arlene was the one responsible for this ungodly mess. Who else could it be?

There could be no other explanation in light of the money found in that house she leased. The box with the head inside had been addressed to that property. No question. Arlene's friend, Mr. Cotton, had said she used the house on High Street for deliveries.

There just wasn't any other explanation.

To pretend otherwise was beyond ridiculous at this point. She looked out the kitchen window at the lab. A swarm of federal agents had arrived and spread out over her farm. People were coming in and out of the lab. She felt like a rat watching the comings and goings and uncertain when the trap would snap, catching her in its lethal hammer.

She had to do something.

Naomi grabbed her jacket, tucked her phone into the pocket and walked out the back door. This was her property. She had agreed to whatever searches the authorities needed to do but she had a right to know what was happening.

She hadn't seen Sheriff Tanner or Chief Brannigan today. This was the FBI's case now so she wasn't sure when or if she would hear from them again. She felt confident they were being kept in the loop. At least, that was the way it worked in crime shows in the movies and on television.

The ground was drying up, which was a good thing. There was work that needed to be done. Until this week the rain hadn't let up. The only thing she knew to do was to carry on with the fall planting and winter prep. This farm was now her livelihood. If the farm went under, so did she.

The idea that Arlene could have more money hidden around the property crossed her mind. She really had to be losing it to think that way. And would the government seize the farm as a criminal venture?

More knots formed in her belly.

The lab door opened and an agent exited. This one was a woman. She smiled and nodded and hurried to a vehicle parked near the house. Naomi had no idea exactly how many agents were here or what they were all doing. Sometimes ignorance was bliss. Hopefully this was one of those times.

She opened the door and stepped into the lab, breathing in the familiar scents. She surveyed the faces she saw in search of Casey. Some of the agents looked familiar. She'd seen them around before. But others were strangers.

"Is there something you need, Ms. Honea?"

The voice behind her startled her. She turned to face the man who'd spoken. "I'm looking for Agent Duncan."

"He's in the office on a Zoom call with our forensics team leader back at headquarters. It shouldn't be much longer."

She glanced toward the office—her office—and spotted him immediately, seated behind her desk. Another agent sat in the chair Arlene always used. Both were in deep discussion with a face on the computer monitor. A briefing, she supposed. Or maybe news from another source.

"I'll wait."

The agent wandered away.

Naomi walked to the storeroom door, noted the two agents going through boxes and packages, canisters and jars. They appeared to be taking samples. Made sense. Everything was suspect now. She wandered to the greenhouse area and checked the plants. They were really only seedlings at this point but soon they would be ready to move to the larger green-house for growing winter greens. Once they were moved out, new seeds would be planted to start the spring plants.

No matter that winter brought dormancy to much of the farm, there was always work to do in the greenhouses. Always a step that led into another on the land. An endless cycle that reaffirmed the beauty and endurance of nature.

As a little girl she'd loved playing in the dirt. Her mother had adored flowers and she'd planted all sorts around the house in pots and beds. But as the or-ganic farm operation grew, the time to spend with her flowers had grown less and less. Naomi had in-tended to start growing a few of her mother's fa-vorites again next spring. Just a pot here and there around the porch. The house needed some color. Starting with a few potted blooming plants seemed an easy enough place to start. She'd also considered getting a dog. Growing up there had always been a dog on the farm.

Just another of the things that had changed after she moved to California.

Not for the first time she wondered if she had stayed would she have been able to make life easier for her mom. Maybe her dad wouldn't have had that sudden heart attack. Why hadn't she come back after her mom died and stayed? Some part of her had recognized her dad likely needed her. But the part in that movie had just been offered. Even her dad had urged her to go back to her life. He and Arlene could take care of the farm.

She should have stayed. Whatever happened over the past years led to this.

Naomi scanned the comings and goings around her.

Murder.

Why hadn't he said anything?

She'd visited at least once a year. Called two or three times a month. He'd never said a word.

Guilt weighed down on her shoulders. Made her feel sick.

Drawing in a deep breath she kicked aside the self-pity. This was no time to worry about what-if. She couldn't fully depend on anyone else to clear her dad's name. It was up to her to make sure the authorities found the truth. Like Casey said, she was the only one who could advocate for her parents.

The office door opened, and Casey and the other agent emerged. As if he'd sensed her presence his gaze landed on hers. He said something to the other agent and then started in her direction.

Despite everything else that was going on, she couldn't help admiring the way he moved. The ease with which he pulled off that sexy, masculine swagger amazed her. *So not smart, Naomi.*

The instant he reached her, he asked, "Everything okay?"

She was fairly certain nothing would ever be okay again, but she didn't bother explaining the feeling. "As okay as it can be. Any news from your people?"

"We have a DNA match for one of the three victims in the freezer. The name likely won't mean anything to you. Jimmy Bagwell of Chicago. The word was his boss caught him skimming the weekly takes. He disappeared about a month ago."

"Are you serious? Another connection to organized crime?" What the hell had Arlene been doing? Running a disposal service for the mob?

"We should talk in your office."

Something in his voice warned that things were about to get worse. Defeat tugged at her as she followed him across the lab.

He closed the door of the office and waited for her to sit. She took her rolling chair and he settled into Arlene's. Except Arlene didn't need it anymore. She was dead. Never coming back. Arlene had been involved with bad people, doing very bad things. Getting rid of evidence—bodies. The realization jarred her. She pushed back the emotion and held on to her composure with both hands.

"It's becoming clearer and clearer that Beck was providing a disposal service."

"I actually just had that very thought." Her head was spinning now. It was one thing to consider an off-the-wall theory but to have an official confirm the possibility was mind-blowing.

"Whether it was disposal or whatever, she was working with very dangerous people. Considering she was murdered, we can safely assume something went wrong. She made a mistake. Crossed a line, ticked somebody off. Take your pick. The concern now is if there's another shoe going to drop. Did Arlene owe them something they didn't get?"

"Like maybe all that money in the walls on High Street?" But weren't they supposed to be paying her?

"Maybe it was about the money," Casey said, "but I'm guessing they knew about the address and would have torn the place apart if they were looking for money or something easily stored in a wall or under a floor."

Naomi felt ill. "But there's something. Something she did or didn't do."

"Most likely," he said. "You were going to talk to someone? An uncle, maybe? Were you able to find him?"

Oh, good grief. She had completely forgotten about her visit to Donnie and then the hermit over in Shake Rag. "Yes, I'm sorry. With all that's been going on I completely forgot to share what I'd learned with you."

"Anything significant?"

"I'm not sure. My uncle couldn't remember where Arlene lived before moving to Winchester. He did recall that she had a sort of thing, maybe only a friendship, with this man—Mr. Cotton, over in Shake Rag. I was able to catch him at home. It was a strange conversation. He said a good deal without saying anything that meant a thing as far as I could tell. When I told him Arlene was dead, he mentioned that they— whoever they is—were probably on to what she was involved in. He was very cryptic."

"He didn't explain what he meant?"

She shook her head. "He said I would know soon enough. And he mentioned that Arlene had learned from the master."

"Sounds like we need to talk to him again." Casey stood. "You free now?"

"Sure." She was surprised that he wanted her to go with him.

"He may speak more openly since you've talked to him before."

Made sense. "Okay."

"Besides—" he reached for his jacket "—you know the way, right?"

"Yes. I…I do." She hoped the man didn't shoot at them this time.

Most folks in Franklin County kept at least a shotgun or a rifle in the house. Then again, Casey had a weapon. She supposed that evened the odds. But a man like Cotton—already on the edge and obviously troubled—probably lived by the motto that he had nothing to lose.

Guess they would find out.

Chapter Ten

Shake Rag, 10:15 a.m.

"Did I mention this was a bit off the grid?"

Casey parked. "You mentioned it, yes." He glanced around the woods that marched right up to the narrow dirt road that stopped a good distance from the cabin barely visible in the distance. "You came out here alone?"

"I grew up here, so I'm used to this sort of thing." Naomi reached for her seat belt. "Mainly, I think I was running on adrenaline."

He grunted. The lady was definitely pretty fearless. The weight of the weapon nestled against his torso was reassuring. Off-the-grid types like the individual in this case could be a little sensitive to strangers.

"Let's see if he's accepting visitors." Casey emerged from the vehicle and adjusted his jacket. He really didn't want to get himself shot today. As he moved beyond the hood, he glanced at Naomi. He definitely did not want her to get hurt. "Stay behind me."

"Somehow it didn't look quite so ominous before."

"Desperation sometimes prevents us from seeing the danger before we make the leap."

"I've taken a few leaps like that in my time," she confessed.

"You were fearless even at eleven," he pointed out as they started moving toward the small ramshackle structure ahead.

She laughed, then covered her mouth and stared forward as if expecting the hermit to start calling out threats to halt or else.

God, she had the bluest eyes.

Focus, man.

He parked his attention back on the potential danger lying ahead. This was no time to go wandering off the task at hand.

"I have no idea what you mean, Agent Duncan," she said in a stage whisper. "I've never considered myself fearless."

"The rule was no diving off the pier."

She stalled, looked at him. "Oh my God. *I* jumped."

The words came out in a sort of awe as if she'd only just remembered that long ago day.

"You did. We had decided we were going to do it.

Before either one of us had the good sense to stop, we were both standing on the railing. Someone shouted, *No diving*. The next thing we knew people, including security, were rushing toward us. We looked at each other and you just grinned and said, *Are you brave enough to jump?* Then you jumped. I didn't have the guts."

"My parents had a fit. I didn't understand all the fuss. I was a great swimmer. It was amazing. Those moments in the air before I hit the water were incredible."

"I think it had to do with sharks, rough waters and pilings. You know, all that dangerous stuff."

The image of strands of her red hair in the breeze, those blue eyes sparkling with mischief. And that smile. He'd never forgotten that moment.

"I thought I was a mermaid in disguise. There was nothing to fear."

A *mermaid*. The perfect description.

"I almost gave my mom a heart attack." She shook her head. "It really was a foolish thing to do."

Now he felt guilty. "It may have been my fault."

She stared at him now, but he kept his eyes on the shack ahead. "How could it have been your fault? I'm the one who chose to jump."

"I recall there being a double dog dare involved."

She gasped. "You're right. I dared you to jump and the challenge escalated from there."

The great diving incident had been the last day they spent together without the cooler kid from Cali. He'd heard about Naomi's escapade and wanted to meet her. He and his mother were in the high-end condo community next door to the one Casey and Naomi were at. From that point on the west coast kid spent his every free moment on their side of the brick wall that separated the two communities.

"We were kids," he said, continuing on the path to the shack of a cabin. "Kids are reckless sometimes."

"I'm just glad to have survived."

Casey moved more fully in front of her as they reached the narrow porch on the shack. At the door he raised a fist and knocked a couple of times. It was way too quiet. They'd made plenty of noise on the walk up. The last thing he wanted to do was surprise the old guy.

"Mr. Cotton," Naomi called. "Are you home? It's Naomi Honea. I brought a friend." She glanced at Casey. "I hope you don't mind."

"We're friends?"

She smiled. He forgot to breathe. He gave himself a mental shake and knocked on the door again.

No response. Not even the slightest sound.

An old truck sat next to the house. There were other vehicles, too, but none that would run without taking a sapling or two with them. "You know if that truck is his current ride?"

"No idea. It's the same one that was here before. The others, too."

Casey knocked again. Louder this time.

Still nothing.

He hitched his head to the right. "Move over there."

She did as he asked, and he reached for the door. The knob turned without any resistance. Unlocked.

"Stay put," he ordered as he drew his weapon.

He moved beyond the threshold. Exigent circumstances were questionable. He actually had no real reason to believe Cotton was in danger. But he wasn't answering the door. An operable vehicle sat in the yard. The resident was a hermit and the door was unlocked. Casey doubted he would go anywhere without locking the door.

"Mr. Cotton?"

The house was dark with only narrow slats of light slipping in through the closed shutters on the windows. He used the flashlight app on his phone to look around. No light switches, not even a pull string from an overhead fixture. Cotton was obviously a hoarder. Stacks and stacks of newspapers and magazines and boxes sat around the perimeter of the room. Otherwise, it was surprisingly clean and tidy.

A fireplace appeared to be his heat source. Beyond the living room area was a small kitchen as well as a bedroom. He checked the bedroom first. Narrow

bed tucked against the wall. Small dresser with drawers. No closet. He walked back into the kitchen. A
window over the sink drew his attention. He crossed
the small room in three strides and looked out over
the small clearing that comprised the backyard before disappearing into the dense woods.

Then he understood why Mr. Cotton wasn't answering.

"Naomi!"

She stepped in through the front door. "Did you
find him?"

"I did." He turned to her. "I want you to stay here
in the house. I'll be right back."

He exited the back door, which was also unlocked,
before she could question him. The grass was knee-
deep in the back. There was a small shed at the edge
of the woods. An old-fashioned hand-operated well.

Elmer Cotton hung from an orange nylon rope.
The ladder lying about three feet away appeared to
be the way he'd reached the sturdy tree limb and tied
the rope there. It would seem that he'd made a noose
on the other end, put it around his neck and then
jumped from the ladder. There was no question he
was dead. The lividity in his bare feet was obvious.

"Oh my God."

Naomi stood at the back door, her hands over her
mouth.

"Stay where you are," he ordered, "until I've had

a look around." The unknown subject could still be in the area.

He moved all the way around the clearing. Scanned the ground for trampled grass. At the front of the house he found no indentation showing a vehicle had been in the yard other than his SUV. The killer likely parked on the road and slipped through the woods. Taking the elderly man completely by surprise. He moved back into the house then. Naomi waited in the kitchen near the back door just as he'd asked her to do.

"Don't touch anything," Casey warned. "This is now a crime scene."

It was possible the old man had taken his life. He'd been pretty upset when Naomi told him about Arlene's death. But Casey never liked a scenario that was too easy. Too convenient. Until he was certain, he wasn't taking any chances.

Casey was grateful for enough bars on his cell to call Sheriff Tanner and report the situation. Once the call was made, Naomi followed him back to his SUV where they donned gloves. They'd already been inside so no point in bothering with shoe covers.

"Let's have a look around." He glanced at her. "Let me know if anything looks different than the way it was when you were here before."

She nodded. "Got it."

Fearless Naomi was a little shaken at the moment.

Her lower lip had trembled when she spoke. Jumping off a pier and breaking the rules was vastly different from murder and so far she'd stumbled into several murder scenes. This may or may not be another but it involved a death nonetheless.

He surveyed the wall of articles and photos Cotton had collected and displayed. Definitely a conspiracy theorist. His focus appeared to have been primarily on politics from decades ago. More recently he'd gone off on a tangent about pesticides and food additives. A few articles were related to climate change. But most of the recent articles were about how humans were being poisoned in an effort to depopulate the earth.

"Hey! I think I found something!"

The shout came from the bedroom. Casey joined Naomi there. Above the small dresser was a painting. Maybe eleven by fourteen. The woman was nude, seated on the edge of a pool or fountain, looking back over her shoulder at the artist.

"I think this is Arlene," Naomi said. "She looks much younger, maybe thirtyish, but I think it's her."

Casey reached out and carefully lifted the unframed canvas from the wall. He turned it around and there was a large envelope tucked into the back.

"How about holding that for me while I put the canvas back?"

Naomi removed the envelope. He placed the canvas back on the wall and took the envelope from her. "Let's have a look."

With the top of the dresser clear, he opened the envelope and spread the contents there. More yellowed newspaper articles. A few pages cut from magazines. A couple of photos. *Old* photos.

"Some of these are in German," Naomi pointed out.

One article showed the date: 1958. November.

Casey carefully laid out the articles in German and snapped photos. "I'll send these in for translation."

"Here's one in English." Naomi pointed to another article. "This one is from 1964." She pointed to the photo next to the article. "This is the woman in the painting."

"Has to be." Casey quickly read the article. Naomi did the same, hovering close to see over his arm.

Ursula Becker escaped East Berlin with her five-year-old daughter, Anna. Becker, a brilliant scientist, defected to the US and has been offered a position at the prestigious Johns Hopkins.

"Anna," Naomi said. "Becker. Beck. This must be Arlene and her mother, which would mean the painting is her mother, not Arlene."

"That would be my assessment, as well." Casey

moved through the articles. The newest one was from 1975. "Ursula Becker was murdered in 1975."

Naomi took the article from him and read it. "The police believed her to be a victim of a so-called Nazi hunter for crimes against humanity during the Holocaust." She moved her head slowly side to side. "What in the world is all this?"

Dread thickened in Casey's gut. Were they looking at mob murders or something else altogether?

Honea Farm, 2:00 p.m.

NAOMI ENTERED DIFFERENT words into the search box. There had to be more about Ursula Becker. Naomi had come back to the farm an hour or so ago. A deputy had driven her home. Casey was still at Mr. Cotton's shack—the latest crime scene. She shuddered.

For her sanity's sake, she had stayed away from the news and social media. Reporters were all over town. She'd seen all sorts of different news vans on the drive back through town. They had descended on the Cotton property right behind the forensics team. Naomi had hunkered down in the rear floorboard of the county cruiser to escape without the reporters seeing her.

To occupy herself, she had been searching for information since she got back to the farm. If Arlene was Anna Becker, Naomi had never once heard her use a German accent or a German word, much less a phrase. But she'd been in the United States since she was five years old. It was possible she didn't remember living anywhere but the US. Her mother may have worked hard to avoid the use of her native tongue—even going so far as to erase her accent. Had her mother changed her name to Beck, as well? No, no. The article from 1975 had used the name Ursula Becker.

Ursula Becker came to this country as a renowned geneticist. The accusations against her as cited by the words scrawled on the wall above her dead body all those years ago were for her crimes against humans at Auschwitz alongside Josef Mengele. A handful of survivors from Auschwitz insisted she had served as Mengele's closest assistant.

Naomi reminded herself to breathe. Had her parents known who Arlene really was? About her family history? If any of this was true—and Naomi was so blown away by the idea that she couldn't quite make the leap—how could they not have known? This was beyond the scope of anything she could have imagined when this nightmare began.

The portrait in Mr. Cotton's house and the photo in the newspaper article of the woman, Ursula Becker, certainly resembled Arlene. The likeness was uncanny. At this point there was no confirmation, but it couldn't be anything else.

Had Mr. Cotton discovered Arlene's true identity?

Naomi gave herself a mental shake. She had read about these horrors in history class. Watched the occasional documentary. A movie with her dad once. But this wasn't something that happened in small-town Tennessee. This was truly stranger than fiction.

Unquestionably more horrific than fiction.

If it was true that Ursula Becker was guilty, that didn't mean Arlene—her daughter—was guilty just because of the family connection. She left Germany when she was five. How could she have known or even remembered?

How on earth had Mr. Cotton gotten involved with this? How had he figured it out? She thought of all the political articles she'd seen posted at his place. Maybe she should have read them instead of assuming what they were. No doubt Casey's people were combing each one thoroughly.

Mr. Cotton had asked her what she knew about him, then he'd said there were things about him that were dangerous.

Is this what he'd meant?

At least now she had some inkling as to why Arlene appeared not to have existed before coming to work on the farm nearly forty years ago.

Where had she been between 1975 and when she showed up here? In hiding? After her mother's murder, maybe she had been on the run. But why? At five years old when she fled Germany it was doubtful she had harmed anyone or knew things that could be helpful to anyone. Why would she have no choice but to hide? Why would anyone want to harm her?

Unless she'd followed in her mother's footsteps and had done some inhumane work here. On the farm. The remains she'd found…the body parts in the boxes—all of it made Naomi's chest constrict.

This was all too over the top. Like a bad movie. And if there was one thing Naomi knew it was bad movies.

She stared out the kitchen window toward the lab Arlene had loved so much. What kind of person kept human remains in their freezer? Had recently decapitated victims delivered on dry ice to their secret address? Terror, black and inky, slithered through Naomi.

Good grief, what had her parents gotten themselves into? Her mom and dad had been very intelligent people—her mother was a physician, for God's sake. Surely they weren't fooled for all those years.

Naomi hoped they had been.

She really, really did.

A rap on the front door drew her to the living room. She peeked beyond the curtain and spotted Casey. She unlocked the door and welcomed him in. Her mind needed a break from this new level of her ongoing nightmare. Not that he likely had any good news but at least she would stop coming up with more terrifying theories if she were distracted.

She didn't even want to consider the rumors likely going around the community. Honea Horror Farm. She shuddered inwardly.

"Were you able to get the articles translated?" What was she saying? Of course he had. He was the FBI. They could make anything happen.

"Is that coffee I smell?"

"Yes. You want a cup?"

"I would love a cup."

Naomi hurried to the kitchen and filled a mug, then joined him in record time.

"Tell me," she urged. She lowered into her chair and waited.

He sat down on the sofa. Sipped his coffee and smiled. "That hits the spot."

Her nerves were jangling. She forced a smile. Silently she urged him to get on with it.

"The articles were lauding the brilliance of a young scholar, Ursula Becker. She was mentored by the top research scientists in Germany. There is no mention in her history about being at Auschwitz or any of the other places used by the Nazis. The trouble comes later, after the war, when her name showed up on a list put together by a group of survivors. Her murder was never solved, and no one openly took credit. Her daughter, who was a senior at Harvard no less, vanished. They kept their lives very private, so we haven't found a lot of background yet, but we've got people on it."

"How did Mr. Cotton play into this insanity?"

"We don't know. He was a research scientist at NASA. About twenty-five years ago he had what was referred to as a breakdown. No one has heard from him since. I guess that's when he went off the grid here."

"So, Arlene shows up here. Then Cotton. They had to know each other before. It's the only logical conclusion."

"We're leaning toward that scenario, but we have no proof just yet."

Naomi took a breath. "I need to know what conclusions your team has reached regarding the farm and all that's happened here." Right under her nose, she didn't add. Under her parents' noses!

"I can share with you what we have so far." He savored another slug of coffee. "The remains found in the freezer were filleted from the bones. There are no parts of organs present."

Her heart thumped harder with his every word. "The red market," she said, her words hardly more than a whisper.

His gaze narrowed. "What do you know about the red market?"

"Only what I found on my internet searches since

finding what I did in that freezer. Sometimes the organs and bones are sold separately from the rest."

"We believe," he went on, "that is likely the case. The organs were obviously harvested before the rest ended up here. We're investigating the possibility that Beck was using the rest of the tissue in her work on your farm. The part we haven't been able to work into the scenario is the absence of the bones. Like you said, they were likely sold. Separately obviously. It just seems strange not to find a single one. Did she sell those first? Who knows? But we have some measure of evidence on the rest but nothing on the bones beyond the probability that they arrived here like the intact remains we found on her High Street porch. From there, we don't know yet."

The shaking started deep inside Naomi. This nightmare had reached new, unfathomable levels. "You have to believe me when I say my parents would never have gone along with something like this. She had to be doing this on her own. Maybe after my mom's death, during my father's grief."

His steady brown eyes held on to hers for a long moment. "You have my word that we are exploring every possibility, including that one."

Naomi wanted to feel relieved but honestly it was impossible. To ask this man—his team—to assume all of this happened right here on the farm where her parents lived and worked without their knowledge was a stretch. She was aware.

"I've worked with Arlene for over a year and I had no clue."

He nodded. "It's possible. Some people are very good at hiding the bad things they do."

Was that an agreement with what she'd just said or a warning to brace herself for learning what her parents may have been doing?

"What happens now?" she asked, her voice sounding hollow. She was so tired. More tired than she had ever been before.

"I'd like you to help me with the search. You grew up here. If I know you as well as I think I do, you probably explored every square inch of this farm."

A real smiled touched her lips then. "I did. I'd roam the woods and the fields daydreaming about my escape."

He chuckled. "I think we all did some daydreaming about escaping as kids."

An escape would really be nice about now. Except reality was not going to allow that to happen anytime soon.

"Let me grab my hiking boots and we'll get started."

"The temperature is dropping, and the wind is up, so you might need a hat of some sort."

"Good idea."

She hurried upstairs, used the bathroom, then located her most comfortable boots, a scarf and a beanie. As she passed her parents' room, she hesitated. "I hope you weren't keeping secrets from me."

Not these kinds of secrets, anyway.

She rushed back downstairs and found Casey waiting for her at the door.

"You ready?" he asked.

"As ready as I'll ever be."

But not nearly ready enough for what might be coming next.

Chapter Eleven

Honea Farm, 4:00 p.m.

Sheriff Tanner and his deputies had shown up with UTVs for roaming the farm. For the past going on two hours, they had covered the open fields and pastures. More deputies, federal agents and officers had taken the woods, moving on foot in a grid pattern to ensure nothing was missed.

So far Naomi had noticed nothing unusual. Nothing different than it had been when she was a child. Her hopes were dwindling.

Yet, she knew there had to be someplace Arlene carried on this evil part of her work. There was nothing in the lab—other than the remains found on Monday—that even hinted at an operation like Arlene appeared to have been running. Naomi wanted to feel guilty for thinking such bad things about the woman, but she was so far past that point now she felt nothing but anger.

Casey stared across the latest field they'd explored. "Think hard, Naomi. What we're looking for could as easily be underground as aboveground."

He'd reminded her of this about a dozen times already.

"I get that but…" She heaved a weary breath. "I haven't seen anything that jumps out at me."

"I'll check in with the other teams and see how they're coming along."

The disappointment in his voice made bad matters worse.

Surely there was something she was missing. She closed her eyes and thought of all those days she had roamed this farm, unafraid of running upon anything she couldn't handle.

"Idiot," she muttered.

Her mom had always scolded her for running off in the woods. She'd remind Naomi that there were sinkholes and caves around Franklin County that could swallow up little girls.

Caves.

"Casey!" She turned all the way around looking for him. Found him only a few feet away deep in conversation.

She waited, barely able to contain herself, until the phone call ended. "There's a place," she blurted. "In the woods near a spring that comes out of the hillside. I used to sneak over there all the time. There are lots of rocks and trees. It was like a grotto in the hillside. I didn't consider it as someplace Arlene might use until just a moment ago when I thought about all the caves in this part of the state. There was a narrow opening in the mouth of the hillside where the water came out. It might lead to a deeper cave."

"Show me."

They climbed into the UTV and headed toward the woods on the back side of the farm. The grotto wasn't in the woods but it was nearby. Casey spoke to Sheriff Tanner en route and had him and a couple of his deputies meet them at the location.

By the time Casey parked not so far from a cliffy side of the hill, she was ready to leap off the UTV and rush down the hill. How had she forgotten about this place? Maybe she'd erased more than she realized from her memory banks. When she'd gone to Hollywood, she'd worked hard to keep the memories of home at bay.

She'd been homesick but refused to admit it even to herself.

As they approached the spring-fed pool, she stalled. "This isn't how I remember."

There was no narrow opening next to the water. She recalled vividly having to wade through knee-deep water to reach the narrow opening and peer inside.

"You're certain it was here."

She nodded. "Positive."

Sheriff Tanner, hands on hips, surveyed the terrain. "We didn't run upon any other underground springs in our search."

Naomi was as certain as she could be and at the same time terrified that she might be wrong. Still, she insisted, "This has to be the place."

"Sometimes these hillside cave openings collapse," the sheriff suggested. "With the water coming out there, you can bet there's been an opening at one time."

"We need to get an excavator in here and start digging," Casey suggested.

"We'll likely run out of daylight before we can get set up," Sheriff Tanner warned.

"If you have the resources," Casey said, "let's get them in place so we can begin first thing in the morning."

"I'll make the call now," he assured.

Naomi walked closer to the small pool. The runoff from the pool traveled beyond her line of sight down the hillside. Even in the hottest part of summer there was water here. Sometimes in the winter ice would form on the pool. She remembered trying to skate on it and almost falling through.

She really had been too adventurous. Fearless, as Casey said.

She remembered all the times her father had to

take her to the clinic and have her stitched up. Or to get a tetanus shot. Naomi was forever stepping on old rusty nails or ripping open a wound on some rock or what have you. The nurse who worked for her mother for as long as Naomi could recall would always say, "Uh-oh. Here comes trouble."

Nurse Sarah. Sarah Holland.

Naomi had forgotten about her. She always gave Naomi whatever shots she required. Sarah would whisper to Naomi that her mom couldn't bear to stick a needle into her little girl.

"Sheriff." She walked over to the man who'd just ended a call. "Do you know if Sarah Holland is still around?" Naomi hadn't heard anything about her or run into her since she'd been back in Winchester this past year.

"She is," Sheriff Tanner confirmed. "She's the administrator at the Happy Valley assisted living facility near the hospital."

"She was my mother's nurse when she had her clinic."

He smiled. "That's right. She came to the school on career day once when I was in high school."

Naomi walked over to where Casey was crouched by the pool. The way he studied the terrain she hoped he could see what she saw. Rocks and shrubs and secret places that ignited a child's imagination.

He pushed to his feet. "If there's anything here we'll find it."

She felt confident he only said this to make her feel better since the opening she recalled was nowhere to be seen. "There's a nurse who worked with my mom when she had her clinic. I'd like to go talk to her."

"We could go in the morning," he offered.

"You need to be here. My security detail can take me, right?"

"Sure. We can arrange that."

Anticipation fluttered in her belly. They could be getting closer to finding something useful in the search for answers. At least she hoped.

Happy Valley, 5:00 p.m.

HAPPY VALLEY ASSISTED living was one of the newer facilities in the Winchester area, Naomi learned as she waited to see Ms. Holland. According to the brochure on the lobby table, the facility was state of the art and the first of its kind in middle Tennessee. A very expensive and classy joint. Naomi was surprised. The rooms, if the photos in the brochure were any indication, were like high-end apartments only smaller. The shared dining room and kitchen were every bit as sleek and well-appointed as a five-star restaurant.

If a senior needed help with everyday living, this was the place to be.

"Ms. Honea."

Naomi looked up. "Yes."

The woman smiled. Her hair was gray, and she was now pleasantly plump, but Naomi recognized Sarah's face.

"Ms. Holland." She stood. "Thank you so much for making the time to see me."

"I'm sorry we haven't done this sooner. Let's go to my office."

Naomi followed her along the corridor to a large, airy office that overlooked the grand fountain out front.

"You've done a marvelous job of creating a sanctuary," Naomi said as she settled into the offered chair. "I'm amazed at how peaceful and lovely it is here. I'll bet you have a waiting list."

Smiling broadly, Ms. Holland nodded. "We do. We're very lucky that people have recognized and appreciated the priceless value of a place like this one."

Naomi figured the priceless part was the one sticking point.

Sarah's smile slipped into a frown. "I'm so sorry to hear about the horrors you're experiencing at the farm. It truly is quite awful. Your mother would be beside herself. Is there anything I can do to help?"

"Actually, that's part of the reason I'm here. In all the years that you worked with my mom did she ever mention any issues at the farm? Maybe with any of the people who worked with my dad?"

Her mom had spent countless hours each evening after a long day at the clinic to help out on the farm. It hadn't seemed strange at the time. To a nine-year-old there was no difference between a doctor and a farmer. They were both jobs. But now she understood that what her mom did was above and beyond the call of duty.

Mrs. Holland pursed her lips. "You might not remember but one of the reasons your mother decided to work so hard with your father on the farm was because of Lanita Carlson. She was only four and she suddenly fell terribly ill. Your mother felt as though she didn't diagnose her in time to save her life. She never got past it. Every physician loses a patient eventually, but this one haunted her. She started to second-guess herself in everything she did. It was quite painful to watch. After you left for California, she actually spent more time on the farm than at the clinic. A nurse practitioner took care of the patients."

Naomi felt sick. "I had no idea."

"It wasn't something she wanted to talk about. Instead, she devoted herself more and more to the farm. Truth be told, your mother was the one who turned it around. Nolan, bless him, worked very hard to make a go of things. But he just wasn't as savvy as your mom. He had the vision but couldn't quite pull off the execution. Your mother really was a genius. To her way of thinking, the way to a healthy life stared with healthy eating."

"My dad seemed happy to have her with him in any capacity." Naomi didn't recall any tension between them, but she'd been a kid. She may not have noticed.

"He was thrilled. As I said, she was the brains behind the vision. With her help, he had the farm thriving in no time flat."

"Arlene Beck had been working for my dad for a good number of years already when my mother started pitching in. They seemed to work well together also."

"Arlene was another one who had cutting-edge ideas about how to elevate the farm to an organic farm. She and your mother became quite close, I think."

"I guess you heard she was murdered." It was ridiculous to think for a second she hadn't. The debacle at the farm was big news. National news.

Something flashed in Ms. Holland's expression. "It's all quite tragic. Your parents loved the farm. I know they would hate to see it torn apart this way."

On Naomi's watch at that. How had she allowed

this to happen? Surely there were signs. Had she just not been paying attention?

"It's unsettling to say the least." Naomi considered how to best frame the next question. She'd already ventured into this territory but she needed to be sure. "When you were working together at the clinic, did Mom ever mention anything about Arlene? I don't recall there ever having been any issues at all."

"I can't think of a time when there was an issue. But then, your mother was very private when it came to her personal life."

"Did you know Arlene very well? I haven't been able to figure out where she lived before Winchester. Or if she had any family I need to contact."

Ms. Holland frowned. "She was already here when I moved to Winchester. I suppose I've never thought of her as living anywhere else. I don't recall her ever saying."

"No accent that suggested a particular part of the country?"

Ms. Holland considered the question for a moment. "There was a bit of an accent. Nothing like ours down here. I assumed it had to do with where she'd been educated. These kids go off to college and come back talking like strangers."

Naomi could vouch for that scenario. She'd spent ages trying to conquer her Southern accent. "She never mentioned family or friends from somewhere else?"

"Not that I recall." She smiled, but the gesture was obviously forced. "I really didn't know Arlene well." She glanced at the clock. "Oh my, it's time for my next appointment. I hope we can chat again soon." She stood, broadening her plastic smile.

"Thank you for your time, Ms. Holland. Please let me know if you think of anything that might help us learn more about Arlene."

"Of course."

Naomi left with the strangest feeling that she'd said something that made the woman uncomfortable. She'd seemed fine until Naomi pushed the subject of Arlene. She hadn't wanted to go too deeply into that past.

Certainly it was possible she did have an appointment but no one had been waiting in the lobby as Naomi left. Or perhaps she simply didn't want to get involved in this bizarre case.

Maybe Donnie would have some insight into Ms. Holland's relationship with Naomi's mom and Arlene. Didn't hurt to ask.

Dogwood Apartments, 6:00 p.m.

DONNIE WAS SURPRISED to see Naomi again so soon. She was surprised herself. Her uncle wasn't one to keep in touch and Naomi hadn't really put forth the extra effort to try to change that reality. Frankly, she'd been a little busy.

"This is wild," Donnie said after listening to her rundown of the latest news. "You're saying Arlene's mother might have been some sort of war criminal?"

"I can't say for sure, but that's the way it looks so far. I'm having trouble accepting that Mom didn't know any of this. Dad might have overlooked it. You know he didn't like to get into people's business. But Mom was so keenly perceptive. I can't see her missing all this."

She thought of the story about the patient—the child—her mom had lost, and her heart ached. Why hadn't her mom ever talked about it? Had her dad known? What was worse, all these questions were making her doubt everything she thought she knew about her family. Naomi didn't like that feeling at all.

"I can't see it, either," he agreed. "Muriel was always the smart one. She was far too perceptive for anything to be happening around her and not recognize it. There's something off with all this, Naomi. I'm very concerned. Would you like me to come to the farm and stay with you for a while? It's not like I have anything pressing to do around here. The fresh air might even do me good."

"You're always welcome, Uncle Donnie." She thought of how Casey Duncan had slept on her couch and likely would tonight and instantly regretted having extended the invitation.

"Oh, snap," he muttered. "I did promise Heloise I'd look after Mr. Grumpy this weekend. She's going to visit her sister in Indiana. He's quite the feisty little pooch and her sister hates him. I'd have to come back and forth through the day and evening to take care of him."

"It's not necessary right now, Uncle Donnie. I have my own personal bodyguards."

"Just like a celebrity," he teased.

She rolled her eyes. "One more question," she ventured. "Do you know of anyone in the area who might have emigrated from Germany after the war? Anyone who might have known Arlene's mother?"

"You mean like a Holocaust survivor?"

"Yes, I suppose I do."

"There were a couple I remember reading about, but that was years ago. I can't recall their names."

"Maybe I could find something at the library?" If it was still open. Damn. She always seemed a day late and a dollar short.

"I'd call that lady who owns the newspaper, Audrey Tanner. She's the sheriff's wife. I'll bet she can tell you right off. I just remember that it was in the newspaper a while back."

Naomi started to go but decided she had another question or two.

"Do you think Arlene could have done something like this? I mean, really, was she so coldhearted?"

He stared at his clasped hands hanging between his knees. "You know, she was a little cold. Stand-offish. Not with your folks, I don't think, but she rarely spoke to me." He chuckled. "Everyone likes me. But like I told you before, I sort of stepped on it where Arlene was concerned."

Naomi smiled. "You're just a likable kind of guy."

Her uncle gave her a half smile. "Try talking to Audrey over at the *Winchester Gazette*. She'll know if I'm recalling right."

Before leaving Naomi asked, "You remember that cave-like opening by the underground spring I used to talk about all the time? The one Mom told me time and time again to stay away from?"

"Sure do. I even went in it one time. I was hoping for lost treasure or hidden booty of some sort. But I didn't find anything at all."

"You could actually climb inside?"

"Yep. I saw it with my own eyes."

"There was only one on the farm, right?"

"As far as I know. Why do you ask?"

"We went out that way this afternoon and it must have fallen in or something."

"That's too bad. It was pretty cool once you got past the part that required you to belly crawl through it."

"Cool how?"

"It was a big room. Like a cavern. Seems weird that it would just fall in like that. But it happens. Usually something causes it."

Very weird, she agreed. She could only imagine what had caused it.

Something more to add to this horror story.

Tanner Home, 7:00 p.m.

THE *WINCHESTER GAZETTE* was closed so Naomi asked her driver, the deputy assigned to her security detail this evening, to drive her to the Tanner home. Casey had called to check on her—he was heading to the chief of police's office for a big conference call with all the entities involved with this ever-evolving case.

Just her luck to have the most bizarre criminal case to ever happen in Winchester. Her family would likely end up a part of some documentary.

Not at all the fame she'd hoped for when she ran off to Hollywood.

Naomi knocked on the front door of the Tanner home and waited. She was bone tired. When she got home she was having a long, hot shower to relax her muscles and her mind. Maybe some wine to take off the edge.

The door opened and a very pregnant blonde woman smiled at her. "Naomi Honea. Nice to finally meet you."

See, the sheriff's wife already knew her. "Likewise," Naomi offered.

She didn't know very much about Audrey except that her family had owned the local newspaper forever, it seemed. Like Naomi, Audrey had left Winchester to follow her own dreams but then returned to take over the family business.

They apparently had a good deal in common.

"Do you have a few minutes to talk?" Naomi asked, hoping her impromptu visit wouldn't be too much of an inconvenience.

"Sure. Come in. Colt is still at work but I'm on maternity leave and bored stiff."

Naomi hoped one day to have children of her own. That dream seemed a long way off these days.

"I'm sure Sheriff Tanner has filled you in on what's happening at the farm."

"To the degree that he can, yes. Please have a seat."

They settled into chairs facing each other near the fireplace.

"Has your paper in, say, the past thirty or so years done a story on Holocaust survivors living in the area?"

Audrey thought about the question for a bit. "We did. I think it was about ten years ago."

"Could you share names with me so that I might speak—?"

"I'm afraid they've both passed away since then.

But I can round up next of kin for you if that would help."

"I'd appreciate it. I'm trying to make sense of all this and it's just not happening."

"Sometimes it doesn't until the final piece of the puzzle is discovered. I'll locate the information and text it to you."

They shared cell phone numbers and Audrey showed Naomi to the door. Back in the county cruiser she thought of how lonely life would be on the farm now. Her parents were gone. Arlene was gone.

If there was even a farm left when this was over.

Chapter Twelve

Thirty-five minutes ago, Naomi had arrived home. Her first thought as she stood on the porch was, *What now?* All the official personnel and vehicles appeared to be gone for the day. Her surveillance detail had told her that Casey was still in the teleconference in town with the sheriff and the chief. A moment later as she entered the house, it occurred to her that it had been days since either of them had the opportunity for a decent meal. She had no idea why food even entered her mind. It certainly hadn't before now.

Even so, she rummaged through the fridge and the freezer to see what she had on hand. Stocking the shelves had been the last thing on her mind, but now, tonight, she was suddenly starving.

It was weird. Her emotions and senses had been in some sort of partial limbo and suddenly they were all roaring at once.

She was hungry. She was confused. She was alone. All of it swirled inside her like a cyclone.

Thankfully she dug up a box of frozen lasagna that was not out of date. Frozen rolls that only had to be browned and frozen green beans that could be steamed in the microwave. It wouldn't be five-star cuisine, but it would be edible.

She had forty-five minutes before the lasagna would need to come out of the oven. A shower was essential to her feeling human again. Sweats would be comfy. While the water in the shower heated up, she grabbed a comfy pair of sweats and fuzzy socks. The weather app on her phone alerted her to cooler than usual temps tonight. Since the rain set in, the weather had been unseasonably cool. Maybe she'd have her first fire of the season. One of the things she loved best about this old farmhouse was the big fireplace in the living room.

Wine, too. Definitely wine.

The water felt fantastic as she closed her eyes and allowed it to sluice over her body. For a long time she only stood there, allowing the heat to envelop and relax her. Her muscles loosened and the insanity of the day slowly started to drain away. She washed her hair, working her fingers over her scalp, massaging and kneading.

She continued on to her neck muscles, urging the tightness and the tension away. Before she could stop herself she imagined how it would feel to have

Casey's long fingers and wide hands moving over her body this way. She sighed and smiled a secret smile.

Maybe it was the desperation she had felt for days now or the shock radiating through her again and again as each day brought some new harsh reality. Another stunning jolt…another murder. Somehow at this moment it coalesced into a need so strong she could hardly contain it.

She placed her hands against the cool shower walls and took slow deep breaths until control was hers once more. A few moments passed and she felt ready to face the world again. She refused to allow the events of this week to take her down. Her parents had worked too hard to make this farm what it was. She owed them her every effort to right things once more.

After drying her skin, she stood before the mirror and considered her hair. Wild and even redder when it was wet. She toweled it dry and applied the tiniest bit of product to stave off the frizzies. The sweats felt soft and warm and the fuzzy socks were the finishing touch.

Descending the stairs, the smell of lasagna filled the air. It wasn't homemade but it sure smelled good. Her stomach rumbled. She took the final step down and stalled.

A blast of cold air slipped around her, made her shiver. She walked to the front door and ensured it was fully closed. Then she headed for the kitchen. She froze in the doorway.

The back door stood open.

For three beats she couldn't move…couldn't even scream.

The timer sounded on the oven, shattering the eerie silence.

Naomi forced one foot in front of the other until she reached the door. She pushed it closed. Locked it.

Had she failed to shut it properly?

No. She had come through the front door. She hadn't touched the back door.

Someone had been in the house.

She reached into the pocket of her hoodie and closed her fingers around her phone. Then she went to the counter and pulled out the biggest knife in the block. The silver blade gleamed against the light.

With her back to the sink versus one or the other exits from the room, she moved to the stove and silenced the timer, then reached for the knob to turn off the oven.

It was already off.

She stared at the knob. Closed her eyes. Looked again. *Off.*

This was an old stove. Not one of the new ones that turned off the oven when the timer signaled. You had to manually turn off the stove. The timer was just a timer.

The blood pounding in her ears, she moved toward the front door. The deputy on duty was right outside. No more than a dozen yards from the porch. All she had to do was go outside and wave to him.

She backed across the living room, splitting her attention between the kitchen door, the hall and the stairs. Those were the only three usable routes to get to her...if someone was in the house.

Her back bumped the door. She reached behind her, flipped the lock. In one fast move she whirled around and pulled the door open. She was on the porch and moving forward. Didn't bother waving. She rushed down the steps and across the grass in nothing but her fuzzy socks. She didn't stop until she reached the deputy's car.

Where was he?

She moved closer. Peered through the window.

Empty.

She checked the back seat.

Nothing.

Fear pulsed in her veins.

Before she could consider another option, she got in behind the wheel and hit the lock button.

She called 911.

Honea Farm, 10:30 p.m.

CASEY BURST OUT of his SUV before it stopped rocking in the driveway. He rushed to the county cruiser. Naomi stared up at him, blue eyes wide with fear.

"Unlock the door," he said gently.

The click sounded and Casey pulled the door open. He grabbed her and pulled her out of the car.

Deputies and officers poured across the property to start the search for the missing deputy. The security detail who had apparently vanished.

"You okay?"

She nodded. Dropped the big knife she'd been clutching. It clattered on the ground. "I am now."

"Let's get you inside." He urged her forward, to the house.

By the time they reached the porch Tanner was coming through the door.

"House is clear."

"Thanks." Casey breathed a little easier.

Naomi looked from him to Tanner and back. "Where's the deputy who was here? The one who drove me home?"

Tanner gave her a nod. "Don't worry. We'll find him."

Inside the smell of marinara sauce reminded Casey that he hadn't eaten since before lunch. Didn't matter.

Naomi dropped into her chair and he sat down across from her. "Tell me what happened."

"I put food in the oven and went upstairs for a shower." She shivered. "When I came down the back door was open. I closed and locked it. Thought maybe I hadn't shut it properly. But the stove was turned off. I didn't turn it off. Then I realized I came in through the front door. I hadn't been near the back door since I came home. Someone was in the house while I was in the shower."

"Let's take a walk through and see if anything is missing."

"If something happened to the deputy or if he is dead…" A shudder quaked through her.

"Let's hope he's after whoever came into the house."

She nodded.

They moved from room to room, checking the closets, drawers, cabinets. In the downstairs study Naomi stopped.

"He was in here." She glanced around. "Assuming the intruder was a he."

"Can you determine if anything is missing or what he may have been looking for?"

"It'll take a minute."

"Take your time."

Tanner stuck his head in the door and Casey stepped into the hall to join him. "I hope we don't have another body." The count was already far too high, and they were no closer to finding the answers they needed.

"Almost. We found the missing deputy. He'll pull through but he took a hell of a blow to the back of the head. He spotted someone at the rear corner of the house and went after him. He didn't get a look at his face, just a general size. It was an ambush. Looks like it bought the perp some time to get into the house."

Damn it. "Keep me posted on the deputy's status."

Tanner assured him he would and headed back outside. Casey returned to the study to see if Naomi had discovered anything missing.

"The deputy's going to be okay?"

"Looks that way. He confirmed there was an intruder. Have you noticed anything missing?"

"I can't be certain, but it really looks like he only riffled through papers. Whatever he was looking for must not have been here."

"We'll check for prints," Casey said, "but chances are he protected his identity with gloves."

This was what they'd found throughout the lab and other areas of the property. No prints other than those of the people who worked there.

Within the hour the deputies and officers had cleared out for the night. Naomi had insisted on finishing the dinner and sitting down to a civilized meal. The bottle of wine surprised him.

"Would you like to share notes from our afternoons?" She tested a bite of lasagna.

"We found evidence to prove Cotton not only knew Arlene, but he had also been watching her for years. He left endless accountings of dates and codes. The final pages from the past month were all the same."

Naomi looked at him expectantly waiting for him to go on.

"'She has to die. She has to die. She has to die.' Every entry was exactly the same."

"Is it possible he killed her?" She lowered her fork back to the table. "He seemed so overwrought when I told him she was dead."

"Maybe he was upset because he felt we were on to him."

"But we weren't." She frowned. "So, if he was Arlene's killer, who broke into my house tonight?"

"A very good question to which I do not have an answer." He took a bite of lasagna and made a satisfied sound. "This is really good."

"Please. It came from a box in the freezer." She suddenly looked paler than usual. "I'll never be able to reach into the freezer and think nothing of it again."

He smiled reassuringly. "You seemed to have managed tonight."

"Maybe." She speared a green bean and brought it to her lips.

He watched with far too much interest. Caught himself and focused on his plate. "GPR picked up on some anomalies near your grotto so we're excavating a small location to have a look."

"GPR?"

"Ground-penetrating radar. It's a way of look-ing beneath the surface of a location without dig-ging randomly."

"Wow." Emotions flickered across her face. "I'm beginning to wonder when this nightmare is going to end."

He understood this entire situation was incredibly overwhelming. Murder and puzzles like this were his work. Steps, routines and methods he went through with each case. For her, it was foreign, intrusive, more than a little scary.

"How about you?" he asked, moving on. "You learn anything useful today?"

"I talked to the nurse who worked closely with my mom when she had the clinic. She operates an as-sisted living facility now. She only had good things to say. She was unaware of any problems and didn't know Arlene very well. She did mention that Arlene had a bit of an accent in the beginning but not one she could readily identify."

"Sometimes you have to beat the bushes for a while before something pops out."

"No kidding." She sipped her wine. "I told my uncle what we had learned and suspected so far. He wasn't a lot of help, but he did mention that there were two Holocaust survivors in the Winchester area. I spoke to Audrey Tanner, the sheriff's wife.

She owns the local newspaper. She confirmed what Uncle Donnie said, but unfortunately, the two had passed away. She's going to look up the names for me and get us the information."

"We should hear more from my sources in the Bureau tomorrow. I have my doubts as to whether this relates back to Beck's family history, but it's important that we thoroughly investigate every possibility."

"I guess the mob connection is more likely." She picked at her lasagna.

"You don't agree?" He sipped the wine. One glass was his limit.

"I'm not sure. It feels like this is bigger than the mob connection. Arlene is dead. Why keep coming back? Why murder Mr. Cotton?"

"If he was murdered," Casey countered.

"If," she agreed.

"The only reason for anyone to persist beyond her murder is if there's something more they need or want. Something she hid from them."

"So, we keep looking." She cradled her wineglass.

"We keep looking until we've done all we can to find answers. At this point we have at least six victims. I want to make sure it ends now."

From this point forward if he had to be away from her for any reason, he would have a second deputy or officer stand in his place. The risk was too great. Whoever was behind this business, he wasn't finished yet. He had come into this house with her here and alone and left without harming her. Casey would like to say that meant he had no intention of hurting her. But he wasn't fool enough to believe anything of the sort. Without a doubt, he was searching for something.

People who killed to accomplish a goal sometimes had rules, lines they didn't cross and even a modicum of honor. But those same people would typically do whatever necessary to protect themselves.

"I suppose when this case is over, you're off."

Casey watched her as she gingerly tasted another green bean. "Back to Nashville," he agreed.

"You have someone there?" She dared to look at him this time.

"My mom. My dad died a couple of years ago."

"I'm sorry to hear that."

"Thanks. And I have a sister—if you remember—who is bossy and nosy and better to me than I deserve."

A smile spread across Naomi's face. "I do remember her. Blonde? Very pretty? About sixteen that long ago summer?"

"That's the one. She's married, has four kids and thinks she knows everything. I cannot tell you the number of blind dates she has arranged for me. Generally, without my advance knowledge."

Naomi laughed out loud this time. "She sounds

like a wonderful sister. She and your mother have probably got your wedding planned already. They just have to find the right bride."

"I'd lay odds on it."

They picked at their foot in silence. Casey imagined she was as exhausted as he was, but he wasn't ready to crash. He wanted to talk to her. To *be* with her.

"What about you?" he said. Turnabout was fair play, right?

"Me?" She shrugged. "I've been so busy with the farm I haven't had time to think about a personal life."

"You mean all the single guys in Winchester haven't been knocking on your door?"

"Are there single guys in Winchester? I'm pretty sure they're all taken. Not that I've been looking, mind you."

The pink blush that crept over her cheeks told him she wasn't entirely comfortable with the conversation.

Casey allowed another taste of his wine. "You just turned thirty, right?"

She made a face. "Is that supposed to mean something? Is my life over because I'm thirty and single?"

He held up his hands. "No, no. That's not what I meant at all."

"Good." She sipped her wine. "I can assure you

I will never forget my thirtieth. I found human remains in my freezer."

"That's too bad. Definitely made for a memorable event."

"I'll get over it. As my father would say, just another day."

Except it wasn't just another day. It was a really bad day.

Casey stood, gathered his plate and glass and took them to the kitchen. Naomi trailed him. Without further conversation they cleaned up the kitchen and tossed the remains of dinner in the trash.

Naomi poured more wine and Casey wished he could indulge but he wouldn't take the risk. The sweatpants and hoodie sweatshirt made her look like a little girl.

"What are you smiling about?" She held up the bottle. "You want more?"

"I should pass."

She stared at him over the rim of her glass. "What's the smile about? I swear, I can't think of a thing either of us has to smile about at the moment."

If he told her would she be flattered or annoyed? "I like the sweats. You look relaxed."

She tugged at the baggy top. "When I came home all I could think about was standing under the hot spray of water and getting into something utterly comfortable."

He had to remind himself to speak since his brain was still stuck on the image of her under that hot spray of water.

She set her glass aside. "Okay, I don't know if it's the wine or the insanity of the past few days driving me, but I have to do this. I cannot take it anymore."

He frowned. "What can't you take anymore?"

"Kiss me." She planted her hands on her hips. "I know you're feeling the attraction just like I am so let's get it over with. See if the real thing can stand up to the memory."

"You want me to kiss you?" he confirmed, his pulse already hammering.

"Only if you want to—if you're as curious as I am, then I'm certain you want to."

She had no idea.

He took her face in his hands, glided the pad of his thumb over her cheek. "I've dreamed of doing this again for a very, very long time."

He kissed her.

His lips melted into hers and the rush of sensations made it impossible to breathe.

He drew back just far enough to look into her eyes. "How's that?"

"I'm not sure. Can we do it again?"

A knock on the door sent them stumbling apart.

Grappling for his composure, he held out a hand

for her to stay put. He walked to the window and checked the porch.

Deputy Lawton.

Breathing easier, he moved to the door and opened it just enough to hear what the man had to say.

"Just wanted you to know that I'm on for the night. You have any trouble you let me know."

"Keep your eyes open, Lawton," Casey warned. "I'm sure you heard what happened to the deputy earlier."

"Got it, Agent Duncan."

He turned on his heel and walked back to his car.

Casey closed the door and locked it.

When he turned back to Naomi she was standing at the bottom of the stairs.

"See you in the morning."

Then she was gone.

One thing was for sure. That long ago kiss didn't hold a candle to the one they'd shared just now.

The memory would haunt him for another twenty years.

Chapter Thirteen

Casey had just poured his second cup of coffee when he got the word. He was needed at the excavation site. They'd found something.

He hadn't heard a sound from upstairs. He'd worried that when he showered she would wake up, but she hadn't stirred. It was late when she went to bed. Considering the recent events, he doubted she went to sleep immediately. Probably didn't sleep well, either. He'd wanted to follow her up those stairs last night something fierce. But she hadn't extended the invitation and he knew better.

At least they'd had that kiss. The memory warmed him.

Whatever happened when this investigation was done, he would think of that kiss for a very long time to come.

Casey found paper and pen in a drawer and left her a note to call when she was up. He pulled on his jacket and headed out the front door, locking it behind him. It was warmer this morning than last night. He hurried down the porch steps and to the cruiser parked next to his SUV.

The deputy powered down the window. "Morning, Agent Duncan."

Not Lawton. There must have been an early-morning shift change. Casey was surprised he hadn't knocked on the door to announce the change.

"Deputy." Casey gave him a nod. So far this week he'd met a different deputy for each shift. Except for Lawton. He'd showed up for the detail three or four times now. "I'm heading across the field to the excavation site. I'd like you to move to the front porch until Ms. Honea is up."

"Yes, sir."

While Casey loaded into his SUV, the deputy climbed the porch steps and took a seat in a rocking chair. Casey backed up, then turned toward the narrow dirt road that led deeper onto the property. He could drive most of the way. A ping warned he had a text message. He stopped and had a look.

Call me.

Casey put the SUV in Park and made the call to

his ASAC. Assistant Special Agent in Charge Preston Wagner answered on the first ring.

"Duncan, this case just elevated to the highest priority."

Casey braced for whatever profound news he was about to receive. "I'm listening."

"Dental records and prints confirm your vic, Arlene Beck, was Anna Becker. Those numbers on the file jacket are showing up as foreign bank accounts that go back decades. There's a lot we don't know. But we were notified to stand down. I need you to wrap up and get back to Nashville."

"Wait—" Casey took a second to slow his frustration. "What does that mean, *stand down*?"

"You know what it means, Duncan."

"I know what it means," he growled. "I'm asking you in what capacity should I stand down on this one? We have multiple homicide victims and no confirmation that they're all related. If—"

"It means that whatever you find, it has nothing to do with Becker or that history. It means this is bigger than the Bureau and a task force will be taking over."

"Give me the day at least," Casey argued. "There are loose ends to tie up here."

"I can give you that," Wagner agreed, "but you cannot move forward on this investigation. It's above our pay grade."

"I can live with that," Casey relented. "But I want

to know how did this Anna Becker end up in Franklin County, Tennessee, as Arlene Beck?"

"I don't know much," Wagner admitted, "but I know that after the death of her mother, Becker— Beck—disappeared. She was the one to turn her mother in to the authorities. I have no idea why and probably never will. Before the authorities could move in on her mother—Ursula Becker—she was murdered. The daughter was never heard from again. It was assumed that the daughter was dead, as well. Apparently, that was not the case."

"Thanks. I appreciate that much." He had a feeling this information explained a lot more than maybe Wagner understood.

"Duncan, I know this isn't what you want to hear, but the order came from above."

"Got it." Casey ended the call before more could be said. No need to give the man time to toss out any other restrictions.

Casey had never been one to break the rules. But this was different. He wasn't going to pretend he didn't know what he knew. He damned sure wasn't leaving Naomi in the dark when she deserved far more. This was her home. Her family.

When he reached the grotto, the excavator sat dormant, but judging by the amount of dirt and rock lying in a pile to one side, the digging had been going on for a while this morning. He was glad he hadn't gotten the call from Wagner before the excavation began. Maybe they'd uncovered more pieces of the puzzle Naomi would need to get on with her life.

Whatever was going on, he wanted the whole story. He wanted to protect Naomi from anything that might be coming. Hell, at this point they still had no idea who the bad guy was.

Casey parked and headed for the half a dozen people huddled around the open pit that had been unearthed just above the pool of water below. One of the team members, Ted Letson, glanced up at him and shook his head. When Casey reached the other agent and had a look into the pit for himself, he understood the reaction.

What the hell?

In the pit was a pickup and a car. Both were damned rusty and bent up from being dumped into the pit and then covered with dirt. The vehicles looked to be thirty or more years old.

"One of the Franklin County deputies who is licensed in cave rescues," Letson explained, "is down there trying to locate a license plate on one or both vehicles. He had his gear in his truck, so we let him have at it."

Casey snapped a pic. "You called Tanner or Brannigan?"

"On the way. Called them right after I called you."

Casey opted not to mention his conversation with

Wagner. He intended to push forward as far as possible before the new investigators arrived.

"Yo!" the deputy in the pit called out.

"What have you got?" Letson called back.

"We got bones in both vehicles. Like entire skeletons. One in each."

More victims. At least two. Damn. Casey said, "We need a bigger forensics team."

"I think you're right," Letson agreed. "I'll call Wagner."

"Don't worry about Wagner. Call Jensen directly. He'll get someone down here ASAP."

Rule break number one. Wagner would not be happy when he found out.

Letson made the call. While he did, Casey removed his jacket and donned the proper gear. He was going down there. Every minute they wasted put them closer to being shut down. He'd made a promise to Naomi that he'd find answers for her. He wasn't going to let her down.

Casey used the same ladder rope the deputy had put in place to make his way down to the vehicles. The car appeared to have been dumped on top of the pickup. The scent of disturbed soil rose up and filled his nostrils.

"Have a look," the deputy said as Casey found his footing atop the car.

The driver of the car was still strapped into the

driver's seat. Like the deputy said, the skeleton re-mained intact. The clothes were mostly rotted away, but a pearl necklace hanging from the neck area sug-gested the remains were female.

"Can we get a good look into the cab of the truck?" Casey asked.

"It landed kind of canted to one side so there's a good slice of cracked window right beneath the right front tire of this car."

Casey slipped down lower to a crevice where dirt had not filled in around the truck.

"Be careful," the deputy said. "I don't think this car will move, but you never know."

"Got it." Casey eased closer to the blue truck's driver side window. It was necessary to force his head into the small area between the car and the truck to see inside. Another set of bones. Mostly intact. No seat belt this time. The bones lay against the passenger side door as if the victim had been slung there when the truck landed in the hole. Like the other victim, the clothes were mostly gone, but a good portion of a set of sneakers remained. He was only guessing, but judging by the length and width, this was likely a male victim.

His assessments would need to be confirmed but he was usually on the money.

"I can make out part of the car's license plate," the deputy called out to him.

Casey climbed back in that direction using the occasional rock protruding from the earth and parts of the vehicle's undercarriage.

"I can see the first number but nothing after that."

Casey looked around. "Let me climb over the quarter panel and see if I can get a shot with my cell phone."

The deputy pushed on the car. It rocked ever so slightly. "Better be careful, this thing is not as stable as it looks."

"With that in mind," Casey said, "you get back on the ladder while I do this."

"I'm not sure," the deputy began, "it—"

Casey shot him a look that warned this was not a debate. The deputy moved back to the ladder and climbed up a couple of rungs.

When the deputy was safely out of the way, Casey moved up onto the vehicle. The car rocked slightly, and he stilled to wait for it to settle. Then he started to move again. When he was lying facedown across the quarter panel over the rear tire, he slid just far enough to lower his arm between the rear end and the dirt wall. He took a couple of pics and checked the screen.

He got half the license plate, but he needed the whole thing.

He slid on his belly, moving closer to the bumper, and reached deeper this time. Angled his phone a little more.

The car moved.

This time it didn't stop.

Honea Farm, 7:00 a.m.

NAOMI SPREAD THE covers over her bed.

She'd smelled the coffee and roused half an hour ago, but she hadn't wanted to go down and face Casey just yet. It was silly, she knew, but she was a little embarrassed about having insisted he kiss her.

Sleep had eluded her last night. Between finding Mr. Cotton hanging from that tree and…

Good grief, how could this all be happening? Murders rarely happened in Franklin County. Suddenly the homicide rate had quadrupled and her farm was the primary crime scene. It was totally crazy. Beyond crazy.

She walked down the hall and paused at the door of her parents' room. Surely they had no idea all this was happening.

But how could they not? It wasn't just one thing, it was so many things. So many bodies. So many puzzling pieces. The hidden money. The strange strings of numbers. The remains in the freezer. A human head in a box!

Still, big questions remained. Where were the

bones? Who did this? Why? Beyond the money obviously.

She thought of Arlene and all the years she had been part of this family. Other than Sarah Holland, her mom's nurse, Arlene was the closest friend her mom had. Between the farm and her mom's medical clinic, her parents basically knew everyone in town, but they were busy people. Always working either at the clinic or on the farm. There was the occasional community function to which her parents felt obligated to attend but there wasn't a lot of socializing. Hellos and updates were provided in passing at the Piggly Wiggly or the Farmer's Co-op.

Naomi wondered if the lack of close friends was related to all this somehow.

No. No, her parents had nothing to do with any of this. The idea was ludicrous.

She moved away from their door and headed downstairs. The coffeepot was calling her name. She hoped Casey had received an update that answered questions rather than piled on more.

The final step down, she called out, "Good morning."

Footsteps in the kitchen drew her in that direction. At the door she almost bumped into a deputy.

"Morning, ma'am."

She blinked. Scrambled to recall his name. "Good

morning, Deputy Lawton. Sorry, I was expecting Agent Duncan."

"He got a call to go out to the excavation site, ma'am," Lawton explained. "He asked me to stay in the house since you were still asleep. He's a little worried after last evening's scare."

So was she. She pushed a smile into place. "Well, all right, then. I am dying for a cup of coffee."

"Just made a fresh pot. The other was a little stale."

"Thanks." Casey had likely made coffee before daylight. A fresh pot was a good thing.

She poured a cup and savored a long, warm swallow before moving back into questioning mode. She leaned against the counter and turned her attention to the deputy. "Have they found something near the pool?"

"I'm afraid I haven't heard anything specific, only that they needed Agent Duncan there." He, too, leaned against the counter on the opposite side of the kitchen.

Naomi enjoyed more of her coffee. Lawton's cell phone made a sound and he pulled it from his belt and checked the screen. News, she hoped.

"Looks like they have found something, ma'am." He put his phone away. "Sheriff Tanner says the two of us should have a look around here. See if we find any old keys. They found an old car and old truck buried out there by that underground spring."

Naomi's breath caught. "Oh my God. How is that possible?"

"I don't know, ma'am." He shrugged. "Sometimes our folks don't tell us all they know. They keep secrets. I suppose they think it's for the best, but it usually turns out to be not good at all."

No kidding. Naomi set her cup aside. "It's the craziest thing I've ever seen. I always considered my parents very honest people. I can't believe they were keeping secrets like this. And Arlene." She shook her head. "It's just stunning that she did the things it appears she did. I still can't fully believe it. Did you know her?"

Lawton shook his head. "Not really. I mean, I've seen her around, but I didn't know her. One of the other deputies told me she was cutting people off the bone. Wonder what happened to all those bones?" His eyes bugged out a little. "And I heard about that box with the head in it. You're right. That's pretty dang crazy."

"I've tried to think of where she might have hidden the bones, but it's possible she sold the bones to a buyer on the red market. I'm sure you've heard of the red market."

"I've heard talk about it," he said, "but I don't know much. It's not something you like to think about. And we don't get a lot of that kind of thing around here. There was that one time Chief Brannigan discovered an employee at the funeral home was taking things—pieces—from folks they prepared for burial."

Naomi had almost forgotten the incident. She supposed it was possible there was a connection. She straightened away from the counter. "Shall we start the search? Keys, you say?"

"He said keys and I guess it wouldn't hurt for us to look for any kind of hiding place we can find. Like you say, those bones have to be somewhere."

She would certainly rather be doing something than standing around waiting for more bad news. "Sure. You're probably more of an expert than me. Where would you suggest we start?" She had checked all the places in the house she could think to look already. But then she was so close emotionally to this, it was hard to know if she had been thorough enough.

"We can start at the top and work our way down. I've found that's usually the best. Could be a trap door or a hidden room."

Naomi managed a smile. "See, I knew you would have better ideas. I didn't really consider a secret door *or* room."

She shook herself as she trudged up the stairs. These were her parents they were talking about. Would her parents really have a secret room of some sort they hadn't told her about?

At this point she wasn't sure of anything anymore.

What if she never knew the whole truth?

The thought shuddered through her like a mini earthquake. She didn't want to feel this uncertainty about her parents for a minute longer than necessary.

She stopped at the door to their room, couldn't help the guilt that sheared through her. "This is their room."

"First we check behind anything hanging on the walls and under anything in the room."

"No need to go through the drawers?" She was surprised he didn't want to start there.

"You probably already looked through those."

She nodded. "I did."

"Well, there you go. You check under the bed and under chairs and side tables. I'll take the closet."

"Got it." Naomi got down on all fours and started with a visual search under the bed.

Once she had moved aside shoeboxes and dust bunnies she confirmed there was nothing under the bed but dusty hardwood floor. One by one she dragged the bedside tables away. Nothing on the floor or the wall where they had stood. With that in mind, she went to the footboard and tugged until she slid the headboard a few inches from the wall. She inspected that area as well and found nothing but plaster. Pulling the narrow rugs on either side of the bed aside, she found nothing there, either.

There was a chair on each side of the bed. Her

parents each had their own chair for reading or taking off shoes at night. Just in case, she removed the cushions and found nothing. Then she also pulled the covers back on the bed and checked there, then under the mattress all the way around. It was fairly easy to lift each side as she moved around the bed.

Back to the chairs. She turned them over, checked the floor beneath them and the bottoms of the chairs.

Since Deputy Lawton was still in the closet, she decided to remove the drawers in the night tables and check under them. After that she did the same with the dresser drawers. She had looked in all the drawers, but she hadn't pulled them out or looked at their bottoms.

By the time she'd finished she had drawers scattered on the floor all over the room. She'd even pulled the dresser from the wall and checked behind it.

Deputy Lawton came out of the closet. He glanced around. "I think we can call this room clear."

Naomi nodded. "What's next?"

He lifted his eyebrows. "Your room?"

"This way." Naomi led the way to her room and started the same process.

"You sure you don't mind me digging around in your closet?" The deputy looked a little skeptical.

"Have at it." At this point Naomi had nothing to hide and doubted anything would embarrass her.

While he started on her closet, she took the same steps with her bed and the rest of the furniture in the room as she had in her parents' room. Like before, she found nothing. The deputy found nothing. They moved on to the guest room and the two bathrooms.

With no luck on the second floor, they moved downstairs.

Naomi checked her phone repeatedly. Nothing from Casey. She'd sent him a couple of text messages to see how it was going. It hadn't been that long, maybe an hour since she and the deputy had started searching. Hopefully, she would hear something soon. One of his fellow agents, Letson, had called to check in with her a little bit ago and he'd assured her Casey would be in touch soon.

The bathroom and hall closet downstairs were the same as upstairs. Dusty but little else that wasn't expected. Nothing in the study, either.

The living room took only ten minutes since there was no closet and only a few drawers in the side tables.

Naomi sat her hands on her hips and surveyed the disarray. "Should we move into the kitchen or take a break?"

Deputy Lawton's face was red and he seemed to struggle for a breath. "No, no, I'm good. Let's keep going." He checked his phone.

"News?" She sure hadn't gotten a word from anyone.

"Just checking the time. Does the house have a basement? A lot of these old houses do."

Basement? She shook her head. "If there's a basement I've never seen it or heard my parents mention it. As many storms as we spent time hunkering in this downstairs closet, I feel like if there was a basement we would have been there instead."

No basement for sure.

He nodded thoughtfully. "How about in the barn? Any hiding places you remember as a child?"

"We can check." She wanted to be cooperative. "I remember climbing around in the loft, horsing around in the stalls. But not much else."

"Your daddy had a workshop."

"I'm sure the forensics technicians went through the shop and the barn, but we can have a look if you'd like." Even a trained specialist could overlook something.

"I think that's a good idea. Do we need keys for the shop?"

"Yes." She crossed the kitchen and reached into a cabinet for the old stoneware saltbox. It was empty save for a few keys. It was also an antique.

"Well, I'll be," Lawton said, pushing his cap up a little off his sweaty forehead. "Who would have thought of looking for a key in an old saltbox?"

"Dad said there was no use making things easy for thieves."

"Your daddy was a smart man."

The deputy followed Naomi out the kitchen door and toward the workshop. She glanced across the fields, wishing she'd hear something from Casey. He usually stayed in touch.

Usually.

That was a stretch. They'd only met on Tuesday and this was Friday. Their meeting nineteen years ago didn't actually count. Well, maybe a little.

Once the shop was unlocked, she and Deputy Lawton spread out and started the search. The place smelled of grease and tools. Her father had one of most anything one might need to work on the old farm equipment and the buildings. He never threw anything away.

They checked all the shelves—the wall lockers, Deputy Lawton called them. They looked like metal cabinets with doors to Naomi, but she would take his word for that.

"What about that?" Lawton asked. "Has it always been there?"

He pointed to the ancient hydraulic lift. When she was a kid, her dad would drive his truck or her mom's car onto the lift and send it up into the air for changing the oil and any other maintenance that required going under the car. Her dad had always been a little claustrophobic. She couldn't help smiling at the thought. He had gotten trapped in a closet when he was a child and he never could stand to be shut up in a small space again. It was his one fear. Otherwise, her daddy had always been the bravest man she knew.

"It has." She shrugged. "At least as long as I can remember."

"You don't mind if we check it out?"

She shrugged. "Go ahead. It might not even work. Dad hasn't done his own maintenance like that in years." Age changes everything.

Deputy Lawton crossed to the little door on the wall. Her dad had put the control in a sort of electrical breaker box that could be locked. He didn't want Naomi or any of her friends messing around with it.

He picked through the keys they'd taken from the saltbox and unlocked the panel. He pressed the necessary button and with a low growl the lift started to rise.

When it was about halfway up, four or so feet off the floor, Naomi blinked, stared at the concrete floor again.

What in the world?

Instead of just two tracks that car tires usually sat on, a portion of the concrete went up with the two tracks.

Now, with that section up in the air, there were stairs going down.

"Has that always been that way?"

Naomi shook her head. "I have no idea. I've never seen it before."

"Come on." He pulled a flashlight from his utility belt. "Let's have a look."

Chapter Fourteen

Excavation Site, 10:00 a.m.

Casey held stone-still while the crane struggled with the weight of the car.

He was trapped.

When the car moved, he had slid down between the truck and the bottom of the pit. The car had tipped and then wedged over him. He had no idea where his phone had landed.

More than an hour had been spent trying ways to dig him out, but the consensus was any additional dislodging of dirt would only send the car further off balance. Now a crane had been brought in to extract the car from the pit.

Letson had checked on Naomi half an hour ago and she and the deputy on detail were searching the house again.

She was fine. Safe. Keeping herself occupied.

The problem was, Casey was between a rock and a hard place.

Metal whined and the crane strained as the car started to move. Casey eased deeper against the dirt wall. The smaller he made himself, the less of a target he would be if something went wrong.

The noise ceased.

Casey braced for bad news.

"You still okay down there, Duncan?"

"I'm good."

"All right, then. The car is a few inches above the truck so we're going for it."

"Let's do it!" Casey called back.

The whining and groaning began again. Casey steeled himself and waited it out.

Another few inches of space appeared between the car and the truck. Casey relaxed just a little. Another foot, then a second one. Now they were getting somewhere.

The sound of metal shearing jerked his attention upward. The car was a good four feet above the truck now, but something had torn.

Rusty metal ripped.

The car dropped.

Casey covered his head with his arms.

Shouting above.

Silence.

Casey looked up. The car had stopped. They'd

only lost about fifteen inches, but could they go any farther?

"Duncan!"

"Yeah?"

"The guys up here are worried the metal is going to tear even more if we keep pulling the car upward. We're thinking you should try to get out of there. Fast, man. Really fast."

"I'm coming."

Casey scrambled up from the ground and over the hood of the truck. He'd made it to the other side of the pit where the ladder hung when one end of the car dropped, slamming into the hood of the truck.

Damn. That was close.

"Get outta there." Letson was at the top of the ladder waving him up.

Metal screaming, Casey propelled himself up the ladder and out of the pit. He sat on the ground and watched as the car dropped completely onto the truck.

Letson clapped him on the back. "The good news is while the car was in the air I got a shot of the license plate. The numbers were readable. Alabama tag, thirty-one years old. Hopefully we'll have the owner's name soon."

Casey stood, dusted himself off. "I should get back to the house, check on Naomi."

"Naomi?" Letson echoed, his eyebrows raised.

"Ms. Honea," Casey amended, not appreciating the man's pointed question.

"Duncan!"

He turned to Tanner, who was jogging in his direction. Damn. He hoped there hadn't been another body found.

Worse, Wagner may have called Tanner and informed him they were to back off and wait for whoever the Bureau was sending to continue this complicated investigation.

"I just received some interesting news from Rowan," Tanner said as Casey met him a few yards from the pit.

Rowan was Chief Brannigan's wife, the coroner. Casey said, "Something I hope will fill in some of the missing pieces on this one." The case had just taken another complicated turn with the find in the pit. Two more victims who had been missing for at least three decades.

"When I was bringing Rowan up to speed on this business with Beck/Becker and Cotton yesterday, she got a hunch and had some lab work done. You know, she used to work with Nashville Metro. She made a lot of invaluable contacts. Anyway, she got one of her friends at a private lab to run DNA comparison for us on Cotton and Beck."

Judging by the excitement in Tanner's voice,

Casey figured this was big news. He needed a turning point. He was running out of time.

"Elmer Cotton," Tanner went on, "and Arlene Beck are siblings."

"That is an interesting turn of events. Considering the age difference, if Ursula Becker is the mother, then she had another child after arriving in this country."

"Makes me wonder if Cotton decided his sister was too evil to live. Maybe he killed her and then himself to end the line."

"A definite possibility," Casey agreed.

Now the question on Casey's mind was how did Arlene Beck entwine herself so deeply in the Honea family? Were she and Naomi's mother related somehow? Of like mind? Or maybe it was the dad, Nolan. It was becoming more and more difficult to believe they had nothing to do with all that was happening on their farm.

Casey stared at the pit. Digging that pit, transporting the vehicles with the bodies inside, had taken teamwork. Careful organization. And complete trust.

Based on the age of the vehicles and the time frame they were buried, Naomi either hadn't been born or was a little baby. A hell of a lot had been hidden from her all these years.

The need to talk to Naomi was stronger now. "I

should go back to the house and give Naomi an update."

The distant *whomp whomp* filled the air. The sound drew Casey's and Tanner's gazes to the sky. A helicopter came into view, lowering as it neared their location.

"Friends of yours?" Tanner shouted over the din.

Casey spotted Wagner in the passenger seat as the helicopter sat down in the middle of the field. He decided not to mention it was probably trouble. Instead, he nodded. "Yeah, the assistant special agent in charge."

Tanner looked from Casey to the helicopter. "I guess he has something important to say since he made such a grand entrance."

Casey made a sound of agreement. No doubt. He strode toward the helicopter as it powered down. Wagner jumped out and hunkered down as he rushed to meet Casey. This was probably not going to be pleasant.

The engine shut down and silence fell over the field. Deputies and agents watched, waiting for whatever orders the brass was about to relay.

"Duncan," he said when they came to a stop a few feet apart.

Casey gave him a nod. "Wagner."

"I couldn't reach you by phone and this was too important to wait. Between the State Department and various other agencies, we've been ordered to turn over all evidence ASAP. I need your team to pull out now. Locals, as well. I believe I mentioned this in our previous conversation. I had a feeling—" he glanced at the excavator "—you might have some difficulty extracting yourself from the scene. I thought I'd give you a hand."

"This was already happening when we had our previous conversation." Casey gestured to the crowd gathered. "There was a bit of a glitch and I haven't had a chance to pass along your order."

Wagner appeared to let that go. "We should sit down with the locals and debrief."

"You can say whatever it is you've got to say now, sir." Tanner moved up next to Casey. "I'm Franklin County sheriff Colton Tanner." Rather than extend his hand, he planted both on his hips. "Coming there—" he nodded to the cowboy striding toward them like a character out of an old Western movie "—is Chief of Police William Brannigan. We're more than happy to hear what you've got to say, but this is our town, our case. We won't be shutting anything down."

Wagner looked to Casey and he shrugged. He wasn't about to give an assist on this one. Whatever had happened here, Tanner and Brannigan had a right to have the full story. Their community deserved the full story.

While Brannigan and Wagner were discussing how they could all proceed together, Casey intended to slip away and check on Naomi. "Can you give me a ride back to the house?"

"Sure thing," Tanner said. "We should bring Naomi up to speed."

They loaded into the sheriff's truck and headed back across the field.

"It's wild how you can know someone your whole life and never suspect what they might be hiding," Tanner commented. "I guess even being a lawman doesn't make you immune to deception."

"Being a lawman just makes it harder when you discover you've been deceived," Casey commented. "You feel like you should have seen it when no one else did. But we are only human."

Casey relaxed when he saw the county cruiser parked in the drive next to Naomi's pickup. But he wouldn't be satisfied until he laid eyes on her. She was the biggest victim of all in this mess. She had been deceived by everyone around her.

Inside, the house was empty. Casey's guard went up. "She said she and the deputy on detail were searching the house again." Though this looked a little intense, maybe she'd reached her limit on patience. Naomi wanted answers more than anyone.

"Let me give my guy a call and find out where they are."

Casey would breathe easier when he knew where she was. He waited while Tanner made the call. When he frowned and ended the call, he said, "No answer."

They walked back outside and to the cruiser. Tanner looked it over, glanced inside. "I thought Higgins had detail this morning, but this is Lawton's vehicle."

Worry niggled at Casey. "I was going to ask—there's been a different deputy on detail every shift except for Lawton. He's covered several shifts this week. Is he one of your most trusted deputies?"

"They're all trusted," Tanner said as he put through another call on his cell. "Lawton volunteered for extra shifts because his sister is a long-time friend of the Honea family. She was Dr. Honea's nurse for years."

"Is that right? He never mentioned it." Casey thought about all Naomi had said about her mom's clinic. "As a matter of fact, Naomi didn't, either. She mentioned the nurse but not the connection to Lawton."

An uneasy feeling welled in his chest. Casey had to force himself to hold still while Tanner did what he had to do.

Tanner ended the call he'd made. "Lawton's not picking up, either." The sheriff made a third call then, ordering someone on the other end to find Deputy Higgins. He surveyed the parked vehicles in the driveway before turning his attention back to Casey. "Naomi's vehicle is here. So is Lawton's. Let's operate under the assumption they're both on the grounds somewhere."

"I'll get my people over here searching." Casey reached for his phone, realized he didn't have it.

Tanner nodded. "I'll have my people bring your people." He made another call. "While I'm at it, I'm having Lawton's sister picked up and brought over here. I think we need to talk to her. Clear up this confusion."

Casey was fairly convinced there was no confusion. Only desperation.

"I CAN'T BELIEVE THIS."

Naomi had been pouring through ledgers for the past half hour or more. Arlene kept precise notes on every incoming "product" and each sale. Naomi was equally stunned and horrified.

She looked up, surveyed the rows and rows of glass containers. Each held carefully stored bones. Every imaginable human bone. All carefully cleaned, from the looks of them, and stored. The room—basement, whatever it was—was climate controlled. It wasn't that large, maybe twelve feet by twenty feet. Spotless, immaculate. The floors, the walls and the ceiling were white. Boxes of gloves sat on a table, she suspected for handling the bones.

"It's pretty incredible," Deputy Lawton said. "Can you imagine how long it took to build a collection like this?"

Naomi stood from the desk and moved toward the wall of bones. "I can't even imagine."

"The prep area is state of the art," he pointed out.

She turned to the opposite side of the room. He was right. Stainless-steel tables and sinks. Refrigerator, supply shelves. How on earth had this room gotten here without her parents' knowledge? It just didn't make sense.

"I don't understand," she murmured. "How is this possible?"

"I'll bet it took lots of money."

Naomi glanced at the deputy. He seemed astonished, as well. Who wouldn't be?

"My parents couldn't have been part of this. It's impossible. They would never do this."

"You're right," Deputy Lawton agreed. "It takes a certain kind of person." He tapped his temple. "A certain genius, too."

Naomi wasn't sure she would call it genius, but she understood what he meant. Maybe. She walked back to the desk and opened more of the drawers. Arlene had been meticulous in her record keeping. The buyers were recorded as numbers. Now all Naomi needed was the key to the numbers. The buyers should go down for their heinous parts in this, too. She thought of the numbers on that file folder. There had to be a connection. Now that she thought about it, the patterns were similar.

"What you looking for?"

She glanced up. "There should be a key or a legend somewhere that tells us who the buyers are or what these numbers mean. I'm certain the FBI will want to round up the buyers, too."

"I can't let you do that, Naomi."

She looked up from the middle drawer. "What?" She must have misheard him.

"You see." He sat his hand on his service weapon and started toward her. "My sister and I have worked a very long time to help build this business. We started a very long time ago, but it wasn't until we met Arlene that everything clicked. She truly was a genius. It's a shame her disturbed brother thought he had to save the world from her. We told her to get rid of him a long time ago, but she wouldn't." He laughed, a deep one that shook his round belly. "Can you image, she couldn't bear the idea of killing her brother when she did all this." He waved his free hand around the room. "Oh, and far more. You have no idea all the things she did."

Naomi backed away from the desk.

He continued coming toward her.

As much as she wanted to charge him and try to get past him, the gun be damned, she desperately needed him to keep talking. She needed to know the truth.

"How did she hide it from my parents? I can't believe they missed all of this." She looked around the room. "It's too much." He only grinned. So, she took a different tactic. "Maybe I'm wrong. It must have been my mother. She was a *true* genius. I'll bet she's the one who arranged everything. The mastermind. Arlene probably took orders from her."

Fury tightened his face. "Oh, no. Poor Muriel was like you, she believed the best in everyone. But then she let herself get in the way." He shrugged. "She may have gotten a little suspicious, but Sarah took care of that. Did you know there are certain chemicals you can add to a person's food and drink that will cause cancer? Really fast, fatal cancer."

Pain followed immediately by outrage roared through Naomi. "Are you saying she poisoned my mother?"

He shook his head, grinning like a fool. "I said no such thing. But while she was sick and with you so far away, it was easy to set all this up. To expand the business. We took every opportunity to construct the things we needed but after you moved to California your parents just didn't take vacations the way they used to. A couple of days here or there but nothing extended. Your father wouldn't leave her side in those last months. We accomplished a lot during that time."

Ice slid through her veins. "What about my dad?" Every fiber of her being screamed in pain at the idea of what this man—this monster—was telling her.

"For a long while he only muddled through, allowing Arlene to do as she pleased, but then he started to get a little nosy. Maybe it was all those extra deposits she made for him. He started to wonder where she was getting all that extra cash."

Her heart seemed to rip apart in her chest.

"Exchanging his heart medication for something stronger was simple. Took no time at all. He didn't suffer. Not the way your mother did. It was too bad, but it was the best way to do it, my sister said. No one is ever suspicious of cancer and, you know, heart attacks happen all the time."

For the first time in her life, Naomi wanted to hurt someone. No, rage exploded in her chest—she wanted to…

What she wanted didn't matter. She had to find a way to escape. Casey and Sheriff Tanner needed to know what had happened here. They needed to stop these people. Otherwise, her parents would end up being blamed in the end.

She would not allow their reputations to be destroyed.

She held up her hands to stop his advancement. "Just tell me what you want. The farm? What? They're probably going to blame my parents, anyway. I'll just go back to California and never look back. We all get what we want."

Another of those deep rumbling laughs burst from his throat. "Don't try pulling that on me. I've got your number, lady. My only job was to find this place. You see, Arlene didn't trust us completely. She liked hiding certain things like the records." He nodded to the desk. "And the money. She doled it out like she was the only one in control. All I have to do now is set this place on fire and leave you to burn up with the evidence of our buyers."

She had to get out of here. "But what about the money? Don't you want it? I know where she hid the money."

His gaze narrowed. "Don't lie to me."

Obviously Sheriff Tanner and Chief Brannigan had not briefed all their deputies and officers about the find at High Street. Thank God.

"You remember where I found that head in the box?" She held her breath. Prayed he would believe her.

"'Course. I heard about that. I'm a deputy, after all."

"Well, what I didn't tell anyone was that I found money, too." She shrugged. "I didn't know what was going to happen with all this and I thought I might need to run away if the police tried to blame me. So

I hid the money. It's a lot of money. A whole lot of money."

He studied her a moment. "I don't believe you."

"It's in bundles. All small denominations. A whole lot of money." She emphasized the last part.

"Where did you put it?" His fingers tightened around the butt of his weapon.

"I'll show you, but I'm not telling you. And you already know it's not in my house. I'll bet you've checked the barn and the lab."

His lips pursed with anger. "Tell me or I'll kill you now." He drew his weapon.

She shrugged. "Then I guess you'll never get your hands on the money because you will never find where I hid it. Never in a million years."

For a moment she was certain he wasn't going to go for it, then he motioned with his gun. "Let's go. You do anything I don't like, and you'll regret it."

She nodded.

"First, take out your cell phone. Turn it off and leave it on the desk."

She hated to give up her cell but if it got her out of here, she would have a far better chance of survival. She took it from her pocket and turned it off as requested and then placed it on the desk.

"This way." He motioned with his gun again.

She moved in front of him. She should have known something was wrong when he lowered the hydraulic lift after they came down the stairs. But the sight of all those bones had thrown her off balance.

No problem. He had to raise it again for them to get out. When he did and they got to the top of the stairs she was running, gun or no.

Rather than go to the stairs and press the button behind the locked glass panel, he went to the cabinet next to the sink. He opened the doors and checked inside, then moved around the wall on that end of the room, sliding his hand over the white surface. What the hell was he doing?

"There it is." He stood back and watched as a panel opened in the wall.

Okay, this was too much.

"I thought you didn't know where this place was." What a liar!

"I didn't, but my sister said Arlene talked about it all the time and the escape tunnel she installed." He hitched his head toward the wall of bones. "I figured it probably wasn't there or behind the desk where all the files are. This was just a guess." He gestured to the small opening. "Ladies first."

"Why don't we just go out the way we came in?" This is not how she had planned this happening.

"Your FBI friend is probably back at the house by now. For all we know, the place could be crawling with feds and cops."

Exactly what she'd hoped for.

"Let's go," he repeated.

She ducked into the opening, grateful for the dim lighting, and walked two steps before she could straighten to her full height. About every ten feet there was a small dim light overhead. Like emergency lighting in a stairwell. He came in right behind her.

"Let's go," he ordered.

"I thought you were burning the place." If he set a fire, surely smoke would set off an alarm in her dad's workshop. There had to be ventilation.

"I'll do it after I have the money."

She got it now. He didn't care about destroying the evidence. He had just assumed the money would be here with the bones and ledgers, but it wasn't. He had searched the place while she studied the ledgers. The money is all he wanted.

"Fine."

She started forward. "Do you have any idea where this goes?"

"Nope, but I'll go back the way we came if you run into a booby trap."

Her heart skipped a beat. She hadn't even thought of that.

They walked onward. The tunnel was narrow and she was surprised his broad body didn't scrape the sides. The floor and walls looked like concrete, but she couldn't be sure. Finally, the tunnel ended at an iron ladder that led upward.

"Start climbing," he ordered. "When you get outside, if you run, I'll shoot you in the back. I'm not going to prison."

He was if she could do anything about it. "Okay."

Naomi steadied her breathing and reached for the ladder. She was halfway up when he said, "Don't forget I'm right behind you."

She reached the top of the ladder and the exit appeared to be one of those round hatch openings like the ones in submarines—at least in the movies. She had to grab hold with both hands and twist with all her might to open it. When the lock released, she pushed the hatch upward as she climbed the last few rungs.

The opening was narrow. If she was lucky, he'd get stuck.

Looking around, she took her time climbing out. She needed to get her bearings before his head was out of the opening.

Woods. Had to be only a short distance from the house. They hadn't walked that far. She climbed out, pulled herself up onto the ground.

All she had to do was run.

A strong hand clamped around her ankle and jerked.

She hit the ground face-first.

Lawton was out of the hole and towering over her with his gun before she could scramble up. "If you scream, I will shoot. If you run, I will shoot," he growled as if he'd been reading her mind all along.

She eased into a sitting position and stared up at him. "So, shoot."

He grabbed her by the arm.

She grabbed the weapon with both hands.

Chapter Fifteen

Tanner's missing deputy had been slugged from behind, secured in the trunk of his cruiser and left on a side road less than a mile from the Honea farm.

Casey found no relief in his statement of events. Lawton had arrived and told him there was a problem at the barn. Halfway around the house Lawton had attacked. When Higgins had awakened he had been secured in the trunk of his own cruiser. Naomi had still been in the house at the time Lawton showed up, only minutes after Casey had left. Naomi had likely still been asleep.

Fury whipped through Casey. He and the others, including Wagner, had fanned out around the farmhouse and started the search. The barn, the lab and workshop, and the woods around the perimeter of the front and back yard had yielded nothing so far. Brannigan had ordered a team with dogs but it would be a bit before they arrived.

The cell phone Casey had borrowed from a deputy vibrated. *Tanner.* "Is the nurse here?" he asked the sheriff.

"My deputies just arrived with her. Two others stayed back to search her property. You want to question her, or do you want me to do it?"

Casey considered going back to the house, but he needed to be on the ground. "See what you can find out. I'll stick with the search."

With all the vehicles accounted for, unless someone picked Lawton and Naomi up, they had to be out here somewhere. If the sister had picked them up, hopefully they would soon know.

"I'll call you back as soon as I know anything."

Casey put the phone away and started walking again, deeper into the woods.

"Agent Duncan!"

The shout came from his left. Good distance away. He shouted a response and started in that direction.

"We've got something over here."

Casey found the two officers from Brannigan's department maybe a hundred yards from the workshop. They were huddled around something on the ground.

His gut clenched and his heart slammed against his sternum.

"It leads down a ladder into a tunnel," one of the officers said. "You want me to check it out."

"Call for backup first," Casey said. To the other officer, he ordered, "You come with me."

They started forward as the officer left at the tunnel opening called for backup.

"Which direction is the road?" Casey asked. If that was an emergency egress, there was no doubt a way to get away from the farm. A vehicle or something stashed nearby.

"This way, sir."

The urge to call out to Naomi was so strong he barely held it back. They couldn't take the risk. The element of surprise might be their only leverage at this point.

Casey and the deputy covered a good distance when a sound…a whisper or wheeze…stopped Casey in his tracks.

He held up his hand, then motioned with a finger to his mouth for the other man to stay quiet. The sound came again. A gasp or wheeze.

Fear, icy cold, rushed through Casey's veins.

Was Naomi injured?

He moved silently toward the sound. Gasp…whoosh…gasp.

The sound grew more frantic and louder as he neared a patch of thick undergrowth between two trees.

His weapon at the ready, he rounded the first of the two trees.

Lawton sat on the ground, leaning against the tree, service weapon in his hand. Red painted the front of his shirt, originating at a hole mid chest.

His shuddered with the violent gasps sawing in and out of his sagging mouth.

"Where is she?" Casey demanded as he took a step closer, his bead on the man's head.

Lawton stared wordlessly at him while attempting to raise his weapon.

Casey tensed. His finger curled around the trigger.

The hand grasping the weapon fell back to his thigh. The weapon slipped free of his grasp.

Casey collected the weapon and pitched it aside.

The officer who'd come with Casey rounded the clump of trees and underbrush.

"Call Tanner," Casey ordered. "Then, if this bastard tells us where Naomi is, call an ambulance. If he doesn't, just leave him here to die."

While the officer called Tanner, Casey started walking away.

A frantic attempt at a howl echoed behind him. He turned around and Lawton managed to raise his left arm and point into the woods on his right.

Casey nodded at the officer to call for an ambulance, then he lunged in the direction Lawton had pointed. He called Naomi's name. He raced through the woods, dodging trees, shouting her name at the top of his lungs.

His own name echoed back to him. It was a distant cry. An anguished cry. But it was her and she was alive.

He rushed toward her voice.

She raced right up to him and threw her arms around him. "He was going to kill me."

"You're okay now." He set her back. "Are you injured?"

She shook her head. "I'm okay." She glanced beyond him. "Is he still alive?"

"Barely."

"We struggled. The gun went off, he staggered back and I ran." She blinked repeatedly to staunch the flow of tears, her words coming in a rush. "I just kept running even after I realized he wasn't chasing me anymore. I was so hysterical I couldn't remember the way to the road. I think I've been running in circles."

He hugged her close to his chest. "It's over now."

She drew back, stared up at him. "His sister. She poisoned my mom and caused my dad's heart attack." The tears turned to a river now.

"Come on." He pulled her close and started back toward the house. "We'll make sure they don't get away with what they've done."

"My parents never knew," she said. "They didn't do anything wrong."

He tightened his arm around her shoulders. "I don't think anyone ever believed they did."

"I know where the bones are now," she mumbled against his chest. "There's a bone room. Under my dad's workshop."

This was going to take a long time to sort out.

Casey wasn't leaving until it was done.

"Naomi."

She was pretty sure she was dreaming. In this dream she could hear his voice. Casey's voice. It was about the sexiest voice she'd ever heard.

"Naomi."

A hand touched her shoulder, gave it a little shake.

Her eyes opened and she sat straight up.

It took a moment for her mind to orient itself. Sheriff Tanner's office. Sofa. She'd fallen asleep in the sheriff's office.

Casey smiled and sat down beside her. "Hey."

She leaned into his warm body. "Hey."

The case was solved, and he would be leaving. Maybe tonight. She wasn't ready. At all.

She looked around the room for a clock. "What time is it?"

Where was her cell phone? Oh, yeah, in that underground bunker bone room. She shivered.

"Midnight," he told her. "I came to tell you it's okay to leave now."

She could leave? It really was done. She could not go back to the farm. Not right now. Maybe not ever. The idea of what those people had done to her family…the reality that if she had been there instead of chasing a dream in California…

"I can't go to the farm." She barely got the words out without bursting into tears again. She'd cried so much already her eyes were raw from it.

"I was thinking about a place where you'd feel more comfortable and where the reporters won't think to look."

She stared up at him then. Even as exhausted as she knew he was—not to mention his near-death experience in that pit—he looked amazing. "Where?"

"I'll be able to confirm that any minute now."

"Okay." God, she was confused. "This is way too crazy for a movie or a book. No one would ever believe it."

"I think you might be right." His arm went around her.

She snuggled into his side. Arlene—Anna, whatever—killed her own mother. Of course she hadn't thought twice about killing Naomi's parents.

Sarah Holland—aka Juanita Tripp—claimed in her statement that Arlene had bragged about learning everything her mother knew and then getting rid of her. Her only mistake, she'd said later, was in not killing her little brother at the time. He'd only been a kid. She hadn't expected him to remember that Nazi hunters hadn't been the ones to kill their mother. She certainly hadn't expected that he would one day find her again and try to get close. Once he confirmed that she was doing the same heinous things their mother had done, he'd killed her and then himself.

If that wasn't weird enough, there was Deputy Lawton and his sister—who was really his wife. The people in the pit—the ones whose identities Lawton and Holland had stolen—were just innocent victims who fit the profile of what the depraved couple were looking for.

Tripp had needed a nurse identity in order to get close to Naomi's mom so she picked Sarah Holland. Holland had no children. No husband and no close family. She was easy to become. Lawton was a little more complicated. He was a cop in Mobile, Alabama. But like Holland, he had no close family or friends. A loner. Easy for Richard Tripp to become him. Claim he had to suddenly move up to Tennessee for a sick relative, eventually getting a position with the sheriff's department. His background checked out. It was easier back then to change personnel files. Not like now in this electronic-driven world.

"But this is your story to tell," he offered. "You might be surprised and end up with a book deal and a movie deal."

Could she? "This is Winchester, Tennessee," she

argued. "How does something like this happen in such a small town?"

"It's the perfect place to disappear," Casey said. "It's small, quiet. Not much happens in the way of crime. So, nobody looks too closely."

He reached into his pocket and retrieved his cell. "We are confirmed."

"Confirmed?"

He stood and offered his hand. "We are the guests of Sheriff Tanner and Chief Brannigan at the Falls Mill Bed and Breakfast."

"Really?" She'd only been there once on a tour. Years ago. But she remembered that it was charming and tucked away from the world.

"You game?"

She accepted his hand and moved up beside him. "Are you my bodyguard for the night?" She really, really wanted to believe this part was not about work. The investigation was done for the most part. But that only meant that he would be going back to Nashville. Her chest hurt just thinking about it.

"I was considering making an offer to guard your body for the foreseeable future." He shrugged. "As long as you need or want me. Especially if you end up starring in your movie."

A smile stretched across her mouth. "I guess that kiss sealed our fate. The one the other night, I mean."

He cupped her cheek and smiled back at her. "I'm

fairly certain the one from when we were kids did the trick. I've never wanted anyone the way I want you."

"Well, Agent Duncan—" she tucked her arm in his and turned him toward the door "—I think we should explore these wanton desires you have and see where they take us." She paused at the door and looked straight into his eyes. "All we have to do is be brave enough to jump."

* * * * *

COMING NEXT MONTH FROM

INTRIGUE

#2031 TEXAS STALKER
An O'Connor Family Mystery • by Barb Han

While fleeing an attempt on her life, Brianna Adair is reunited with her childhood friend Garrett O'Connor. Trusting others is not in her nature, but Brianna will have to lean on the gorgeous rancher or risk falling prey to a stalker who won't stop until she's dead...

#2032 STAY HIDDEN
Heartland Heroes • by Julie Anne Lindsey

Running from her abuser is Gina Ricci's only goal, and disappearing completely may be the answer. But local private investigator Cruz Winchester wants to arrest her ex and set Gina free. When everyone in Gina's life seems to become a target, will Cruz be able to save them all...without sacrificing Gina or her unborn child?

#2033 ROGUE CHRISTMAS OPERATION
Fugitive Heroes: Topaz Unit • by Juno Rushdan

Resolved to learn the truth of her sister's death, Hope Fischer travels to the mysterious military-controlled town where her sister worked at Christmas. Teaming up with the enigmatic Gage Graham could lead to the answers she's looking for—if Gage's secret past doesn't find and kill them first.

#2034 K-9 PATROL
Kansas City Crime Lab • by Julie Miller

After his best friend's sister, KCPD criminalist Lexi Callahan, is attacked at a crime scene, K-9 officer Aiden Murphy and partner Blue will do anything to protect her. But being assigned as her protection detail means spending every minute together. Can Aiden overcome his long-buried feelings for Lexi in time to save her from a killer?

#2035 FIND ME
by Cassie Miles

Searching for her childhood best friend requires undercover FBI agent Isabel "Angie" D'Angelo to infiltrate the Denver-based Lorenzo crime family. Standing in her way is Julian Parisi, a gentleman's club manager working for the Lorenzo family. Angie will need to convince Julian to help even though she knows he's got secrets of his own...

#2036 DEADLY DAYS OF CHRISTMAS
by Carla Cassidy

Still recovering from a previous heartbreak, Sheriff Mac McKnight avoids Christmas at any cost, even with his deputy, Callie Stevens, who loves the holidays—and him. But when a serial killer's victims start mirroring *The Twelve Days of Christmas*, he'll have to confront his past...and his desire for Callie.

YOU CAN FIND MORE INFORMATION ON UPCOMING HARLEQUIN TITLES, FREE EXCERPTS AND MORE AT HARLEQUIN.COM.

HICNM1021

"So, tell me who you *think* is stalking you," he said in more of a statement than a question.

She shrugged her shoulders. "I don't know. That's a tough one. There's a guy in one of my classes who creeps me out. I'll be taking notes furiously in class only to get a weird feeling like I'm being watched and then look up to see him staring at me intensely."

"Has he come around the bar?"

"A time or two," she admitted.

"Is he alone?"

"As far as I can tell. He never has worked up the courage to come talk to me, so he takes a table by the dance floor and nurses a beer," she said.

"Any idea what his name is?"

"Derk Waters, I think. I overheard someone say that in a group project when his team was next to mine. By the way, there should be no group projects in college. I end up doing all the work and have to hear complaints from everyone in the process," she said as an aside.

Garrett chuckled. "Maybe you should learn to let others pull their own weight."

She blew out a sharp breath. "And risk a failing grade? No, thanks. Besides, I tried that once and ended up staying up all night to redo someone's work because they slapped their part together."

"Sounds like something you'd do," Garrett said.

"What's that supposed to mean?" She heard the defensiveness in her own voice, but it was too late to reel it in.

"You always were the take-charge type. I'm not surprised you'd pull out a win in a terrible situation."

Well, she really had overreacted. She exhaled, trying to release some of the tension she'd been holding in her shoulders. "Thanks for the compliment, Garrett. It means a lot coming from you. I mean, your opinion matters to me."

"No problem." He shrugged off her comment, but she could see that it meant something to him, too. He picked up his coffee cup and took another sip. "Okay, so we have one creep on the list. What about others?"

"I wouldn't classify this guy as a creep necessarily, but he has followed me out to the parking lot at school more than once. He's a TA, so basically a grad student working for one of my professors. He made it known that he'd be willing to help if I fell behind in class," she said.

Again, that jaw muscle clenched.

"Doesn't he take a hint?"

"Honestly, he's harmless. The only reason I brought him up was because we were talking about school and for some reason he popped into my mind. He's working his way through school and I doubt he'd risk his future if he got caught," she surmised. "Plus, this person is trying to run me off the road."

"You rejected him. That could anger a certain personality type," he said. "What's his name?"

"Blaine something. I don't remember his last name." Up to this point, she hadn't really believed the slimeball could be someone she knew. A cold shiver raced down her spine at the thought. "I've been working under the assumption one of the guys at the bar meant to get a little too friendly."

"We have to start somewhere. I believe my brothers would say the most likely culprit is someone you know. I've heard them say a woman's biggest physical threat is from those closest to her. Boyfriend. Spouse. Someone in her circle." He shot a look of apology. "It's an awful truth."

She issued a sharp sigh. "I can't even imagine who would want to hurt me."

Don't miss
Texas Stalker *by Barb Han,*
available November 2021 wherever
Harlequin Intrigue books and ebooks are sold.

Harlequin.com

HIEXP1021

BY EVELYN ANTHONY

The House of Vandekar

The Scarlet Thread

The Relic

The Doll's House

Exposure

Available from HarperPaperbacks

EXPOSURE

·EVELYN ANTHONY·

HarperPaperbacks
A Division of HarperCollinsPublishers

HarperPaperbacks   *A Division of* HarperCollins*Publishers*
          10 East 53rd Street, New York, N.Y. 10022

Copyright © 1994 by Anthony Enterprises Ltd.
All rights reserved. No part of this book may be used or reproduced in any manner whatsoever without written permission of the publisher, except in the case of brief quotations embodied in critical articles and reviews. For information address HarperCollins*Publishers*,
10 East 53rd Street, New York, N.Y. 10022.

A hardcover edition of this book was published in 1994 by HarperCollins*Publishers*.

Cover photograph by Anthony Loew

First HarperPaperbacks printing: February 1995

Printed in the United States of America

HarperPaperbacks and colophon are trademarks of HarperCollins*Publishers*

❖ 10 9 8 7 6 5 4 3 2 1

EXPOSURE

CHAPTER 1

JULIA HAMILTON HAD DODGED THE PRIVATE detectives watching her. She had booked her seat on the morning flight to Jersey using another name and traveled to Heathrow by Underground. Timing had been vital; she had to arrive at the terminal at the last minute, check in, and speed through to the departure lounge.

Once airborne, she couldn't be followed. The flight was bumpy, but Julia didn't mind. She was never airsick and loved flying.

The skies were gray and heavy with rain; as they began their descent, she leaned to look out of the window. Below, the sun was shining through a break in the bank of clouds. The land below was green, and the sea dashed against the craggy shoreline, whipped by a sharp wind.

Her cousins had been waiting to meet her at the airport.

It had been so easy to manipulate them; they were kind, straightforward people. When she said she needed a few days' holiday, they responded with a warm invitation. Julia refused to feel guilty; what she had come to find out was more important than a mild deception. Richard Watson was on that island, and she had come to find him. Richard Watson, she was certain, held some of the missing pieces in a jigsaw of betrayal and death.

It had been easy to gain the introduction. Her cousin Janey Peterson was thrilled to have such a celebrity to show off to her friends.

Julia Hamilton, the Fleet Street megastar, author of a famous book on the Rhys child murders, now head of the *Sunday Herald*'s much publicized new feature, "Exposure." Everyone, Janey had said enthusiastically, would be dying to meet her.

Including their friend Richard Watson. A telephone call had secured an invitation to dinner. And there she was, sitting at Richard Watson's right hand, the guest of honor. There were six people around the table that night: Watson and herself, David and Janey Peterson, and a couple called Thomas. He had a booming voice and an avuncular manner. His wife was small, spoke just above a whisper, and was, as Julia had discovered during the predinner drinks, quite Waspish.

Julia knew that Richard Watson was observing her. It was the price of a high profile. She was used to paying it, able to deal with men who felt the need to be aggressive and women jealous of her success. And her good looks. She had enough scars not to be conceited about that either.

"We're all such fans of yours," Bob Thomas said. "You must tell us what 'Exposure' has up its sleeve. . . . Rumor has it you're going after a politician?"

Julia said gently, "You should never listen to rumors.

I'm afraid you'll have to wait till the paper comes out." She gave him a charming smile. He grinned.

"Well, it was worth a try, anyway. So what brings you to our little island—hot on the trail of some juicy scandal?"

Julia shook her head. "Afraid not. I'm having a lovely pre-Christmas break staying with David and Janey. Just relaxing and being spoiled." She smiled at them as she said it. They were so generous and hospitable. So genuinely proud of her.

So different from the ruthless, grasping denizens of her professional world. Fiona, the Waspish little wife of Bob Thomas, leaned across and said to her, "You wrote that book, didn't you—the one about the Rhys murders—a few years ago? I can't remember the name, but it was so much better than Truman Capote's book . . . I can't remember the name of that either. . . ."

Julia said, "*The Color of Blood*."

"That's right," Thomas bellowed. "I thought yours was wonderful, brilliant analysis."

"Thank you," Julia said. "I'm glad you liked it."

"Well," his wife whispered, "I wouldn't say I exactly liked it because of the subject. Horrifying actually. Dreadful having to deal with child murders like that. Didn't it bother you? You must have been very young?"

Julia said, "Yes, putting it mildly, it bothered me a great deal. I felt afterward I had to write in depth about what happened and why. It was the only way I could get it out of my mind."

Then her host, Richard Watson, joined in. "I'll admit I didn't read your book," he said. "I found the reporting harrowing enough, even though it was brilliant. You've never followed up with another one?"

"No, I just haven't the time. My publishers have given up nagging me. I'm really a journalist, that's what I love doing. The book was a catharsis. I don't think I'll ever do another."

"I envy you," Bob Thomas said. "I wish I could write a book. Couldn't put anything down to save my life."

"I've talked enough about myself," Julia said, turning to Richard Watson. "Tell me about you. How did you come to live here?"

Not rich, her cousin Jane Peterson had said. But very comfortable. Retired from a senior job in industry. Widower, rather a self-contained man, although everybody liked him. He lived in a fantastic house, part of Jersey's past in its way, and he entertained beautifully. Julia was sure to like him. He'd often talked to them about her articles in the *Sunday Herald*. He said she was the main reason he bought the newspaper.

"Well." He leaned back and looked at her. He was a good-looking man, with remarkably blue eyes that were warm and friendly. Also shrewd. "My wife died, and I took early retirement. We had no children, you see, and I'd nobody to worry about but myself. We'd spent holidays here and made friends, so I decided to live here. You didn't have to be a millionaire in those days, or I assure you I wouldn't have qualified. And what clinched it was seeing this house for sale."

"Oh, yes," the small-voiced woman called Fiona Thomas whispered from her place on his left, leaning across him to make herself clear to Julia. "Do tell Miss Hamilton all about that."

Julia leaned toward her. "Call me Julia," she said. "Please."

Fiona Thomas smiled and sat back. "Julia," she murmured. "How sweet of you. . . ."

"This house is rather an oddity. But I was absolutely bowled over by the site and the views. It was very run down when I saw it; the garden was a wilderness, and it was very bleak—pouring with rain, I remember. I was intrigued by it, and, let me say, even more intrigued by the price. It had belonged to someone called Hunter—

long before your time, my dear," he said to Julia. "She'd married a succession of rich men, and the last husband was one of the richest. She was very beautiful, and apparently very good fun. But in the end she drank like a fish and became quite impossible. The equivalent of our tabloids absolutely adored her. She was always saying or doing something outrageous, and she was always in the news."

"I remember," Janey said. "'Mink is too hot to sit on,'—wasn't that her?"

Richard Watson laughed. "It certainly was. She had a new car with gold-plated fittings, door handles, ashtray, and the seats were covered in leopard skin. She'd have been lynched by the antifur people today. When the press asked her why leopard skin, that's what she said. 'Because mink is too hot to sit on.' It made headlines all over the world. She really knew how to get herself into the papers."

"She certainly did if she came up with quotes like that," Julia said. "I love it, I really love it. 'Mink is too hot to sit on.'. . . " She laughed. "So what happened to her?"

"It all ended sadly," Watson said. "They had this big yacht, Paradise, I think it was called, and her antics got her husband kicked off the board of his family business, so they spent their lives cruising from one tax haven to another. She used this house as a pied-à-terre when they berthed here. It was a forties time warp when I bought it. My drawing room was fitted up as a private cinema—screen, projector—everything left just as it was. Apparently one day she got bored, or had a row with the Jersey authorities—she was always rowing with people—it was drink, unfortunately. They just left, didn't even bother to put the house on the market. When she died, her executors put it up for sale. And I bought it."

Someone said, "You've done wonders with it, Dick.

You ought to see the garden he's made. And all that clever lighting at night."

"Dawn and sunset are the best time," he said. "Not that I'm up in time for the sunrises these days. But I've had a lot of fun getting it the way I wanted it. Sheila, that was her name. Sheila Hunter. Such a shame she went to pieces like that."

"I must read up on her," Julia said. "She sounds interesting."

"Very small beer compared to the scandals we get these days," Thomas boomed cheerfully. "Hardly rate a mention in the Sun, would she?"

"Now, that could be a subject for a book for you," his wife suggested to Julia. "I don't think there's been a biography. Of course, nobody dared when she was alive. She was a great one for suing. She had some famous black pearls. They became very fashionable."

Julia let Richard refill her glass. The food and wine were as well chosen as the candles and winter-flower arrangements on the table. He was a man of taste and style. She liked him. She felt he liked her. She refused to feel guilty because she had come to his house under false pretenses to make use of him.

As she was using her nice cousins, Janey and David Peterson, who'd been so delighted to see her. So welcoming. She withdrew from the conversation, adopting the role of a listener.

"The definition of age," Richard Watson was saying, "is a desire to talk about the past. I find myself doing it more and more. I spent a few nights with my nephew in London . . . the solicitor, you met him, Janey, he came over for a sailing holiday last summer—"

"Yes, I remember him, charming young man," Janey said brightly.

Richard Watson grinned. "Not particularly, he's rather

bumptious and pleased with himself, but at least he's kin, so I keep in touch. He took me out to dinner at his smart club—excellent food, much better than restaurants—I found myself talking about the time I spent as a prisoner of war. I don't think I'd thought about it, let alone talked about it, for years! And there I was in full flood, banging on about being captured and spending three years in a camp in Germany. I suddenly realized he was bored stiff, poor chap. So I cut it short and changed the subject. I felt what a boring old fool I'd become."

"That's the trouble." Bob Thomas snorted. "The young think they know it all."

Richard Watson said gently, "Didn't we? I know I never listened to a word my father said after the age of eighteen. Sad thing was, you know, when I did come back from the POW camp, we couldn't communicate at all. Of course they were delighted to see me—my mother cried and rushed off to make tea; my old father managed to put his arm around me and then hurried upstairs with my bag. He just didn't know what to say."

Julia judged the moment had come. "Did it affect you badly? It must have been awful trying to adjust."

"It wasn't easy," he admitted. "I'd come back home a stranger. To myself as much as to them. I didn't realize what the loss of freedom had done to me. I couldn't make my mind up about anything. I'd lost the habit of taking decisions. If someone had told me what socks to put on in the morning, I'd have done it."

"How long did that last?" Julia leaned close, engaging his full attention.

"Couple of years. I tried several jobs, couldn't settle into anything; it was quite a common manifestation of POW fatigue. Then I was taken on by ICI as a trainee, and I got interested. Absorbed actually. And it all started to come right after that."

Julia took a breath. *Now.*

"I read your book," she said. "I have a friend who's mad on the last war and he gave it to me to read. I really enjoyed it. Did you map it out while you were in the prison camp?"

"Yes," Richard Watson said. "I did. It was so desperately boring and miserable, and so damned cold in the winter. . . . We were always hungry too. Most of the chaps spent their time talking about escape or playing chess or bridge. I worked on my insignificant wartime memoirs. I can't believe you found them interesting, but I must admit I'm flattered."

He smiled at her.

Bob Thomas boomed out, "Book? What's all this, Dick— been keeping secrets from us?"

"It was years ago—long before I came over here," Richard Watson protested. "I had some copies privately printed. I didn't know there were any circulating anywhere. I just wanted to get it off my chest, I suppose."

"Hidden talents." Bob Thomas had their attention. "Better watch out, Julia, or you'll have a rival in Dick here. . . . I'd like to read it sometime. I bet you've got a copy of the great work stashed away. The army was the best time of my life. I often regretted not making a career of it. Too young to get into the actual war, but I enjoyed my national service." He looked around for approbation.

Julia said quietly, "Did you feel like that, Richard? Your book didn't read like that."

He turned to look at her, and then, suddenly, he turned away. "I hated the army," he said. "I hated everything about it. And I wasn't a good soldier. The idea of killing someone absolutely appalled me. I had no blood lust."

"Did you ever kill anyone?"

He hesitated for a moment. Then he said, "No. But I did save a man's life."

· · ·

Julia had borrowed Janey's little Ford runabout to get to the dinner party. She was determined to meet Richard Watson before anyone else arrived.

As they got into the two cars, Janey complained.

"What a pity you made such a fuss about being on time. We could have driven back together and had a lovely postmortem on the evening."

"Knowing you, darling," her husband retorted, "we'll have one as soon as we get inside the front door. Do you know, Julia, she really enjoys talking about the party afterward more than the party itself. I warn you, you'll be in for a long session unless you're firm. Janey, you'd better drive. . . ."

"I should think so"—his wife giggled—"after the size of that last brandy. Julia, you can follow us, all right?"

Julia started the car and set out after them, keeping the rear light in view. In spite of the cold wind blowing in off the sea, she opened the window and breathed in the salty air. She couldn't believe it. She went over Richard Watson's story in her mind; he had made it so real, so vivid. No one had spoken a word till he'd finished.

And then, as if some high tension had been released, everyone changed the subject and took refuge in banter and small talk. The last hour after dinner was the longest Julia could remember. Coffee was followed by an exodus of the women from the dining room, leaving Richard Watson and his male guests to port and cigars. The only other man Julia knew who continued the archaic practice of separating the sexes was William Western. But then, he was a law unto himself, and he said so. He was also Julia's boss. . . . She remembered a Saturday night spent at the mansion in Hampshire, when her dinner companion had announced that this was the part of the evening he enjoyed most, as she got up to leave.

She had ignored him when he tried to talk to her afterward.

When finally the men rejoined them in the big drawing room with its spectacular sea views, everyone moved around, and she found herself sitting beside her cousin, David. Liqueurs were brought for what the booming Mr. Thomas called "the girls." Julia refused anything.

"This is nice," David said, sinking deeper into his chair, cradling a half-full balloon of brandy. "At last I've got a chance to talk to you. My darling wife's monopolized you from the moment you arrived. Tell me, how are Hugh and May? We must look them up when we come over next time."

Julia assured him that her parents were well and would love to see them both.

"And tell me about the job," he went on, lighting a cigar and bent on enjoying himself. "What's it like working for Western?"

Julia checked her screaming impatience to get out of there and get to a telephone. She said, "Impossible, most of the time. He's impossible as a person. Totally demanding and absolutely ruthless. He's also a genius, if that excuses it. I'm not sure it does. Just don't ask me if I like him, will you!"

"I don't have to, after that. But then you love the rat race, don't you, Julia, and look what a success you've made. Top job, big salary. You're a public figure. And the really nice thing about you is it hasn't made you the least big-headed. You're just as sweet as you ever were." He stretched over and patted her knee. Julia judged he'd had a little too much of Richard Watson's brandy.

"I've no reason to be big-headed," she said. "I've had all the lucky breaks, David. Starting with Western picking me out. Otherwise I'd still be plugging away on a provincial newspaper with nothing more in my sights than editing the women's page. David—"

He grinned at her. "Yes? You're fidgeting, aren't you? Sorry. Here, I'll move and let Bob Thomas come and talk to you. Watch out for your eardrums, though. He's a nice fellow, but, my God, he's got a voice like a bloody fog-horn—"

"No," she said quickly. "No, don't. I was really thinking of the time."

"You in a hurry to get home? Tired?" He peered at her.

"No, I'm not tired. But I did want to call someone. . . ."

"Oh," he said. "Oh, I see. Janey said you had a special boyfriend. Is that it?"

"Yes," she said eagerly. "It's nearly a quarter to one. I promised I'd ring him, but I don't want to make it too late. He gets up at the crack of dawn every morning."

"Right." He put out the cigar and heaved himself to his feet.

"Dick," he announced, "you've wined and dined us all too well. And I've got an early appointment in the morn-ing. So we should be on our way."

Julia whispered, "Thanks, David," as she moved to shake hands with Richard Watson and say good-bye.

She didn't want to go into the kitchen and drink coffee with them when they arrived back at the Petersons' house. But Janey insisted. She ushered them inside and started putting coffee into mugs and filling the kettle.

"How did you enjoy it?" she asked Julia. "Interesting, isn't he? And what an extraordinary story—I suppose it's true. What do you think, darling?" Julia gave her cousin a pleading look.

"I think," he said, "that it was absolutely true. And what's also true is that Julia wants to ring the love of her life, and you and I are going to bed. Switch the kettle off and come on. 'Night, Julia. Don't forget to put the lights out when you come up. And I do have an early stint tomorrow. Bless you."

Julia waited till they had gone upstairs. She went into the passage and listened till she heard their bedroom door shut. Then she went into the sitting room and closed the door after her. She picked up the phone and dialed London. He wouldn't be asleep; she knew he sat up till all hours, reading, watching late-night TV. And there was nobody there to nag him about going to bed. He would be awake and waiting.

Waiting for her call.

It only rang three times before he answered.

"Ben," she said. "Ben, it's me. I'm fine . . . fine. . . ." He was already interrupting. She cut in on him. "Just listen, will you? It came right out of the blue tonight. At the dinner . . . yes. Yes . . . Ben." She took a deep breath. "You're not going to believe this, but I think we've found our man."

At ten-thirty next morning Ben made the call as they'd arranged; there were two days of her visit left, and she had to get back to London. She came in and said to Janey, "That was the office—I've got to go back early. I'm so sorry to cut it short like this—I've had such a lovely time."

Janey drove her to Jersey airport. "I'll miss you," she said. "You made such a hit with everyone, you'll have to come back."

"I will, I promise," Julia said. "And thank you for giving me such a lovely holiday. Bless you." She kissed her and went off to the departure lounge.

What an incredible coincidence. She let her mind roam during the short flight. Just when she was losing hope, luck smiled on her.

A dinner party in Jersey with a retired business executive had provided the missing clue. A clue so carefully concealed that every lead after Germany and the interview in a Sussex village had ended in nothing. For want of a nail the battle was lost in the end, as the old doggerel ran. She had found the nail.

So many things depended on trifles, a snap judgment, a decision taken without any inkling of the ultimate consequences. And it had all started with an invitation and a distant dream.

The letter had been signed by a secretary to Lord Western of Western International Newspapers. He would like her to come down to his house in Hampshire for a personal vetting, with a view to offering her a job.

Julia had thought it was a practical joke till she telephoned the number. But it was no leg-pull by a colleague. It was real. The invitation was to come down for dinner, stay the night, and leave after breakfast. "Black tie," the brisk voice told her.

She, the voice, would send her a map of how to get there. She, Julia, should reply to Lady Western direct. She nearly lost her nerve and backed away from it. Her father was a country solicitor, her background middle-class. Life peers with country mansions issuing one-night invitations were not part of her experience. She'd worked for five years on provincial papers starting at sub-NUJ rates on a small weekly till she got her job as junior reporter with the *Yorkshire Post*. When her news editor wanted to entertain his staff, he took a room in the local pub.

It had been a daunting experience; her old Renault looked like a battered beetle as it turned into the sweep of drive and drew up before the façade of Hollowood Park. A butler took her suitcase, and she followed him up the steps and into the hall.

A woman came forward to meet her. Julia never forgot her first sight of Evelyn Western. She was astonishingly beautiful, with white hair and a delicate face that was still lovely in old age.

She came up and shook hands with Julia and smiled down at her; she was nearly six feet tall and straight as a rod.

"Miss Hamilton—how nice of you to come. I'm Evelyn Western. Now, would you like a drink before you go up to change?" She didn't wait for an answer. "Of course you would, after that long drive. Come along, you're the first to arrive. I do admire people who are punctual. I'm hopeless myself."

Julia got an impression of nice pictures and comfortable furniture in a big paneled room, but she was too nervous to observe her surroundings in detail.

She asked for a glass of sherry, which was not what she wanted. Evelyn Western sat down next to her.

"You're very young," she said. "Twenty-six?"

"Twenty-seven," Julia answered.

"My husband believes in young talent. He's had his eye on you for some time—did you know that?"

"No, I didn't. I just got the letter mentioning a job with the *Herald* and I couldn't believe it. It's like a dream come true."

"What a nice thing to say," the older woman remarked. "I shall tell William. He reads the good provincials; he's always on the lookout for new people with fresh ideas. He spotted you quite early on. I remember him saying to me one morning, 'There's a girl here, Evie, Julia Hamilton. *Yorkshire Post*. I like what she writes. She might do for us one day.'" Julia hadn't known what to say. She sipped the sherry. There was a pause, and Evelyn Western said, "I'm telling you this so you won't be frightened of my husband when you meet him. He'll grill you to see what you're made of, but stand up to him and you'll be all right. He knows I'm going to say this because I always

do when someone comes here for the first time. Some of
the young men don't like it, but I feel you won't mind."

Julia looked at her. She had very blue eyes, cleverly
made-up to emphasize their color.

"I don't mind, Lady Western. I'm very grateful to you.
I was so nervous coming here, I nearly turned around and
went home. But I won't forget what you've said. Thank
you."

"Not at all. Now, I think you should go up and change.
We'll gather in the drawing room at a quarter to eight.
Baker will take you up. See you then."

Much of what followed was indistinct in her memory
when she tried to describe it to her parents. Her mother
wanted to know what the bedroom was like, avid for
details, but Julia couldn't supply them. It was full of
chintz and bright colors, and a handsome bathroom with
an enormous round bath. She'd been too frightened of
being late to try it before dinner. Afterward, when she
came up and it was all over, she slipped into the bath
and thought about the evening. There were twelve for
dinner, three couples, another girl, two single men and
herself, and the Westerns. Evelyn Western introduced her
to the other guests and then steered her toward her husband. Julia knew the face; it was well publicized, but she
was shocked to see how slight he was. His wife stood
over him like an elegant giraffe. Julia was somewhere
around five foot eight—she'd never bothered to find
out exactly—and she was at eye level with William
Chancellor Western. He had graying hair; a fresh, un-
lined complexion; and pale-gray eyes like ice chips.

He repeated his wife's greeting. "How nice of you to
come. I shall call you Julia. Did you have a good journey? I hope the directions were clear."

"Perfectly clear, thank you, Lord Western. It's very
kind of you to have me. What a wonderful house." It

wasn't mere politeness. She'd never seen a more beautiful drawing room in any coffee-table book of great houses. The plasterwork was exquisite, the ceiling soared above a massive chandelier lit with real candles. The pictures . . . Julia had studied the history of art among her degree subjects, and she recognized works by the greatest English portrait painters, from a massive Van Dyck group to a lovely joyous Raeburn of a mother and two children playing with a spaniel. Western saw her looking around.

"You like pictures?" he asked without waiting for more than a nod. "Know anything about them?"

"A little," Julia answered. His manner was disconcerting. He asked a question and then followed on without bothering about an answer.

"You studied history of art, I remember," he said. She was amazed that he should know such a detail.

"I make it my business to research anyone thoroughly before I offer them a job. A lot of people can write a good newspaper piece. It takes intelligence and intuition to be a good reporter.

"You're seated next to Leo Derwent, over there. Foxy-faced young man, very pushy. He's a politician. See what you think of him, and tell me about it after dinner." Then he had moved on and left her standing, staring after him.

Julia felt her face burn at the peremptory manner and the rude way she'd been abandoned in a roomful of strangers. Don't be afraid of him, his wife had said.

Well, I bloody well won't be intimidated, Julia decided. *He's not going to walk over me just because of a job.* She finished the glass of champagne that had been handed to her by the butler and walked straight across to the man so aptly described as foxy-faced.

"I think we're sitting next to each other," she said. "We were introduced, but I never catch anyone's name. I'm Julia Hamilton." And she gave him her most charming smile.

Leo Derwent had never heard of her—neither the name nor the face registered in his personal computer of people worth cultivating—but it was a very pretty face, with fiery-red hair standing out like a halo. And big dark eyes. Unusual.

A very sexy little piece, he decided, and wondered whether that cunning shit Western was offering him a tit-bit. He had a way of putting politicians in his pocket. No doubt he knew Leo's weakness for sexy girls who enjoyed playing games. He looked down the front of Julia's dress and said in a careful accent. "Aren't I lucky? Leo Derwent—your glass is empty. So's mine. Let's see if we can catch the Admirable Crichton's eye—" He was a dreadful specimen; with his phony vowel sounds and his self-promotion.

It would have been easy to dismiss him as shallow and pretentious. But under the veneer, so painfully acquired, of manners and attitudes that were not natural to him, Julia sensed there lurked a predator as cunning and ruthless as the animal he unfortunately looked like. He monopolized her during dinner, setting out to impress her with his achievements.

"I really think," she whispered at last, "I'd better say something to the man on my left—I don't want to be rude—you've been so interesting."

And she escaped him, leaving him uncertain whether she had snubbed him or she knew something about social customs at smart dinner parties that he hadn't picked up for himself. The dining room was as spectacular as the drawing room. The table was laden with early silver, the food and wine were superb. When dinner was over, Evelyn Western stood up. "We'll have coffee in the drawing room, and don't be too long, Billy, please!"

After a quarter of an hour she said to Julia, "I won't have them sitting for hours in the dining room. Why should we have to wait, twiddling our thumbs, till they've fin-ished the port. Ah, here they are—come along, go and sit down next to William. Over there on that sofa. And remember," her voice lowered, "don't let him bully you." For a moment she touched Julia on the arm. "He likes you, I can always tell."

He turned those slate-colored eyes on her. "Good dinner, wasn't it?"

"Delicious," Julia answered.

"I love food," he announced, "it's one of life's great pleasures. I hate women who diet. My wife never had to bother, she's always been thin. You didn't pick, I noticed."

Julia took a deep breath. He was doing his damnedest to disconcert her. If she gushed, he'd despise her.

"I was starving," she said. "I hadn't had any lunch."

To her surprise he laughed. "Neither had I. Didn't have time. I saw you getting on well with Leo. What did you think of him?" Again without waiting for an answer, "Clever fellow, come up by his bootstraps. Could be prime minister one day, only I won't see it."

Julia said coolly, "Well, I hope I don't. I wouldn't buy a new car from him, never mind a secondhand one."

"I see," he said. "Not afraid to speak your mind, are you? Good. And you're right. He's a sharp little crook and one day he'll be caught out. Ever done a profile?"

"Not the kind you'd publish, Lord Western," she answered. "The papers I worked for wanted nice, cozy articles about local people. 'Head of the Hospital Management Committee Councillor Bloggs at home with his family'—that sort of thing."

"Well, I want you to do a piece on Leo Derwent," he said. "Not for publication—you're not going to run before you can walk—but just to show me what you might be able to do. Send it up to my office by Wednesday. You'll be starting under Harris; he's been news editor for ten years and he's a very good man. But he's jealous of new blood. He won't take you seriously, he doesn't rate women beyond fashion and features, so do what he says, smile sweetly, and be patient. Are you patient? Not with that hair, I bet. Never mind. You'll have to learn."

"I'll try," Julia promised. "Can I say something?"

"In a minute, I haven't finished. You aren't patient, are you?" He laughed again. "Get the feel of the paper, and don't mind the boys; they'll all have one thing on their minds, but I expect you're used to that. What's your own situation—regular boyfriend? Don't blush, I like to know everything about my protégés. You're a protégée; I think you've got promise."

"Thank you," Julia said. "I wasn't blushing. I didn't think you had a right to ask, that's all."

"I have all the rights," he said firmly. "You'll have to accept that. Now—you wanted to say something?"

He paused, and they looked at each other. He had a hard, cold stare, and she hated being transfixed like that. She mustered her courage and stared back. "I just wanted to say that this is the opportunity of my life and thank you for giving it to me. I won't let you down."

He did something that made her jump. He patted her hand. "I'm sure you won't. And make no mistake, Julia, you'll be fired if you do. Now, I can see my dear wife looking bored, so I must go and rescue her."

He stood up. He moved on without glancing back at her. One of the women moved across and sat beside her. Her husband had been on Julia's left at the dinner table. She was in her forties, beautifully dressed but there wasn't a line or a laughter crease on the smooth surface of her skin. "I hear you're going to work for William," she said. "How exciting!"

"Yes," Julia said. "Yes, I'm sure it's going to be. If I can stand the pace."

●　●　●

What a long time ago, she thought, buckling her seat belt as they came into land.

Five years had passed since the naïve country reporter had come face-to-face with the great man and gone away determined to prove herself. Now she recognized the technique. He liked putting people on their mettle; if they failed to measure up, they were of no use to him. She remembered sitting up for two nights, reference books and *Hansard* by her elbow, writing and rewriting the profile of Leo Derwent. Western hadn't even acknowledged it. She remembered crying in the lavatory because she was sure she hadn't got the job, but a week later, she got a letter telling her to report to Harris. But nothing happened and slowly she settled into the routine of the newsroom and made her best effort to get on with Harris.

The first day she had introduced herself, she felt so nervous that she stammered slightly. The man pushed thick, horn-rimmed glasses off his nose and looked at her without interest.

"Mr. Harris? I'm Julia Hamilton," she said. "I . . . er, I've come to start . . . " He didn't help her. He was somewhere in his early forties, with graying hair and an unwelcoming manner.

"Yes, I know. Your spot's over there. Find your own way around. Davis'll give you something to do." Then the glasses came down and he went back to reading a printout. Julia didn't see him glance up when she turned away and watch her go across to the bank of WPs and screens and find the vacant place he had indicated. He saw Davis, who was next to her, grin and offer a hand. Davis would be nice to her; Davis was always nice to women—the secretaries, the messenger girls, even the odd cleaner, if they were attractive. Harris wondered how the pretty redhead, blushing to her ears with first-day nerves, would cope with Davis. He shrugged men-

tally. Not that he cared. The old man liked to foist someone on him from time to time. Like all tyrants, he
enjoyed springing surprises. There'd been a number of
Young Turks brought in from outside, potential rivals for
his job. Ben Harris had seen them all off. He had nothing
to worry about with a girl. She was the first girl Western
had introduced, which must signify something, he supposed. Some whim, some mischievous quirk had prompted
Western to single her out and land her in Harris's lap.

She wouldn't last; he didn't think he had to make it
difficult for her, though he was ready to do so. She'd cut
her teeth in the newsroom, and if she was ambitious,
and sensible, get herself into the Women's Feature,
where she would have a future.

Ben Harris had come up via the provinces, working as
a teenager on freebie news sheets, on to the weekly newspapers, running errands, at the end of everyone's boot.
But he had talent; he could write and he could angle a
story for maximum news impact. He worked and pushed
himself upward, ending on a quality Midlands newspaper, where he became news editor. And then the offer
came to move to London, to the mecca of the Western
Group. He was married by then, with two children.

His wife hadn't wanted to move. She liked her home
in Birmingham; she had friends, the children were doing
well at school. The marriage started to break up when
they moved down to London. They'd been divorced for
many years. Ben Harris lived for his job. Sometimes,
with a few too many drinks inside him, he boasted he'd
sucked printer's ink instead of mother's milk. He was
tough, he had no friends, only colleagues in the office
and potential rivals. He had one motto, and it was the
only thing he believed in: Watch your back. He wouldn't
have to watch it with J. Hamilton.

She'd been there a month when he told Davis to give

her a few minor stories to cover. He noticed that she had seen Davis off, without taking an enemy; nobody else had got closer to her than a drink in the pub after work.

He gave her grudging credit for that. Everything she produced was cut to pieces by the subeditor. Most of it went into the shredder and was never used. Ben Harris waited for her to whine. Most people would have complained, not to him—he didn't waste time with the minnows on his staff—but he'd have heard about it. He knew everything that went on.

But J. Hamilton, as he called her, disdaining a Christian name, got on with the next assignment and said nothing. He began to think of her as a pro: quiet, dedicated, and adaptable. One morning he asked to see her copy. She'd been covering a protest over a stretch of dangerous road near a school. It was bottom-of-the-page, half-inch stuff, not important enough to rate a photograph. Just a group of parents parading with placards. Routine, dull. . . . He read the piece. He called the sub who murdered Julia's work as part of his job. Ben Harris said, "This is good. Don't fuck about with it. Don't say I said so."

He watched her progress; it was steady, and it showed decided flair. She had taken the tough period of initiation with dignity and guts. She was popular with the rest of the staff, who'd begun to accept her as a colleague. They'd stopped making bets on who would get to lay her first. Incredibly, as Harris realized, she had become one of them. She went out on her stories—often with a photographer now—she stood her round in the pub after work, she asked no favors of anyone because she was a woman. He called her in one day.

She had matured; she was confident now. She called him Ben, because he'd snapped at her once, saying, "Drop the Mr. Harris, for Christ's sake—I'm not a bloody shop walker!"

"How's it going, J?" he asked her.

He never smiled, Julia noticed. When he said something complimentary, it was with a scowl. "Fine, I think. I'm getting a lot of stuff in these days. I hope you're happy with me."

"You'd know if I wasn't," he said. He dropped his heavy glasses on his table. "I didn't think you'd last," he said flatly.

"I know," Julia answered quietly. "That made me all the more determined."

He glanced at her quickly and then said, as if the words were chewed-up glass, "You're doing all right. Don't try and run before you can walk, that's all."

Julia smiled. "I won't, because you won't let me."

"Too right," he agreed. "Now, I'm busy, even if you're not."

Julie had been on the staff for nine months when William Western exploded his bombshell. A big news story had just broken. The mutilated and abused bodies of two five-year-old twin girls had been discovered in a wood outside a Welsh village on the border.

It was shaping up to be one of the most gruesome sex murders of children since the Moors killings thirty years ago.

When the directive came down to Ben Harris, he couldn't believe it. *I want Julia Hamilton to cover this. Let's see what she's made of. Western.* Ben slammed the note down on his desk and shouted an obscenity. He didn't care who heard him. Send an inexperienced young woman up to cover a horrendous child murder like this?—Western must be off his trolley.

He opened his office door and yelled into the bedlam of the newsroom. "Tell J. Hamilton to come in here!" Then he banged the door shut. Davis, who had become a good friend to Julia, raised his eyebrows in a comic grimace.

"He's yelling his head off for you. Stand up to him, Julia—it's the only way. If he fires you, we'll all come out on strike!"

"Like hell you will." She managed to smile at him. "I can't think what I've done. . . ."

When she came into his office, Ben Harris looked up and glared. "I've just had this come down from the top floor," he said. "You can read it, but you're not bloody going."

Julia scanned it quickly.

She said quietly, "I've got to go. I haven't any choice."

"Sit down a minute," he told her. "Just listen to me. You're a good reporter. You're doing well. I like your stuff, and I'm bloody difficult to please. But this isn't on. This is the biggest murder story we've had in decades, and it's going to be one of the worst. Those kids were tortured and raped. Whoever did it, mutilated them while they were still alive. I wouldn't send a woman to cover this story in any circumstances. And you've never touched a murder story, have you?

"This isn't going to be just human interest, grief-stricken parents, shock horror in the community, all that crap—this means inquests, police-incident rooms, autopsies, the lot! It's no job for you. If you foul up on this, you're finished. That's the way he works."

"If I refuse the job, I'm finished," Julia said. "That's why he picked me. He said it, let's see what she's made of—I've got to go, Ben, or I might as well resign now."

He looked up at her. She was pale, he realized, shocked by the prospect. But she was right. Western would write her off if she refused.

"You know, it might be better if you did just that," he said slowly. "I've seen tough men gutted by something like this. Don't do it. Call the old bastard's bluff. I'll back you."

"I know you will," she answered. "But it's not the

point. I can't walk away from it, or I'm not fit to be in the job. I'll go, Ben, and I'll show him what I'm made of. Now, will you back me up?"

He stood up. "I'll back you, J. Hamilton," he said. He looked angry. "But only so long as you don't screw up."

"Thanks," she said. "I'll try not to."

The double murder was a sensation. The tabloids shrieked with gory headlines, the quality papers reported with restraint and sobriety; the *Sunday Herald* gained plaudits from all sides for the concise, unsentimental coverage under the byline J. Hamilton. The reports were a masterly analysis of the horror that had engulfed a family and a small community in a Nonconformist village. There was no sensationalism, just clear prose of depth and integrity, exploring the personal and social elements in the sexual perversion of the crime.

No one suspected that the writer was a woman.

When the arrests were made, Julia was called back to London. A local man, married with children, was charged with the double murders. They were close neighbors of the twins' family.

On her first day in the office she was fêted and congratulated. The grinning Davis smacked a kiss on her cheek. A personal note of commendation was sent down from Western. That evening she was borne off to the pub to celebrate. Ben Harris came up to her.

"It's about time I bought you a drink," he said. "You deserve it. Come and sit down over here." He seldom socialized with his staff. He kept himself remote, immersed in his job. Nobody else liked to join them.

"You look completely gutted," he said. "Take a few days off."

"I'd rather work," Julia answered. "I cope better if I keep going."

"I told you what it would be like," he said. "You

wouldn't listen. But it's marked you, and it shows. Drink that up and have another. I don't often buy people drinks, so make the most of it." A rare smile softened his face. He pushed his thick, gray-streaked hair back and said, "You did bloody well. I was amazed; and you got better and better."

"Thanks." She smiled back at him. "It's heady stuff, coming from you. Thanks, Ben."

"Excuse me for butting in—" He looked up sharply. A young man was standing by their table. "I just wanted to say what a great job you did on those Rhys murders. I'd no idea it was a woman when I read them. My name's Felix Sutton." He held out a large hand, and Julia shook it. "I'm on the political desk. I hope you don't mind me crashing your party. I just wanted to say it was great stuff."

He had a friendly, self-confident grin. "Mind if I sit down?"

"Of course not," Julia answered. Ben Harris pushed his chair back. She realized that he looked at the intruder with hostility. He gave the young man his well-known scowl. "I'll be off, then," he said.

Felix suggested they go to a trattoria in Covent Garden. He didn't argue when she said of course she'd pay her half. Sitting opposite him, Julia realized how attractive he was. He wasn't conventionally handsome; he looked like a boxer, with a broken nose and a boxer's body. He was certainly younger than she was, but it didn't seem to matter.

"Before we order," he said, "do you want to talk about the case, or have you had enough blood and guts for to-night?"

Julia winced. "Don't," she said. "It was a nightmare. I just had to shut off any feelings, or I couldn't have done those interviews or gone to the inquest. All I could do was hang in there to see whoever did it got caught. It kept me sane. Now I've got to put it out of my mind. Or try to. I haven't slept a night through since I went up there," she admitted.

"I'm not surprised. Let's start with a bottle of wine. The talk around the office is you're marked for stardom. They're all buying drinks and chatting you up now, but some people aren't going to like it. Ben Harris, for one," he said.

"But I've only just started," Julia protested. "I couldn't be a threat to him in a million years."

"That's not how he sees it," he countered. "I'll bet he stabbed a few backs on his way up, why shouldn't you? Especially with the old man behind you. Have you been down to the house yet?"

"I went before I started working. He wanted to have a look at me. He said he'd noticed my stuff on the Post."

"I've heard that's how it goes. But only if it's someone he's picked out specially. I wish I'd get a chance to meet him."

"Maybe you will." She was careful not to discuss William Western. He didn't pursue it; he talked about himself without bombast, but without modesty either. He'd come to the newspaper as a junior reporter straight from Keil University. He had a first-class degree in Modern History and PPE. He had done some amateur boxing—he touched his nose and grinned—reached the all-England semifinals, but that was just a hobby. He liked keeping fit and worked out at a gym on the weekends. "What I really want," he said as the second bottle of wine was opened, "is to get to the top. One day I'm going to be sitting in old Warburton's office." Clive Warburton was chief political correspondent, and a powerful pundit on the Westminster scene.

"You *are* ambitious," Julia remarked. "But you've got plenty of time, anyway."

"No, lady, that's where you're wrong." He was quite serious, the cheery grin had changed to a look of steely purpose. "Anyone who thinks they've got plenty of time isn't going to get there. I'm the original young man in a hurry. I want it all, and I want it yesterday."

Suddenly he laughed. "As you can see, I'm an ambitious bastard. Changing the subject, I love your hair. Is it for real?"

"Of course it is," Julia protested. He smiled at her, and it was a naked sexual invitation. "I suppose I have to take your word for it."

"You do," she said firmly. "It's late, and I'm shattered. Let's get the bill." She paid her share, and he took it. "This was great, let's do it again?"

They were in the street, and he was looking down at her.

Julia had ended an affair when she left Yorkshire. There'd been no man in her life since then. "Why not? I liked it too."

"Can you drive me back to Islington?"

"Yes, of course."

He squeezed himself into the little car; he was too tall and too big to fit comfortably. "Mine's on the bloody blink," he explained. "We had a little argument with a truck coming up the A-ten and the truck won. Just here, number twenty-eight. It's not as grotty as it looks outside. Quite nice. Want to come in for a drink?"

"Not tonight," Julia said. "I'm on my knees, I'm so tired. I hope to God I sleep."

"You would if you came up with me," he said coolly.

"You're very sure of yourself, aren't you?" She felt suddenly angry. Angry with herself, too, because she was tempted.

He grinned and, bending down, aimed a light kiss on her cheek.

"No harm in trying," he said. "I hope you'll say yes next time. See you, Julia." He got out and ran up the stairs and let himself in. He didn't look back as she drove off.

That was five years ago, and his prophecy had come true. She was the brightest young star in the Fleet Street firmament, with her own byline and a book analyzing the Rhys murders, published to general acclaim. And she and Felix had moved into a flat together.

Felix had planned a weekend at the pub on the Avon. He liked fishing and he waved her objections away by saying he'd teach her. "It's a nice place, not fancy, but they hire out rods and a boat." Julia had been looking forward to it; London was hot, and she'd just come back from a hectic trip to the Midlands to write about a prominent industrialist who had committed suicide before he could be arrested for fraud.

His company was in receivership. He'd walked out of his Queen Anne house near Melton Mowbray and blown half his head off with a shotgun. A couple of days lazing on a river and making love to Felix would take her mind off his wife and two teenage children.

But on Thursday afternoon the call came through. Western's personal secretary. The same smooth voice, well known to Julia now.

"Lord and Lady Western would like you to dine with them on Saturday and stay the night."

"This Saturday?"

"It is rather short notice, but they're sure you'll understand."

There'd been several invitations since that nerve-racking initiation. Julia knew the formula: down for dinner; a smart gathering of politicians, diplomats, people Western wanted to make use of, or who hoped to make use of him. Then leave promptly after breakfast. He called it

Dine and Sleep, mocking the royal protocol at Windsor Castle.

"I had something planned," Julia protested.

"I know they're counting on you," the voice said. "Surely you can rearrange it, Miss Hamilton. When can you let me know?"

It wasn't an invitation, it was an order. As the voice was well aware.

"I'll change my plan," Julia conceded. In a necessary show of independence, she added, "But you're right, it is short notice. I suppose someone else dropped out."

"Not to my knowledge. Arrive at six-thirty, black tie as usual. I'll let Lady Western know."

She'd put through a call to Felix. He had been promoted to Clive Warburton's "gofer." Go for this and go for that. But it was a start, and he was making himself very useful.

"Darling," she said, "I've got to cancel our weekend. The old man's asked me for a D and S on Saturday. I'm so sorry, but I've got to go."

"Of course you do," he answered. "Might be something in it for you."

"I was looking forward to going with you," she insisted. "I tried to get out of it, but it was impossible."

"Don't get your knickers in a twist," he said cheerfully. "We'll do it another time. The Warbler wants me to go to the all-night debate tonight, so I won't be home. He's out to dinner, lucky old fart. See you."

Julia put the phone down. He didn't mind about canceling the weekend. Of course it was easier for her that he wasn't jealous or possessive.

He took life as it came. Their personal life, she corrected herself. He had tunnel vision when it concerned his career. He expected her to feel the same. They had fun together; they had mutual friends, though most of them tended to be Felix's age and with his interests. But he was good about escorting her to anything important. He could be charming and well mannered when he chose. "You catch more flies with honey than you do with vinegar," he quoted. They had a very open, civilized relationship, and it suited them both. She just wished he had been as disappointed about losing their weekend as she was.

The flat they shared was a long way from the basement in Pimlico, where she lived when she first came to London, and from the shabby chaos of Felix's Islington pad. It was a smart conversion in Chelsea Square, and it belonged to Julia. The furniture belonged to her, and the modern pictures, picked up from local art galleries. Felix said they looked like a lot of daubs to him; he didn't contribute anything but a sophisticated stereo and record player that cost nearly as much as Julia's pictures. She was a star and earning a star's salary.

He didn't resent the disparity; it didn't worry him that she carried three-quarters of their living costs. He was still comparatively low-paid, but he had everything to play for. He had Clive Warburton in his sights. His break would come. And when it did, he announced to Julia, then he'd pick up the bills and keep her! And laughed in his carefree way. Sometimes he reminded her of a great, casual child, convinced that the world and everyone in it owed him something just because he was there. But he made no personal demands. He lived his life, and he expected her to live hers.

She came into the sitting room and put down her overnight case. It was dark-blue leather with her initials stamped on the side.

"I'd better be off now," she said. "I hope to God the traffic's not too bad." She'd heard him come in while she was showering; he'd called out and settled himself to watch the England v. Germany football match. He was mad for all sports, and nothing was allowed to interfere with his gym sessions and football.

She might keep him, in actuality, but she was never going to own him. He had made that plain from the start. His nickname in the office was Toy Boy; Julia had heard it and blazed with anger. But he only shrugged and laughed. "They're jealous I got there first. I don't give a fuck what anyone says." And he didn't.

He looked up and got to his feet. "Come and kiss me, beautiful. We've just scored the equalizer."

He always kissed her hard, using his tongue, and she couldn't help the surge of sexuality when he touched her. He knew it, too, and traded on it. "I have to keep my end up with my megastar," he liked to tease her, and pulled her laughing into bed.

He was a marvelous lover, but on his own terms. He had never said he loved her, even in their closest moments.

"I wonder what the old sod is up to this time?" he said, letting her go. "You won't have a ladder left to climb—I wish I could get a toe on it. Put a word in for me, will you, darling?" He always said it, half in earnest, but not expecting anything. She had never promoted him, she never would. He had his terms for their relationship, and integrity in the job was hers.

"I'll be home on Sunday, lunchtime. Will you be here?"

"Don't know, might go down to the club and get a game of squash. Have a good time, darling, and we'll go fishing another weekend. See you sometime Sunday." As Julia let herself out, she heard him exclaim in disappointment. The Germans must have scored another goal.

The secondhand Renault had gone a long time ago. She drove a sleek BMW; the evening dress hanging in its initialed sleeve in the back came from Bruce Oldfield. She had made it early, and she wasn't shy about showing her success in terms of a smart car and good clothes.

Appearances counted; Julia had learned that early on.

It was all face value and hype; success was more than talent. She knew she had that, and it made sense of the gloss she had deliberately applied to her lifestyle. She had followed Evelyn Western's advice for the second time: "Spend on yourself; dress well. You mustn't be afraid to stand out. Not that you can help it, Julia. You did that the first time you came down here. Poor child, you looked like the new girl on her first day at school. . . ." She had smiled kindly at the memory. "Now you're a personality, a name people recognize. Make the most of it. And I'll help you if you like. I do know about clothes. But don't let William know; he'd say I was being bossy."

She had made the introductions, the tactful suggestions, and Julia realized how much Evelyn Western was enjoying herself. There was no hint of patronage. Once, she turned to Julia, with her extraordinary blue eyes bright with pleasure, and said, "You know, this is such fun for me. We never had a daughter."

And with equal tact she bowed out and left Julia to make her own choices and develop her own style.

She knew the route down to Hampshire, the turnoff from the highway, and the descent into deep countryside. She eased down at the entrance to the drive, slowed for the speed bumps, and rounded the sweep to the front of the house. The butler had changed since her last visit. Western was a demanding and temperamental employer. He hired and fired in his domestic scene as he did in his business. Or businesses. He controlled a chain of middle-ranking hotels, an investment bank in the City, and mining interests in Brazil and West Africa. And three commercial radio stations and a Midlands TV network.

Her bag and the dress were taken upstairs for her by a maid, and the butler, a Filipino, she noted, said Lord Western was waiting for her in the study. There was no sign of his wife, and Julia was disappointed. Western was business, career colleague, a human iceberg. Evelyn, she felt, was a friend.

William Western was reading when she came in. He looked up, smiled briefly at her, and said to the butler, "Whiskey and soda, and vodka on the rocks for Miss Hamilton. Hello, Julia. Good journey down? Saw the smart car driving up scattering my gravel—sit down, over there. How are you? You look well." She was used to it by now. The questions didn't wait for an answer. She sat opposite him; he even told his guests where to sit. He said, "I hear you had another engagement."

"Yes," she answered. That bloody secretary had passed it on. . . .

"Glad you canceled it and came here instead. I've got something in mind for you. I think you'll like it. Where's that idiot with our drinks? He's been here a week; you'd think he'd know his way around by now. What have I interrupted? Off for the weekend somewhere with Sutton?"

She kept her temper, but it showed, and he seemed amused by it.

"Yes. We were going to fish on the Avon. Felix was going to teach me."

"About the only thing he could teach you," he said. "He's a bloodsucker. Don't waste too much time on him. Ah, at last!" He glared at the Filipino. The man gave a quick, nervous glance and offered the drinks. "The lady first," Western snapped at him. "God almighty—" He spoke as if the butler were part of the furniture. "You wouldn't believe the references—must have written them himself."

It was shaming, and Julia said thank you, very loudly, to make up for his appalling rudeness, as she took her drink.

"I can't stand stupidity," he said. "Drives me mad."

"Perhaps if you didn't frighten him to death, he wouldn't be stupid."

He looked sharply at her. "Siding with the underdog, are we? Evelyn does the same. She doesn't have to pay the salary. And don't presume to criticize me, I don't allow it. Now, let me tell you who's coming to dinner." He paused; he liked to playact sometimes. Julia waited. He was a bully and a tyrant. As a person she disliked him intensely. But she couldn't resist the firecracker mind, the supercharge of energy. It glowed around him like a nimbus.

He took a large swallow of his whiskey.

"Nobody," he said. "You and Evelyn and me. Almost a family gathering."

Julia said quietly, "Lord Western, I'm very flattered."

"Then don't look disappointed. It'll be worth your while. You can fish with the boyfriend another time. But this could be the most important evening of your life. Now—" He finished his drink, and got up. "Time to go and change. Evelyn's coming down from London by car, she'll be here in a minute. Seven-thirty. Don't be late."

"I'm never late," Julia pointed out. "You know that."

"My wife is; hopeless about time. She's fond of you, you know. Thinks you're a nice girl. I think you're a clever one. Much more important." He left the room so quickly that it made her blink. He never waited for anyone. He left, and that was the end of it, even if someone else was in mid-sentence. He was a dreadful, egotistical bulldozer, and she hated him, she thought, refusing to gulp down her vodka and hurry after him. But when he said it could be the most important evening of her life, she knew he meant it.

CHAPTER 2

WESTERN WAS WALKING ABOUT STABBING A big cigar to emphasize his words.

Dinner had been tense; she could feel the atmosphere building up, and it wasn't just Western generating drama. His wife was as charming and friendly as always, but there was something wary about her. Anxious. Julia couldn't make it out. And then they gathered in the study.

He spoke abruptly.

"How would you like to head up a new feature?" He saw Julia's expression and said irritably, "My dear girl— for God's sake, you don't think I'm talking about some kind of *women's* page?"

Julia said, "Well, yes, I did—"

"Don't be stupid," he snapped. "I'm talking about a major feature with a new angle. I'm going to call it 'Exposure.'"

The Herald's commitment to honesty in public life. Watchdog of the nation. Investigative journalism on the American model. No holds barred, take on all comers. It'll make The Sunday Times' 'Insight' look like a snoop after the Parish Council!" He stopped. "Well, what do you think of it? Can you do it?"

Julia shook her head; she saw Evelyn Western watching her. She looked tense. Head up a controversial feature. . . .

"I don't know what to say," she said.

"Well, it's the first time since I've known you," he retorted. "You're not being modest, I hope. I wouldn't offer you the job if I didn't think you could do it."

"No," Julia answered. "I know you wouldn't. Do you really mean I'd be in charge—not responsible to anyone?"

"Only to me," he said. "Directly responsible to me. If you get this right, you could be the Herald's first woman editor in a few years—"

"Billy, don't overwhelm her," his wife cut in. Then to Julia, "It is a wonderful offer."

"I know," Julia answered. "And I'll take it. Lord Western—I really don't know what to say. 'Thank you' sounds so inadequate. . . . I can't believe it's going to happen." She gave a nervous laugh. "It's incredible."

Western turned to his wife. For a second longer than usual they held each other's gaze. Then he said, "Ring for that half-witted Filipe and tell him to bring some champagne. We've got something to celebrate."

"To the birth of 'Exposure,'" he announced, raising his glass.

"And to you, Julia," Evelyn Western added.

She stood up, reed-thin in her straight black crêpe dress; a double row of enormous pearls gleamed in the light. They were the only jewels she wore apart from a very small sapphire surrounded by tiny diamonds on her wedding finger. Given to her before Western had made his first millions. He'd been a small-town accountant when they married. It was an endearing touch of sentiment.

"I know you'll want to get down to details with Julia, so I'll go to bed," she said, "and leave you to it. Try not to stay up all night, will you?" She gave her husband a fond smile, bestowed the last of it on Julia, and was gone. How could she love him? Julia had often wondered. What was there to love in William Western?

And she was such a fundamentally nice woman. Julia gave up. She'd never understand it.

Western finished his champagne. "I don't really like this stuff," he remarked, "but it's supposed to be lucky to christen a new venture. I'm switching to brandy. Like some? No, all right then, stick to your fizzy. But don't drink too much—you're going to need a clear head.

"Now, I suppose you're wondering where to start— well, I've got your first program mapped out for you. 'Target' would be a better word. I like the sound of it— target. We must work that into the format, it sounds good. . . ."

Julia was caught up, enmeshed beyond objective judgment by the speed and energy of the man. Target. Yes, it would catch the reader's eye, whet the public appetite for blood. He knew his public. . . .

He had a bumper half-full of brandy in his two hands, leaning toward her. The sheer power of his personality was at full throttle. She felt a rush of exhilaration not too far from the sexual high she got from Felix.

"I want you to go after Harold King," he said. "I want that bastard's head on a plate. Money's no object, hire what staff you want—go where you need to—just nail him for me." He stared hard at her. "Do it, and you can name your price."

• • •

Julia went to the usual guest room. She'd risen on the Richter scale of Western's approval. It was twice the size of the one she'd occupied that first night five years ago; it had a spectacular view of the lake.

Ideas were spinning like tops in her brain. Harold King. The most controversial figure in the public domain. A genius, a billionaire, a brutal adversary; a power figure that reveled being in the spotlight.

There were legends about him, fostered by himself; other rumors spoken in a whisper. Arms dealing, corruption, financial tentacles reaching deep into Eastern Europe.

And friends in very high places who protected him.

"Nail him for me. . . ." Western had said. "And you can name your price!"

As he promised, it had been the most important evening of her life.

"I can't help feeling guilty," Evelyn Western said. "She's still an innocent, Billy. Nobody else would have taken this on."

"That's why I chose her," he answered. He was in his dressing room and he came and sat on the bed and took hold of his wife's hand.

"Evie, she's clever, she's ambitious, and she's determined. That wasn't a bribe—I meant it. I'll make her the *Herald*'s editor if she brings this off. And because she's a woman, she can get to people and places that won't arouse suspicion."

"For how long?" his wife countered. "How long before King realizes she's investigating him? And then what will happen to her? I wish I hadn't encouraged her. She trusts me."

He squeezed her hand and held it between both of his. He looked tired suddenly, as if a light had been extinguished.

"You did the right thing," he said. "I've got to destroy

him before he destroys me. And I'll use anyone—anyone—to stop it from happening. Now, you settle down and take a sleeping pill. I don't want you lying awake fretting. Come on, here's the water, swallow it down. . . ."

"Felix," Julia called out, closing the flat door. "Felix?" There was no answer. She felt a chill of disappointment.

Why couldn't he have been there to share the excitement with her? Why did he have to go and play his bloody squash when he knew she was coming home?

"Selfish bugger," she muttered, feeling quelled. "I'll go home, I'm not sitting here all afternoon till he comes back. I'll ring up and see if they're in for lunch."

Her parents lived in Surrey. Her father was retired; Julia's brother had taken over the partnership in the family firm of solicitors. He was doing very well and talking of opening an office in London.

He and his wife and two young children lived in the same suburb of Hampton. They were very close to his parents, who doted on their grandchildren. It was not disloyal, Julia admitted, to say that since her career took off, she had drifted apart from the family unit.

Her mother answered the telephone. She sounded surprised and delighted when Julia suggested she drive down.

"That would be lovely; I'll turn down the beef—how long will you be? Oh, don't worry, don't drive too fast—Daddy'll be thrilled to see you."

It was warm and welcoming. Just what Julia needed. At least brother Tom and his brood of children wouldn't be there monopolizing her parents. She could tell them about the new job. They didn't appreciate the finer points of journalism, and secretly she knew they'd rather she had married a suitable man and settled down, but they were always supportive.

Felix could come back to an empty flat for a change. She jumped into her car and set off. She'd brought him down to Sunday lunch once, and she knew her parents didn't like him. She didn't like him much herself at that moment, and the realization surprised her.

The trouble was, as soon as he put his hands on her, she'd melt like a candle under a match.

It was an excellent lunch. Good, plain English food, as her father liked to tell an audience, was the best in the world. He couldn't stand meat mucked up in sauces, and tarted-up vegetables you couldn't get a tooth into. Julia listened with affection. He never changed; he was solid as a rock in his integrity, his political right-wing bias, and his basic decency as a husband, father, and professional. A lifetime spent as a solicitor had given him sharp insight into people's characters without making him a cynic. That was remarkable in itself. He beamed across at her.

"You're looking very chipper, Juliette." He used the pet name from her childhood. "Anything up?"

They'd cleared away, and she'd helped her mother load the dishwasher. They were sitting outside in the garden with their coffee. It was a lovely spring afternoon. "Yes," her mother interposed, "you look like the cat that's got the cream."

"Well, I have," Julia answered. "I've been staying with the boss. I got back this morning. Mum and Dad, he's offered me a tremendous job. My own feature."

"Oh?" Her mother's bright smile faded a little. Julia realized she'd been hoping for a different kind of cream. A nice man, a possible wedding. Not Felix, who'd behaved like a conceited lout when she introduced him. "What sort of feature?"

"Well, something like 'Insight,' only much tougher, more aggressive." Her father was an avid *Sunday Times* reader.

"Good Lord—well, that is exciting. Are you going to run it?" he asked.

Julia nodded. "Yes, Dad. It's my baby, I'm the boss; except I'm answerable to Western. And Western wants me to start off by digging up any dirt I can find about Harold King! Isn't it amazing? Big salary, expenses, staff, anything I want."

Her mother didn't say anything. The phrase about digging up dirt didn't appeal to her. Her father said after a pause, "Harold King. . . . Didn't he ruin a high-court judge because of some investigation some years ago? Yes, I remember. I'd be a bit careful before you make an enemy of him. He's got a nasty reputation."

"I know his reputation," Julia answered. "And it's pretty obvious that he's cultivated it because he's got plenty to hide and he wants to scare people off. I'm not scared, Dad."

"I know you're not," her father said. "You were always a gutsy girl. But just be careful, won't you? Even in my little backwater practice we heard some very disturbing things about that gentleman and the way he manipulated the law." And then, because he felt he was damping her enthusiasm, he added, "But congratulations, darling. We're very proud of you—aren't we, May?"

"Oh, yes, very," her mother responded. And it was true. They were proud of their daughter, even if she had moved into a world they couldn't relate to; her success was visible in the very expensive car, the smart clothes, and the generous presents she gave them at Christmas and on their birthdays. But her lifestyle was alien. They admitted to being old-fashioned and tried not to judge.

But they felt more at ease with their son and daughter-in-law, a nice, sensible girl—and the darling grandchildren. Glamour and high-flying were all very well, but in the end a woman needed stability.

It would come in time, they assured each other. They

were indeed proud to have a daughter who was such a star in her profession.

It was a happy afternoon for Julia. It went past tea-time, and she was easily persuaded to stay for supper. It was, inevitably, lunchtime beef served up cold, with a salad and hot potatoes, and it took her back in a rush of nostalgia to her childhood. It had been very happy. No traumas, no teenage upheavals, just stable and pre-dictable, from her earliest memories. She owed them a lot, these elderly parents, caught like the proverbial flies in the amber of their class and upbringing.

With the money she would be making, she had the happy idea of buying her father a new car. And she resolved, on the drive back to Central London, to make more time to go down to Hampton and see them.

When she came into the flat, she knew Felix was back, because he'd dropped his racquet and sweatshirt in the hall. He was untidy, and she usually picked up after him to avoid an argument. He didn't mind a bit of a mess, he said; if she did, then, okay, it was up to her to clear it up. He didn't care if *she* left things lying about.

She went into the sitting room. He was sprawled in the chair; for once the TV wasn't on. He was reading the *Observer*. He looked up, grinned at her, and threw the paper aside.

"Hi—where've you been?"

"Down to Hampton; I had lunch with Mum and Dad."

"Oh—good for you. What news, sweetheart? Come on, tell."

If you'd been here when I got back, you wouldn't have to ask, Julia thought, but didn't say it. They had an independent rela-tionship, mutually agreed. "I've got a very good offer." She sat down and said, "How about a drink for me?"

He brought her a vodka swimming in ice. "Great. What is it?"

She told him, but without the rush of enthusiasm. She sounded quite cool about it. And for some reason, born of resentment, she didn't mention Harold King, as if she were punishing him by keeping the best part back.

He was very pleased for her. He wasn't jealous—sometimes she thought it was because he was so confident in his own abilities. No trace of a chip on the shoulder with Felix. Thank God.

He got up and stretched, and looked across at her.

"It's late and there's nothing on the telly. How about bed?" She wanted to say, "No, you go ahead, I'm not tired," and dent that maddening self-esteem, but she didn't. It wouldn't have worked.

She'd tried that approach once, after a row, and he'd simply shrugged and said, "Suit yourself." In the morning she'd capitulated and initiated sex between them.

"You're a clever little piece, aren't you," he murmured, biting and poking at her ear with his tongue. He used low-grade slang during lovemaking; he called her a bimbo and a piece, and she didn't care. He hoisted her on top of him, and for a few seconds Julia thought, *I can't go on with this, I've got to stop.* And then the flame seared the candle and it began to melt.

Julia's phone rang just before lunch. She'd been making a list of staff she was going to need. Western had offered a suite of offices on the penthouse floor, and she'd taken it, and asked for a private telephone line, not connected to the switchboard. She was glad she hadn't mentioned the name of Harold King to Felix. They'd gone their ways the next morning, and she had felt diminished by the sex they had shared.

It was no longer making love. It was just having sex. It was an unhappy sensation. She put it out of her mind and got down to work. Reflection had convinced her that secrecy was paramount to get the project going. It was one thing to tell her parents, and a phone call bound them to discretion. Very different to set the hare of rumor running through the office and then through the tight little world of media.

One of the conditions of joining her new staff had to be secrecy on pain of immediate dismissal. She picked up the phone. "Julia Hamilton."

Ben Harris's voice said, "I've had a private memo from upstairs. Don't come to my office. Meet me at the pub in half an hour."

He was sitting in a corner when she came in; the lunchtime crowd were gathering. "Hello, Ben, sorry to keep you waiting. Something came up just before I left."

"No problem. I haven't wasted good drinking time. Usual for you?"

"Why don't I get it?" she said. "Scotch for you?"

He nodded. "I'll get the next lot."

She sat down beside him. "Why didn't you want me to come to the office?"

"Because I wanted to talk to you," he said. He lit a cigarette. He was a heavy smoker. "I got a memo about you from the old man. About the new job."

"Yes," Julia said. "I knew he was going to tell you himself. I didn't ask for it. I didn't go behind your back."

"I know you didn't," he said gruffly. "You never have. Unlike some. My contract is up in five years. I wouldn't have minded handing it over to you, Julia. Never thought I'd bring myself to say that to anyone, but I mean it. You'd make a bloody good editor."

"That's a real compliment, coming from you. You're the best."

He narrowed his eyes against the cigarette smoke and then peered at her.

"Remember the time I told you not to go on the Rhys murders? You wouldn't listen. And you were right. You coped with it, wrote your book, made a name for yourself. But before I say anything else, I want you to know I'm not trying to knock you or cramp your style.

"You're a clever girl, and you're not a cow either. Quite an achievement in this game. I like you. So listen to me this time.

"For Christ's sake, don't touch this one. Don't go after Harold King!"

Julia set down her drink. "I didn't know he was going to tell you that. Nobody is supposed to know at this stage—"

"He had his reason," Harris muttered. "I know about King. He wants me to help you. I said no."

"Oh, God," Julia exclaimed. Her anxiety was for Harris, not herself. "You didn't, Ben—you know what he's like. He'll think of an excuse and throw you out on your ear."

"No, he won't," Harris said sourly. "Let me tell you a few things about King. No, just listen. I'm not talking about public knowledge. He thrives on that. I'm talking about who and what he really is. He came out of nowhere, and he's covered his tracks so well, no one's ever been able to find his country of origin or anything about him. Except that he says he's probably Polish, but even that's a guess.

"He speaks it like a native son, but he speaks German fluently. Apparently without an accent. He could be anything. You've heard about the business deals and the borderline stuff. Anyone opposed him, he wiped them out with lawsuits.

"It's rumored he has links with the Mafia, contacts with drugs, illegal arms shipments. He's up to his armpits in every dirty deal you can think of—he's bought people with money or blackmail or both."

"How do you know all this?" she asked him. He stubbed out the little butt of cigarette and fumbled for another.

"Because I started looking into him myself. Ten years ago. Western told me to call it off or lose my job."

"I don't believe it," she protested. "After what he said to me—he made you drop it? Why?"

"King had something on him," he said, and his voice was very low. "My guess is, he's about to break it, and that's why Western is going to stick his neck out and strike first. Or stick your neck out. That's the bottom line."

"What is it?" she asked. "What could he have on the old man? Why hasn't he used it before? They hate each other, everyone knows that."

Ben Harris didn't answer her. He pushed back his chair and stood up. "I'll get us a drink. You want a club sandwich?"

"I'm not hungry and I don't want a drink. I'm working this afternoon. Ben, you can't just throw out hints like that. Tell me!"

"Are you going to take my advice?" he demanded. He was still on his way to the bar.

"No," Julia said. "No, I'm not."

"Then you might as well get back to your smart new penthouse," he snarled, and it was the old Ben Harris—jealous, difficult, a man nobody liked.

Julia shook her head. "You're not getting rid of me," she said quietly. "All right, I'll join you. Vodka on the rocks. Make it a small one."

He came back and sat down. He had a cheese-and-pickle sandwich on a plate. He took a bite out of it. "Ben," she said, "please. Look at it this way. If King is what you say, someone ought to do something about it! Instead of putting me off, you ought to help me expose him."

Ben Harris looked at her. "Publicity is a funny thing, Julia." He went on, "If a man gets himself into the public eye by being a self-confessed shit but a bit of a character, the great British public takes him to its heart. They

say to themselves, He's been a naughty boy, but he's not
so bad. Look what he did for those refugee kids from
Romania, and didn't he rescue Brighton Soccer Club
when the lads went to see him—deep down he's got a
kind heart. You know the kind of con trick, and it always
seems to work. I don't understand the mentality, but
then I wouldn't. I'm Welsh. King has built himself up
into an institution. The poor refugee boy picked up from
a DP camp by a kind-hearted UNRRA official.

"People have got a sneaking admiration for him. They
think, 'Look where he's got. All that money, all those
businesses. Perhaps he has cut a few corners, so who
hasn't?'"

"Ben," Julia said softly, "why won't you help me?"

He looked at her. She'd never noticed his eyes before.
They were as dark as Welsh coal.

"Because I'm scared for you," he said. "There were two
people rich enough to call King's bluff. Alfred Hayman,
the boss of Eros Films, and J. D. Lewis, the head of Lewis
Publications. Big men, and tough. King wanted their outlets; movies and TV and a big publishing and magazine
network. He went after them in his usual way, buying
into the shares, rumor mongering to depress the price—
clever articles placed in the financial columns speculating
about profits spiraling down—Hayman and Lewis fought
him off. They routed the bastard in his takeover bids,
and each of them set out to get him." He looked at her.
"They're dead. Hayman was actually murdered in the
Bahamas, and Lewis was run off the road one night on
his way home to Kent. Nobody was ever charged. King
couldn't stop them, so I believe he had them murdered. I
traveled to the Bahamas to look into the Hayman killing.
I talked to the police. I even got to see the body. It was a
contract killing, dressed up to look like a robbery. I
remember having a drink with the Bahamian copper in

charge. He was a smart man, very impressive. He said to me, 'This wasn't done by any of our people. They don't shoot a man at point-blank range in the left ear and then turn his place over for valuables. They use a club or a knife. This killer came from outside on a contract. From the U.S., I'd say.' Hayman was fighting King with his own weapons. He'd been buying into King Media Promotions through nominees, and he was gearing up to go public and throw him off the board."

"And the other man—Lewis, the boss of the multinational publishers?" Julia asked him. "Did you look into that too?"

"Yes, on my own time. I'd been told to drop the story after Hayman, but when Lewis was killed, I couldn't leave it alone. It nagged at me. I knew King was involved. I didn't find out anything I could use. Just a hit-and-run accident at night on a wet road. Lewis was driving a Bentley. They're built like bloody tanks. It must have been a hell of a big truck that hit him, because the car bounced through the barrier and went down an embankment. It was smashed up like a matchbox. If you're going to take on a car like that without getting hurt yourself, you hit them sideways with a three-tonner.

"From the tire marks they reckoned Lewis was going at about eighty miles an hour. As I told you, they never found the truck or the driver. Case closed. Like Hayman. Now, do you still want to mount a personal campaign against Harold King? I tell you what, go away and think about it. Sit in that plush office with the nice view and imagine what it would be like to wake up one night and find a man in a hood bending over you with a knife.

"There are contract killers who specialize in sex crimes. It puts the police off if the hit is a woman."

Julia stood up. "You've no real proof, Ben," she said slowly. "You're just trying to frighten me. And if you really believe it, then you ought to help me stop him. You go back to your office and think about that. Thanks for the drinks."

Ben Harris watched her leave; several men looked after her, raking the back view. Slim, very neat, elegant legs. And that mane of red hair standing out like a beacon.

She wouldn't listen to him. She was stubborn and she was courageous. And Western had hooked her. Just as years ago he had hooked him. And then, Harris addressed his remaining inch of whiskey, cut him off short and gave him the news editorship as a consolation prize. He wasn't afraid of Western, and he showed it. On the few occasions Western had tried to manipulate a news story, Ben had stood up to him, true to his calling. If his marriage had failed and his grown-up children did their filial duty with a Christmas card, Ben had been true to the job.

He had been jealous and suspicious of all comers because he couldn't bear to face the future without his work; even jealous of Julia Hamilton after the success of her stories on the Rhys murders.

Jealous but, in his professional heart, admiring of a talent and the guts that went with it. She was a nice girl, he couldn't deny that. Success hadn't spoiled her; it hadn't made her conceited. He remembered his remark when she came back from Wales—"Christ," he muttered, it seemed like yesterday. She'd looked gray and hollow-eyed. Western had thrown her in at the deepest end, sending her on a vile murder of two helpless toddlers. "It's marked you, and it shows." He'd been grudging and angry, because he was shocked at what the experience had cost her.

He had a daughter of his own, even if she never bothered to come near him. Julia Hamilton had looked into the darkest pit of human evil and survived without losing her faith in people. When Ben Harris realized that, he decided to back her. She wasn't out to knife him and get his job; others might like to, but it wasn't her style.

He had been what he termed friendly, until she took up with that bumptious prick Sutton. Then he was irritable, nit-picking, and nasty for some time. He had never understood the female mind. So his ex-wife complained, and he didn't argue. He just went off to the pub or back to the office.

Julia hadn't been scared off the assignment. He knew that. She'd been shaken, he could see, but still determined.

She'd go ahead, and King would soon hear whispers that someone was poking around trying to uncover his past.

He bought himself another Scotch. "If you really believe it, then you ought to help me stop him. You go back to your office and think about that. . . ." He did think about it. He thought about it when he went in to the big steel-and-plate-glass Western building and as he finished off his day's work. He thought about it sitting at home with the TV screen flickering in front of him.

He hadn't much to lose. He'd backed off himself once, because Western told him to; was he really going to let a pigheaded young woman take on Harold King, and sit on his hands? He pressed the off button on the remote control. The picture faded to a tiny crimson eye, and that, too, diminished and was gone. Then he got up and unlocked a cupboard in his bedroom, and took out an unmarked file.

CHAPTER 3

"LET'S GO OUT TO EAT TONIGHT," JULIA suggested. Felix looked at her and grinned. "Good idea. Who's paying? I bought a new suit and some shirts this afternoon—I'm penniless."

"I'm paying," Julia said. "And you'd better put on the new suit. We're going to Mario's."

"We are?" he stared at her. "Sweetheart, you *are* paying—it's ten quid for an orange juice. . . . Are we celebrating something?"

"No," Julia answered. "It's down to expenses. I just want to go there and see the place. I've booked a table for nine o'clock. I'm going to change."

The head waiter at Mario's was a friend of Ben Harris's. Julia was discovering that there were unexpected facets to his character. He knew a lot of unlikely people, and he could call in favors when he needed information. Like which evening this week Harold King was dining at Mario's with his family. He always took his wife and daughter out to dinner at Mario's; it was a weekly ritual. He had a special table that was always reserved in case he called up at the last minute, and Harris said he always ordered the same menu. Foie gras, followed by steak Diane, ending with a *bombe surprise*. His wife and daughter would drink claret at a hundred and twenty pounds a bottle, Ch. Haut Brien '82, and a vintage Krug to go with the pudding. King never touched alcohol. He was a life-long teetotaler.

Julia dressed in a short black skirt and a sequined tank top, with long fake diamond earrings that swung like waterfalls against the blazing hair. Felix whistled when she came in, and said, "You look good; you ought to take me out more often. How do you like the suit? Nice, conservative House of Commons uniform?"

"Very smart," Julia said. "You look good too. Let's go. We can have a drink at the bar and see who's there."

They took Julia's car, and on the way he said to her casually, "What are you up to? You're not going to the most expensive watering hole in London on expenses just to have a look at the decor. Who are you interested in?"

She made it sound unexciting. "Harold King. I've heard he's angling for a life peerage. Have you heard any buzz about it? Might be an interesting profile."

He frowned. "No. And I don't believe it. He's a bloody crook, he'd never get an honor. It may be a stupid, lousy system, but nobody'd stand for him going to the Lords. You going to do a profile on him?"

"No," she said. "It's just an idea at the moment. We might be taking a look at the honors system."

"Oh, I see." He settled back in his seat. "'Exposure' on the trail of corruption, selling honors—great stuff, Julia.

So long as you don't expect to get a DBE yourself one day. . . . They've got long memories."

"Hey," Felix said, looking around as they took a seat in the upstairs room. "This is rather smart. I think I could get used to this lifestyle, don't you?"

It was a long room, paneled in eighteenth-century pine; there were big, comfortable sofas and occasional armchairs, fine sporting pictures on the walls, fresh flowers, and piles of newspapers on the center table. It was a pastiche of the English country house, and in clever contrast to the chic Italian decor of the restaurant below. There was no bar in sight; orders were taken and drinks brought to the customers.

Julia saw them sitting in a corner. Harold King, with his wife and his daughter. He was familiar enough from TV and photographs, but the reality was different. He was much taller than she expected, with a shock of pure white hair that framed a semicircle of bald scalp. The eyebrows were white, too, and they bushed out over heavy-lidded pale eyes. It was a powerful, ugly face, the flesh sagged in a dewlap onto his collar. He had a powerful body with heavy shoulders. His skin was coarse and tanned a deep brown, whether from sun or artifice, she couldn't tell. He was sitting in a big chair, and he seemed to sprawl over it, legs spread, feet planted on the carpet, his hands moving constantly as he spoke. To his right a very thin dark woman listened and smiled and occasionally nodded. She was beautifully dressed, and wearing a massive ruby-and-diamond brooch on the neck of her black dress. When she gestured, a diamond as big as a pebble flashed blue fire. The wife of thirty-two years. Marilyn; ex-model, ex-bit-part actress. Incredibly, the delicate creature with her birdlike frame and little painted face was the mother of the hulking blond girl on the other side of King. Gloria King, a cruel misnomer, for she was a female version of her father. White-blond hair, the same pale eyes with tortoise lids, the coarse features and heavy limbs; she wore a suite of gold-and-diamond jewelry like fetters around her neck and wrists. She never looked away from her father's face. Her eyes were fixed on him in adoration.

Julia murmured to Felix, "There's King, over there, with the wife and daughter."

Felix stared openly. "Jesus," he said, grinning. "She's going to need a bloody big cash settlement. I suppose if you thought about the money long enough, you'd get it up. . . . Mum looks a better bet. Bit like fucking something out of the Mummy Room in the British Museum."

"Felix," Julia hissed at him. "Keep your voice down." She didn't need to warn him, because at that moment Harold King began to shout.

"Where the hell's the menu? Where's Phillipe?"

"He's on his way up, sir," a nervous wine waiter assured him.

King scowled at him. His voice rose over the quiet room, so that everyone stopped talking and turned to look at him. "I want him now—go and tell him to hurry up!"

The head waiter was already hurrying across the room. King waited till he reached the table.

"I want another bottle of Perrier and the menu. What the hell's going on here? You call this service?"

Phillipe was a man of international reputation and part-owner of the restaurant. He held out the leather-covered menu.

"I have it here, Mr. King."

"Take it away; you know perfectly well what we always have."

He dismissed the man with an angry wave. Phillipe gave

a slight bow and said smoothly, "Of course. Your Perrier will be here immediately."

"My God," Julia said. "Did you see that? What a pig!"

Felix shrugged. "He was playing games, drawing attention to himself. It's part of the act. I bet he gives Phillipe What's-his-name a socking-great tip when he leaves and the oily little bugger will take it and bow low. Put the moral indignation away, darling, and let's enjoy ourselves."

Julia said angrily, "Nothing bothers you, does it, Felix? How can you excuse behavior like that?"

"Because I don't sit in judgment like you do," he said quickly. "You're the crusading journalist, not me. After all, if I'm going to spend my life with politicians, I can't afford to side with the underdog. There's just no future in it."

Julia said quietly, "Then you'll never get to the top, Felix. You make fun of Warburton, but he's got real standards and integrity. That's why he's trusted. Let's go to our table." She got up, and he followed her with a slight shrug. She was in a touchy mood, and he was irritated because he wanted to enjoy himself. He didn't want a moral lecture, he decided, he wanted lobster quenelles. . . .

Harold King noticed the redheaded woman when he passed them on the way to the table specially reserved for him. It was in the middle of the room, giving him a vantage point where he could see everyone and everyone could see him. He noticed her because he hated that color hair. He had never considered any woman cursed with it to be attractive. One day he'd seen a secretary in the main office with red hair and ordered her to dye it or be sacked.

With the temper typical of the coloring, she'd told him to stuff his job and stormed out in tears. He had told personnel not to give her a reference.

But this one was familiar. He recognized Western's star protégée, the reporter who'd covered the Welsh child murders and written a serious psychological study of the murderers afterward. Julia Hamilton.

He read every word in Western's newspapers, both London and provincial. He noted his staff, his main advertisers, his political stances, his attitude to social, economic, and world issues. King always studied his targets in depth while he was preparing to attack them.

This girl was outstanding; he watched her narrowly, dismissing the companion as some young hanger-on. She'd be a good catch for him when the time came. If the bribe was big enough in terms of money and power. Every human being had a price. It would gratify him to rub Western's nose in the shit by employing Julia Hamilton.

For a moment their glances met. King was extraordinarily sensitive; the coarse, bullying persona he presented concealed a deeply intuitive understanding of people. It had given him power over them, precisely because he knew what made them tick.

Her contempt and hostility were tangible in those few seconds of eye contact. He registered her reaction to him and stared her down. He also registered that it took quite a long time before she turned her head away. There was contempt in that gesture, too, not submission.

He swallowed his glass of Perrier and glared around for the waiter. Yes, he decided, *I'll employ you. I'll make you an offer you won't refuse, because nobody could. And then I'll break you. As I've broken other fools who tried to stand against me. And I'll enjoy doing it.*

He gave his attention to the first course and dismissed Julia Hamilton from his mind.

His wife was talking trivialities about some charity committees. He didn't bother to listen. She had social ambitions, and he despised her for it. He knew, if she didn't, that all the high-society ladies wanted out of women like her was fat donations from their husbands. In return they patronized them. Money was the key; he didn't mind if Marilyn indulged her silly fantasies. It kept her out of mischief. What he wouldn't allow was his daughter being dragged into the charade. Luckily she wasn't interested in female time wasting. He looked at her with affection. She was his clone; she looked like him and she wanted only one thing in the world: to be like him. She was his compensation for the son he never fathered. Better than a son. He realized that. A son would have competed. Gloria worshiped at his shrine. "How's the foie gras?" he asked her. She smiled up at him. "Delicious, Daddy." He went on; he was needled by that other woman's refusal to be overborne, and he felt spiteful. "Enjoying yourself, darling?" "I'm having a wonderful time," his daughter answered. "I always love coming out with you." He reached across and patted her hand. "You're my girl," he said. He turned to his wife. "Isn't she my girl?" The pretty doll nodded obediently. "Yes, Harry, darling." He knew she had given up competing against her daughter long ago. He also knew that she and Gloria hated each other.

A son, he often reminded himself, might have sided with his mother.

"Good dinner," Felix remarked. Julia had hardly spoken through the meal. His irritation was growing. Excellent food, exceptional wine—he'd insisted on choosing from the list and he hadn't spared the cost. Why not—Western was paying. And he knew it annoyed Julia.

Why the hell did she have to be so sour? Working herself up into a froth of righteous indignation because Harold King had been rude to some greasy waiter. . . . He always shouted the odds in public; it was part of the image. He was surprised she couldn't see it in perspective.

Julia said, "Let's have coffee, and I'll get the bill."

"I'd like a brandy," Felix announced. "Or are you getting into a moral dilemma about the expense account?"

"Order what you like," she said curtly. She knew him in this provocative mood. Like a spoiled child.

"Okay—let's see—Armagnac." He scanned the wine list. "The sixty-eight should be nice. I'll have that."

"And for madame?" the wine waiter inquired.

"Nothing, thank you." Julia wanted to finish her coffee and go. She had hated the whole evening, and it wasn't just because of Harold King. Felix returned to the attack.

"My old man was a wine merchant," he announced. "He knew a lot about wine, but not a lot about business. All the old bugger left me was a champagne taste on a beer income. Julia, what the hell's the matter with you?" He leaned toward her. "You've been so fucking sour the whole evening. What's the matter?"

She stirred her coffee and then put the spoon carefully into the saucer. She looked up at him. "You are, Felix. I don't think I like you very much."

Red seeped up his neck and into his face. He said, "What is this—some kind of message?"

"I don't know," Julia admitted. "Look, don't let's argue about it. I'll get the bill."

"I haven't finished my drink," he said loudly. "Anyway, I think I'd like another one."

"Please yourself," she said quietly. "If you want another, you can pay for it." She signed the bill and pushed back her chair. "I'll see you later," she said.

"You'll be lucky," Felix snapped. "Thanks for a lousy evening."

The head waiter came up to her. He had noticed the little scene of friction and the young man scowling at the table as she walked away.

"I hope you enjoyed your dinner," he said.

"Very much, thank you," Julia answered.

"May I order you a taxi?"

"I have a car." Her wrap was brought, and she draped it around her shoulders. Felix hadn't followed her. Phillipe saw her to the door.

"Give my regards to Mr. Harris," he said. "I hope he will come and see us soon."

"I'll tell him," Julia promised. She couldn't imagine Ben Harris in a restaurant like Mario's. Perhaps because she knew so little about him. She didn't drive home directly. She detoured around Hyde Park and on an impulse headed toward the embankment. She loved the river at night. Unfortunately it wasn't safe to park the car and get out and walk. She didn't want to go back to the flat. She wanted a little time to think.

The relationship was changing; it had been happy in the beginning, deeply sexual on both sides, carefree and without ties. Like a passionate friendship. The few years' age difference hadn't seemed significant. Even the disparity in money was glossed over. He thought it was a joke to be called her Toy Boy. And she realized, in that pause for introspection, that she had begun indulging him like the spoiled child she chided him for being. But he wasn't a child; he was an ambitious, selfish, unscrupulous man with a talent for sex.

Suddenly, foolishly, Julia's eyes filled up with tears. It couldn't go on. It was demeaning to both of them. She didn't love him, she admitted that. But the truth was worse. She didn't like him anymore, and she'd been goaded into saying so that night. It was time to put an end to it. She wiped her wet cheeks and started the engine. When she opened her front door, the flat was in darkness. He had gone off somewhere, spending the night with a friend. In the morning he'd turn up and expect her to take him into bed and pretend nothing had happened. It wasn't the first time he'd taken off. But it would be the last.

Inside, she kicked off her shoes. She was glad Felix wasn't there. On an impulse, checking her watch for the first time, she dialed Ben Harris's number.

"It's me," she said. "I hope I'm not interrupting anything."

"Only a bloody boring program on ITV," was the answer. "How did you get on?"

"He was having dinner with his wife and daughter. He actually gave me the hard stare."

"I bet you gave it back," Ben said.

"I did, but it wasn't easy. He's horribly intimidating."

There was a slight pause.

"It hasn't made you change your mind?"

"No," she said firmly. "Quite the opposite. You're right, Ben, he's bad news all right. It was a good idea of yours; I'm glad I've seen him. I couldn't see that file of yours tonight, could I?" Again there was a pause.

"I could drop it around in half an hour. Where's lover boy?"

"He's not here," Julia admitted. "We had a row."

"Glad to hear it." Harris sounded laconic. "He's a sponging little prick. Take my advice and don't have him back."

She said slowly, "I'm not going to. Can you really drop the file over? I don't think I'll sleep much tonight anyway. I'd like to get started."

"See you," he said, and hung up.

She opened the flat door to him. "Thanks for coming over," she said. "It's very good of you."

"No problem." He looked around the sitting room. "Nice place. Do you collect the pictures?"

"Yes; I'd like to get one or two abstracts one day, but they're just too expensive. Sit down, I've made some fresh coffee."

"I couldn't have tea, could I?"

"Of course you can. Won't be a minute. Tea bag do?"

"Never have anything else," he called after her.

It was an attractive room. He liked the pictures; they gave color and originality, a reflection of their owner. He opened the file and leafed through it. She came back with two mugs. He liked her for that. "Before I give you this," he said, "I'm going to ask you one more time—are you still going ahead with this investigation?"

"One more time," she said, "yes, I am. And I'm going to ask you something. You are going to help me, aren't you?"

"I wouldn't be giving you this if I wasn't," he said. "Against my better judgment and all my instincts, I'm going into it with you. But on one condition, and it's not subject to argument." He looked at her obstinately. She knew the expression. This was his sticking point, whatever it was. "Name it," she suggested.

"That you pull back when I tell you to and leave it to me," he said. "Otherwise, J, no file, no deal. And don't promise anything you don't mean."

Julia hesitated. "Why should I have to pull out?"

"You won't," he answered, "unless I think it's getting dangerous. Which I think is certain, especially if we come up with something. Do you want to think it over?" He had closed the file and put it under his arm. He meant what he said.

"No. You have a head start. I need the file and I need you, Ben. We have a deal. Western won't like it, but he doesn't have to know."

"The less anybody knows from now on, the better," he said. He finished his tea. "Are you getting rid of Sutton? You won't be persuaded by him?"

She shook her head. "No," she said. "It's not good for either of us anymore. Don't be too hard on him, Ben. It's not really his fault."

"You're too much for him," Ben Harris remarked. "Too bright, too successful, too much of everything. You haven't talked to him about this, have you?"

"No. I just said we might be doing a feature on the honors system. He doesn't know anything else."

"Good. I'll be off now, J. Read this through and we'll get our heads together tomorrow. After office hours. Thanks for the tea. I'll see myself out."

The file started in 1948 with the release of a displaced person from the UNRRA rehabilitation center in Nessenberg. There were ten thousand men, women, and children in that particular camp, human flotsam thrown up by the tidal wave of war. People without papers, identities, or proven nationalities. The young man who called himself Hans Koenig was typical of the victims of national chaos and breakdown. He had no papers, claimed he was brought as slave labor from the Polish borders in 1939, but couldn't remember his name or place of birth, or what had happened to his family. He thought they'd been shot. He'd been beaten and traumatized. He remembered nothing. The history was quite common. Teenagers and children were seized, transported, Germanicized if they were Aryan types, or worked as slaves in factories or on the farms. Girls were sold into domestic service. Hans Koenig insisted he didn't know who he was or where he came from. He had been found in a refugee column fleeing the Allied advance. The medical records said he was suffering from acute emotional trauma. He had been in the camp for four years.

Hans Koenig was just one more statistic in the register of human misery that the officials of UNRRA, the military, and the civilian authorities in the British Section were trying to sift through and sort out.

There were guilty hiding among the innocent: deserters from the German army, SS masquerading as civilians, minor war criminals from the Ukraine and the Balkan States hoping to evade punishment. The SS were easier to identify because of the number tattooed under the armpit, but most had burned or scarred themselves to avoid detection. There was no evidence of guilt in Koenig's medical record. He was a stateless person, without a past and with no future. Julia read slowly through the photostats of those early reports. Suddenly the aftermath of that dreadful war seemed real to her. The grainy newsreels and staccato broadcasting style of documentaries had meant little to someone who hadn't been born at the time. Past misery, hopelessness, and human evil spoke to her with a clear voice as she read of the only known origins of the man she had seen in the smart restaurant that night. The coffee was cold beside her. Her watch said it was two forty-five in the morning.

"Nobody even knows his real nationality. He says he's probably Polish . . . but he speaks German fluently. . . . He could be anything."

She remembered Ben's description of Harold King. He'd Anglicized the name he'd given himself in the camp. Koenig. King. Some subtle indication of the man he would become perhaps, or a mere fancy on her part, looking for motives. . . . She started to read again. He had been released into the care of an UNRRA official who stood surety for him and obtained a set of temporary papers from the British Control Commission in the Munich area. The copy of the document showed faded signatures: the Control Commission officer in charge of refugees, a Major Grant, and the UNRRA official, Phyllis Lowe. A woman had got Hans Koenig out of the camp. The rest was Ben's work, the result of his detailed and careful investigation into what happened after that.

Phyllis Lowe had continued to work with the United Nations organization among the refugees for another six months. She had lived in requisitioned accommodation in Nessenberg itself, and the young man had stayed with her. She had employed one of the many destitute German civilians to teach him English. The man had been a schoolteacher, and exempt from the army because of a clubfoot.

At the end of the six months Phyllis Lowe had resigned her job and returned to England, taking Hans Koenig with her.

And there, like a line drawn across the page, Ben had come to a dead end. There were no official records, nothing. Nobody in Nessenberg knew Phyllis Lowe or remembered the young man. The schoolteacher had died in 1953, and his family had left the district. The work of UNRRA went on for several more years before it was disbanded.

Phyllis Lowe went to England with her protégé. Dead stop. Everything known about Harold King from the fifties onward came from one source. Himself. Harris had included the relevant chapters on King's early life from the biography he had had printed by one of his own publishing companies. The hack wrote movingly of his time in the camp and of the English lady who had rescued him. She came across as a kind-hearted spinster who treated him as a substitute son and died tragically of cancer a few months after bringing him to England with her. She had bought him a few hundred pounds' of savings certificates, and with this he had founded his fortune.

It was the standard story, part tearjerker, part eulogy. With his benefactor's small legacy King, as he now called himself, bought a stock of remaindered books and an old van. He sensed that people needed escapism. They were sick of war and hungry for entertainment.

Everyone wanted books, and books was what King gave them. He traveled the country, selling from his van, buying up books wherever he found them, renting a small shop that became a chain of retail bookshops, then a printing business, and in the early sixties he had enough money to acquire a small publishing company that had gone broke publishing quality books and unknown authors. King had pulped the whole stock. The hack made the act of vandalism sound like an instance of his genius. King recruited his own new authors, and King Publishing was born. "I sold dreams to people," was the famous quote, "because I had a dream myself. And I made it come true."

Ben Harris added his own footnote to the story.

King's stable of writers specialized in crime novellas. Cheap to produce, cheap to sell. Lurid mass-market trash that peddled violence and sex in tune with the new fashion for permissiveness. They made a fortune for him. This was well known; he boasted of it, sneered at his critics, and branched out into soft-porn magazines.

Nothing new there. But Harris had ferreted out a less well-known detail of how he founded his publishing empire. He had lent money to the philanthropic owner of that early publishing house, promising to maintain its literary standards, and then called in the loan without warning.

The man lost his business and died penniless a few years later. No one had bothered to ask what had happened to him.

It was a technique King had perfected over the years. He had a sixth sense; he could smell a business in trouble as a predator smells blood. He bought into them, usually under nominees, then took them over and turned them into profitable enterprises that he either sold or enlarged for his own purposes. Within twenty-five years he had acquired a major publishing house, two quality London monthly magazines, and a substantial stake in Midlands Independent Television. Not to mention property interests and a construction company engaged in building work in the Middle East.

It was common knowledge, and he announced it regularly, that his next project was to run his own national newspaper.

At forty he had got married to a beautiful model who had done a stint as an actress, and told the world that from now on he was going to be a family man. The string of mistresses he had run with maximum publicity were sent packing. There were no more photographs of King at functions and first nights with "friends" hanging on his arm.

There hadn't been a whisper of a woman since. King was presented as the devoted husband and father of his little Gloria. And it had all begun with a kind-hearted English lady in a camp full of refugees in ravaged Germany after the war. Hans Koenig, the nameless, hopeless young man traumatized by his experiences, had touched her heart. And when she died, leaving him friendless in England, he swore to justify her faith in him. There was another famous quote. "She believed in me. I wasn't going to let her down. I owed it to her to get out and make myself a success."

It was an incredible story. A sharp dealer, a tough business opponent, a genius without mercy for those less able than himself—a man without morals or scruples who didn't give a damn for his reputation. The sentimentalist beating his breast about his benefactress. The faithful husband and doting father. The impulsive philanthropist who helped orphaned children in Romania and saved a football club because the players came to see him.

The man whose most dangerous adversaries had met violent deaths. Julia closed the file. "Incredible" was the right word.

•   •   •

She was in the kitchen eating breakfast when she heard Felix come in. She had managed to sleep for a few hours; it had been fitful and troubled by dreams related to what she had read. She felt a little jump of anxiety as the kitchen door opened.

"Hi," he said. "I'm back." He came in and closed the door. He looked puffy-eyed and unshaven. Julia looked at him and thought that wherever he'd spent the night, there hadn't been a razor.

"Hello," she said. She spread marmalade over her slice of toast.

"Any breakfast for me?"

"Yes, if you make it," she answered.

"Oh. Still hating my guts, are we? Any use saying I'm sorry? I behaved like a stupid shit last night." Julia had never heard an apology from him before. And with painful insight she knew why. He'd been with a woman. He was feeling guilty because he'd slept with someone else. She sighed.

"There's plenty of coffee. Sit down, Felix. Don't worry. I'm not hating anyone this morning. I think it's time we had a talk."

"I meant it," he said. "I was bloody to you. I'll make it up to you." He reached over and caught her wrist. "Kiss and make up," he suggested. He brought her hand up to his mouth and licked her palm.

Julia pulled sharply away. "That won't work anymore, Felix." He shrugged. "Okay, if you're still humpy with me—" He picked up a mug and poured coffee. "What do you want to talk about? Got any aspirin? I shouldn't have had that second Armagnac." He tried a grin, making a joke of it. It had always worked with her before. The cheeky-boy act followed by a good session on the mattress. She shook her head. "I meant what I said last night. That's why I don't want to sleep with you this morning. I don't want to go on living with you anymore. It's not working for either of us. Is it—truthfully?"

"It's working all right with me," he said. "I don't make demands on you, Julia. You do your thing and I do mine."

"You did your thing last night, didn't you?" She said it calmly, and he reddened. "I don't want to hear about it—it doesn't matter. It just proves what I'm saying. We don't love each other, and now we're not even friends anymore."

He sipped his coffee. "We never were," he said, surprising her. "All we ever really had was sex. I loved it with you, and you couldn't get enough of it with me. But we didn't have a lot in common. Ambition maybe. I always felt you wanted something more, some kind of emotional hook. I wasn't ready for it. I'm still not. Sorry."

"I'm sorry too," Julia said. "But we did have some happy times, so don't let's forget that. I know I won't. You'll find someone else, Felix. If you haven't already."

He looked at her honestly. "I haven't," he said. "I've had the odd bonk here and there. Like last night. But it didn't mean anything. I think a lot of you, Julia. I mean it. You're bright, I admire that. You'll go far up the old ladder. And one day I'll be up there too. What do you want me to do—move out?"

"Yes," she said slowly. She chided herself for being so tired that she felt very near to tears. Not enough sleep, that was all. She'd be too busy to be lonely. "Yes, but I don't want to rush you. You've got to find somewhere else that suits you. We can—well, keep out of each other's way till you do. I've got to go, Felix, or I'll be late."

"I've got to shower and shave," he agreed. "Or I will have the Warbler giving me black looks. I'll see what I can fix up. And do me a favor, will you? Don't cry. We'll always be friends." He sat on at the table when she hurried out. It was a pity. He felt depressed. She was a great girl. But she was right. He'd started cheating on her in the last year.

His afternoons weren't always spent at the squash court or the gym. It was time to move on. Time to get out from under her shadow. Spread his wings on his own account. Some of his friends had been telling him that for a while now. She was just that bit older and she had the status and the money. Deep down he felt belittled and he was beginning to resent it. So he cheated on her. Which didn't enhance his self-image. He got up, dropped the mug in the sink, and went out to get ready for work. He heard the front door close and knew that Julia had gone.

"Well?" Ben Harris asked. "Where are you going to start?"

Julia said, "Right at the beginning. Page one, line one. How do we know Phyllis Lowe is dead?"

He looked up sharply, scowling. "What do you mean?"

"Did you check? Has anybody seen a death certificate? No, they haven't. Everyone took King's word for it. So I sent someone down to Somerset House first thing this morning to look up every Phyllis Lowe who died between April and June in 1949. Those are the dates given in that load of rubbish he had written about himself. Cancer was diagnosed in April, just as the daffodils came out, and she died as the roses bloomed in their back garden. No one called Phyllis Lowe died in the London area in that year during that period. In fact"—she put the list in front of him—"the only single women of that name who died of cancer in the whole of London during that year were all fifteen to twenty years too old to be her! See for yourself."

Ben scanned the list.

"Christ," he muttered. "You're right. But let's say he gave all that crap to his author, about the date and time of year, just to make it sound good—it doesn't mean she didn't die—"

"But not when or where he said," Julia pointed out. "Ben, this could be a wild guess, but I'm going to follow it up."

He said, "What's the wild guess?"

"I think she may still be alive. And if she is, I want to talk to her. Now, let's work out where we start looking."

"UNRRA had records of all their personnel. They must be somewhere, and they'd give her family personal details—home address, next of kin, that sort of stuff. But, J, it's forty years ago—"

"I know," she agreed. "But didn't people have ration books, identity cards? Listen, they've traced medical records back to the First World War just recently. They'd been lying about in local hospitals and nobody had bothered to throw them out. I've got a good team of researchers."

Ben Harris said, "How about the area where King says he was living with her—it's in that book—the house with the fucking roses in the back garden. Tell them to try the local doctors. Some of these practices keep medical records for years—even after the patient's dead. Nobody bothers to chuck them away—"

"And," Julia interrupted, "if they moved on, their records were forwarded to the new doctor. Tell me"—she changed the subject suddenly—"why do you think King lied about her? It wasn't just to make a good sob story. Why not tell the truth instead of inventing a whole scenario?"

"Because the truth wasn't quite as pretty as the lie," Ben Harris said.

"Then we've got to find it out," Julia told him.

She tapped the file with one finger.

"Everything else came to a dead end. You went to Germany, you went to Nessenberg; there was a record of a Hans Koenig among the ten thousand DPs who were there in 'forty-nine. We know this woman got him out and took him in to live with her. Then she says she's going to England, and that's the last anyone hears of her. He could have entered this country illegally and made up the whole story."

Ben Harris had a rare smile. She saw it then.

"I'd love that," he said. "I'd really love to prove something like that. Just for starters. How many people can you put on to this?"

"You tell me," Julia answered. He considered. "Three pairs. A pair works better in this kind of job; one sees something the other one's missed. Two to work through the Hammersmith medical centers, ask around the neighborhood where this Phyllis Lowe had a house—if she did—two to track down any former British employees of UNRRA, and another couple to go back to Nessenberg and do a better job than I did. UNRRA worked very closely with the military authorities, but also with the German civil administration."

He'd pushed his glasses up onto his forehead, his eyes narrowed in concentration. "I may have missed something, but what?"

"There's only one way to find out," Julia answered. "How's your German, Ben?"

He looked up. "Pretty good—why?"

"Because I think we should go to Nessenberg. Can you take a few days off?"

"I haven't been away from the office in God knows how long. I've plenty of time owing to me. Brennan would love warming my seat for a bit." Brennan was one of his assistants, and Ben suspected him, as he suspected everyone, of eyeing his job.

"Then that's settled," she said. "Wednesday suit you?"

"Wednesday's fine," he agreed. "You don't take long making up your mind, do you, J?"

"What's the point of waiting? Anyway it would help if

I was out of my flat for a bit. Felix is looking for some-where else to live. It'll give him time."

He said, "It's none of my business, but I'm glad you didn't chicken out. It's about time he got off his butt and looked after himself."

"Don't be too hard on him," she said. "He took it very well; I don't want to be unkind. We did have some very happy times together."

"Glad to hear it," he sounded snappish. "You'd better book the flight and the hotel—the Nessenberghof is a good one, or it was when I was there. May have changed now; ten years is a long time. We'll need to hire a car."

"I'll get that organized," Julia promised.

"Right," he stood up. "How long do you reckon to stay?"

"As long as it takes. I can't help it, Ben. I just have this gut feeling. It all starts with Phyllis Lowe."

"It ends with her, that's the trouble," he answered. "I'll be off now." He had reached the door, when she said, "I'm off too. Why don't we stop off and have a drink on the way home? I could do with one."

Ben took his glasses off and stuffed them into his breast pocket.

"Well, I've no pressing engagements for this evening. Why don't we make it dinner?"

"I don't see what they hope to find out in Germany," Evelyn Western pointed out. "All that's been gone over and over, and nobody got anywhere."

She was driving to London with her husband. The glass partition was shut, so the chauffeur couldn't hear their conversation.

"That's exactly what I said to Julia," he answered. "But she's got some idea in her head about the woman who brought the bastard to England. There's no record of her dying when King's biographer says she did. She's following up on that. I don't believe it matters. He's lied about himself so often, one more lie doesn't make much difference. Good thing is she persuaded Harris to work on it with her. He said no to me. I told you."

"You can't blame him after last time," his wife said.

"I hadn't any choice," Western insisted. "They'd found Richard Watson. I had to back off."

"I know," she placed her hand over his, comforting him.

"It might have been a bluff, but I couldn't risk it. The honors list was up for confirmation, we were going at full throttle with the TV franchise—I *had* to pull Harris off the story."

"We should have gone to see him," she said slowly. "I said so at the time. But you wouldn't listen to me, Billy."

"I knew him, you didn't," he retorted. "He wasn't the sort to be bought off. That's all King needed—proof that I'd been to see Watson or made some attempt to bribe him. Then he'd have crucified me."

"He's going to do that now," Evelyn answered. "It's just a matter of time."

"Time is what it's all about," he said. "He wants the *Herald*, and he's waiting for the right moment before he pulls the rug out on me. But I'm going to get there first, Evie. I'm going to show him up as a liar and a crook, and nothing he says will be believed after that."

"And you really believe that Julia can do it?"

"With Harris to help her—yes. I have to believe it. I have to."

Evelyn Western looked out of the window. It was raining, and the glass was blurred and opaque in the failing light.

"I wish he was dead," she said.

Western didn't answer. He had thought that often enough. It was the last desperate option. But he didn't say so to his wife.

CHAPTER 4

HAROLD KING SWIVELED HIS CHAIR SO HE could look out of the enormous plate-glass window. It offered a magnificent panoramic view of London, with the broad, silver sweep of the Thames so far below, it looked like a ribbon. In the distance he could see the pointed towers of Westminster and the House of Commons. Once, when he had made his first million, he joined the Liberal party; he liked the idea of becoming an MP. He had run for office during the next by-election and been roundly defeated by the Labor candidate. Since then he had conducted a merciless campaign against the MP in particular and the party in general. The defeat had wounded his pride, and he never forgave anyone or anything that touched his self-esteem. Beyond the Commons lay his ultimate goal. The Lords.

But that was some way in the future. That would be his next target after he had increased his power and sphere of influence by the acquisition of the *Sunday Herald*. And with it the political journalists that had made the newspaper famous, and the financial section that was so well respected that it had inside information from the Treasury and the Chancellor's office. Western had built himself a power house in that newspaper.

He had recruited the best people, paid them the top salaries, and got himself a life peerage. He was the friend of ministers in the government and was courted by the Opposition. He was everything that Harold King intended to be at the apex of his own career. And his train of thought, sunny and optimistic on that morning, like the weather outside his enormous window, switched to something his daughter Gloria had said on their way home from dinner at Mario's. He listened to Gloria. She had his sharp eye for people, his jungle instincts.

"Did you know that woman, Daddy—the one with the red hair?" He'd felt his wife's eyes on her, knew that she tensed against some discovery of a fresh liaison, which Gloria would have enjoyed bringing into the open. Gloria didn't care if he slept with women. She knew she was the only one that counted.

"No, why? I know who she is—she's a journalist on the *Herald*. Why, Gloria?"

"Because she was looking at you, Daddy. The way you look when you hate somebody."

"Don't be silly, why should some stranger look at your father like that?"

"Shut up," he said curtly. "Gloria notices things. I got the same feeling. Funny you felt it, too, sweetheart. Maybe I should run a check on her."

He hadn't done anything about it until now, when one thought led from the *Herald* to its staff members.

He reached into a silver box and brought out a cigar. He smoked and ate what he pleased. He had the blood pressure of an eighteen-year-old. He enjoyed flaunting it in the face of his doctors, proving that the rules for lesser men did not apply to him. And he was as potent as ever. Joe took care of that side of his life. Joe took care of a lot of things.

Julia Hamilton. He'd follow Gloria's instinct. Joe could nose around and see what he could pick up on her.

He dialed an outside number. A woman on the other end said that Joe was in the sauna.

"Tell him I'll boil his ass if he doesn't get out of there. Now." He didn't have to hold more than a couple of minutes.

"Mr. King—sorry you had to wait."

"Tell that stupid cow not to fob me off when I call," King snapped. "I want you up here right away. I've got something for you."

"Give me fifteen minutes," the man named Joe said.

"Ten," King commanded, and hung up.

On the other end of the line the man, standing soaked in sweat, with a towel wrapped around his middle, turned to the black girl.

"Next time my boss calls, you just say, 'Hold on,' and you get me—you understand?"

She had big, frightened dark eyes. "I'm sorry, Joe—I'm sorry."

"Next time," he said, "you will be. Now, get my fucking clothes."

Nessenberg was much smaller than Julia had expected. It curled up like a cat, snug, neat, and prosperous. It was unaffected by the turmoil of reunification and the problem of refugees from the war-ravaged Balkans. The

Nessenberghof was still there. Harris remarked that it looked exactly the same as it did ten years ago.

It was comfortable and conservative. Their rooms were pleasant with views over the garden at the rear.

"It feels strange," she said. "I've never been to Germany, and it's not what I expected. Everyone smiles and seems so friendly."

"And so they are. The south isn't like Prussia; the southerners are famous for their charm, and for being the cradle of the bloody Nazis. I've found it easier to deal with the easterners. The Berliners are something else again. A race of their own. You'd like them. They enjoy life, and they stuck out after the war with that bloody Wall running through the middle of them. You must go there one day."

"How do you know it so well?" she asked him.

"My wife is German," he said. "We used to come over for holidays. I got to know the country and to like it."

"I didn't know you were married."

He brushed it aside. "I'm not; we got divorced fifteen years ago."

"Do you have children?" Julia asked him. They were drinking coffee after a snack lunch in one of the cheerful cafés on the main street.

"Two. Son and daughter. I don't see much of them. I don't see them at all," he remarked, and there was a bitter note in his voice.

"I'm sorry," she said awkwardly. "It must be hard for you."

"They took their mother's part. That was it. I didn't try to argue the case. They were old enough to make up their own minds."

It must have been a bad divorce; she didn't like to pry any further. To her surprise he started to talk. He drank his coffee and leaned back in his seat and said, "I met

Helga when she came to stay with my parents as an exchange student. My kid brother went over to her family
to learn German, and she came to us to learn English. She
was very pretty. Blond, blue eyes, real Herrenvolk type.
Nice girl too. I fell like the proverbial ton of bloody
bricks and married her. I was a reporter on the Birmingham
Advertiser. We lived in a rented flat, and she went out to
work as a mother's helper. We hadn't any money, but
we were pretty happy. Shame it all went wrong."

Julia leaned a little toward him. It still hurt, she could
see that. No wonder he said his German was good.

"What went wrong?"

"I moved to the Herald," he said flatly. "We'd been in
Birmingham for twelve years. We owned a nice little house
in the suburbs by then, she had a lot of friends, local
bridge club, golf twice a week—solid middle-class lifestyle. The kids were at school and doing well. I was news
editor of the Birmingham Post by then, and it was a good job.
But I wanted more challenge, J. I didn't want to stand still.
And a job on the Herald was the big opportunity. So I
took it and moved them all down to London. Long and
short of it was, Helga hated it, the kids hated it, and I
escaped into my work. We rowed, I stayed out more and
more—it's not difficult in our job, you know that—and
in the end she left me. Moved back to Birmingham, got
a job, met another man, and remarried. End of story.
Want some more coffee, or shouldn't we try to make a
start?"

He'd said all there was and he wanted to close the topic.
Julia said, "Yes, but thanks for telling me about it. Where
do we start, Ben?"

"No harm in retracing my steps. We start with the
Bauhaus. The town hall and the records office. They
weren't very helpful last time, but now that we're all one
happy European family, it may be easier."

"May I ask the reason for your request?" The clerk at the inquiries was a woman in her middle thirties; she wore the disdainful and suspicious look common to civil servants the world over. What, it conveyed, did these foreigners want, asking to see the old records of the late 1940s? . . .

Ben answered. "We're trying to trace a missing relative."

"You've left it rather late, haven't you? A German national?"

"No—" Julia interrupted. They were speaking in English. "My uncle. He had no nationality; he was in the DP camp."

The woman raised her thin eyebrows. "Then we would have no records of anyone like that. I don't know who would; it's so long ago. I'm sorry."

She had turned away in dismissal when Ben said, "But you would have records from the British Control Commission. I saw them here some years ago. And I found some documentation. My friend's uncle was discharged into the surety of an English woman working among the refugees. This was sanctioned and approved by the military authorities and he was allowed to live here with her."

Julia took it up again. She felt that Ben had antagonized the woman. She tried a soft approach. "If we could just look and see if there is anything connecting her with him afterward. It means so much to my mother, and she's in poor health. There might be some clues we could go on. Please?"

There was a hesitation, then with a slight shrug of resignation the woman did her good deed for the day.

"You can look through what we have," she said. "But I don't see what you hope to find. Unless you missed something last time." She spoke curtly to Ben.

"That's why we need to look again." Julia headed him off. "Just to make sure. I'm very grateful to you."

"Sign this form, please. I'll get someone to take you down when it's been authorized. Sit over there; I don't know how long it will be."

It was a full half hour before a girl came with the form duly signed and countersigned. Ben murmured to Julia, "I think she's a dyke. I wasn't getting anywhere."

"You should try turning on the charm," she whispered back.

"Haven't any." He followed her down the stairs onto the lower floor.

There was the musty smell of disuse and slight damp, and the artificial light emphasized the bare and ugly room with its stacked files and the metal table with a single hard chair.

The girl spoke in German. "The file for the Control Commission on refugees in 1948 is number one-seven-two-oh-three. I can leave you. You have two hours before we close. There's a bell by the door. Please ring when you have finished."

"I will," Harris said. He gave her a big smile, and said to Julia, "Was that better?"

"Not much. She thought you were going to bite her. Leave the soft soap to me, Ben. It's not your style. Now— I'm in your hands."

"Nothing!" Ben Harris exclaimed. The air was dusty and cold; their time was almost up. "Same stuff. No clue. Phyllis Lowe got him out of the camp, we know where they lived—I tried that and it wasn't even the same house anymore. Official notification she was leaving for England. Nothing," he repeated. "Come on, J, we're wasting our time here."

Julia leaned on the table; her elbows hurt from the hard surface. There was dust in her throat from the old paperwork, and her hands were dirty. "It can't be right," she said. "It can't just stop like that. It doesn't read right. Ben, if we can come in here and be left alone with this stuff, what's to stop someone else coming and taking something out?"

"What? You suggesting King's been here?"

"I think someone has. Look, don't you realize that there isn't any address or reference given for Phyllis Lowe apart from the bare details of her position with UNRRA. They wouldn't have accepted her guarantee for a displaced person without knowing she was a respectable, responsible person. She'd have had to make an official application to start with. There's no copy of that. No copy of the officer dealing with it, replying, or giving his recommendation. Just that one release document. Let me have another look at it. Let's see the page numbers."

He turned the file backward. "There," he said. "No luck. No page number. Nothing else was attached. But you're right. There would have been correspondence, references, all that sort of cross-checking. Why the hell didn't I see it before?"

"Because you weren't looking," she said. "What you saw was what's been left for anyone to find. Proof that she got King out and then applied to leave the country with him. You didn't look because you weren't looking for Phyllis Lowe. You were looking for something about King. Wait a minute—this signature—Major Grant." She stood up quickly. "Ben, if we can track him down, we'll get the information."

"If he's alive," Harris said slowly. "There were some very young majors at the end of the war. He could be in his seventies. You're pretty bright. Major A. B. Grant, liaison officer, UNRRA. Right there, under the signature.

Let's go. We can get someone working on it right away."

She shivered; the temperature had dropped, and the room with its dusty archives was dank and cold. *The files had been doctored. Which means that they were on the right track. Harold King had built up Phyllis Lowe into a surrogate mother. But he didn't want the world to know any more about her.*

Harris rang the bell, and after a few minutes the same girl came in. She was obviously anxious to get rid of them. It was time to close the offices. "You are satisfied?" she asked. "Yes, thank you. We found some useful information," Ben answered.

"Sign here, please." She put a release form in front of them; it was a pledge that file number 17203 had been examined and returned and that nothing had been altered or removed. "Both signatures, please," she said.

Ben pushed the form across to Julia with his pen.

"You must have a lot of these," he remarked. "Do you keep them all?"

"There's not so many," the girl told him. "Not for such a long time ago. We have everything up to date on computer now. But this old stuff"—she raised her shoulders slightly—"it just lies here getting dusty. One day some-one will clear it out. We could use the space."

"I'm sure," Ben agreed. "How long have you worked here?"

"Three years. Thank you, Fräulein." She took the form from Julia.

"Where will you keep this form?" he asked her. She moved to the door, urging them out. "We don't keep it. It goes on computer. Excuse me, but we must hurry. I'll take you upstairs." She locked the filing room behind her, and their steps clattered on the stone floors and up the stairs to the main office. They stepped outside into the late-afternoon sunshine.

He called out, "*Danke schön*," and the girl said, "*Bitte*," and shut the door.

Julia and he began to walk to the hired car.

From the ground-floor window the girl watched them go. Then she went into the receptionist's office and called out "Frau Walter?" No answer. She had gone on the tick of the clock, as she always did. Other members of the staff were talking and getting their coats on as they prepared to leave. The old porter-cum-caretaker would lock all the doors and check the windows before he, too, left.

The girl picked up the telephone in the office and punched a number. It was an answering machine at the other end of the line. She spoke quickly but clearly. "This is Minna. An English couple came here poking around the exchange commission file—1948. I'll take a note of their names." She hung up and looked around to make sure nobody had seen her make the call. Then she joined the trickle of secretaries and local officials leaving the Bauhaus.

"I've got a friend," Ben said, "he's got contacts in the War Office. He might be able to check on the records."

"You've got friends everywhere," Julia remarked.

"Part of my job," he answered. "Contacts are eighty percent of getting a story first. I did this guy a favor a few years ago. A well-known general was caught buggering rent boys in some gay club. He was retired on the usual grounds, ill health. He'd been a good soldier and he had friends. They didn't want to see him crucified. I killed the story." He looked at her. "I'm old-fashioned, J. I don't believe in character assassination just for the fun of it. Even though it sells newspapers. They'll find Major A. B. Grant if he's still alive." He checked his watch. "Too late to call up now. I'll get on to him in the morning. I know a nice little restaurant where we could have dinner, if you like—if it's not closed down."

"Why not? I'll meet you at the bar at eight."

"Seven," Ben corrected. "This is provincial Germany. They eat early."

Felix had found a one-bedroom studio in Pimlico. The girl he had casual sex with noticed a "to rent" sign in the window of the converted house and rang him to suggest he look at it. He knew that it was close to where she lived, but shrugged that off.

She was a fun girl, but he wasn't going to get involved. He had packed up his clothes and the stereo and his CDs; it was lucky Julia was going to be away. Meeting, however briefly, in the flat would be awkward for both of them. He had arranged to sleep out for the two nights before she left. He felt no animosity toward her.

He was surprised to feel relieved that the relationship was over. He had never admitted to himself until then that in spite of his determination to be independent and live his own life, he had found the last year increasingly oppressive. He owed Julia, and he didn't feel comfortable about it. That discomfort had made him more selfish and wayward to offset the obligation. "I'm a free man," was what he was saying to her and to himself, but it hadn't been true. "Toy Boy" had stung her to indignation. Typically he had shrugged it off, but he recognized that it was just bravado. The jeers had rankled, and he had punished Julia by being extra macho in his attitude. His dominance was sexual, and he used it to subdue her and even inflict little humiliations. He looked around the flat they'd shared together, at those bloody-awful pictures she was so pleased with, and heaved a huge sigh of relief that it was over. And because the burden was lifted, he left her a note. *Hope I haven't left too much of a mess. Thanks for some great times. I'm at 832-8474, if you feel like a drink sometime. Felix.* That made him feel better still, and he went out with his belongings with a light heart and put the keys back through the mailbox. The retired detective keeping watch from a parked car on the opposite side of the street saw him go. He'd been one of a forty-eight-hour watch on the place, ever since Joe said he wanted it staked out. The woman had driven off with luggage, and now the boyfriend had moved out. It was clear for them to get into the flat.

Joseph Patrick was a fixer. He'd learned to manipulate from his childhood in a Dublin orphanage. They'd given him the surname Patrick because he'd been dumped on the doorstep on Saint Patrick's Day. He was a small, weedy child who had to use his wits to survive the bullying of bigger boys and the pitiless Christian discipline of the brothers who were in charge of human refuse like himself. Bastards, slum children, abandoned through shame or cruel economic necessity. Children from respectable families who were smitten by death or debts or the curse of alcoholism. The orphanage opened its doors to them all. Few left unscathed when they reached adulthood. Joe Patrick learned two lessons in survival very quickly. Make yourself useful to the people with the power—that applied equally to the bully boys, who ruled inside the dormitories, and to the members of the staff, who ruled the whole community. And never, ever, give trouble or support anyone who did. He knew no loyalty except to himself. He conformed to the rigid religious routine without absorbing any moral sense. He became known as someone who would run errands, spy on troublesome fellows, accommodate homosexual demands if they were made upon him. He left the orphanage with a good reference from the brothers and an introduction to a small shopkeeper who employed youths at their behest. Within three months Joe had opened the back door to a gang that beat the old man unconscious and robbed the till. They knocked Joe on the head for good measure, so he was not suspected.

His entry into the criminal community of the city was on the same pattern as life in the orphanage. He made himself useful and he didn't show a high profile. He knew he was much cleverer than the men who gave him a few quid for doing their dirty work, watching shops or private premises that were targets for burglary.

He went on to scout for girls likely to turn prostitute, hanging around the bars and pubs, looking for runaways or teenagers who wanted drugs. He supplied the drugs and introduced the users to the pimps who ran them. He had a couple of tarts himself, and he beat them as mercilessly as he had been beaten as a child if they slacked off or tried to keep some of the money. He was tall and thin, with Irish good looks and bad teeth. He combed his curly dark hair and dressed in trendy clothes, and the police employed him as a snout. It was a dangerous tightrope, even for someone as agile as Joe Patrick. He had a drinking partner, a drunken copper who had more in common with the crooks he spent his time with than with the police force. It was time for Joe to get out of Dublin. The word was out for him. Time to get out while he was still on two legs. Joe took the advice. He had some money, a lot of clothes, and an address his pal had given him. He went to London and introduced himself to a small, seedy firm of private detectives.

They hired him as a legman.

And that was how Harold King found him. He'd worked for King for eighteen years, starting with a small surveillance job on a journalist who had written uncomplimentary articles about King Publishing and its pornographic output. Joe was told to dig dirt. He didn't find any, so he supplied it. He still ran two or three girls on the side, and he set the journalist up with one of them. He photographed her giving him a blow job in the back of the car. There were no more articles about King's porno magazines. Impulse and curiosity made King ask to see him.

The man had initiative. Nobody had told him to set up the victim. King saw the cheap, flashy man in his mid-twenties, with all the cunning of the petty criminal in his sharp eyes. But there was a brain under the mophead of curls. King sized him up and came to a decision.

He could use someone like this gutter rat. And he would always be able to control him. He looked him up and down and drew on his big cigar and said, "You want to work for me?"

The bad teeth, legacy of poor diet and neglect, fanned out into an ingratiating smile. "Sure. Sure I do."

"And you don't mind what you have to do?"

The shoulders lifted under their overwide pads.

"I'm not partic'lar. Whatever." He had a thick, nasal Dublin whine that offended King. It would amuse him to take this piece of human garbage and remodel it.

"Then see a dentist and get something done about your teeth. If you work for me, you look the way I want you to. You talk the way I want and you dress the way I tell you. Understand me?"

Men with power over him had been talking to Joe Patrick in those terms all his life. He had no pride, only a price.

He ran his hand through the curls on his head.

"You're the boss, Mr. King. That's great by me."

As he waved him out of the office, King called him back suddenly.

"And get that nit nest cut off!"

Joe Patrick had been his man ever since. He was barbered and well dressed now, his accent smoothed into phony American; when he went to the States to sort something out for King, he lapsed back into the brogue. He had a smart flat off Hyde Park and he drove a BMW. He was a businessman, with cards printed to prove it. Joseph G. Patrick, export/import, and an office address in Covent Garden. He lived with two black girls, and he had supplied King with women since he married and the "starlets" and "models" he liked to be seen with in public were given the shove. No girl who serviced King would have dared talk about it. Joe Patrick had maimed women if they crossed him.

And he paid handsomely, because that was King's way. He bought discretion with money, and implicit in everything was the threat of Joe if they stepped off the track.

King wanted this woman Hamilton looked over. Joe had done many similar jobs over the years. They were the bread-and-butter jobs, like providing the right girl. He had done other, more complicated things for King. They put the jam on his daily bread. And they had taken Joe to some interesting places. He knew the States quite well, and parts of Europe.

Responsibility had given him a certain gloss. He had self-confidence and he had learned how to behave with people better educated than the waif beaten into learning by the good brothers at home.

Joe was a chameleon, he could blend into his surroundings. The flat was empty, but there wasn't much point in waiting. The Hamilton woman could come back at any time. He fixed for an entrance to be made that afternoon.

There was a double mortise on the front door, but it didn't trouble Joe's expert. He picked both locks and stood aside for Joe to enter.

"You stay here," Joe mouthed at him. They were on the first-floor landing of the Chelsea conversion. The front door had opened on a buzzer from one of the top-floor flats; stupidly the woman pushed to open before she asked the name on the intercom. Joe's man had his answer ready.

"Interflora," he said. "I'm delivering to number two. Hamilton? No reply so I'll leave the plants outside the door. Thank you."

And he and Joe were inside the building and up the first flight of stairs. "Anyone comes, you call me." Then he was in Julia's flat.

He knew how to search without leaving any signs. He opened drawers, lifted clothes, and felt underneath them; he shoved his hands under the mattress of the double bed, rifled through the fitted cupboards, opened the one remaining big suitcase and the hat box. He knew where people hid money and jewelry and personal papers. He found nothing, but some gold trinkets and a little spare cash in a drawer. He didn't touch them.

There was an answering machine. He switched it on, listened, made quick notes, and reset it. He was looking for business papers, anything connected with her job on the *Herald*. She didn't bring stuff home. The messages were personal. A call from her mother, two from friends asking her and someone called Felix—the boyfriend who'd moved out—to dinner.

And Felix's note with his telephone number. Joe copied it. Then he went through the wastebasket in the living room. Among the empty envelopes and a few circulars he found a screwed-up piece of scrap paper. Someone had jotted down a rough schedule.

8:30 *Heathrow. arr. Munich 12:15 C. time check in Ness. approx* 1 p.m. Joe put the note in his pocket. He had been in the flat for under ten minutes. He came out. "Okay, close it up." His man relocked the door, and they slipped downstairs and out into the street.

Joe didn't know what he'd found, but he had a number that might come in useful. He knew where the ex-boyfriend could be contacted.

There was no trace of the camp outside Nessenberg. A housing development had been built on the site. Julia and Ben drove out the next morning.

"It's incredible," she said, "seeing how they rebuilt everything after the war. I never realized till I came here."

"They're a resourceful people," Ben answered. "Disciplined and industrious."

"More than that, surely," she questioned. "I've seen newsreels and photographs—the whole country was devastated."

"They're proud," he said. "My wife said to me once, 'We were defeated, but we're not going to be beaten.' Her family had been bombed out, and two of her uncles were missing in Russia. She came from Hamburg.

"That was really pasted. But they'd rebuilt it by the time we came over. I don't think her father and mother were too pleased she'd married me, but they put a good face on it. They were crazy about the grandchildren."

"I'm sorry you don't see them," Julia said. "Maybe you'll get together when they get older."

"I don't see why," he said. "I wasn't a very good father. They're going their own way. Let's talk about something else."

He looked grim and irritable. She was beginning to understand him better. Bad temper was his cover for feelings. For hurt and, she suspected, for real loneliness. She was beginning to like him as well as understand him. In a good mood he was wonderful company. They had enjoyed an excellent dinner the night before in another restaurant—his old stamping ground had become a grocer's shop. He ordered German food and wine, and the conversation was wide-ranging and easy.

He talked about Germany and the resurgence of the neo-Nazis, the problems of reunification for a country that had been split in half ideologically, with a generation brought up with different work and social ethics. He was extremely intelligent and well informed, and she was fascinated.

She said so then, as they drove back to the hotel.

"I really enjoyed last night, Ben. I learned a lot from you. I've learned a lot from this trip."

"I thought I'd been a bloody bore," he admitted. "It's just that it was a part of my life because I married Helga. Don't know why I go on about it now. Anyway we got something out of our trip. Major A. B. Grant."

Julia said, "When will your War Office contact let you know?"

"We should get something today," he answered. "All they've got to do is track down the records of who was here and whether there's a 'deceased' after the name. Everything's at the touch of a computer key."

"If he's dead"—Julia shook her head—"we're back to square one. Somehow I don't think he will be."

He smiled slightly at her. "You're an optimist, J. I'm a pessimist. I'm the guy who says the bottle's half empty. You say it's half full."

The hotel proprietor was a plump, efficient lady with a friendly smile. She greeted them as they came in.

"Good morning! Herr Harris, there is a message come through on our fax machine for you. I have it here."

Julia craned over his shoulder. He read the script quickly and turned to her. "It's better than a half-full bottle," he said quietly. "Major Grant married a local girl. He retired to live over here in seventy-four. They've even got the address for us. He draws a disability pension."

Impulsively Julia grabbed his arm. "Ben—this is our breakthrough! Where is he?" For a moment his hand came over and gripped hers. Then he released himself. "At Hintzbach, about thirteen miles away. I'll call him."

The owner of the town's biggest supermarket was also head of the local Veterans Association. He had been a panzer sergeant in his twenties and suffered a wound in the Western Desert that saved him from the Russian front. He had ended the war as a civilian stores administrator for the 101st Division which was engaged in fighting the American Sixth Army. He had watched his country be overrun, its towns destroyed, its population driven onto the roads in search of shelter from the fighting. He had seen his people starve and die, and his comrades penned up in POW camps where the rations were so short that thousands perished. He had escaped because he was a civilian with the lower part of his leg removed. But he was a soldier in his heart, and everything he saw in the new Germany convinced him that the defeat of Adolf Hitler was the worst disaster in his country's history. His views had not changed with his prosperity. He and his wife had worked and saved, and the result was his business, a big modern house on its own grounds, and his position as a respected member of the community. He was also the unofficial liaison with old soldiers who needed help.

Help had come from many unexpected quarters. From America, where the members of the old Bundt were still loyal; from South and Central America, where sympathizers hadn't forgotten their homeland. The Veterans Association had used its resources to rehabilitate men still suffering from the war in the early years and to build homes for the elderly and incapacitated, even providing small pensions for their widows to supplement the state allowance. The branch at Nessenberg had recognized his work by making him its president. He was very proud of that position. More proud than he was of the big modern shop that had grown from his first venture into trade and the money that came from it.

He could still serve, albeit silently. His three sons were his grief and disappointment. They were liberal-minded, enlightened, and quite alien to him. They were shamed by the past; they rejected racism and deplored any militarism or nationalist feelings. They were the new Germans, and their father couldn't understand them. Politics was not discussed at home. He hoped that the criminals and layabouts pouring into their country under the guise of refugees, taking state money and jobs from their own people, would teach them how wrong they were. But he said nothing anymore. He had his friends and his contacts, and they belonged to his past. His answering machine was in his private office, and only a few people knew the number. He took note of Minna's message.

Minna was the daughter of a colleague who'd served with SS Panzer Division in the East. He belonged to the fighting unit, not the prison guards and execution squads so emphasized by their enemies. All countries had their undesirables. Atrocities were common in a war. He had erected a mental barrier against history. The camps had existed, but they were exaggerated out of all proportion by the Jews. Already the numbers of dead were being called into question. Minna was her father's daughter, imbued with his loyalties and ideals. Years ago—many years ago—he had had a visitor. A fellow soldier from the Western Desert where his lower leg had been torn off by a British mortar. The man said he was acting for other ex-soldiers who had shed their uniforms and taken refuge from the enemy in the DP camps at Nessenberg. The alternative had been to starve as prisoners of war.

The DPs were fed and given medical care. They were the lucky ones in that dreadful period. He was asked to protect those who had bluffed screening officers and UNRRA officials. Over the years there had been people snooping, looking for someone in the records. He had made sure that anything incriminating was removed, leaving one or two documents as instructed. Now the snoopers were back. They had been looking at the same file, the file for the Control Commission 1948. He remembered them, those well-fed, sleek British officers, quartered in his town, sifting and questioning, looking for so-called war criminals or deserters. He hated still, remembering them. They were long gone, and the interfering busybodies from the United Nations with them.

From England these two had come. Minna had noted their names. He decided to pay Minna a call and find out more before he fulfilled his obligation.

And paid back some small part of the handsome donation he'd accepted for the association's hardship fund.

The road to Hintzbach took them through some pretty Bavarian country, and the place where Major Grant and his wife had retired to live was a picture-book village, with clapboard houses and narrow streets. Everything was clean and orderly, and the street cafés and beer halls were full of customers. It was lunchtime, and the shops were closed. The house they were looking for was next to the wine store. Window boxes full of bright flowers and an incongruous British nameplate painted in garish colors. "Rooks Nest."

They left the car in a side street—it was forbidden to

park in the main road—and went to the front door. Ben had spoken to the wife. The major was not very well, but she would ask, and who wanted to see him, please? An author, Ben explained, doing some research for a book on the work of the Control Commission with refugees. They promised not to stay too long, but would be grateful for a short interview.

She opened the door to them. Julia saw a slight, dark woman with a little gray in her hair. She was pretty, even in age, and she must have been at least seventy. She wore a flowered apron and a blouse with a crisp frill at the neck.

"I'm Mr. Harris." Ben stepped forward, holding Julia by the elbow. "And this is Miss Hamilton."

"Come in, please." The hall was small and dark and smelled of furniture polish. "My husband is very excited to see you." She had a charming smile. "But he does get tired. He's in here. Shall I get you some coffee? Or a glass of beer?"

"Coffee, please," Julia answered. It was a downstairs room converted into a bedroom. Major Grant was sitting in an armchair with a knitted rug over his knees. A fire was alight in the grate.

Ben went across and shook his hand. Julia did the same. It was cold and skinny, like a bird's claw. He looked frail, with sparse white hair and hollow cheeks. "It's very good of you to see us, sir," Ben said.

"It's a pleasure." The old man smiled at them. "I don't get visitors from home these days. Do sit down, make yourselves comfortable. My wife will bring us some coffee and some of her cake. She makes marvelous chocolate cake." They talked about the weather, he asked a few questions about England—he hadn't been back for five years, since then he'd had a minor stroke, and he didn't get about much. Julia felt he had lost touch with his own country. He gave his wife a devoted look when she came back with a tray. "I'll leave you," she said. "I have things to do."

"No, no," he protested, "stay and talk, darling. After all, you were as much a part of that time as I was." He turned to Julia, who was sitting closer to him than Ben Harris. "Gerda was a DP. That's how we met. She can be a great help; she can tell you what it was like from experience."

"That," Ben said gently, "would be invaluable."

They had talked for an hour before Julia raised the subject of Phyllis Lowe. "I'm particularly interested in the Englishwomen who came to work for UNRRA; I've contacted many of them who are still around"—she avoided saying "still alive"—"but I can't find any trace of Phyllis Lowe. I know she befriended a DP, a young man called Koenig." She looked inquiringly at them. They had left England in seventy-four, King was not then a public figure. The old man looked up and said sharply, "I knew Phyllis. And I knew Koenig. I tried to warn her about him, but she simply wouldn't listen, would she, Gerda?"

"No," his wife answered. "She was completely taken in by him. My nationality had been established by then, and I was working for Alfred. Millions of documents were destroyed during the bombing, mine were lost at Frankfurt, but my parents' marriage certificate helped to prove I was who I said. So I was released from the camp. I didn't know Koenig inside—there were thousands of us—but I did know Phyllis Lowe. She was a nice woman—"

"She was a fool," the major interrupted. His wife reproved him quietly; they were in a dialogue that excluded Ben and Julia, reliving their own past. "She was in love with him," she said. "Crazy in love. She wouldn't listen to anyone."

"In love with Koenig?" Julia asked. "Were they lovers?"

"Of course they were," Grant said irritably. "They made a fool of me to start with. She was nearly forty, and he must have been around twenty-five or -six. She convinced me he was a poor stray with a traumatic past—

dragged out of his home when his parents were shot, working as a slave laborer on a farm, hunted like an animal with all the other poor devils when the Russians invaded. She wanted to take him out of the camp, educate him, and give him a chance of a new life. A lot of the DPs settled in Europe if they couldn't get to the States, for example. I believed her.

"She was so damned convincing, and I knew she had a reputation for hard work on behalf of the refugees. She was well liked and respected. So I recommended he be released in her surety. He'd never given any trouble, he seemed a decent lad. Very respectful, rather gauche. I interviewed him several times. He told the same story as Phyllis did. The Fräulein had been so kind, she was like a mother. I remember the swine squeezed out a few tears on one occasion.

"It was put up between them, but I didn't find that out till later. As soon as he left the camp, they were living openly together."

"Did she educate him—I read somewhere she employed a local man to teach him English?" Ben asked.

"Huh—she did indeed. She spent money like water on him. She got clothes for him, she scrounged and bribed for cigarettes—she even had the cheek to ask me for Players because he liked them! And didn't he change his spots, eh, Gerda?"

"Yes," his wife said, "he did. He was arrogant, greedy, and he even humiliated the poor woman. She seemed to like it. He'd go around the cafés boasting about his rich English mistress and how she did exactly what he wanted. Alfred had a serious talk with her, didn't you, darling—he tried to point out that she was making a complete fool of herself, that the man was exploiting her. And what did she say to you?"

"She said she had never been so happy in her life and I didn't understand her Hans, as she called him. 'He's young and full of life, and whatever you say, he loves me. I know he does.' And then she told me she was going to marry him and take him to England."

He sighed, as if he had exhausted himself reliving the past. For a moment there was silence, his wife looked at Julia and nodded, as if to say, "Please, that's enough."

Julia stood up, "Major Grant, we mustn't keep you any longer. Just one more question. Did she marry him?"

"Yes," he answered. "She did. She was a civilian, you see, and we had no jurisdiction, or I could have stopped her. She married him six months after he got out of the camp, resigned from UNRRA, and said they were going to England. She did come and say good-bye to me, at least.

"'We're going to be so happy,' she said to me. 'I'll keep in touch, Alfred.' But she never did. We never heard of her again."

"Thank you very much, sir," Harris shook the thin hand. "You've been a great help."

The major said, "Are you writing this book together?"

"Collaborating on it," Ben answered.

"Good-bye, Major Grant, and take care of yourself." Julia didn't shake hands with him; he looked as if he'd fall asleep as soon as they left. In the hall she turned to his wife.

"I do hope it hasn't been too much for him," she said. "He looked so tired."

Gerda Grant shook her head. "He's old," she said. "We both are. But we have our two sons and grandchildren, and we've had a happy life together. It wasn't easy for Alfred, being married to a German. But we loved each other, and that's what mattered."

"What was she like—Phyllis Lowe—to look at?"

"Very handsome. Very smart. I think she was an upper-class English lady—a lot like her came to work for UNRRA.

Sophisticated and superior to him in every way. But she was blind, quite blind. I wonder what happened to her, when they got to England."

"I wonder too," Julia said. "Good-bye and thank you. I hope your husband goes on well."

They walked to the car in silence. Ben started the engine.

"Well," he said at last, "that was a turn up for the book!"

The last person to use that phrase was a betting-mad friend of her father's.

"No wonder we couldn't find a death certificate," Julia answered. "We'll get on to that right away. She'd have been Koenig, that's why we drew a blank. Ben, you realize we've sent out teams looking for everything under the name of Lowe. Come on, let's get back to the hotel—I can call through to the office."

"He married her," Ben muttered, the car picking up speed, "to get to England. But why lie? What's he got to hide, J?"

"Something more than making a fool of a woman old enough to know better. Very convenient, getting cancer, leaving him a bit of money. . . ."

"You think she did die, then?"

"Yes, but I'll be very interested to see that death certificate." She looked at him and said suddenly, "They were a sweet old couple, weren't they? You forget there are people around like that." He didn't answer. Julia felt she had unwittingly touched a sore spot. He put up a tough front, but that failed marriage had left a scar.

The girl called Minna nodded. "He said it," she insisted. "He said they had found something."

He had gone home at lunchtime, and she had come over from the Bauhaus. His wife had left them together in the sitting room. She never concerned herself with her husband's activities for the Veterans, and she knew Minna's father was an old comrade. She hoped the family wasn't in trouble. If they were, her man would sort it out.

"You've got the names?"

"Here." She passed him a slip of paper.

"Describe them to me," he said.

"The man was around fifty—dark, wore glasses—the woman was younger than him. She had very red hair, she was pretty, and she had expensive clothes."

"Good," he said. He consulted the scrap of paper. Minna had copied all the details on the form. "Staying at the Nessenberghof," he muttered. "I can make a few inquiries. Leni is a friend of my wife's—I can see the hotel register. Thank you, Minna. Always watchful."

"Always loyal," she finished the motto for him. "I must go, or I'll be late."

She looked at him silently, a friendly-faced, attractive young woman who had been born twenty years after the war ended. She gave the forbidden salute. Slowly he returned it. Then the door closed behind her.

Julia put down the telephone. "They've got to go back over the same ground. One thing did come up, though," she frowned, looking at her own scribbled shorthand notes. "There's an elderly couple next door to the house where Phyllis Lowe lived with King. They remember a young man and a much older woman moving there. My team has it all on tape. Ben, I think we should fly back. There's nothing more we can do here." She stood up and stretched a little. He noticed how full her breasts were as she made the movement.

He said, "Let's stay tonight. I'll show you Munich. We could fly out in the morning."

"We could," Julia agreed. "All right, let's do that. I'll call through and book the flight."

"I'll do it," he said briskly. "Do you drink beer, J?"

"Not if I can help it." She laughed at him.

"You can't go to Munich and not go to a *Bier Keller*," he said. "See you downstairs at six."

It was a new experience for Julia. The city was beautiful, rebuilt after its travails during the war; there was an atmosphere of gaiety as evening approached. The shops were brightly lit and crammed with goods. The cafés and bars and beer halls were full of Bavarians setting out to enjoy themselves. She was struck by how many of them were dark, far removed from the blond Aryan ideal that had been born in that very place over half a century ago. Ben took her to a *Bier Keller* as he'd promised. It was hot, smoky, and noisy, but the good spirits of the people around them were infectious. A group at a nearby table started to sing, and soon everyone was joining in, steins banging in rhythm on the tables.

"It's crazy," she said to Ben. "It's like a Hollywood movie—but don't they know how to enjoy themselves!"

"We came to the Oktoberfest one year with the kids," he said. "They loved it. The whole place goes wild, drinking, singing, wearing national costume. You'd never think Nazism started here, would you?"

"No," she said, brought down to earth suddenly. "No, you wouldn't."

He stood up. "I think you've had enough beer, so let's move on to something more civilized."

She took his arm as they came out into the street. "I enjoyed that, I wouldn't have missed it for anything. Where are we going now?"

"To the Bernerhof," he said, and he looked down at

her and smiled. "From the ridiculous to the sublime, depending how you look at it. The best food and wine in Bavaria." She didn't let go of his arm as they walked.

They sat in the bar and had drinks while they studied the menu. A pianist was playing sentimental sixties music, the lights were low, the atmosphere relaxed and leisurely.

The women were elegant and the men very different from the boisterous beer drinkers in the *Bier Keller*. It was low-key, luxurious, and subtly sensual as if to say, "Everything is here for your pleasure. Whatever form that pleasure takes, it's our pleasure to provide it!" They dined in a cubicle in the restaurant; it was intimate, and they sat close. She drank more wine than she intended, and reveled in the rich food.

When the coffee, frothing with cream, was brought to them, she said to Ben, "I haven't had a cigarette in ten years. I'm going to have one now."

"I know the feeling," he answered. "That's what this place does to you. You feel you're king of the world and you can do what you like and to hell with it. You look very pretty."

He was not looking at her when he said it. She could feel his body against hers on the cushioned seat.

He hadn't touched her, not even her hand as it lay on the table. He didn't need to; his desire suddenly ignited hers, and she said softly, "Never mind the cigarette. Why don't we spend the night here?"

He half turned to her and then put his hand on her face and raised it. He kissed her slowly, not like Felix, with his importunate tongue and greedy technique, but in gentle exploration.

Then he said, "Are you sure, J? Are you sure it's what you want?" She laid two fingers on his mouth. "After what you've just done, I'm sure."

When he undressed her, he said simply, "You're beautiful. I want to look at you." She saw their naked reflections in the big gilt mirror on the wall opposite the bed and turned around for him, pivoting slowly until he caught hold of her and they sprawled on the bed, locked in a frenzy of desire.

It was a long night. They made love and slept and then made love again. She thought hazily as she drifted into an exhausted, sated sleep, *Felix was a boy. I've been with a man.*

When she woke in the morning, he was already up. She could hear sounds in the bathroom. He came out wearing a terry-cloth robe.

"I let you sleep," he said. He sat beside her on the edge of the bed. He took hold of her hands and held them.

"If you're sorry about last night, we can forget about it. No strings."

"No strings," Julia agreed. "You'd already booked the room, hadn't you?"

"Yes," he admitted. "Just in case. I've wanted you for years—ever since you walked into that office looking like a scared kid on your first day. I wouldn't admit it to myself. But I mean it. I'll back off if you want me to."

She took her hands away and leaned back on the pillows. She sighed.

"Oh, Ben, you are a bloody fool." She smiled at him and held out her arms. "I don't mind missing breakfast if you don't."

As the plane began its descent to Heathrow, Julia glanced at him. He had closed his eyes, stowed his glasses away in his breast pocket. *I must get him a case to put them in,* she thought. *Nobody's looked after the details for him for a long time.*

She loved flying; she leaned forward to watch the ground coming up to meet them. It exhilarated her to anticipate the touchdown, the force of braking and the smooth transition from hundreds of miles an hour to a gentle taxiing across the runway.

She nudged him gently. "Ben—wake up. We've landed."

He opened his eyes. "I wasn't asleep, just dozing. I'm shagged out, and it's all your fault." He unbuckled her seat belt for her.

"You look sensational," he murmered. "How is an old man like me going to cope?"

"You don't have any problems," Julia whispered back. "Come on, I want to see what's on that tape."

Ben Harris eased her out into the gangway. "I think we're going to make a very good team. You're a pro, J. And so am I."

They set off for the Western building, with Julia driving. As they eased into the reserved parking space, she turned to him.

"Thank you for taking me to see Munich," she said. "It was all wonderful."

"Thank you for coming with me." He turned her face up to him and gave her a firm, short kiss on the lips.

"Now, let's get to work."

"Lord Western?" He was conferring with his advertising director when his personal secretary came in. She never interrupted him unless it was important. Even so he scowled at her. The revenue was down on the last quarter, and he had been roasting his executives.

"What is it?"

"Miss Hamilton called in; she'd like to see you sometime after five, if that's convenient."

"Am I free?"

"You have two half-hour appointments, then nothing from six o'clock on. Mr. Osborne at five and Peggy Beaumont from Features at half past. Shall I say six o'clock to

Miss Hamilton? I do have a note that Lady Western is expecting you to go to the Park Lane for drinks with Princess Margaret on that NSPCC appeal—"

Western didn't hesitate. "Cancel Osborne till nine o'clock tomorrow. Pick a slot for Peggy in late morning. Tell Julia to come up here at five. I can give her an hour and a half clear."

He went back to bullying his advertising director.

"I've brought the tape," Julia said. "I'd like you to hear it when you've looked over what we found out in Nessenberg." She placed the typed report in front of him. He opened it, skimmed through the pages, and then looked up at her.

He said coldly, but with triumph, "Lying bastard. The saintly spinster lady was a randy forty-year-old who liked screwing boys."

He went on, tapping the paper with his finger. "He got into England because he was married to a British subject. Then she dies and he gets his hands on her money—this is good stuff. We're just beginning to lift the stone and see the maggots."

"It gets better," Julia said. "Let me play you this tape." She'd brought a small cassette player with her. She slipped the tape inside and switched it on. "Louder," Western commanded. "I can't hear it." She turned up the volume. The voices were old, and sometimes they talked through each other.

"Yes," the woman spoke first. "Yes, I remember them. She was much older, very tarty-looking, used to smoke in the street—"

"Nice-looking woman," the male voice interrupted. "Too good for that fellow. He was just on her. Never did a day's work, lounging about till all hours. They didn't mix with anyone. They went out a lot at night." "And they had awful rows," his wife spoke up. "You could hear them shouting. I rang up and complained once, and she was rude to me. She drank a lot." The researcher's voice. "How do you know? Did you see her drunk?"

"No, but you heard him, didn't you, Dick, yelling when the window was open. Accusing her of being drunk—"

"I'm sure he hit her," the man broke in. "He was just the type. Foreigner, nasty, conceited brute. I'm sure he hit her. Don't blame her for drinking, living with him. They were said to be married. They called themselves Mr. and Mrs. Koenig."

"They had a char," his wife reminded him. "She said there were bottles all over the place."

"A char?" The researcher wasn't old enough to recognize the term.

"A cleaner. Charwoman. She worked part-time for us, and she gossiped to my wife."

"How long before Mrs. Koenig got ill?"

There was a pause, and the question was repeated.

"Ill? She wasn't ill. She had an accident, but she wasn't ill." They were both talking at once.

"What kind of accident?" Julia was watching Western. He was pale and crouching forward, his body tensed over the little machine.

"She fell, didn't she, Alfred? Fell in the garden and fractured her skull. I expect she'd been drinking." The note of an old animosity to the tarty but attractive Mrs. Koenig sang through the recorded voice.

"Jesus," Western said, and then checked himself, as the interview went on. "He called an ambulance, and she was taken off to the hospital. He told the char she'd died a few days later. He was crying, she said. I said it was an act."

"You took her part." The voice was shrill. It was obvious that the Koenigs were not the only people who had quar-

reled all those years ago. "He wasn't as bad as you made
out. You didn't like him because he was a foreigner. He
was a Polish refugee, that's what I heard."

"What happened after that? You're sure I'm not tiring
you?" The researchers were trained not to harass anyone or
apply pressure to the elderly. And these were very elderly.
The preliminary information at the start of the tape placed
them by name and gave their ages as eighty-five and eighty-
seven. They had been resident in the old-people's home
for thirteen years. The husband was in a wheelchair, and
his wife was partially sighted.

"No, no, we're enjoying talking to you. I can't remember what I had for lunch, and she's worse, but I can remember what happened forty years ago as if it was yesterday.
You want to know what?"

"After Mrs. Koenig died, did the husband stay on?"

"No. He moved out, and the house was sold very quickly.
There was a real shortage of houses in those days. Never saw
or heard of him again." Julia leaned forward and switched
the tape off.

"I'm getting this transcribed, and my girl will go back and
get it signed by them both and witnessed by a solicitor."

"What did she tell them?" Western asked. "They didn't
connect anything with King?"

"She said she was trying to trace Koenig because of a
legacy. She had to edit the tape because they talked their
heads off. She was rather sorry for them. They were shut
in together all day, bickering and nagging at each other.
The place was very dreary."

Western wasn't listening. Other people's problems didn't
interest him. "Convenient for him, wasn't it?" he muttered.
"Lucky chap, getting rid of her so quickly. And getting
some money. Well done, Julia. Follow this through."

"You think it wasn't an accident?" she asked him.

"It doesn't matter what I think. What we want is some

kind of proof. You've done good work, but it's not enough."
His tone was sharp. "We can show him up as a liar, but
not a criminal. So far he can't be accused of breaking any
law. And that's what I want. Evidence, proof. Something
I can nail him to the cross with."

He stood up abruptly. Julia said quietly, "Lord Western,
there's something I've got to ask you."

The eyes narrowed suspiciously. "I don't pay you to ask
me questions. I'm in a hurry." She didn't move. "Why did
you pull Ben Harris off the investigation ten years ago?"

He was on his way to the door. "Because he wasn't getting anywhere. He was wasting my time."

"He was looking into two suspected murders of men
who were business rivals of King. You stopped him. Why?"

Western opened the door and called his secretary. "I
wish you'd trust me, Lord Western," Julia said. "If there is
something, I ought to know about it. Otherwise how can
I protect you?"

Suddenly, unexpectedly, he shut the door. He turned
around and looked at her. For a slight man he had enormous
physical presence.

"It's a nice thought, my dear. You find me the right kind
of dirt on Harold King, and I'll protect myself." His secretary knocked, and he opened the door. "Bridget, I'm going.
Ring down for the car." Then he was gone.

"You take the private elevator, Miss Hamilton," the secretary said briskly. "Lord Western won't be leaving for a
few minutes. Excuse me." She stood aside, and Julia walked
past her.

Ben had gone to his office; she went to hers on the floor
below Western's eyrie and sat down to think through that
interview.

She stared unseeing out of the massive windows with its
fine views. Western was out to get Harold King for personal reasons. He had begun a fresh crusade after ten

years of neutrality, and there was only one explanation. He had been threatened once and submitted. Now he was threatened again, and no deal with his enemy was possible.

That was what this was all about. Not a question of morals but of two jungle predators, circling each other looking for the jugular.

Suddenly she felt tired and low-spirited. She wanted to call Ben, but she hesitated. No strings. That was the agreement. They were lovers and colleagues, but they were professionals first. He wasn't the keeper of her conscience, and she had no right to burden him.

And yet when he at first refused to work with her, she'd used a moral argument to get her way. "If King is what you say, you ought to help me stop him."

So why wasn't that reason good enough to apply to herself?

She wasn't the keeper of Western's conscience either. It was doubtful that he possessed one. She was a journalist, a seeker after truth in the public interest. If she wasn't that, then her job had no integrity.

Her outside line buzzed, and she picked up the phone.

"Julia Hamilton."

"How'd you get on?" It was Ben, and she was flooded with relief.

"Come around for supper and I'll tell you."

"Wasn't he pleased? What the hell did he expect?"

She smiled at the familiar irritable tone. "He doesn't pay compliments, you know that. 'Well done, but it's not enough.' He wants a criminal charge so he can nail King to the cross. He actually said that."

"He would. Bugger cooking, we'll go out, get a pizza or something. I'll come at around eight. I've got a lot to catch up on."

"'Bye, Ben," she said. "Thanks for ringing. I was feeling quite pissed off."

"You're tired," he said. "Why don't you go home and put your feet up for a bit?"

In all the years she and Felix had lived together, he had never considered that she might be feeling tired or downcast. She was always in top form, and if she wasn't, he didn't want to know. "I will," she said. "See you at around eight."

She drove home, and as she went up to the first floor, she met the girl who lived in the flat above.

"Hello." They were neighbors, but like most London flat dwellers, they had never got to know each other.

"Hope you got your flowers," the girl said, pausing.

"Flowers? I haven't been back for a few days." Julia shook her head. Flowers . . . not from Felix, surely? Never from Felix.

"I let them in when they buzzed. They said they'd leave them outside your door. I should have taken them in for you. They'll be dead by now."

"I expect so," Julia agreed. "Thanks anyway."

There was nothing outside her front door. No card notifying nondelivery either. She sorted through her mail; it was collected by the caretaker every morning and put into the mailboxes. Three circulars and a bill. Flowers from Felix? She must be out of her mind to think such a thing. Maybe the girl upstairs was mistaken. Most likely they weren't for her at all, and they'd simply taken them back. She forgot about it and went to run a hot bath. She was looking forward to seeing Ben. "Bugger cooking." She smiled. No male chauvinist either.

He didn't stay the night. They ate at a local pizzeria, and he came back for a cup of coffee.

"You don't have to go," Julia protested.

"Yes, I do." He slipped his arm around her. "You're

whacked out. Ask me tomorrow. Anyway I've got to go home and feed the cat."

"I didn't know you had a cat?"

"Had it for years. Found it in the street, poor little sod. It's company. My housekeeper looks after it if I'm away, but she doesn't come in on a Wednesday." It was so unexpected, it was touching. Julia asked him, "What's it called?"

He grinned at her. He seemed embarrassed at admitting the cat's existence. "Pussy," he said. "I couldn't think of anything else. Good night, love. Sleep well."

"You too." Julia kissed him at the front door.

As she locked it for the night, she remembered the flowers. She'd forgotten about them. Felix's note with his telephone number was in her drawer. She saw no reason to call him. Maybe one day, just to be friendly; but not yet. She slept very deeply that night and dreamed that Ben had given her a cat as a present.

"Daddy?" Gloria King came up to her father's chair, and, bending down, she kissed him on the cheek. He had escaped the weekend guests and was sitting in the library with his eyes closed. He liked to relax when they went to the country. He had bought a big estate in Gloucestershire, which he ran as a farm and a commercial shoot, and he'd built a golf course, well out of sight of his house. He believed that everything should pay for itself, and his four thousand acres were not excluded. "I didn't wake you, did I?"

He looked at her tenderly, reached out, and pulled her onto the arm of the chair. He loved having her near him. The ash-blond hair and blue eyes, the physical makeup of her body, woke a folk memory of his own people and his roots. He came from the land, from a line of men and women who were built on a scale to work it. Big bones, heavy muscles, coarse hands and feet for hard labor, like the slow-moving beasts they drove before the plow. But he had been born with brains; God knew what genetic freak was responsible for putting such an extraordinary intelligence in his peasant-boy head. But he knew it was there from an early age. And he concealed it. He read and studied in secret, fearful of his father's scorn. He got a sound beating when he was caught reading one of his schoolbooks. It had been torn away from him with a curse. There was work to be done outside, while he idled. His mother understood him. She was proud that he could read and was eager to go to the local school, though it meant trudging for miles there and back. She didn't dare stand up to his father, but she encouraged and protected him from his three older brothers when they bullied him. He loved his mother. Gloria reminded him of her. When he hung expensive jewelry on his daughter, gave her a Porsche for her birthday, spoiled her with the world's luxuries, he felt his mother shared in it. Too late for her, for his family. They were all dead. His brothers killed in the East, his parents lost in the blood tide of invasion. Nothing left of his past.

He had made his own future, and he owed nothing to anyone.

"No, darling," he said, "I was just being lazy."

"You shouldn't work so hard," she murmured, leaning against him, one arm around his shoulders. He had a warm, comforting smell, a mixture of aftershave and cigar smoke. When she was a little girl, she used to insist that she would marry him when she grew up. It made him roar with laughter. He used to swing her up in the air and say, "Shall I get rid of Mummy, then?" She always said yes, with great vehemence.

"Who's going to pay the bills if I don't work?"

"Don't tease. I'm being serious. You come in here to sleep because you're tired. You shouldn't have to."

"I come in here to get away from your mother and her bird-brained friends," he retorted. "So many women are so stupid. And men. I listen to them sitting around my dinner table talking cock, and I can't believe it sometimes."

"Why do you let her do it?" his daughter said angrily. "You come home to relax, and she has dinner parties and lunch parties, and there's never any time for you to put your feet up."

"She enjoys it," he explained. "She likes being social. And sometimes it's useful. What did you think of that fellow Leo Derwent? Was he interesting?" He'd watched Gloria talking to the junior minister for trade and industry during dinner. He might enter into Gloria's conspiracy against her mother, but he told his wife whom to include on her guest list, and the rising politician was one of them.

There were murmurs about his addiction to tying up his girlfriends and beating them. Low murmurs, but they'd come to King's ear through Joe, who knew what he called the service industry inside out.

Leo Derwent liked S and M. So King suggested that Joe might make some amenable ladies available, and two of them were among the guests that weekend. One of them had already made a mark with the minister, and just to camouflage the ploy, King told Marilyn to seat him next to Gloria at dinner. And, to whet the appetite, the sultry lady was placed opposite.

"He was banging on and on about the *Sunday Herald*," his daughter said. "He says Western is running a campaign to discredit him because he's against a federal Europe. He was quite paranoid about it; he says they've run through articles criticizing his handling of various issues where he showed bias against Brussels. Now he says they've started some 'Insight'-type feature, and he told me he'd met the woman heading it when he went to the Westerns' house about five years ago." Harold King sat up, moving his daughter's encircling arm away.

"Did he?"

"Yes, he talked about it all through dinner. Ego. Ego—they're all the same."

"Politicians' disease," he remarked. "Big heads and little minds. What did he say about this feature? It's called 'Exposure.' There's been a lot of hype about it in the *Herald*, but they haven't run a story yet."

"Well, he thinks they'll have a go at him."

"He's not that important," King muttered. "He says a woman's heading up this feature—they haven't come out with any names."

"Julia Hamilton—she's one of their stars. He said she was a tough bitch when he met her." Her father got up, heaving himself out of the deep chair.

"Hamilton? She's a news reporter. . . . How the hell would he know that?"

Gloria had a flawless memory. She stored everything she thought would be of interest to her father.

"Because he was having a drink at the house with some political journalist filling in for Warburton. Said he used to be her boyfriend but they'd split up. She'd got this high-powered new job. Creepy said the ex had had a few drinks and was throwing hints about her having a go at some VIP. He's sure it's him!" She laughed at the folly and conceit of the man. Like her father, she had scant respect for human beings in general, and cold contempt for human frailty.

"Julia Hamilton," her father said. "We saw her at Mario's when we had dinner last month. Redhead." His face was set, and he was frowning.

"I remember. She was giving you hate looks. I mentioned it."

"You did," he agreed. "You did. Go back to the party,

darling. Say I've had to take a business call and I'll be with you as soon as I can. Be nice to Leo Derwent. He could be useful to me."

"He was getting stuck into that girl Freda, who came with Ted Ellis. I don't think he'll want to talk to me. I'll try."

Freda was the bait sent down by Joe. A very high-class, educated call girl, who brought a touch of genius to her act of sexual humiliation. The junior minister was hooked. King found himself a cigar and sucked hard on it, bringing the end to a glowing red.

Julia Hamilton. Heading a team of investigative journalists. He knew the *Herald* promotion by heart. *Watch out for "Exposure." Watchdog of the nation.* Joe had found nothing in her flat but scrap paper with some jotted timetable for a flight to Germany. And the contact number for the boyfriend. The ex, who'd talked to Leo Derwent.

It was time he asked him a few questions. He got Joe on his car phone. Joe listened, not interrupting. Then he said, "Yes, don't worry, leave it with me. Is it urgent? I need a few days to set it up. Oh, okay, no problem. How are my girls doing?"

They were handpicked, and they had clear instructions: Aim for the one guy and don't mess with anybody else.

"Freda's taken his fancy," King snapped. "She knows not to fuck him in my house?"

"Jesus, no, she wouldn't do a thing like that—I told her. . . ." Joe sounded shocked at the idea. King liked a varied sex life himself, but his home was sacred. Must be the generation, he thought. And the foreign background. He changed the subject hastily. "I'll meet up with our boyo. I'll try it the easy way first time." King cleared the line.

"Julia Hamilton." He said it out loud. Something was in the wind, and he scented it like an animal. He went out of his library to mix with his guests. He made a show of being loud and self-important, dropping names and puffing on a huge cigar. He played the vulgarian and the power figure with the skill of an actor. He dominated them all.

In his modest sitting room in Nessenberg, the president of the town's Veterans Association was finishing his confidential report on the English visitors and their examination of the Control Commission's 1948 file to his contact in Stuttgart. Munich had a core of pro-Nazis and was under close police surveillance. His contact had been changed to Stuttgart. He went through it, checking everything, and then sealed it. It would go by Express Special Delivery on Monday morning. Stuttgart would route it through from there. He didn't know its final destination, and he didn't permit himself to wonder. He had done his duty to their benefactor. That was enough.

CHAPTER 5

"THERE'S NO DEATH CERTIFICATE. NOBODY called Koenig died in the borough during that year or the following two years. They checked, just to make sure." Julia shook her head. "I don't know what to make of it."

Harris played with his glasses, turning them around so that the lenses caught the light. "Any success with medical records?"

"Not yet. One local practice had no records, everything was cleared out when they rebuilt the surgery— just our luck if she was a patient there. They're working on two other practices that were operating at the time. We know," she went on, "we know she had an accident because there were witnesses. But there's only his word that she died afterward. So what happened to her?"

"Wait for the medical check," he suggested. He sat forward suddenly. "Accident victims go to the local hospital. Get someone over to the Putney Royal and the Hammersmith. They may have chucked out stuff forty years ago, but it's worth a try."

"Thanks, Ben. I'll put someone on it now. And I bought you a present."

"Present? What for?"

"To stop you breaking your glasses," Julia said. "Here, put them in this." It was a dark leather sleeve; he knew by the feel of it that it was expensive.

He fitted his glasses inside and put them in his breast pocket.

"I'm not used to presents. What do I say?"

"Nothing," Julia smiled at him. "Stop looking grumpy because you're embarrassed."

"I'm pleased," he said. "Really. Thanks. I've got to get back to my office. Meet me afterward?"

"We can start at the pub," she suggested. "Then you can take me home and introduce me to your cat."

She met Felix going down in the elevator; they hadn't encountered each other since he'd left the flat. "Hi," he said as she got in. "Nice to see you." He looked cool and friendly, without a hint of awkwardness. Julia felt herself stiffen at the sight of him. "Nice to see you too," she said. "How's it going?"

"It's going well. Matter of fact, I'm off to meet some tout who says he's got inside info on a front-bencher. Something juicy."

Julia said coldly, "You know Warburton doesn't deal in that kind of thing."

"I know—he's a stuffy old fart, that's why. I'm going along to see what this creep's got to offer. I'll have to put him down to expenses."

He laughed, and as the elevator doors opened, he

pushed out ahead, calling over his shoulder, "'Bye, Julia—see you!"

Julia followed slowly, watching him stride down toward the parking lot. There had been no spark left. He had become a stranger, a man she couldn't relate to; a reminder, she admitted, of a period in her life when she'd allowed sexual dependence to sway her judgment.

It wasn't Felix's fault; she was older and should have put an end to the relationship before it deteriorated.

Now a very different man had come into her life. They were drawn closer by work and respect for each other's talents. And making love to Ben was a mutual experience, not a male dominance that satisfied a baser instinct in her nature. Perhaps she'd had a need to submit to Felix because of the imbalance in their ages and their finances. She hadn't considered that before, and it surprised her. Working on the enigma of Harold King, complemented by the acute mind and experience of Ben Harris, she had become more intuitive, more self-aware. She walked to the pub where they usually met after work, and she was looking forward to seeing him. The anticipation made her happy; it was an odd feeling, to be happy because you were about to meet a man who'd only left you a few hours ago. To want to see his pet cat that he brought in off the street. And to spend the night with him and eat breakfast with him in the morning. She pushed her way through the bar, and he was waiting for her.

Felix thought he'd never seen such a sleaze bag in his life. The expensive, trendy clothes didn't deceive him, nor did the phony Irish-American accent.

He took an instant dislike to the man with his smooth talk, and the overchummy manner. "I'm Joe," he had said, introducing himself. "Joe Patrick. Pleased to meet you. What'll you have?"

"Beer," Felix said, looking around. He wasn't familiar with the Soho pub his caller had suggested. It was wall-papered with old boxing posters and photographs of fighters posing with some tubby little jerk he supposed was the publican.

"Ever been here before?" Joe Patrick asked him.

"No," Felix said. He sipped his beer. Joe Patrick had a straight whiskey without ice. "Who put you on to me?" Felix asked him.

"Journalist friend of mine. I was telling him the story, and he said you were the guy to talk to; so I called. I think you'll find it interesting."

"What's it going to cost me?" Felix finished the beer. "My boss doesn't print your kind of information, so it's got to come out of my own pocket."

Like fuck. Joe smiled to himself. He had formed his own judgment of Mr. Felix dickhead Sutton. He'd been the journalist's fancy boy till she threw him out. Bigheaded, macho pig with his brains in his crotch. Looked as if he'd boxed or played rugby, with that broken nose. Joe put his head to one side. "Is that straight? You'd be paying yourself?" Felix nodded. "Well . . . " Joe pretended to hesitate. Then he gave Felix a broad smile, displaying the fine white teeth that had been grafted on to his own stumps. "I'll make a special deal with you. We might be useful to each other. Fifty quid, cash."

"Let's hear the story first."

Joe raised a manicured hand with a big gold ring on the middle finger. "Fifty quid on account and five hundred if you print it. That's fair, isn't it?"

"Fair enough." Felix nodded. He took the hand held out to him in token of a pact agreed between men of their word.

"What's the dirt, then?"

"Over here," Joe suggested, leading the way to a small table. "We can talk here. I'll start with the name."

Felix looked up quickly. A leading member of the Commons, no less. Subscribing to a pedophile mailing service. Videos, porno photographs, some of the children were three and four years old. "Very, very nasty stuff," Joe murmured in mock disapproval. His journalist friend— he was a freelance, and his market was strictly tabloid—he'd heard it from a contact in the Vice Squad. They were watching the man after his name had been found on a list kept by a well-known Dutch supplier. Some of the dirt had been confiscated in the post. Then the word came down. Kill it; he'll be given a private warning, but there's heavy pressure not to show him up, or there'll be repercussions that'll hit the other side on the front benches. The copper thought there might be some money in it if a suitable market could be found.

"If he works for the tabloids," Felix interrupted, "why not go to them? They'd love a Scotland Yard cover-up sex-and-scandal story on a politician."

"They wouldn't touch it," Joe insisted. "Same pressure. It's a powder keg, this one. These pricks are in some very high places. So I thought of you. Your paper's doing 'Exposure,' aren't you? I've read all the advance hype, and it seemed just the sort of thing you'd latch on to. You're not scared off by the heavies. . . . What'd you think?"

Felix said flatly, "'Exposure' wouldn't touch it."

"You sure about that?" The blue eyes focused on him, gutter bright with cunning.

"I know who's in charge of it," Felix retorted. "She wouldn't touch it with a barge pole. And I'm the wrong guy. I cover the political scene. I've nothing to do with this new feature."

"How do you know they wouldn't be interested if you haven't asked?" Joe persisted. "Why don't you give it a buzz and see what she says. It's a lady, is it?" He made the noun sound like a sneer.

"A very clever lady," Felix snapped. "She's already got someone in her sights, and it's a much bigger fish than some dirty old pervert."

"Oh? You sure about that?" Felix was irritated by the repeated question. "'Course I'm bloody sure. I'm her boyfriend, for Christ's sake!"

Joe noted the present tense. Pride still touchy. . . .

"I've got a bloody good idea who it is, too," Felix insisted.

"You could be wrong," Joe mused. "The kid fancier's in line for a job at the next reshuffle. . . ." He let the sentence die.

"I told you, it's not a politician! She's going to do some exposé on the Honors List. Shits like Harold King getting a peerage. If that crook gets a seat in the Lords, I'll give up on this lousy country. Here, I brought some cash with me. Fifty quid, but there won't be any more. No story for us. Sorry."

Joe took the packet of notes. "Pity. Next time maybe. I'll keep you in mind."

"Yeah," Felix said, "do that. Thanks for the beer."

He elbowed his way out. Joe, out of a lifetime's habit, counted the tenners and then put them in his inside pocket. He'd got the information like squeezing milk out of a full tit. The boss was right. Joe didn't know how he knew things before they happened, but it wasn't the first time. He was right. This cow Hamilton was out to make trouble for him.

The contact in Stuttgart was not a veteran. He had been ten when the war ended, and luckily for him his family were still together, their home intact. He owned a small engineering business, which was thriving.

His father had been invalided out of the German army

after the defeat of France. A civilian sniper's bullet had left him in a wheelchair.

He had brought up his three children to believe that only treachery from within had deprived Germany of victory. His eldest son left the university with an engineering degree and a secret commitment to the outlawed neo-Nazi movement. He was a fund-raiser and supporter of a political renaissance that was in the open now, encouraged by resentment of the influx of Turkish migrant workers, busy organizing violent opposition to the thousands of refugees from Romania and the Balkans. Jobs were short and times were hard for Germans after the euphoria of unification. Restructuring the shattered economy left by the Communists was crippling, despite the strength of the mark and the industry of the people. Resentments grew, and the movement fed on such feelings.

The engineer from Stuttgart was one of a chain of contacts throughout Germany, with links in France, Italy, and Spain. Fascism was not dead, and it had many sympathizers prepared to help its cause.

One of those causes was the protection of ex-German soldiers who had found a haven abroad after defeat. The report had come in from Nessenberg.

He read through it, bitter at the interference from the old enemy, still hunting patriots after forty years.

He knew where to send it, but, like for the shopkeeper in Nessenberg its ultimate destination was unknown to him, except that it was tied to generous donations to the movement from abroad. The report was packaged and sent off by airmail to an address in Dublin.

It arrived by special messenger at King's house in Mayfair. It was marked PRIVATE, PERSONAL, AND CONFIDENTIAL. No one but King was allowed to open anything labeled in that way.

Gloria put it in his desk drawer in the study. It would

have to wait till her father got back from his latest trip to New York.

He talked his plans over with her; she understood the complexity of his financial dealings, and she was a good sounding board. Sometimes her sharp instincts had an idea to contribute. She treasured that intimacy, not least because her mother had always been excluded. She was too stupid, Gloria thought triumphantly. And one day she knew Daddy would take her on to the board of his conglomerates and she'd be like his son. She had wanted to be a boy since puberty; rejecting the female image in favor of father imitation, Gloria didn't like men. At school she discovered the pleasures of sexual activity with other girls. She was not very motivated; the lesbian affairs were short-lived and very discreet. Her father didn't know about them because she chose her lovers from her circle of friends. They were usually married and dissatisfied.

She'd gone up to Oxford, where she got a two/one in economics and modern languages and then spent two years at the Harvard Business School, where she graduated with Honors. Everything was geared to her succeeding her father; she wasn't brilliant, but she was intuitive and she worked relentlessly to succeed. For five years she had been investment manager in the London office of a firm of merchant bankers in American ownership. She was disappointed he hadn't taken her to New York with him. Lately they had started making business trips together. This time he had refused her, explaining that it meant a series of confidential meetings with bankers and money brokers where she couldn't be present. She'd be bored out of her mind with nothing to do all day. Unlike her mother, Gloria wasn't interested in shopping.

"I'm never bored with you," she wheedled, but she couldn't move him.

"You would be this time, sweetheart. I'll bring you something special back. Tiffany's? How about that?"

"I'd rather come," she persisted. "I'll miss you. Two whole weeks. Call me, won't you?"

"I always do," he had protested. He would bring her something spectacular from Tiffany's, and an equally expensive present for his wife, just to keep both women at each other's throats. He was pleased with Marilyn at the moment. She was looking more beautiful as a result of some discreet surgery, and she was getting a lot of coverage in the social columns. It was all crap, but it was good groundwork for the coveted peerage. He flew by Concorde to New York. It was a heavy schedule. He was going to get the crucial financial structuring he needed to launch his attack on William Western.

It took the research team four days to track down the records, but they found them in the basement of Hammersmith Hospital. In April 1950 a Mrs. Phyllis Koenig had been admitted with severe head injuries following a fall. She was in a coma. The case notes said she had been transferred to a private nursing home after regaining consciousness and severely limited speech and movement. The impairment was permanent and the prognosis poor, as she had a blood clot on the brain that was impeding the blood supply. The nursing home had long closed but it was in the Sussex area, near Midhurst.

They began another search for the death certificate, going forward for five years from the time of the accident, and found it in 1954. The unfortunate woman had lived until then, little more than a vegetable if the hospital prognosis was correct, and had died in the nursing home from a cerebral hemorrhage.

Julia went over the details and phoned Ben. She couldn't

keep the excitement out of her voice. "We're getting some-where," she told him. "Phyllis Koenig didn't die in 1950. She was brain-damaged and she ended up in a nursing home in Sussex. She died there four years later."

"Why Sussex?" Ben said. "Was King keeping her hidden?"

"Looks like it. We'll have a copy of a will by this after-noon. You know, I really think we're on the right track!"

"It's about time," he said. "Take my advice J, don't wind up the boss till you've got something more. He'll only lean on you."

"Like he did before," she agreed. "I haven't forgotten the lesson, teacher. Same place tonight—what time?"

The pub around the corner from their office building was their staging post. They met there, had a drink, and then went home, sometimes to her flat, sometimes to Ben's. Julia had made great friends with the cat. It liked sit-ting on her knee, digging claws into her skirt, and purring.

Their affair was common knowledge now; the clientele at the pub were mostly *Herald* men and women, and they were used to seeing Ben Harris and Julia Hamilton closeted in a corner. Nobody bothered to comment anymore. They were an item, like other couples working on the newspaper.

Ben said, "Eight-thirty," and she promised to call if she learned anything significant from the will.

As soon as he saw her, he quickened; he knew that expression and what it meant. Bright eyes, a slight color, and an air of expectancy. He knew her moods and her foibles and he couldn't fault anything. He sat beside her. She'd ordered him a whiskey.

"Come on, what've you got?"

She opened her bag. "This," she said. It was a photo-copy of the last will and testament of Phyllis Koenig, née Lowe. Dated 29 March 1950. Ben read it and said "Christ" under his breath at one point, and continued reading to the end. Then he looked up.

"She cut him out," he said. "She left everything to her niece. The house in Fulham, the stocks, shares, everything. Over a hundred and fifty thousand pounds of estate. That was a fortune in the fifties!"

"We've traced the niece," Julia said. "She lives in Sussex; that must be why Phyllis was in that nursing home. I talked to her on the phone this afternoon, and she's agreed to see me tomorrow morning. Ben, I know we're on to something now. All the dead ends, all the damned blind alleys, but at last we're seeing light!"

Ben said, "Phyllis must have suspected him when she made that will. She knew she'd made a bloody big mistake by then. And a couple of weeks later she has a fall that nearly kills her. My guess is she probably told King she'd looked after him, just to keep him sweet. So he decided to collect before she changed her mind."

"We'd never prove it," Julia said.

"No, but it's got his stamp on it. Nobody proved who murdered Hayman in the Bahamas or drove Lewis off the road. But I know King was behind it."

On the way back to her flat Ben said suddenly, "We had a bargain, remember?"

"Now, Ben, you're not going to start that—"

"I'm just reminding you, that's all. When I think we're getting too close, you back off this thing."

"*When* we get close," she agreed. "But we're not close enough yet."

Next morning Julia drove to Midhurst. The address was just outside the charming town, with its narrow streets and antique shops. It was a mid-Victorian house just off the road. Her appointment was for eleven o'clock, and she was ten minutes early.

When she rang the bell, it was opened by a small, plump

woman in her sixties. She had bright blue eyes and short, crisp gray hair.

"Mrs. Adams?"

"Miss Hamilton? Come in. You're very punctual—no trouble with traffic? Midhurst can be a nightmare with all these awful trucks blocking up the roads. I've got some coffee ready for us."

She was brisk and confident in manner. Very on the ball, as Julia had expected. The sitting room was pleasant, comfortable, and chintzy. A black Labrador lay in front of the fire, which was lit; it raised its head briefly and then went back to sleep.

"Poor old Daisy," she said. "She's fifteen now, and nearly blind. Can't bear to think of losing her. Do sit down. Milk and sugar?"

"Just milk, please," Julia answered.

"Now," Jean Adams said, "before I tell you about my aunt, I'd like to ask you exactly what kind of feature on that dreadful man you've got in mind."

"I'm not sure," Julia admitted. "I'm trying to find out the truth about him. He's built up a legend and backed it with every lie under the sun. So he must have something to hide, Mrs. Adams, and I want to find out what it is. All that nonsense about your aunt dying of cancer—I suppose you read that biography."

"I did," she said. "Pack of lies. As I expected."

Julia said quietly, "But you did nothing to disprove it?"

"No." The answer was sharp. "To what end, Miss Hamilton? To show up my poor aunt as a woman who took to drink because she'd fallen victim to a wicked man young enough to be her son? That she died brain-damaged and bedridden? No, thank you. And anyway he was too powerful, too rich. I couldn't have fought him. He'd have dragged us through the courts and ruined us before I got a proper hearing. I let Aunt Phyl rest in peace. I still feel the same. That's why I want to know what you're planning to do before I tell you anything."

"I hope to expose Harold King for what I believe he really is. His relationship with your aunt is the tip of an iceberg. It only confirms what a lot of people suspect about him but can't prove: that he's very bad news and he's becoming more and more powerful. You called him wicked, didn't you?"

"Oh, he was," Jean Adams agreed. "Poor Aunt Phyl knew it. That's what destroyed her. She told me he was a war criminal. More coffee?"

The pieces were fitting in, one by one.

"Aunt Phyl was rather a rebel; I knew that even when I was a child. Unconventional—wouldn't marry and settle down. And she was well-off too. She lived—well, I suppose it was a raffish life in those days—wouldn't raise an eyebrow now. She liked the men, and they liked her. She was terribly smart and good-looking. Great fun. She joined the Red Cross in the war, worked in London all through the bombing and the V-ones and those frightful rockets. Then she simply couldn't settle down. It was too dull, she said, after all the excitement. So she joined UNRRA and went off to Europe to work with the refugees and DPs, displaced persons. You know, Miss Hamilton, it changed her."

"I'm not surprised," Julia said. "It must have been horrific."

"Yes, it was. So much suffering, such terrible devastation. She wrote long letters describing it. She was a very good correspondent, and we'd always been close. I admired her; I thought she was so dashing and exciting." Jean Adams gave a rueful smile. "I wished I'd been able to join in the war and do something useful, but I was just too young.

Aunt Phyl was really affected by what she saw in those camps. She threw her heart into working for the people and trying to help. She came back to England in 1947 and took me out to lunch in London. I was working there as a secretary, and I'd just got engaged to Bob, my husband. I remember her saying, 'I feel I'm doing something worthwhile for the first time in my life, Jean. Not just having fun. I'm helping people who've lost everything—families, homes, hope—' Then she laughed at herself, embarrassed, I suppose. 'If I'm not careful, I'll be a reformed character, and that won't do.' She was a tremendous person. Have you ever hated anybody?"

"No, no. I don't think so."

"You're lucky. It's a terrible feeling. I've hated Hans Koenig for forty years because of what he did to my aunt. I never think of him as Harold King. She wrote to me about him. I was getting married and she couldn't get time off for the wedding. She told me she'd found this wonderful young man, so sensitive and intelligent—quite alone, all his family lost, he'd been a slave on a farm in East Germany, and the traumas had marked him for life. He didn't even know his real name. And then the letters changed." She looked away from Julia, into some grim memory of her own.

"She wrote she was in love," Jean Adams said. "Really in love for the first time in her life. The age difference didn't matter; he needed her so much and he was so grateful and loving—they were so happy together. I remember reading it and thinking, 'Good God, this isn't Aunt Phyl— it reads like a bad novelette.' But I was too wrapped up in my own wedding to worry about it. My mother didn't take any notice. 'Oh, it's just one of Phyl's fancies. She'll get bored with him, like all the others.' I think Mother was a bit jealous of her; she wasn't the one with the looks and personality. Then my aunt came back to England and asked us to Fulham to meet him. They were married. I don't know what I expected. Some romantic Slav with soulful eyes, I suppose. But he wasn't like that. He was arrogant. Yes, arrogant and smug. Very physical. I couldn't help seeing what she found attractive in him. And she was besotted, behaving like a silly girl half her age. He didn't like me or Bob, and it was mutual. Bob said to me afterward, 'I think your poor aunt's in for trouble.' I thought so too. I only saw her a few times after that, and she'd gone rapidly downhill. She'd always liked a drink, but it was never a problem. She was actually tight at lunchtime when she came down here one Sunday. Bringing him with her of course. There was a horrible atmosphere. I'll never forget it. He was so rude to her, so hostile. She looked miserable." She paused. Julia sensed that even after all these years it distressed her.

"When did you see her again?" she asked.

"About ten days before her accident. She rang me up and asked me to come to London. She wanted to talk to me urgently. I thought she sounded very strange. We had lunch together, and she told me this extraordinary story." She paused, and then went on.

"Koenig," she said, clearing her throat slightly, "Koenig never drank. Nothing. Not even beer. He hated Aunt Phyl drinking anything, even in the very early days when she took him in to live with her in Germany. She did tell me that, and said it was rather sweet, but she didn't see why she couldn't have a gin and tonic at the end of a long day. . . . Of course, as she got more and more miserable and he was nastier to her, bullying her for money, she took to the bottle in a big way.

"It drove him mad apparently. He used to hit her sometimes—never in the face where it showed, but on the body. He'd punched her black and blue several times. Then one night he'd been out for a walk—she never knew where he went, but he'd disappear for hours at a time—he came back, and she was tight. And then he did something extraordinary, quite out of character. He poured himself a big gin. She couldn't believe it. He stood over her, and he said, 'Now, you drunken old cow, I'll show you what you are. I'm going to drool and stagger and lie in the bed snoring and stinking of gin like you do. I'm going to be too drunk to fuck you, you old bag, and you won't like that.' Apparently it was the most dreadful scene; she began to cry in the restaurant when she was telling me, word for word. The insults, so personal, so terribly cruel. And he did it. He got blind drunk that night. She said she was so frightened, she sobered up completely. He was like a madman. And he told her the truth about himself.

"He wasn't Polish or a refugee. He'd been in the German army and fought in the Western Desert. He told her he'd murdered a group of British prisoners of war. He boasted he'd shot them down in cold blood after they'd surrendered!"

Julia drew in her breath. "He said that! My God—he admitted murder?"

"Yes," Jean Adams insisted. "That's what she told me. He boasted of it. He thought he'd killed them all, but one of them survived. He found that out afterward. She said he yelled at her—'Bad shooting.' He was afraid he'd be charged with war crimes after the war. So he threw away his uniform, joined the refugees, and invented the whole story. My aunt was trembling. I remember very well. I did say to her he might have been making it up if he was so drunk and out of control . . . but she wouldn't hear of it." She paused for a moment. Then she said in a low voice, "She also told me he raped her that night."

Julia didn't say anything. She waited until Jean Adams spoke again.

"The next morning he denied it all of course. He said

alcohol drove him crazy, made him imagine things. He begged her to forgive him. She said he was crying." She looked at Julia. "Poor thing, she said she wanted to believe him, she really did. But she couldn't. She looked completely broken. I can see her now, sitting there, saying she wished she was dead. "He's not going to get my money," she said. "I'm seeing my solicitor this afternoon, he's drawn up a new will." Ten days later she had the accident. But a copy of the will had come to me in the post. I was amazed to see she'd left me everything. She'd given me the means of getting rid of him. Bob and I confronted him when she had to leave the hospital. Her solicitor backed us up. We told him we were applying for guardianship and we showed him the copy of her will. He'd get five hundred pounds from us if he cleared out of the house and undertook never to see her or contact us again. He didn't argue. He just shrugged. 'I can't fight you'—that's what he said. 'I'm only a poor foreigner.' He signed a pledge and Bob gave him the money. He said he'd go back to Germany. We believed him. We sold the house and moved my aunt down to Sussex. We took care of her till she died."

She got up, putting the coffee cups on the tray. They didn't speak for a while. At the door Jean Adams said, "Some years afterward Harold King was being written up and photographed, and we realized he was the same man. It was too late then. He was a millionaire and a public figure. We had a family and a lot to lose. My husband was a cautious man. He said it was best left alone. I agreed with him because of my aunt. But I've regretted it over the years. I'll just put these things in the kitchen." Julia followed her out.

A young Labrador, black like the old bitch by the fireside, bounded up to meet them. "Daisy's granddaughter," she explained, bidding the puppy firmly to get down. "Bob died two years ago, and I just can't bear to be without one of this family. My son has the daughter, and they gave me Poppit for Christmas. She's a handful to train, but she's great fun. I wish I could offer you lunch, but I'm going out with a friend. We belong to a bridge club, and we always treat ourselves to lunch first. She's a widow too."

"Thanks anyway, Mrs. Adams, but I've got to get back to my office. Would you be prepared to sign an affidavit, setting down exactly what you've told me?"

Jean Adams hesitated. "I'll have to speak to my solicitor first," she said. "I'll let you know what he says."

"Do you have the original pledge King gave you in exchange for the five hundred pounds?"

"The firm would have it; Bob never kept documents at home in case of a fire or a burglary. I'm sure it's still there somewhere."

A cautious man, as she said. She came to the door with Julia.

"What a smart car," she remarked. "Young women have so many opportunities these days."

"I can't thank you enough," Julia said quietly. She held out her hand, and the older woman took it in a firm grasp. "I'm so very sorry about what happened to your aunt. I hope it hasn't upset you too much—talking about it."

"It just makes me angry," Jean Adams answered. "I really would like to see that swine get his just desserts. I hope you do it!"

"I'll do my very best, I promise you. Let me know what your solicitor says."

"I will. Good-bye." She turned and closed the door, and Julia went down the short path to the road and into her car. She felt oppressed, as if the other woman had laid some burden on her. The burden of evil that had gone unpunished. It was a strange, outmoded phrase, dredged up from somewhere in her memory, but it was very apt.

Whatever she had promised Ben Harris, she insisted, she wasn't backing out of this one.

There was nothing Joe could do till the boss got back from America. He had the information for him, and there didn't seem to be any urgency. The *Herald* feature hadn't come out with anything yet. It was still a case of "Watch this space." He took himself and one of his black girls to the races in France. He had plenty of money, they stayed in good hotels, ate well, and he had a run of good luck with the horses. He felt generous and he gave her some spending money. He was sorry he hadn't brought the other girl; he liked threesomes, but it might have been awkward, where they were staying. He met up with some Irish who were over for the meeting, and they had a great time. He picked up the tabs and played the big man, and kept the girl out of sight. He knew his countrymen. They were good at downing the jars, but they were prudes at heart.

When he came back, he put a call through to King's personal secretary. Face like a copper's boot and no tits. King never mixed business with pleasure. She had some surprising news for him.

"Mr. King flew back two days ago," she said. "He's been trying to contact you, Mr. Patrick."

Joe swore softly. "He wasn't expected till the end of the week," he said. "Anything wrong?"

"Not that I know of." The voice was cool. She didn't like Joe Patrick. She thought he was common and cheeky. Once he'd tried to chat her up. She knew he was mocking her. "You'd better call him. He's in his car on the way to lunch at BZW."

Joe was scared. He hesitated, thinking how best to explain his absence without leaving a contact number. That was his mistake. King wanted him and couldn't find him. He wouldn't like that. He said "Shit" several times and then nerved himself to dial the car phone.

King always called his home when he was away. He was in a good mood, because the negotiations with Field Bank were going well, and the funding for a frontal assault on Western International looked viable without too big a borrowing commitment. It was early days, but his confidence was soaring. He smelled blood, and his instincts had never failed him. He spoke to his wife first; she was nearest when the telephone rang. She chattered about her committee meeting for the East London hospices and how they had asked the Princess of Wales's office to suggest a date for a big charity function.

The Princess, always eager to help the suffering, proposed an earlier date than they hoped, and her presence would ensure substantial funds.

King let her run on—he was in a good mood—and then cut in and asked if Gloria was there. Gloria was on her way out to dinner, but, hearing her father was on the line, hurried back. She didn't care if she was late.

"How's my girl?"

"Missing you, Daddy. How's it going?"

"It's going fine. Hard bargaining, but I'm getting there. Anything I should know?"

Gloria remembered the special delivery. "There's a package for you. It came last week."

"Oh—what kind of package?"

"It looks like documents," Gloria answered. "It's marked private, personal, and confidential. I put it in your desk. Do you want me to send it over? Shall I open it for you?"

"No—no!" The change of tone alarmed her. He was shouting at her. "It's been there since last week? For

Christ's sake, you stupid little . . ." Gloria gasped as he spat the filthy epithet at her. "Why didn't you call me at once?"

"Daddy, I didn't know . . ." Tears were welling up.

"You get it over here by DHL. Tonight, so I have it in the morning—you do it, you hear me?"

"Yes." She was crying now. "Yes, I'll do it right away. Oh, Daddy, I'm so sorry. It wasn't my fault. . . ." But the line was dead.

Her mother had left the room when she took the phone. She couldn't bear the cozy telephone calls between father and daughter. Now she came back and saw Gloria in tears.

She smiled. "What's the matter, darling? Lovers' quarrel?"

Gloria swung on her. Hatred flared up openly between them when King was safely absent. "Shut up! Please, shut up!"

Marilyn King kept that maddening little smile on her face. Her daughter looked so ugly when she cried. Her skin was blotched and she blundered about like a wounded animal, making her way to the door.

"You'll be late for dinner!" her mother called out.

"I'm not going to fucking dinner!" Gloria shouted, and slammed the door of King's study behind her. She found the package, the cause of that dreadful burst of anger and abuse. It wasn't her fault. Anything marked private was never opened, that's all she knew. It was just a rule. She couldn't even remember seeing anything marked up like that before. She started writing out a label and began telephoning.

What could be in it, to make him erupt like that? Something to do with his business in New York. The delay must have compromised him in some way. But how could she know? She wailed aloud as she made the arrangements, at exorbitant cost, to get it on the next plane by special courier to New York and then to his hotel.

It reached Harold King just before a working breakfast with the finance director and deputy chairman of Field Bank.

Harold King didn't open it. He knew where it came from, and he couldn't risk losing his concentration by looking at the contents before an important meeting. It had waited a week, bearing its warning message. It would have to wait another two hours.

The meeting was long and difficult. His American financiers wanted more collateral than he had to offer, and he had failed to convince them that it wasn't necessary. No deal had been in sight when they parted with a further meeting scheduled for the next morning. He was short by too many millions to launch his bid successfully. Unless he could come up with guarantees against the money he needed to back his bid, Field Bank was not prepared to bankroll him.

King kept his nerve. He blustered, cajoled, joked, and tried to overbear, but it didn't work. Then he switched roles. He became quietly confident. He had, he said as they were leaving, ample resources that he could call upon if they insisted, but he maintained they were not necessary. He would discuss it further with them in the morning.

The resources were ample, but they were not his to pledge.

They consisted of the pension fund of his thousands of employees in all corporate businesses throughout England and Canada.

When he shut the door on them, he was calm. Crises had this effect on him. He had seen his solution, and he was weighing up the risks. If he was successful, the money would never be called in and he would never be found out. He had gambled before and won. He would win this, the biggest gamble of his business career.

Then he opened the package and started to read the

report. The meeting took place the next morning. He was smiling and almost cherubic with good humor. He had thought the position over, and although he deplored the lack of confidence evident in their attitude, he understood the reasoning behind it. He was a man of responsibility himself, and he appreciated the bank's commitment to its investors. He would therefore pledge the extra money from his personal resources. Details would be made available to them when the agreement was in a draft stage. He concluded the meeting with handshakes and warm expressions of goodwill all around. He canceled the other meetings. They could take place later.

More urgent business needed his attention.

He packed up and flew home to England almost a week ahead of schedule.

King worked on the flight. He had sent his assistant and his two secretaries on a later flight so they could clear up and reschedule meetings with other financial institutions for a month's time. He had promised Field Bank, but he wasn't going to deliver till he'd exhausted one or two other possibilities. Where the moral tone wasn't quite so high. He took his paperwork with him and settled down in First Class, angrily waving away the proffered champagne. But throughout the flight the issues blurred. The report written in German overlaid the columns of figures and financial predictions. He was after Western, but Western was after him. Ben Harris and Julia Hamilton had taken up the old trail in Nessenberg, so long gone cold, thanks to his friends and connections. And the few words spoken to the girl clerk in the Bauhaus as they left the dusty old files in their dusty basement room . . . those words shrilled in his head like a warning siren.

Thank you. We found some useful information.

What information? What had they found that hadn't been excised from the records? King locked his papers away in his briefcase and pulled an eyeshade over his eyes. He wasn't sleeping, but blackness helped him concentrate. Something had prompted Western's clever news hound to say that. Perhaps it was the woman who had spotted something he had missed. "A fresh eye," he muttered. She'd retraced Harris's path and deviated from it in some way. They'd left the Nessenberghof and gone to Munich.

Why Munich? The proprietor of the hotel had answered his contact's questions in all innocence, even showing him the hotel register confirming the names. And added the information that they were going to Munich and had booked into the Bernerhof. The grandest hotel in the city.

Munich. It tormented him. They'd found something that sent them to Munich. He pulled off the eyeshade and reached for the report again.

So painstakingly assembled, every spoken word, however trivial, had been noted down. Thank God for Teutonic efficiency and attention to detail.

Before checking out and going off to indulge themselves—it must be indulgence to stay at the Bernerhof—the couple had asked about the best way to get to Hintzbach. A funny choice, it struck her, there was nothing of interest there for English tourists. But they set off, and left the Nessenberghof afterward. They didn't seem to be lovers. They had separate rooms. No, King thought savagely, they weren't lovers, they were journalists on an assignment. And Harold King, alias Hans Koenig, was that assignment. It all tied in. The schedule of flights to Germany written on a scrap of paper, which Joe Patrick's break-in had discovered, and now this. Western had been stopped in his tracks following the same line ten years ago. Now it was reopened.

He landed at Heathrow and drove straight home. He didn't wake his wife or look for Gloria. He went to his study and dialed Joe Patrick's number. He'd given the bastard a job to do and heard nothing from him. He wanted answers. He didn't get them that night, or for the following two days.

Nobody knew where Joe Patrick had gone. He had left no contact number. All King needed was confirmation of the evidence from Germany. He had looked to the Irishman to prove it. Then he could decide what to do.

The old lever on Western wouldn't work a second time. A drastic solution might be needed. A permanent solution.

Joe Patrick knew how to take a bawling out. He didn't try to excuse himself while King was in full flow. He shrank into himself as if the furious invective were a rain of blows.

He'd seen the boss lose his temper before. There was no stemming it. You just had to wait till it blew itself out like a hurricane. He marveled at the scope of insults; King might have a foreign accent, but he had native vocabulary when it came to swearing. Joe had no pride or resentment; he had the good henchman's mentality. He'd fouled up by not being in reach when he was needed. At last, when King stopped abusing him, he ventured to speak. He knew better than to make excuses.

"I'm sorry. I won't fuck up like that again."

"You do," King exploded for the last time, "and you're fired!" His tone lowered. He spoke normally. "Did you get hold of Hamilton's boyfriend?"

"Yeah, no problem. I needled him a bit, and he spilled. He's a dickhead. Hamilton's the boss of 'Exposure,' the *Herald*'s super snoop, checking on you. He thinks it's tied up with the Honors List. I don't think he knows any more."

"'Exposure,'" King repeated. "That adds up. They say

it will launch its first feature in November." He was almost talking to himself. Then he looked up sharply. He'd chewed the balls off Joe. Most human beings responded to being kicked, but that type needed assault and battery from time to time, to stop them getting lazy.

He said, "I want her followed. And Harris. I want to know everything they do, where they go, who they see. I want to know when they crap! Understand me? Reports come to you on a daily basis, and you pass them to me the same day. Take my advice, Joseph"—he said the full name with heavy emphasis—"don't go to the races while this is on!"

He gave him a cold glare.

"Get out of here."

"She won't sign an affidavit," Julia said.

"Did you call her back?" Ben asked.

She shook her head. "No. I'll have to go and see her again. And this time I want you to come with me. She might respond better to a man. But she's quite a determined lady, and she's not going to change her mind in a hurry."

Ben slipped an arm around her. They were in Julia's flat; she was wondering whether she could persuade him to move in permanently.

"Listen, you tracked her down, you've opened up the real can of worms on that bastard. What we want to follow up is the war-crime angle. If we can prove that—we'll get him! I'll go and see her alone if you like. We don't want to get heavy with a widow."

"No," she agreed, "you're right. If Jean Adams thinks we're trying to push her, she'll dig in, and nothing will shift her. I know the type. You go, Ben. It's her solicitor's advice. He's too scared to let her sign an affidavit in case King slaps a load of writs on her. It makes me furious!"

"Which he would," Ben countered, "if he knew. Come

on, calm down." He smiled, and said gently, "Fiery lady, aren't you?"

And then, unpremeditated, he said it for the first time. "Maybe that's why I love you." Before she could say anything, he leaned over and kissed her. It was a long kiss, tender and then passionate. He let her go and said, "I mean it, I love you. I hope it doesn't spoil anything."

Julia touched his lips with the tips of her fingers. "I never thought you'd say it," she whispered, and then kissed him in return.

As she felt his hands moving on her breasts, she withdrew a little.

"Don't love me," she said. "Not yet. Talk to me. Let me talk to you. That's what I love about you, Ben. There's so much more to us than just sex."

"Like what?" he murmured, still holding her, but now his hands were still.

"Like sharing things, talking them over. Our work, our stupid jokes—I even love your cat!" She laughed at herself. "Why don't you bring Pussy to live here. I think she'd like it."

"I think she would too," he said. "But not yet, my darling. I caught you at the end of a relationship. I want to be sure you're ready for a real one with me. No rebounds, no second thoughts till you've had time to know me and make up your mind. There's the age gap too."

"It's the right way around this time," she insisted. "You're your own man, Ben. There's no competition between us. You said it early on; we make a very good team."

"Then let's keep it that way for now," he suggested. "Let's stay lovers and colleagues and friends till we see how it works out. And if it does"—he looked at her—"I'll want you to move in with me."

· · ·

Jean Adams put the telephone down. She stood beside it, biting at her lower lip. "Don't touch it," her solicitor had begged. He was a family friend of many years, and his alarm had communicated itself to her. "Don't get involved with the press, my dear Jean, they'll promise anything. And then let you down without a moment's hesitation. If you sign an affidavit, they'll use it. You'll be dragged into their campaign against Harold King, and God knows where that would end for you." He'd been sympathetic but adamant. He owed it to Bob to protect her, as Bob would have done if he'd been alive. He'd told her to forget the past a long time ago, and that advice held good today. More than ever.

Let the lady journalist do her own dirty work. She had the might of William Western to fight her battles. Jean had nobody. He went farther. He found the pledge signed by King in return for money in the office safe, among Bob Adams's papers, and suggested that he destroy it. "Tell them what you've done," he said. "Better still, if they try to pressure you, call me in on it. I'll get rid of them."

Jean Adams had agreed, and telephoned Julia with her decision. The call she had just taken was from a man, a colleague of Julia Hamilton's. He sounded pleasant enough, very reasonable. Could he come and see her just once, just to fill in some more details? He accepted her decision not to sign anything, and sounded as if he meant what he said, but he would really appreciate a meeting. Jean had said rather sharply, "With my solicitor present, Mr. Harris?" And he had said, "Of course. All the better." So she found herself agreeing to an appointment. She sighed. Perhaps she'd been foolish to let him talk her into it. Certainly their old friend would think so. But then, it was up to her, wasn't it? She had a mind of her own, after all. She wasn't going to look like a silly, vacillating old woman and ring this man Harris up and say she'd changed her mind again. Let him come down. It might be very interesting. She believed in being decisive. Decision made, why waste time? She dialed the solicitor's office and left a firm message with his secretary.

She was seeing a journalist from the *Sunday Herald* on Wednesday afternoon at two-thirty at her house and she would like him to be there. Then she went out into her garden to tackle the rosebushes.

Joe Patrick didn't deal with sleaze when the client was Harold King. You couldn't rely on the small fry, the ones that were just legal. Only just. He employed the most reputable firm of private detectives in the country, with branches in all the major cities. They had wide-ranging facilities, from business and industrial surveillance to simple domestic.

They charged top rates, but they were absolutely reliable and honest. No operatives of theirs had ever tried to use his information for their own advantage. A twenty-four-hour watch was mounted on Julia Hamilton and Ben Harris. Ben was followed when he drove down to Midhurst to see Jean Adams.

Julia had described her very well, he thought, shaking hands and accepting an offer of a cup of coffee. An independent, outspoken lady, the type that used to be called the backbone of England, before the national spine began to crumble. . . . He put the cynicism away. He didn't think like that so much now. Julia had made him optimistic.

The bottle was half full instead of half empty. She was always slipping into his mind when they were apart.

The solicitor was there. He was tall, with spectacles and untidy, tweedy clothes. But no fool. The eyes were wary.

"Now," Jean Adams said briskly, "I presume you've come to try to change my mind, Mr. Harris."

Ben said quietly, "No, Mrs. Adams. I wouldn't presume such a thing. I only want to fill in the details a little more and to ask you one or two questions, which might help us. Without involving you." He glanced at the solicitor as he said it. He got no response. The old boy was deeply suspicious. He switched back to Jean Adams.

"I'd like to say we understand your decision and we sympathize with it. King has managed to frighten and bully his way out of trouble with a lot of people. Important people with resources. That's why we undertake not to use the affidavit if you decided to sign it—"

"In which case," the solicitor interrupted, "why ask for it if you wouldn't use it? It doesn't seem much point."

Ben had anticipated that question. "Documents can be shown to members of your profession, sir, in confidence. It can influence their judgment and the advice they give their clients. That was the only contingency we had in mind. And the affidavit would be lodged with you, naturally. Mrs. Adams could withdraw it or refuse to produce it if she wished."

Jean spoke up quickly. "You didn't tell me that, Dick. That sounds quite reasonable."

"It sounds very reasonable," he answered, "except that a court can order you to produce evidence once its existence is established. Mr. Harris, I've advised Jean not to get involved with your newspaper investigation of Harold King. I'm here to make certain you don't persuade her otherwise." He gave Ben a look of frank dislike.

Ben hesitated; he wasn't getting anywhere. He didn't want to play his only ace so quickly, but he hadn't any choice.

"Mrs. Adams," he said, "I don't like to say this, but did it occur to you that King might have tried to murder your aunt?"

"Oh, come on—I must protest!"

Ben ignored the solicitor's interruption. He was watching Jean Adams. Her face had flushed, and then the color drained, leaving her very white.

"No," she said. "Please, Dick, be quiet for a minute." One hand rose to silence her adviser. "No, it certainly didn't. It was an accident. She was blind drunk, according to the hospital, when the ambulance brought her in. Good heavens." She pushed back a wisp of hair. "Good heavens," she said again.

"You couldn't have proved anything even if she had died," Ben went on. "Her drinking was his alibi. But just think about it. He'd lost his head and told her the truth about himself. He was in her hands. I'll go farther. I started looking into Harold King ten years ago. I am convinced that the murder of a business opponent in the Caribbean and the so-called fatal accident of another business opponent in this country were orchestrated by him to protect him from a takeover. Your aunt told you he'd admitted murdering unarmed British prisoners. He ill-treated your aunt. He hated her. Do you really think he would have risked being exposed? Look at the timing—ten days after she saw you, she had a near-fatal fall. King wouldn't stop at murder. I'll tell you what I want, Mrs. Adams. I don't want to drag your family through the mud. I don't want to cause you any worry or distress. I want to find out what happened to those prisoners in the Western Desert. That's what I want to hang on Harold King. And you are the only person alive who knows he admitted it." He stood up. Neither of them said anything. He saw the solicitor move close to her chair. She looked pale and very old.

"Thanks for seeing me," Ben said. "I'm sorry if I've given you a shock. I'll see myself out."

He was in the hall when the solicitor caught up with him. "What you've done is disgraceful," he said. "You've no proof, and even if it was true—nothing can be done about it!"

"Please, Dick," Jean Adams came out, "you mustn't abuse Mr. Harris." She came up and opened the front door for him. "I'm going to think about it," she said. Ben Harris took her hand. It was trembling slightly. "I owe it to my aunt if he really did that. Aunt Phyl believed him about the prisoners. I'll be in touch, Mr. Harris. Good-bye."

Ben walked down the short path, past the rosebushes, already trimmed back before their winter pruning, and the watcher in the dark blue Volvo parked on the opposite side of the road, lowered his road map and logged him out on his tape recorder.

"Ben," Julia said gently, "you did the right thing. We need that affidavit. It may never be used—you said it yourself."

"I know," he admitted. "But she looked so bloody shaken. I felt a real shit, J. I suppose I haven't been at the sharp end of the job for so long, I've gone soft. You sit in an office and send other people out to suck blood. I didn't feel good about it."

Julia kissed him. "I know, but you still did the right thing. We both think King tried to kill that poor woman. And if we can follow this lead through and come up with a war crime like shooting British prisoners—we've got him, Ben. Under the new law he can be prosecuted!"

Ben said slowly, "There's no guarantee she'll do it, even now. Her legal chap will bust a gut trying to talk her out of it. But I just felt she'd come to a decision when I left. I think what I said tipped the balance. Anyway she said she'd call us, so we'll have to wait and see. Thanks, love."

"For nothing," Julia said softly. "Stray cats and old ladies—big, tough Ben Harris—you're rather a lovely man. . . . I'm going to take you out to supper and then I'm going to bring you back here and spoil you absolutely rotten!"

· · ·

"Daddy," Gloria King said, "what's the matter?"

He was slumped in front of the TV in his study, a cigar burning itself out in the ashtray. The program was a mindless sitcom that she knew he would usually have switched off immediately. He looked tired and preoccupied. She came and perched on his chair and slipped her arm around him. "Are you still angry about that parcel?" she asked. "I'm so sorry, I tried to tell you. . . ." Her eyes had filled with tears. Whenever he was distant with her, she felt like a miserable, guilty child, desperate to be forgiven.

King looked up at her. He took her hand and held it.

"Don't be silly, darling girl," he muttered. "Fuck the parcel. Fuck everything." She sighed, flooded with relief.

"Then what's wrong?" she persisted. "You're not yourself ever since you came back from New York. Is it the business? Isn't it going well?"

"Not as well as I hoped," he admitted. "I've got to find a lot more money than I reckoned, but I'll do it. It just needs a bit of fixing."

He glared at the flickering screen, the muttered inanities and recorded laughter in the background. Joe Patrick was doing his job. He got the agency's reports faxed through, and faxed the copy direct to King's private-and-confidential number.

Ben Harris had gone down to Midhurst to see a Mrs. Jean Adams. King felt as if his heart had stopped. The shock was so intense, he couldn't feel it beat for some seconds. Jean Adams. The image of her swam in front of him, forty years out of date. Small, sharp-tongued, an enemy. Phyl's favorite niece. It must be the same. Midhurst in Sussex where Phyl had spent her last years, his secret locked in the damaged brain. It must be the

same Jean Adams. He relived in those few moments the
confrontation when she came to see him, her dull husband in tow, and bought him off with a few hundred
pounds. He was poor, when he should have been rich.
But he was safe and free of Phyllis—the albatross he'd
hung around his own neck. Jean Adams. He hadn't
thought of her in years. She'd slipped out of his memory, as if she were dead like her aunt. But she wasn't. She
was alive, and Ben Harris, back from his trip to Germany
with Julia Hamilton, had gone down to see her.

His enemies had been ferreting around for years trying
to discredit him. Without success. His business deals
were shrouded in layers of deceit, impossible to pene-
trate. He was a genius at covering his tracks with nominees, subsidiary companies, and offshore operations. His
criminal activities were protected by their own nature.
Laundered money for drugs in the States, illegal arms
supplied to all sides in Eastern Europe. . . . He'd contacts
among the secret world of the Mafia, which were as
interested in anonymity as he was. He had nothing to
fear there, and he had made a huge fortune, most of
which was banked and invested overseas. He glanced up
at his daughter.

She said, "What is it, then? You're not ill, are you,
Daddy?"

He saw panic in her eyes. He smiled. "Ill? Don't be silly.
I'm like an ox—you know that. No, it's nothing, just a little hiccup. I'll sort it out. I'll tell you about it one day. And
I've been thinking—how would you like to give up that
job with Hart Investments and come and work for me?"

She blushed. "Oh, Daddy! You mean it?"

"Why not," he went on. "It's about time. You're a big
girl and you've got your business degree and five years with
Hart's—I've always had this in mind, Gloria. I want you
working with me. One day, when I'm too old, you can

take over. What do you say? Are you ready for the deep end?"

She hugged him, her face radiant. "I'm ready if you say so," she said. "But you'll never be too old. Never."

"Sweetheart," he said, "I'm not immortal."

Gloria King spoke quietly. "You are to me."

He sat on after she had left him. She was so excited, so happy that her face glowed. She'd need a husband, King decided. Clever, but not too clever. A man to support her, but never able to dominate. Father children. He liked that idea. The dynasty principle appealed to him. Pity if it was a life peerage, because he couldn't pass it on . . . but never mind. Power was what mattered; titles without power and money were a mockery. Gloria would learn from him. Her mind was as quick as her body was clumsy. He'd teach her everything and little by little confide some of his secrets to her. She wouldn't be troubled by scruples. She'd always appreciated that there were no rules in business except the cardinal one: Don't get found out. He dreamed, planning the future for a little while. Then abruptly his heart quickened as he faced reality again.

His past was his one weakness. He never thought about it. He never thought backward, unless there was a reason. Regret, nostalgia—these were a form of indulgence he despised. What was done was done, and necessity was the only rationale. He had set out to survive because that was the only purpose of life. He'd seen other men die, and there was nothing heroic about it. Just waste. Natural waste of the lesser breeds, the victims who would always fall before the strong. He was strong and he was clever. He had used Phyllis Lowe—he sneered mentally as he remembered her—sentimental, oversexed, enthralled to middle-aged passion. A natural victim.

A self-pitying drunk who'd brought her fate on herself. She'd goaded him into an act of madness, and paid the penalty. Not the full penalty as he'd intended. He'd always meant to abandon her in due time. But once he'd lost control that night, he knew he'd lost control of her. So he acted. But the blow hadn't been hard enough. It hadn't killed her. It had locked up his secret in her twilight mind, and she'd died with it unspoken.

She'd left her whole estate to the niece, Jean Adams. The niece had been glad to pay him off, so she knew nothing sinister. And he had genuinely forgotten her existence in the years when he rose in the public domain and became a symbol of ruthless power. He didn't fear exposure by the wife of a small-time stockbroker, if she was even still alive. He feared the German records in Nessenberg, and early on he had made a trip over to see the right people and closed off that avenue into a cul-de-sac. He had sympathizers with his story, men he could talk to as a comrade, men with secrets of their own. He thought he had blocked any possible investigation. And he had the power to silence his enemy and rival, William Western, when he attempted it, because Western had his own secret to protect.

But battle was imminent, and Western had decided on one last throw against him. Harris had gone back to Germany with Julia Hamilton, Western's brilliant protégée, and this time they had found a lead. And the lead had led to Jean Adams. And back from her to his dead wife.

He got up, heaving himself out of the deep chair. They could expose the truth about Phyllis's death, but it wouldn't be enough to damage him. He could explain the lies in his biography by the need to protect the poor alcoholic woman's reputation. It wasn't enough for Western to deal him a real blow.

He dialed the number, and Joe Patrick answered. "I want Adams's phone bugged."

"It'll be done tomorrow," Joe answered. "The agency

won't do it, but I have another source. How about Hamilton's place? Harris shacks up with her there. I can fix that too."

"You do that," King said. "And I want reports on the hour if anything comes up. You may have to pay Mrs. Adams a visit."

"Just say the word," Joe murmured. King hung up. There was nothing more he could do. Shut off now, slam the mental door. He had other things to think about. His financing of the takeover, his plans for his daughter.

Recognizing his own power induced a surge of confidence. It assured him he was invulnerable. Nobody would ever get near enough to the truth and live to tell the world about it. He could make sure of that.

CHAPTER 6

JULIA WAS IN HER OFFICE. BEN HARRIS HAD rung in to say his daughter, Lucy, had rung up out of the blue she was in some kind of trouble. He was meeting her in Birmingham and wouldn't be in till the morning.

There had been no word from Jean Adams since his visit two days ago. Beyond Julia's window the London skyline shimmered in late-autumn sunshine.

They were getting closer. Some of the smoke screen was lifting here and there, showing glimpses of darker things than she had ever imagined.

Harold King was concealed in the heart of it—a charlatan, a liar, and, by his own admission in a drunken frenzy, a man who had shot down unarmed men and gloried in it. And probably attempted to murder his wife. This, Julia recognized, was not the push-button killing of rivals like Hayman and Lewis by men hired for the job. King had reddened his own hands.

She pictured him in the exclusive restaurant, a crude bully, playacting the part he had adopted as a public face. The man of power, the vulgarian, the genius who overrode opposition like the murderous Juggernaut of ancient India, crushing whatever lay in its path.

That gave him a superhuman image, a larger-than-life perspective that perpetuated the legend. Behind it was someone very different. Someone cold and cunning, with the killer's immunity from conscience. A man with one weakness: He could never drink alcohol; it loosed the demons and took control of his tongue. His well-known abstinence was a discordant note. It was not compatible with King, the self-proclaimed bon viveur who loved the high style. It was part of Hans Koenig, who knew that never again in his life must he touch a drink.

The office was air-conditioned. But Julia shivered as if a draft had suddenly found its way into that controlled atmosphere and chilled her. She would miss Ben that evening. He had sounded worried on the telephone. His daughter was in trouble, and she'd surfaced after years of miminal contact. Julia had said of course he must go and try to sort it out. Lucky girl, to be able to call on him and have him come running. It made her think of her own parents. She didn't feel like spending the evening with friends, though a call would have brought invitations to dinner by most people she knew. She was well known, a social catch. And she wasn't encumbered by Felix any longer. He hadn't been popular with her friends. She hadn't seen him or heard of him, and he had slipped into the background of her mind. She was sure he had replaced her very quickly and that he was getting on with his own life in his own way. She buzzed through to her secretary.

"Call my parents, will you, Jenny—thanks."

Her father was put through. He sounded delighted when she asked if she might come down and spend the evening. No, Julia insisted, her mother was not going to spend the time in the kitchen—they would all go out to dinner. Would he book somewhere really nice—she didn't know the restaurants in the area. Her mother took over the conversation. How lovely—she sounded so pleased, Julia kicked herself for not making time for them more often. Yes, it would be a treat to go out instead of cooking, but only if Julia stayed the night. She wouldn't feel happy if she had to drive all the way back in the dark.

So many dreadful things happened to women these days. Suppose the car broke down? Julia didn't argue. It was protective and warm-hearted; it didn't irritate her anymore as it used to when she was less assured. It would be fun to sleep in her old room. She could start very early in the morning and be in her office in plenty of time. She wouldn't be home when Ben rang, but she could record a message on her answering machine giving him the Surrey number. She felt very happy, and the somber mood had disappeared. She didn't think about Harold King as she let herself into her flat and changed the message on her answering machine so that Ben could get in touch with her.

The hired surveillance reported her leaving the flat at six o'clock. Then they started tailing her BMW as it drove out of London. It was the chance for Joe's other contacts to take over.

They had already called on Jean Adams.

It was quite early in the morning, and she had not taken her dogs out for their walk when the telephone engineer rang to report a fault on the line. Jean was in the kitchen eating a frugal breakfast and reading The Times. She found the *Telegraph* too solidly right-wing; the idea of *The Times*'s impartiality was a legacy from her youth, and she believed it firmly.

"There's no fault on my line," she protested. "I've made two calls out this morning."

"It's incoming calls, madam," the man said. "That's where the problem is. I'd like to send someone around to check the connection. Will you be there in half an hour?"

She decided to postpone the walk till later. She had nothing much to do that morning anyway. Except make the telephone call to her solicitor with her decision. The walk with the dogs had been a planned diversion. She'd slept so badly and worried the problem to and fro before making up her mind. Let the telephone engineer come and put the wretched fault right. "Yes," she said, "I'll be here. I must say your service has improved. I used to wait for up to two days if anything went wrong. Privatization, I suppose."

"Glad you're satisfied, madam. Half an hour and our engineer will be with you."

He sounded a pleasant man, Jean thought. They'd been so surly in the old days. At least the government had done *something* right. She made a fresh pot of tea and finished reading *The Times*. The telephone engineer arrived exactly half an hour later. It took him ten minutes to check the phone in her sitting room and the bedroom extension. He was a dour young man who didn't invite conversation. He came downstairs and said, "It's all fixed."

"What was the matter?" she asked him. She didn't like his manner. He gave her the impression he'd been called out for nothing.

"Loose wire, no fault in the connections. You won't have any more trouble."

"I wasn't aware I had any in the first place," Jean Adams said sharply.

She wasn't going to put up with surliness. She walked into the hall and let him out. She didn't thank him for coming. She lifted her downstairs phone. It was working perfectly. The bug was voice-activated, and the calls were recorded and transmitted by remote control to a central number, which in turn logged them and recorded them. Jean Adams took the elderly Daisy for a short trot up and down the street and then put her back in the house. The boisterous puppy needed a good hour's exercise, and she set off by car for the open countryside.

It was a lovely autumn morning, crisp and sunny. She came back invigorated and calm. At twelve-fifteen she telephoned her solicitor and told him she would come in the next afternoon and sign the affidavit. He hadn't wanted to prepare it, poor man. He'd pleaded and argued and used delaying tactics, which had cost her a lot of worry and lost sleep, but she had always known in her heart that she was going to hold out against him.

At her age there wasn't much future to consider. Let that loathsome creature do his worst, and damn the consequences!

During the day there were other phone calls. Social calls, a query about a bill from the electricity board, and the call to the office of Barrat & Thompson, Solicitors and Commissioners for Oaths. Joe Patrick played the tape to Harold King on a portable machine no bigger than a cigarette pack.

They sat in Joe's office. It was a plush room, furnished in an aggressive, modern style that he felt demonstrated his prosperity. He had an expensive and very graphic female nude, complete with pubic hair, hanging on the wall opposite his plate-glass desk. King sat sprawled in a big leather Swedish chair that swiveled when he moved.

One of Joe's girls had brought them a tray, with whiskey for Joe and mineral water for King. The air was thick with cigar smoke. King listened without movement or change of expression. That deadpan look meant he was at his most dangerous.

The voice of Jean Adams was clear and crisp.

"I know you're going to argue with me, Dick, but I know it's the right thing to do. I'm going to sign the affidavit. I want you to put in it everything I told you, and I'll come in tomorrow."

The man called Dick was pleading with her.

"Jean—what good will it do? You've no proof King tried to kill your aunt—you've let the matter lie since 1950—why bring it up now—?"

Her voice cut in on him. "And what about those prisoners he said he murdered—?" Joe Patrick risked a quick look at Harold King. His florid skin was graying as the blood drained from the surface. Joe kept his eyes averted after that.

"My dear, it's only hearsay. Don't you see that your aunt's alcoholism made everything she said suspect? You didn't really believe her yourself."

"I didn't want to." The tone rose in self-accusation. "Bob talked me around. Just like you're trying to—you men all want a quiet life!" She gave a brisk little laugh. "Dick dear, let's not talk about it anymore. I failed to have the courage of my convictions once. I've got a chance to put that right. I'll be in your office at two-thirty tomorrow. And why don't you and Betty come around and have supper with me in the evening?"

"We'd love to." The voice was resigned. "All right, Jean. See you at two-thirty."

There was a heavy silence as Joe switched the recorder off. He waited for King to speak. At last, clearing his throat of nervous phlegm, he said, "There were other calls, but this was the one I thought you'd want to hear."

Harold King drew on his cigar. He was in shock. He could feel it. His body was cold, and a chill sweat was breaking out under his clothes. His strong heart pumped furiously in response. He tipped ash off the end of his cigar onto Joe's geometric carpet. The ashtray was at his elbow, but he didn't see it.

"She's talking cock," he said. He looked at Joe, and there was such a threat in that look that Joe Patrick blinked and cleared his throat again.

"Absolute cock," King repeated, emphasizing each word. His accent came out as a guttural snarl.

"Yeah," Joe agreed quickly. "Cock," he echoed.

Never explain, was one of King's maxims when dealing with underlings. But instinct counseled otherwise this time. The Irishman was cunning as a rat. "Her aunt was a piss artist." He drew on the cigar again, calming himself. There was no reason to explain who the aunt was.

"She had d.t.'s. She had hallucinations."

"Yeah." Joe nodded. "Sure. Me own grandmother was like that—shoutin' the odds about being robbed and poison put in her food. . . ." Like King, stress brought out his native brogue. King shut him up with a gesture.

"It's cock, but that wouldn't stop the *Sunday Herald* making use of it," he said. "I've got big deals going. I can't afford hassle. Fix it, Joe. No affidavit." He levered himself out of the chair, which swung awkwardly under his heavy body.

Joe Patrick was on his feet. He said in a soft voice, full of the lilt of his native tongue, "I'd best take care of it meself. Leave it with me."

King didn't speak. He just nodded, and the eye contact confirmed what had been agreed. Joe's girl helped him on with his coat and opened the door for him after she'd called up his car on the phone. She was good-looking, he thought, appraising her. He didn't go for color, but she was beautiful in her way.

He had recovered his nerve. His body heat had regulated, and the heart was steady. Joe would make sure there was no signed affidavit lodged where Julia Hamilton and "Exposure" could make use of it. He trusted Joe. He was imaginative. He'd make it convincing. He sat back in his car, and slowly he relaxed. And began to think it through. Germany was where the leak had sprung, in spite of his precautions. Break the Jean Adams connection and there was nothing but hearsay from the past. There was an old business saying he liked to quote: "When you want to break up a syndicate, cut the heads off one at a time." Jean Adams would be the first.

Ben Harris faced his daughter. He'd forgotten how pretty she was. She had her mother's blue eyes and blond hair. It was a pretty face, but it was drawn with worry, and there were dark shadows under her eyes.

"I can't tell Mum," she said. "She'd freak."

She picked up her cup of coffee and sipped from it. She was a stranger to him, although there were traces of the child he used to bounce on his knee at bedtime. A grown young woman with a problem she couldn't share with her mother and her stepfather. So, after years of neglect, she had asked him for help.

"He's the problem," she said. "He's a real pain about this sort of thing. He'd say it was disgracing the family."

Ben didn't answer. He had never met or spoken to the man his wife had married. He had never even been curious about him. He had assumed that he was a good father to his stepchildren. Apparently not in this instance.

"It's none of his business," Ben said at last. "It's your choice."

"Yes," his daughter said quickly, "that's what I feel. I want to keep it, Dad. It's not Pete's fault. I was the one that slipped up." Pete, he had elicited, was the married boyfriend who wasn't ever going to break up his home. He already had three children. "Trouble is"—she bit her lip, hesitating for a moment—"trouble is, I haven't got much money. . . ."

Ben helped her out. It pained him to see her embarrassment with him. He was her father, after all.

"You mean you haven't got any," he prompted.

"I'm in my last year at college," she said. "I've got ninety quid in the bank. My grant pays the rent, and Mum makes me an allowance. . . ." She trailed off again. Her eyes filled with tears. "I feel awful coming to you like this," she said. "I took Mum's part when you broke up, and it just sort of drifted after that." Ben reached across the café table and put his hand on hers.

"Lucy love, you don't need to apologize. I was a lousy father. And your mother was right to pack it in. I'd like to make it up to you. You want this baby, go ahead and have it. I'll see you right for money, that's no problem. But you'll have to tell her."

"I know," she said. "She will freak, though."

"She'll get used to it. She was mad about you two—she'll love it; you'll see." She leaned back and sighed. She took out a pink tissue, which he suspected was torn off a lavatory roll, and blew her nose.

"You're a real star, Dad. I'll get a good degree and I'll get a job. I won't be a burden to you, I promise."

"Don't be bloody silly," Ben told her. "It's my grandchild, too, you know. How does your friend Pete fit in—is he going to be around?" She shook her head. He felt a jolt of anger. "No. He's called it off. I don't blame him. He's got enough to pay for with three kids already. I'm on my own, and that's better really. I'm not scared, it was just I didn't see how I was going to cope and I did want to finish college. You are a star. I mean it."

"No problem," Ben smiled at her. She was an independent free-living product of her age, but her vulnerability touched him as much as her courage. He wished he'd been part of her growing up. Her question took him by surprise.

"What about you? How's your life going?"

"It's okay. I've got a top job and I earn a hell of a salary. No complaints."

"Girlfriend?" his daughter asked. "I thought you'd have got married by now."

"My track record wasn't very good," he said. "And I didn't meet anyone"—he looked at her—"but that's changed. There's someone very special now. I don't know how it'll work out, and we're not rushing into a commitment. I'd like you to meet her one day."

"I'd like it too," she answered. "We'll come and visit, me and my illegit." He realized what an attractive smile she had. The clouds had lifted with the rapidity of youth and optimism. Thanks to him.

He'd planned on staying the night in Birmingham and seeing some old newspaper colleagues if he could contact them. He changed his plans.

"Let's get the bill," he said to his daughter. "I'd like to come and see some of your work. And then I'll take you out to dinner. How's that?"

"I've got my portfolio in the flat," she said eagerly. She was studying textile design. "And dinner would be great. I am eating for two," and she began to giggle. They left the café, and, after a few yards walking on the pavement looking for a taxi, Ben's daughter slipped her arm through his.

Joe Patrick was silent and bad-tempered after King left. He was always nervous, keyed up before a serious job. And there was so little time to prepare. He cursed Harold

King, and raised a threatening fist to his hapless girl when she interrupted to ask him something. She fled, and he sank into contemplation. He roused himself and phoned Julia Hamilton's number. He mustn't neglect other tasks just because King had tossed hot shit in his lap. Hamilton's flat hadn't been bugged. The agency said she'd driven off with what looked like a little overnight case and headed out of London. She was logged in on the M25 by seven o'clock that evening. The phone rang four times and then the answering machine cut in. He listened. It wasn't a normal message.

"Ben darling. I've gone down to my parents' for the night. Please call me." The number was a code and four figures. "I hope it went all right. Love—J." The place was empty. He could send his electronic man along with the lock picker he'd used when he broke in before. They'd fix the phones up and have time to put simple bugs in the rooms. She wouldn't be able to sneeze without Joe having it on tape.

He decided to eat something. He came out and yelled, and the girls came out looking apprehensive. His temper was always unpredictable. One or both of them could get a punching if they weren't extra careful.

"Get me somethin' to eat," he snapped. They knew his preferences. He liked simple stuff when he was alone and not showing off in restaurants. Eggs, burgers, chips—the junk food of his youth, when such fare was a treat.

He poured himself a measure of whiskey. Irish whiskey, which slipped warm down the gullet and heated his cold belly. But not too much. Just one to set him up. "Fix it, Joe. No affidavit." A beating wouldn't be enough. He'd read King's mind and knew what was expected. No contract worthy of hire could be bought at such short notice. It wasn't a job for a greedy heavy, who might foul up and get caught. It called for an expert. Himself, as he'd offered. He ate in the kitchen, washed his food down with a cup of strong tea. Then he looked at his girls. The apprehension in their pretty faces stirred him. He liked to feel a woman's fear. And that gave him his plan of action. He glanced at his Rolex, a present to himself.

It was nine-thirty. He'd be in Midhurst before eleven.

"I'm goin' out," he said. "You two tar babies wait up for me, see? I'll be ready for some fun when I get back." He got up and went to each girl and pinched their cheeks. They'd never heard the term "tar babies" till he used it. It was Dublin slang for black girls, exported from the slave states of America. They hated it, as Joe Patrick knew. He lingered by the older girl, Tina; she was his favorite of the two. "You be ready for me. I'll want something special tonight."

"You'll have it, Joe baby," she promised. She poked out her tongue at him provocatively. When he'd gone, she closed her mouth and looked at her friend. "One day I'm going to bite it clean off," she whispered.

"Like fuck," the other girl said. "He'd kill you. What's up? Where's he off to?"

"Some poor bugger's going to get done over," was the answer. "Joe always gets a hard-on afterward. Come on, let's watch telly."

Jean Adams ate her supper on a tray by the fire. She let the puppy in to sit with the old Labrador bitch, who raised a sleepy head and sniffed, before going to sleep again. It was warm and peaceful, and she enjoyed the TV. She loved police series and never missed her favorite program. Then there was the news, and if she wasn't too tired, she watched "Newsnight." Then bed, with the old lady in her basket upstairs by the radiator in her room and the puppy snug in the kitchen with paper laid out on the floor in case of accidents. She was still young and not always able to last the night. Jean was content. She had made her decision and lifted the burden of that old guilt from her mind. She would sleep with a clear conscience. At eleven-thirty she let the dogs out into the rear garden for a last pee and then locked up.

Slumped down in his seat in the car parked opposite, Joe Patrick saw the square of light in the upstairs window go out. He waited.

At ten minutes past twelve he broke into the house through the kitchen window.

"You're looking bright-eyed and bushy-tailed," Julia's father remarked. She had come back into the sitting room after a long telephone call. She had taken it upstairs. He and her mother had exchanged looks. She had arrived with flowers for her mother and a bottle of special malt whiskey for him. She looked relaxed and happier than they could remember, and they felt it wasn't connected with her new career. Her mother couldn't resist the question.

"Who was that, darling?"

Julia smiled. Why not say something? She knew they'd be pleased, especially her mother, who was convinced that fulfillment lay in a comfortable marriage like her own. "He's called Ben Harris," she said. "We're working together. You'll be glad to know that Felix and I broke up."

"Thank God for that," her father exclaimed. "I thought he was rather a lout—terribly pleased with himself. I didn't say anything at the time—"

"Dad darling, you didn't have to—I could see it on your face. He was all right. I think he needed someone nearer his own age who wasn't always competing with him."

"And winning," her mother interposed. She was shrewd, as Julia knew. Her wisdom came from long experience of life and people.

"And winning," Julia admitted. "Ben's quite different. He's older, he's got a big job, and we're very good together. I think you'll like him. I hope so, anyway, because I do." She looked at them and smiled. Her mother said, "He's not married, is he?"

"No, Mum," Julia said gently. "He's divorced. A long time ago. He's in Birmingham meeting his daughter. She's got some problem she wants sorting out. I'll bring him down one day."

"Do. We'd love to meet him."

They'd gone to a hotel for dinner and come back in a happy mood. They had recovered ground lost through lack of contact over the years, and to her relief the subject of her brother and sister-in-law and their children had only been touched upon, instead of dominating the conversation as before. Julia had been irritated and vaguely jealous; it wasn't an incentive to see more of them when they had so obviously closed the circle. Now, ever since that visit for Sunday lunch when she was upset by Felix's absence, the gap had opened, and she was inside a circle of their own. Just her father, her mother, and herself. Ben would like them, she was sure of that.

He'd talked to her about his daughter, Lucy; his attitude surprised her. She hadn't seen him as paternal. He sounded pleased about the pregnancy, proud of his daughter's decision to keep her child and resist the easy option. Proud of her work, which he said was very original. And then, before she had time to feel a twinge of jealousy, he asked about her, told her he missed her. And said he loved her, rather abruptly, before hanging up.

Typical Ben. Soft words were still drawn out of him like teeth. She went to bed earlier than usual because her father looked tired. He was close to seventy; she often forgot that. Loving someone else had sharpened her perceptions, made her think of other people more.

She woke, made herself some breakfast, and slipped out without disturbing them. She left a little note on the kitchen table.

See you both very soon. It was lovely. And signed it with her childhood pet name, Juliette. She drove through empty roads, listening vaguely to taped music. It was a lovely day, and the autumn colors blazed from the trees in the early-morning sunlight. She switched on the news as she came into London and met the early traffic. It was the usual: signs of a slight economic upturn. A report of bomb explosions in Belfast, Palestinian riots on the Israeli West Bank, a statement on the rise in petty crime in London.

And the murder of an elderly widow in Midhurst.

Ben was waiting for Julia in her office.

"Ben?" She came up to him, smiling, surprised to see him so early. "Did you drive down last night? I thought you were staying—"

"Jean Adams is dead," he said. Julia stared at him in horror. "There was a break-in, and she was murdered last night. I got the latest update. Here."

Julia sat down. She blanched as she read.

Jean Adams had been found dead in the early hours of the morning. She had been sexually assaulted, and bludgeoned to death. Neighbors were alerted by one of her dogs howling and barking and called the police. The animal had been kicked and had to be destroyed. Robbery was the motive, because jewelry and money had been taken and the room ransacked.

"I can't believe it," Julia said. "Ben, I can't believe it's true!" He pulled a chair close to hers. She looked terribly white and shaken.

"I can," he said.

She went on, her voice uneven. "What sort of man would *do* a thing like that? She was near seventy—"

He lit a cigarette. "It's happened before. They break in

to rob, the woman wakes up, and they get turned on because she's terrified. Then they kill her to stop her identifying them. Makes you think about the death penalty. Come on, have some coffee."

"I don't want any," she said. "Have the police got any clues?"

"They're going through the place," he said. "I had a word with the local crime boys. It's the first murder of its kind down there, and they're pretty fired up about it. I said we knew her, and they promised to call in if they find anything. J, I don't want to sound callous, but I don't think she signed that affidavit."

Julia looked at him. "No, I realize that. I suppose we could ring the solicitor to make sure. Later on. God, I hope they catch that brute."

"He won't have a nice time down at the station if they do," Ben remarked. She was upset, and he didn't labor the point about the affidavit. He was sure Jean Adams had told him she was signing it that day. It was a very long shot to imagine she'd advanced the timing. But he had to take it. He, not Julia, would call the solicitor's office. He would be better able to cope with the response.

He went downstairs, and after an hour he made the call. At first the receptionist said her boss was out, then suddenly he came on the line. His voice was shaking with rage and emotion. "You ring up at a time like this about your bloody affidavit! No, she didn't sign it! You're the scum of the earth, all you media people!" And the line cleared as he banged down the telephone.

It was a busy morning and a hectic afternoon for Ben Harris. He cut his lunchtime drink and sandwich with Julia. The murder wasn't top priority, such cases were no longer headline news. There had been too many of them. Political crisis, disasters, a plane crash in northern France killing a group of British students—the stories came pouring in, and the widow lying in the mortuary in Midhurst rated a few column inches on the inside page. Then Harris's phone rang in mid-afternoon. It had been quieter for the last hour, and he swore. He loved pressure, it brought out the best in him, but it frazzled his nerves and primed his temper with a very short fuse.

It was the detective chief inspector from Midhurst in charge of the Jean Adams murder. He talked to Harris for a few minutes. Ben said briefly, "Thanks—thanks very much. No, we won't print anything. Not without your say-so. Keep me posted."

One of the fingerprinting team had chanced on something. Faint marks on the telephone upstairs in the bedroom. Similar marks on the instrument downstairs. They'd taken them apart and found that Jean Adams's phones had been bugged.

Ben put a call through to the penthouse office. Julia was out at a meeting. He didn't leave a message. He sat on in his office with the whirl and bustle of his newsroom eddying outside and thought it through. Then he made another call. He asked to see William Western as a matter of urgency.

"Take her off this," Harris said again.

Western made a bridge with his fingertips. "No," he said.

Ben leaned toward him. Western was sitting behind his desk, and he had kept Ben standing. It hadn't put him at a disadvantage. He came close to the desk and leaned toward the slight man in his big chair and said, "King is on to what you're doing. He knows we're after him. He had that woman's phones bugged, and she was bloody murdered before she could sign that affidavit. That's no coincidence. That's King. You pull Julia off this and I'll see it to the limit for you."

"No," Western said. "You're not as good as she is. You tried before and you got nowhere."

Ben glared at him. "I was looking into two murders, and you made me drop it. Let's get the facts right."

"The facts," William Western cut in, "are what I say they are. You and Julia are a team. Neither of you drops out. If King is behind this, and it's only supposition on your part—don't shout, Harris, just listen—then it means two things. Somehow, somewhere, you've leaked information. So look into that first. If you're right and the telephone bugging is tied into this murder, then King must think he's safe. He's broken the only link you've got with the accident to his wife and the story about a war crime. So what you do now is put it about that the story's dead. No proof. And check your own telephones. Or hadn't you thought of that?" He raised his eyebrows at Ben Harris, almost taunting him. Harris stepped back.

"I've thought of it," he said. "I'm giving you formal notice that I'm resigning. As of now." Western unhooked his fingers.

"And leave your friend Miss Hamilton to carry on alone? I don't think you'll do that."

"I'll get her to resign with me," Harris snarled at him. His fists were clenched at his sides; he looked explosive with anger. Western said coolly, "I don't think you'll do that either. Or you wouldn't have come to me first. Stop behaving like a bloody fool. She won't give up, and you know it."

"She will," Ben insisted. "She promised. She didn't tell you, but it was the condition upon which I agreed to work with her."

"She won't keep it," he said, dismissing it. "She doesn't

quit. If you're worried about her, then do what I've told you. Give out that you've killed the story. Keep your mouths shut and get on with it." He shifted in his chair, making himself comfortable. "I'll run a line on the new 'Exposure' feature hinting at a completely different target."

"Thanks," Ben Harris said furiously. "You'll have my letter by tomorrow morning."

"I hope not," Western murmured. "I shall be sorry to lose you. Miss Gilbey"—he spoke into the desk mike—"show Mr. Harris out and tell Parsons to come in, will you?"

"Ben, for God's sake, what's going on?"

"Just do as I say, will you? Don't make any phone calls from the flat. Meet me at eight o'clock in the bar at Mario's."

He didn't wait for her to argue. He hung up. When his line buzzed back immediately, he switched it through to his secretary.

He must make Julia listen. Western's sneer rang in his head.

"Leave your friend Miss Hamilton to carry on alone? I don't think you'll do that." He was right, he'd called Ben's bluff. He was a ruthless, unscrupulous bastard, only one remove from the man he was trying to destroy.

Western wouldn't sanction murder, but he'd sit back and let someone else take the risk. He wasn't going to risk Julia. Ben went home and checked his telephones, listening for the slightest sound that might indicate they had been tampered with. He heard nothing, but that wasn't any guarantee. The systems were so sophisticated now, they were virtually impossible to detect without taking the instruments apart.

How had King latched on to Jean Adams? The question sent him pacing up and down. How did he find out at this early stage that he was under investigation at all?

Had Julia talked to anyone? He knew he hadn't. It must have come from someone she knew, some chance remark, some off-the-record hint.

He showered and changed into a dark suit. He'd chosen Mario's because the Fleet Street crowd didn't congregate there as they did in the pub or some of the trattoria he and Julia patronized. No eavesdropping. Mario's was safe behind the price barrier.

He arrived early and took his seat on a twin sofa up against one paneled wall. A large Edwin Douglas oil of two spaniels gazed down benevolently from above. He couldn't relax; he fidgeted, swallowed his drink, looked at his watch. Julia was late. It was unlike her. She was a punctuality freak; it amused him, because he was quite casual about being on time. When she came through the door, he started up quickly. She looked different; he'd never seen her dressed up before. They led easygoing lives outside the office. He saw the glitter of the sequined top and the bright paste earrings as she walked toward him.

"You're late," he said. "I was worried."

Julia sat down beside him. She said quietly, "I'm sorry— I had a late call from Western, after you phoned me. He told me what had happened."

Ben hadn't expected to be preempted.

"I should have guessed he'd try to talk you around. I'll get you a drink. Usual?" He summoned the barman.

"Vodka on the rocks, please, Rudi. Another Scotch for me." Then he took her hand and looked at her.

"They'd bugged the telephones in her house," he said quietly. "They must have heard her talking to the solicitor. She was murdered to stop her signing that affidavit."

"That's what Western told me," Julia answered. "He also said you'd gone into his office and freaked out about me. You shouldn't have done that, Ben. Not without talking to me first."

"I tried to call you," he protested. "You were in a meeting. Julia, listen to me." He so seldom used her full name that she hesitated. He was so serious that she bit back her reproach. She had left William Western's office feeling very angry. She didn't belong to Ben Harris. He had no right to interfere in her career.

"I did freak, and I was wrong. I should have waited and talked to you first. But thinking about what happened to Jean Adams got to me—someone breaking in, assaulting her to make it look good, and then beating her around the head. . . . It could have been you. It could *be* you, unless you keep to our deal and drop this whole dirty mess. Please"—he stopped her interruption—"hear me out. You're a fine journalist; you've got talent and insight and integrity. You'll go to the top of the profession without 'Exposure.' That's just the carrot Western offered you to get you to do his dirty work for him. I told him I'm going to resign. I want you to resign with me. I'll pass what we know about King on to certain sources; I've got good friends who might follow it up."

"Without proof?" Julia asked him. "No, Ben, that doesn't add up, and you know it. As for the carrot, it wasn't 'Exposure.' It was your job he promised me. In due time. I know how you feel, and I know what I promised, but I can't do it. I just can't give up and back away from this." She picked up her glass. She said simply, "You can't either. If you do, it's because you're trying to force my hand, and I won't let you. I'm going on till I find something that will bring that man into the dock."

Ben didn't say anything. Couples came in and took their places, the bar was filling up. One or two men glanced at Julia.

At last he said, "You realize Western's manipulating you?"

"Yes, I know he is. But so are you."

"It's not quite the same," he said it bitterly, and his face set.

Julia spoke quickly. "I know that too. But, Ben, I'm not a child that has to be protected. I can see what's going on. I can make my own decisions, and I've made this one. I'm not giving up. After what happened to Jean Adams, I can't! I brought her into this. I'm responsible. So are you. You went down there and talked her into changing her mind. If it wasn't for us, she'd be alive today. That's all there is to say about it."

Ben said, "I asked about the affidavit. She didn't sign it. The old man blew his top at me. He said, 'People like you are the scum of the earth.'"

"People like us," Julia answered, "are the ones who will put a stop to the Harold Kings of this world. One day I'd like to be able to point that out to him."

Her fingers entwined in his and gripped them.

"I love you, Ben, but I've got to live with myself, and I couldn't if I ran away from this. I won't try to influence you. If you want to chuck it in because of Western then I don't blame you. But don't do it to pressure me. I'm committed, and I can't change that. Please, don't let's fight about it. Let's be together."

"If I didn't love you," Ben said, "I'd still feel the same. Let's put the decision on the back burner just for tonight. Let's try to work out what went wrong. How did he know we were on his tail? Who could have known about it and let the word slip?"

Julia picked at the sequins on the edge of her tunic. "I never said a word to anyone. Our researchers only had two names, Phyllis Lowe and Hans Koenig. There was nothing to connect with Harold King. Oh, damn, look what I've done—"

She'd pulled a thread, and a few bright beads scattered on the seat.

"That's pretty, that outfit," Ben said. "Can't you knot it?"

"Yes, it's all right. I wore it the first time I came here—to see him for real."

"Did you?" Ben said it slowly. "You brought Sutton along, didn't you?" She looked at him sharply. "Yes; yes, of course I did. Oh, God."

"You said something to him," he suggested.

"He said it to me," she countered. "'You're after King,' or something like that. I'd blown a fuse over the way he shouted at the maître d'."

"And what did you say?" Ben asked her. She bit her lip, remembering the conversation. Felix had been aggressive, goading her.

"Oh, God," she repeated. "I said I was looking at the Honors List, and he might be on it. But that's all, Ben, that's all. He didn't even pick it up. We were having a row, and I left without him. You came around with the file that night. It couldn't be Felix . . . could it?"

"Only one way to find out. We'll have to ask him. Or I will, if you like. We've got to know. We've got to plug the leak, if it was him."

"We?" Julia asked the question quietly.

"Oh, for Christ's sake, yes—*we*." He banged his glass down on the table. "How the hell else can I look after you?"

The barman saw the pretty redhead lean over and kiss Mr. Harris on the lips. He thought it was quite funny. He'd never seen Harris with a woman before, and he'd have bet a week's wages no one would kiss him in public. He couldn't wait to tell them downstairs.

"Pussy's happy," Julia murmured. The cat was curled up between them on the bed. She reached down and stroked the smooth fur. It purred like a small engine revving up. "So am I," Ben said.

He'd driven her back to her flat after dinner. He wouldn't let her stay longer than to pack some clothes. Tomorrow he would get an electronic engineer to come and check the phones. She had remembered the messenger who had failed to deliver flowers, dismissing it as probably irrelevant, but Harris decided that once inside the building, they'd picked the lock and fixed the phones. A long time ago, he thought, monitoring them every step of the way. It made him cold to think of Julia staying there alone. It was a strange lovemaking between them that night. There'd been a moment when their relationship had almost broken up, and they both knew it. Julia's pride and independence had been threatened; for Harris, backing down in front of William Western might have been too bitter a pill to swallow.

And then, miraculously, they sailed past the rocks. Ben had compromised, and so had she. She agreed to move in to live with him and not to stay alone or put herself at risk. They were a team again, and all the stronger for the crisis. Their love was deeper and more significant when they went to bed; more of a fusion than a frenzied climax. They recognized it without putting it into words, and slept in each other's arms till the early morning.

With Julia at his side Ben Harris went up to see William Western. When they came in together, his eyes narrowed for a moment. A double resignation? He'd lost his gamble with their lives? He thought not.

So he said it, before either one could speak. Always keep control, never let the iniative slip away.

"A double resignation? Of course not. Say what you've come for. I've got a busy morning, but always time for my star girl and a fiery Welshman. God help us poor English, dealing with the Celtic temperament!" He had swept their prepared speech aside in his usual way, answering his own questions.

Ben said, "We're not resigning, Lord Western. Julia wants to stick with it, and I'm not going to let her go it alone. As you predicted." He glared at him.

Western smiled back indulgently. "That's all, then? Good, good. I'll run a red herring with 'Exposure'—think whom we can give a few sleepless nights to, will you, Julia? Some politician with a skeleton rattling about—it might be quite amusing." Then his voice sharpened, and there was no smile left. "And you clear up this security mess. Then get on with the job. I want results and I want them quickly. See yourselves out, and tell Miss Gilbey I want her." He picked up his internal telephone and dismissed them.

Outside, Julia turned to Ben. The secretary had given them a superior smile and hurried into Western's office.

"I hate him as much as you do," she said. "We're not doing it for him. Thank you for being so brave."

"Brave? What the hell's brave about backing down?"

"Everything," she murmured. "For someone like you."

"Hello," Felix said. "Warburton said you wanted to see me."

Ben looked at him; it wasn't a friendly look. "Sit down," he suggested. Felix lounged in one of the chairs, crossed his legs, and gazed at him inquiringly. He wasn't friendly either. This was his replacement; mentally he sneered at the age difference, the heavy spectacles and the hint of gray in the hair. "Julia's got a problem," Ben announced. "That's what I want to talk to you about."

"Oh? Why didn't she tell me herself?"

"She's busy," Ben snapped. "So I'm asking for her." He said, "She's told you about her job with 'Exposure'?"

"She mentioned something, yeah. She was very excited about it. Why?"

"What exactly did she tell you?"

Felix uncrossed one long leg and sat up straight. It was defensive body language, as Ben recognized. "What I said; it was a big career jump, big money, bags of opportunity. You haven't told me why you're asking."

"Because there's a problem, as I said. It could be a serious problem for her. If you'll think back and answer the questions, I'll be able to put you in the picture. Did she ever mention Harold King?"

Felix frowned. "Sort of, yes. It was pretty obvious she had him in her sights. She hated his guts."

"Like a lot of people," Ben said slowly. "Now, this is important. Did you ever talk about it? Ever mention to anyone that Julia was targeting King?"

"No," Felix protested. "Why should I? We broke up on account of that bastard. We'd gone to Mario's, and he was shouting his head off. Julia got all steamed up, and next day gave me the shove."

"Just think," Ben insisted. "Did anyone ask you what she was doing?"

Felix said, "Come on, what's the score? I know King's a rough player—he's not suing Julia, is he?"

"No," Ben answered. He decided to tell part of the truth. Felix wasn't going to make an effort otherwise.

"But her phone's been tapped, and bugs were found in the rooms."

"Jesus—" Felix stared at him. "Why? Who did it?"

"We think it's King. She is investigating him, and that really is confidential. You said he was a rough player . . . that's an understatement. There's been a leak, and we've got to trace it to protect her. She thinks it's you, because you're the only one she talked to. Nobody's blaming you, Sutton, but it would help if you could remember if you passed anything on, and to whom."

Felix scowled in concentration. "Wait on," he said. "I did get a call from some tout with a story to tell. . . . It wasn't any good to me, and it cost me fifty quid." He hesitated, and then said quickly, "That's right, it was a real sleaze bag, peddling dirt. He had a juicy tidbit about—" Harris stared as he mentioned the name, "Porno stuff with kids. A pedophile ring. I told him I couldn't use that sort of thing, and he suggested 'Exposure' . . . I remember I said that she wouldn't touch it." *She.* Ben didn't interrupt him.

"He started arguing; he was that type, cocky little know-it-all. I thought he was probably a pimp. He got up my nose, and I think I said she was after bigger fish." He stopped.

"Go on," Ben said. "He was needling you for information. So what else?"

"I think I mentioned King. I think I did. Yeah, the Honors List. That's what Julia said at Mario's. She might do a feature on the Honors List and scumbags like King getting on it. . . ."

Ben leaned back. "I'd say he was a plant," he said. "You weren't to know. Anyone else apart from him?"

Felix shrugged. "No. He never tried again."

Ben asked, "He didn't leave a contact number? You couldn't find him again?"

"I could try the pub; it was the Jug and Bottle off Dean Street. He gave me a name . . . Patrick. Joe Patrick."

The hostility had faded between them.

Felix said, "You're with Julia now, I hear say."

"We work together, and we're together," Ben admitted. "Look, will you help sort this out for her?"

"Sure. What do I have to do?"

"Go back to that pub, see if you can contact this Joe Patrick."

"And if I do, what then? Say it wasn't true, put him off the scent? I tell you, he was very sharp. He wouldn't swallow it."

Ben said slowly, "He might, if you play it the right way. And I think I know how. We've got to convince King that he's safe. It won't be that difficult, because our one star witness was murdered the other day. I don't have to spell it out for you, do I?"

"No," Felix got up; he moved very lightly for a big man. "Julia's really in trouble—phew! I opened my big mouth. . . ."

"Meet me in the pub at seven," Ben told him. "I'll have the line worked out for you. Don't blame yourself, Sutton, just put it right. Get her off the hook."

"Don't worry, will do," he said. "See you at seven." He held out his hand. Ben took it. "She's a great girl," Felix repeated. "You're lucky."

Joe Patrick was in a sunny mood. King had sent him a present. It was a confirmation of a transfer of fifty thousand pounds to his account in Switzerland. Joe was a rich man. He was secure for life, and so long as King used him for jobs like Jean Adams, his fortune would continue to grow.

He'd brought back the old woman's few trinkets and the stolen cash. The money was safe, the jewelry, such as it was, couldn't be disposed of to a fence. There were a couple of rings, a string of pearls, and a chain bracelet set with tiny colored stones. Nothing worth a toss in terms of real jewelry. He prized the small diamonds and a sapphire out of the rings, tested the pearls between his teeth—they were smooth, not gritty, so they were only costume—and inspected the bracelet. It was hallmarked, but the stones were little more than chips.

He gave the bracelet to his favorite Tina. "Somethin' for you next time," he said to her friend Tracey. Tina grimaced when he had gone.

"Mean sod," she murmured. "Looks like Woolworth's. Wonder where he got it."

Her companion shrugged. She was fond of her friend Tina; they'd grown up together in the black ghetto of Brixton. "Out of a cracker—last year's." She giggled. They had a laugh together, and in spite of the rough times they lived well. They expected to take a beating now and then; both had gone on the game in their early teens, victims of a pimp who ran a string of girls. Joe had picked them out of a cheap nightclub doubling as a brothel. He'd bought them from the pimp. They belonged to him till he got fed up and sold them on to someone else. It was a life of luxury compared with what they'd known. She didn't hate him the way Tina did. "Try it on," she said. "It's pretty. I like it."

Tina slipped it onto her wrist, fiddling with the clasp. "I'd give it to you, only he'd knock my teeth out," she said. "Fuck, I can't get it off." She wrenched at the delicate chain.

"I'll do it, I'll do it," her friend said. "You'll break it." She peered at the clasp. "It's got a catch on it," she said. "Stop it falling off. It could be gold—that's done it."

Tina held it up; the little stones glittered. "Could be."

"Junk doesn't have a catch like that," Tracey insisted. "Might be worth a few quid one day."

"Might be," Tina agreed. "Wonder where he got it . . . "

Felix went up to the bar and ordered a pint of lager. The pictures of the boxers posing with their fists up were faded and dirty, the signatures illegible. There wasn't a recent champion among them, and Felix knew them all from his days as an amateur. "I'm looking for Joe Patrick," he said to the barman.

"He's not here." The answer was prompt, and the look that went with it was wary.

"Know where I can get in touch with him?" Felix persisted.

"I can tell him if he comes in." The offer was grudging.

"I met him here," Felix went on. "We did some business together. Can you tell him to call me—Felix Sutton, *Sunday Herald?*"

The man put down the glass he was rinsing out. Joe Patrick was a big man. He mightn't thank him if he lost out on a deal. "You hang on a minute. I'll see what the boss says."

The boss, the same pudgy figure posing with the fighters like a fat midget, was in his back room watching TV. He picked up the phone and called Patrick's number.

Felix stayed by the bar, leaning on one elbow and drinking the cold beer while he waited. It seemed to take a long time.

The barman was back, serving customers; an obvious tart was eyeing Felix and getting ready to pick him up, when the proprietor appeared, the barman pointed out Felix, and he came up to him.

"Joe's coming around," he said. "Take a seat and order what you want. On the house."

"Thanks," Felix said. "I'll have another pint." He went to a table and sat down. The surface was wet and smelled of slopped beer.

The tart came up behind him. She was young and very pretty with a skirt that just skimmed her upper thighs. The man looked around and jerked a thumb at her. He didn't say anything. She pulled a face and retreated.

Felix grinned at her. She grinned back. He wouldn't have minded, he thought, but he wasn't going to pay for it.

"Hi there." Patrick pulled out a chair. He was swathed in a cashmere coat, and he smelled of strong cologne. Felix felt as if a rat had sat down beside him.

"You wanted to see me?" The bright teeth flashed at him, tribute to modern dentistry.

"Yeah," Felix said. "What are you drinking?"

"Scotch," Joe said. "What can I do for you?"

"You remember that story you offered me?" He lowered his voice.

Joe said softly, "The porno stuff—kids?"

"That's right. I may have a market for it."

"You said you couldn't use it," Joe pointed out.

"I can't. It's not my stuff. But I talked to my girlfriend— my ex, she is now." He shrugged. "And 'Exposure' would be interested. She asked me to contact you. They'd pay good money."

Joe tossed down half the whiskey.

"You said they'd be running something else. I don't want to fuck about with this—it's a hot story."

"Which nobody else will buy," Felix pointed out.

Joe squinted at the Scotch, then put the glass down. "What happens if they don't use it? I'd want money up front. There's my pal on the tabloid and his pal in the Vice—they'd want money up front from me."

"They'd get it. I told you, there's good money."

"What made your bird change her mind, then?" Joe countered. "You said she wouldn't touch it with a barge pole. Your very words."

"She's under pressure from her boss. Western owns the paper. He's my boss too. Difficult bugger. She had a big feature lined up for the first issue in November, House of Lords and Harold King. Dynamite stuff. But it's dead. They can't run it, and Western's kicking her backside. They had some witness who died on them. So I mentioned your proposition to her, and she jumped at it. Western wants a big scandal to kick off with now they've killed the King story. I'd say you can name your price." He looked hard at Joe Patrick.

"So what's in it for you?" Joe asked in his soft voice, losing the phony American twang.

"I might get her back," Felix said. "And I'd want a cut; nothing big, just luck money, as they call it in Ireland."

Joe grinned. "So they do," he agreed. "Are you the go-between, then?"

"No," Felix said. "She does her own negotiating; she'd send someone else to talk figures. You mentioned five hundred."

"That was to you." Joe smiled at him. "For a big feature it'd be in the thousands. You said I could name me price. I tell you what—"

He drained the last of the whiskey. He pushed the glass away, and Felix knew the meeting was over. "Tell you what," Joe was on his feet. "I'll talk to my pals. Then I'll get back to you. I know they had someone else in mind."

He held out his hand; Felix made himself shake it, and gave a powerful squeeze that caused Joe Patrick to wince. He enjoyed that.

"You'll be in touch, then, but make it quick. She's pushed for a story. . . ."

"You'll hear real soon," Joe Patrick promised.

Felix left the pub. It was cold outside with a thin drizzle falling. The girl he'd seen in the pub was walking down the pavement, slowly, looking for curb crawlers.

She came up to him and smiled. "Hello, handsome. Want some fun?"

"Not tonight," Felix said. "Thanks anyway. Buy yourself a cup of coffee. It's bloody cold." He gave her five pounds and then swung off toward Tottenham Court Road. He wouldn't hear from Joe Patrick again. There was no story to sell. There never had been. Ben Harris was right.

• • •

Harold King flew to New York by Concorde. He had decided to take Gloria with him. Her gratitude and excitement touched him. She reached for his hand as the plane took off—its ascent was very steep—and he squeezed it affectionately. She was scared of landing too. The cloud had lifted, and he was in a buoyant mood. "Exposure" had dropped the investigation, because, as Joe repeated, they had a witness who'd died on them. . . .

Joe had been grinning like an ape when he reported his meeting with Felix Sutton. He'd cut the main head off the Hydra by getting rid of Jean Adams. Without her, they had nothing but hearsay. He could dispose of Hamilton and her friend Harris when he took over the *Herald*. Neither would ever work in newspapers again by the time he had finished with them.

He was confident, pleased with Joe, but, as always, he left nothing as a hostage to fortune.

"What do you do about Sutton now?" he demanded.

Joe had seemed surprised at the question. "Call him, tell him no sale."

"You bloody fool." It pleased King to bully him. Too much praise might go to his head. "You drop it like that, he'll see it's a put-up. You're stupid, but maybe he's not. You give him another story. A real one."

"What story?" Joe protested. "I don't have anything."

On a mischievous impulse King solved the problem for him.

"We've set up Leo Derwent. Get the dirt from Freda and give it to Sutton. He likes publicity." He had laughed, and Joe sniggered loyally with him. They had tapes and hidden camera records of Mr. Leo Derwent's sexual preferences, supplied by the call girl introduced to him for that purpose. Harold King set off for America with his daughter, light in heart and full of manic energy. He had decided to short-circuit his financial difficulties by taking the massive pension funds and using them as his personal security. He wouldn't waste time; he'd conclude negotiations with Field Bank, and introduce Gloria into the deal. They might as well accept that she would be side by side with him from now on. It gave him a satisfying sense of continuity to show off his heir.

He had told her about using the funds; it was a test of her business ethics, and she hadn't failed him. "Why not? You need the money—who's going to know?" She was his girl, and he was proud of her.

During the four-hour flight to New York they worked on the figures together. He enjoyed teaching her, initiating her into the way he manipulated money. She would never have his originality or lateral brain power in creative accounting, but all she need do was keep to his guidelines. The businesses would run themselves.

When he reached the Waldorf, he sent several faxes, including one to Joe Patrick at his export-import number.

Retain Harper and Drew until further notice. Surveillance on Julia Hamilton and Ben Harris was to continue.

No hostages to fortune. Once he'd laid hands on those pension funds, he had put his whole business empire on the line.

It was Ben's idea that they rent their flats. They couldn't remove the telephone bugs without blowing Sutton's cover story. And neither place was as secure as Ben wanted. Julia didn't argue with him; she was chilled at the idea that her flat had been penetrated and her movements watched. The thought of Jean Adams haunted her with guilt. And the guilt overcame her fear for her own safety. Ben was right. They needed a place in a high-security block of flats, where nobody would be let in without authorization. The cost would be borne by Western. Ben insisted on that, and Western didn't quibble. They found what they wanted in Chelsea Green, a charming backwater off the King's Road, where a luxury block had a fourth-floor flat for sale. A substantial rent, paid confidentially, secured a year's lease, and it was withdrawn from the market. They moved in together with the ginger cat. Ben had wrung a further concession from Western. Money was available for Julia to redecorate and refurnish it to her own taste. It had amused him to watch Harris turning the screw on him and letting him get away with it.

He would turn a very tight screw of his own when they were safe in the plush little fortress he had provided.

Felix Sutton had come up with a story about the junior minister, Leo Derwent, courtesy of the man they suspected of being in the pay of Harold King. Sutton passed it on as genuine and tended to view Harris's conspiracy theory with some doubt. Ben didn't waver.

Joe Patrick had been a plant, and he was simply lending himself credibility and keeping contact with someone in touch with Julia.

"Are you going to run this muck on Derwent?" he asked her.

"I don't want to, but we've got to fill the November slot with something. I'll talk to Western about it."

Ben had seen the photographs and listened to some of the tapes. Felix had thought they were extremely funny and guffawed at the absurdity of the dialogue between the principals in the fantasy games.

Harris decided his sense of humor was the result of a twenty-year age gap. He saw nothing amusing in human degradation.

Western would have no scruples; if it was a strong story, he would authorize it. Julia made an appointment to see him. She took the evidence supplied to Sutton with her.

He was in brisk, cheerful spirits when she came into

his office. "How is your nice new flat?" He greeted her immediately. "Everything fixed up by now? Good; you want to talk about the November feature—we'll get that over with first. Sit down, Julia. What have you got in that briefcase?" The words came out in a torrent; it was a subtle form of bullying because it deprived the subject of a chance to speak. How well she knew the technique—it always infuriated her.

"I did send you a note of thanks," she said. "We're secure and that's the main thing. I've got the material for November in here. It's not very pretty, I'm afraid, but you had better see it and decide whether we should go ahead." She opened the case and gave him a sealed envelope. He opened it, skimmed through the pictures, his face completely impassive as if he were looking at someone else's holiday snaps.

"Nasty," he said, looking up at her. "I don't need to listen to those." He put the tapes back in the envelope and replaced the sheaf of photographs with them. "Derwent was your first assignment, remember? He was a nasty little specimen even then. Before we use it, we'll have to clear it with the lawyers first. I doubt he'll decide to sue." He smiled.

"I had another angle," Julia suggested. "There is a point, Lord Western that could be argued on moral grounds. Whatever Leo Derwent does in private has no relevance to the performance of his public duties."

"Unless it lays him open to blackmail," he countered. "Which these activities certainly do."

"Exactly," Julia said. "So who took them and why? Who was going to use them to blackmail Derwent? Why don't we chase up that angle and get Derwent to cooperate in exchange for keeping his name out of it? Ben thinks this is a typical entrapment of a politician someone wants to put in their pocket. I believe he's right. Now they're throwing Leo Derwent to the lions. Maybe he wouldn't give in to blackmail?"

"Very clever." Western beamed at her. "We fill the slot and we have the little brute in our pocket. Good, strong stuff. Blackmail attempt on prominent political figure, et cetera, et cetera. It'll have every hare running in Westminister worrying in case they've been found out. But you're not going to do it, Julia. You've got a damned good staff, give it to John Stevens. You and Harris have one target, and you're not wasting your time on anything else. Harold King. A war criminal. That's what I want to hear about from you—not dirt like this." He swept the envelope aside. "What's your next line?"

She had to face him.

"I don't know," she said. "We have an allegation without dates or locations beyond the Western Desert. No charges were ever brought. There's no record in the official histories of the campaign of any prisoner being murdered. It was a clean war out there."

"There's no such thing," Western snapped at her. "Minor atrocities happened everywhere on both sides. I know, I fought in it."

Julia looked up at him. "You did? In the Western Desert?"

"Briefly, yes, till I was captured. I'd been wounded and I was repatriated." He dismissed the subject. "I'm not going to do your job for you. And I have to remind you that one more slip like the last, when a leak cost that poor Adams woman her life, and there won't be a job. For either of you. You've got a month, Julia. I want Harold King in the December issue of 'Exposure.' Good morning."

Julia stood up. She said, "I can't guarantee it by December, Lord Western. But I'll prove him guilty. For Jean Adams, not for any other reason." Then she left the office.

Western sat quietly; he was a very still man when he

was thinking. He knew Harold King was in America. And he knew why. He was gathering his forces for a frontal attack on Western International. Western had contacts in the banking world in Canada and the U.S. He had friends, and he rewarded them for safeguarding his interests. The buzz about Harold King was growing. And he knew that if the scale being mentioned was right, he would lose the battle. December. It wasn't a date plucked out of the air. It would take King time to set up such a huge financial operation, and there was talk of him marshaling private funds. He was throwing everything into the bid. And the opening moves would start early in the New Year. He pressed the red button on his desk. It signaled to his secretary that he was not to be disturbed.

He rested his head in his hands and let his mind roam backward. Back to heat and sandstorms and the danger of death in the desert.

A clean war, that young woman had insisted, with the assurance of the unborn at the time. Nothing in the official history.

Nothing in the laudatory biographies of the two great commanders, Montgomery and Rommel. "A gentleman's war," some idiot had described it.

There had been books written by men who had fought in the Western Desert and had distinguished themselves in battle and viewed it through a romantic haze. Brave men, knights of the desert. He hadn't been one of them.

He had the scars on his body to prove it. They were on his back.

"I'm going to see Leo Cambell Derwent myself," Julia announced.

"Good idea," Ben agreed.

"I want to find out if we're right and King is mixed up

in this. Then Stevens can take over. You know, I almost walked out this morning when he said that about Jean Adams!"

"He was needling you," Ben said. "He doesn't give a bugger about her or anyone but himself. Don't let it get to you. That's what he wants. He was sticking the spur in to get you fired up. Bastard," he added, pouring wine for them both. She had been right to leave King out of it. She was learning how to deal with William Western.

"Do we have a copy of *Who's Who?*" she asked suddenly. Ben's books had come with his sparse furniture. There were a lot of them.

"I've got it, and Debrett's, and all the other references. Over there, top shelf," he told her.

She got up. "I want to look up Western."

She was edgy that evening; the interview had upset her. That barb about the unfortunate Jean Adams had drawn blood. He knew how much she agonized over it.

"Here it is," she said. "Look, 'served with the East Anglian Regiment in North African campaign, 1942, wounded, taken prisoner and repatriated 1943.'"

"So?" he asked her. "What's your drift?"

"The way he talked this morning. 'Minor atrocities happened everywhere on both sides. . . .' I wonder, Ben." She was frowning. She snapped the heavy book shut and put it back. "You said you were sure King had some lever on him, and that's why he pulled you out of the first investigation."

"There was no other reason," Ben said. "He was out for King's blood, just as he is now, and then he backed off. No warning, no explanation, he called me in, told me to drop it and forget the whole thing, and gave me the news editor's job."

"Could it have been something he did in the war? Give me the timetable again. When did he kill the project?"

Ben shrugged. "About ten years ago. Year before he got his peerage. I was sure it was tied in with that. Whatever King threatened him with, he backed down. But why the war? It's a hell of a long time ago—"

"I know, but a lot of things happened then—like King shooting unarmed prisoners. It was the way he talked . . . he wasn't shocked by the idea, he just wanted to prove it so he could finish off King."

"J, darling," Ben reminded her, "you're not investigating Western. He's a cold-blooded bastard. Nothing would shock his conscience; he doesn't have one. You're letting this morning get under your skin. Forget it for a few days, make an appointment to see Leo Derwent, and I'll see if I can come up with anything. I'll ask my pals in the War Office. They helped out before. Your feathers are all ruffled—come here."

After a while she looked at him.

"What would I do without you? I don't deserve you, Ben. I come home and rant on all evening, and I haven't even started to make dinner."

"Dinner," he said firmly, "can wait."

CHAPTER 7

LEO DERWENT WAS ON EDGE. HE'D TAKEN the personal call from Julia Hamilton, and when he put the telephone down, he was uneasy.

She was doing "Exposure," and there were rumors flying about the subject of the opening feature in November. The boast made to Gloria King during that dinner party was suddenly an awful threat.

She wanted a private interview, stressing the word "private."

He had proposed a meeting in his office in the House. When she came in, he appeared to be relaxed and well briefed about her career since they last met.

Very much the junior minister entertaining a member of the quality press, but sweat was beading under his armpits and on the palms of his hands while he went through the small talk. His secretary brought a tray of coffee. "Well," he said at last, "I know you're a busy lady, and my time is limited. What can I do for you, Miss Hamilton?"

Julia opened her shoulder bag and took out an envelope.

"These have come into our possession," she said quietly. "I thought you ought to see them." She watched him as he opened the envelope and saw the first of the photographs. Blood rushed into his face and then drained till he was a ghastly white. He opened his mouth as if to speak. He put the photographs facedown on his desk and looked at Julia.

"Where did you get these? What is this?"

He sounded as if he were choking.

"They were sold to my newspaper," she said. "With some tape-recording sessions between you and the woman in the pictures."

"What do you want?" He was staring at her. "You're not going to print these. . . . I'll sue, I'll fight you to the highest court. . . ." The words were brave, but the man was stricken.

Julia said, "Nobody's going to print such things in any newspaper. I haven't come here to expose you or threaten you, Mr. Derwent. I've come because I don't like blackmail, and I believe that's what has happened to you. I want to run a feature, but you won't be mentioned. I want to scare off the kind of people who took these photographs and set you up. I'm being absolutely honest. You've got nothing to fear from us. I want your help."

He shook his head. "I'm ruined," he said, "completely ruined. If you don't run this story, they'll go to someone else—"

"We bought the negatives," she countered. "It was

targeted at my feature, and I want to know why. Tell me honestly, was anyone trying to blackmail you? Why did you call their bluff?"

"With these? My God. I'd have given my last penny to buy them back. No. Nobody approached me. Oh, my God," he said again. "I need a drink. Excuse me."

He got up and opened a cupboard. Bottles and glasses were assembled for entertaining. He poured a large neat vodka and came back to the desk.

"What a mess," he said. "What a bloody awful mess."

Julia asked him, "Have you any idea who set you up? Do you have any enemies?"

He swallowed the vodka. "I've made enemies—who doesn't in politics?"

"Did anyone know about this affair? Does this woman have other clients? Where did you find her?"

Leo Derwent scowled. "I didn't pick her up, if that's what you mean. I met her at a dinner party." His frown deepened. "She wasn't a tart, she was just another guest. We hit it off, and we liked the same sort of games. I never paid her—just a present or some flowers. . . ."

"She wasn't a guest," Julia said. "She was a plant. Who gave the party?"

He didn't answer for a moment. Then he said, "Harold King. I was down at his house for the weekend. She came with another man."

"And gave you a very heavy signal?" Julia suggested. He nodded.

"She came on very strong. Christ. I never thought for a minute—"

"Why should you?" Julia interrupted. "You met her at a friend's house. Would you describe King as a friend?"

"I know him. I've been down there once or twice. I thought he was aiming me at that daughter. . . . She was always seated next to me, chatting me up. I thought it was rather funny. Christ," he muttered again. "You think it was King?"

"Who else?" Julia asked. "He wanted to get something on you and he fixed you up. Your girlfriend was in on it. She must have set the camera and the tape and handed the stuff over."

"Then why didn't he use it?" Derwent demanded. "Why pass it on to you? He wouldn't give Western the drop off his nose."

"Something more important was at stake. So he sacrificed you."

"What do you want me to do?"

He had recovered his nerve. He looked mean and seething with rage. King had made a bad enemy, Julia decided. A cornered fox that would fly at his throat when he got the chance.

"I want you to do nothing," she said quietly. "Behave as if this hadn't happened. See King, be friendly, ask the daughter out to lunch if you can stomach it."

He watched her keenly. "Why?"

"Because we're working on something that will bring Harold King up on a criminal charge. A very serious charge."

Leo Derwent smiled. "I love it," he said. "What else do I have to do?"

"Tell me anything you hear, anything you pick up. That's why I suggested the daughter. Did she fancy you?"

He shook his head. "I've heard she fancies girls. Wouldn't surprise me. But I'll try. By Christ, I'll give it my best shot if it'll put that bastard in the shit."

Then he said quickly, "What about this feature on blackmail . . . are you going to hint at him? What about security for me?"

Julia stood up. "I'll make it a general feature. I can cite several examples in a vague enough way to throw anyone off. My boss wants a lot of hares running, not just one. And here's proof of his good faith."

She handed him the manila envelope.

"Everything's in it," she said. "Negatives and tapes. I don't expect you'll be seeing her again."

"If I did," he said savagely, "I'd make it for real."

"He's the worst kind of creep," Julia said to Ben that evening. "I wouldn't trust him an inch if I could help it. But he'll do anything to get back at King after this. And we might pick something up. He promised he'll chat up the daughter . . . He said she was a lesbian, but that won't stop him. My God, we do elect some gems of humanity, don't we?"

"You get good and bad in everything. Our own profession isn't exactly lily white. And here's something to take the taste of Leo Derwent out of your mouth. I read it in an hour."

It was a small, privately printed booklet. *Memories of the Desert War*. The author had served as an officer in the East Anglian Regiment. He had won a DSO for bravery at the battle of Sidi Abbas and been captured trying to escape back to the British position at Tobruck.

There was a photograph on the cover of a good-looking young man in shorts and shirt, his cap at a rakish angle, posing with three other men.

"Darling," Julia said gently. "I've had a long day. I don't think I'm in the mood for war stories."

Ben said quietly, "I think you'll be in the mood for this one. There are some good photographs inside. Trust me."

She looked at him and said, "Ben? You're on to something . . . why didn't you tell me? You've let me go on about bloody Leo Derwent—"

"You needed to get it out of your system, that's why,"

he said. "I'll make supper tonight. You get stuck into that."

He was putting steak under the grill when he heard an exclamation.

He came and looked around the door. "Ben," she said. "It's him! In the photograph—Look!"

He said, "I told you it was interesting. Wait till you get to the end."

Joe Patrick went through the reports from the detective agency. He didn't repeat his earlier mistake; he kept King informed on a daily basis, but they'd lost the telephone taps on Harris and Hamilton, and there was no chance of getting into the new flat they shared together.

The building was very secure, with TV, entry-phone system, and resident porter. The surveillance reported Julia Hamilton going to the House of Commons, but that was the only break in her normal office routine. She and Harris led a quiet domestic life, rarely going out. When they did, it was usually to the same restaurant and the pub close by the *Herald* offices. There was a dearth of activity, which King noted and found reassuring. They were at a dead end after Jean Adams. The negotiations in New York were coming to a climax. He had appointed Gloria to the board of the Pension Fund Management before they left England. Her signature, combined with his and that of a terrified accountant who never even read what he was required to sign, released the eighty million investments into King's personal control. When presented to the chairman and board of Field Bank, they appeared as private assets.

He stopped off at Miami, and he didn't involve Gloria in these negotiations. She'd come to that part of his business interests later on.

She accepted the exclusion with her usual docility. He

noticed how she bullied the staff who accompanied them from London and demanded service from their hotels with a high-handedness equal to his own. With him she was a submissive and adoring acolyte.

She went to Mimi's Club, courtesy of King's business acquaintance who owned the place, and sunned herself by the pool while he was busy. She found one of the cocktail waitresses attractive and secured her services by mentioning her need of a personal maid to the manager. The girl understood that if she wanted to keep her job, she had better accommodate Miss King. There'd be a good tip at the end of it. She was used to taking care of the men. It was her first experience of a woman lover. She confided to her friends that for sheer appetite this ugly bitch left the guys at the starting gate. And she was good too. It made a nice change having a woman. She rather liked it.

King spent two days in conference with the local Mafia representative who owned Mimi's Club and three of the biggest hotels in the resort. He was a majority shareholder in the company controlling a string of escort agencies and massage parlors. He fronted for the godfathers who controlled the business in the state. King had obliged him by laundering drug money through one of his own subsidiaries in Lichtenstein. It was more of a courtesy call than serious business, but King believed in keeping his contacts sweet against the time to call in favors. With the takeover planned for the early part of the coming year, he was mustering his allies. On the night before they left for England, King entertained him in his own restaurant and introduced him to Gloria. She was looking very well, tanned from the sun and relaxed after an afternoon spent with the waitress. King was proud of her.

The mafioso was complimentary. When she had left them to their late cigars, he said, "A lovely girl. Not married yet?"

King had shrugged and said, "She's hard to please. She loves her old Daddy too much to leave him."

"Yeah, my daughter's the same. But she's got a good husband and four kids. They make my life, those kids. You find the right guy for her; I picked Maria's man, and they're very happy. A man needs grandchildren when he gets to our age."

King accepted the flattery. He was at least fifteen years older than the American. "There's no hurry," he insisted. "She'll find someone."

But the idea stuck in his mind. Gloria was a catch. Never mind that she didn't bother much with men. King paid no attention to that. She was a big girl and shy. He'd warned her about fortune hunters a long time ago. Maybe that had put her off.

He came back to London in a mood of swelling confidence. Everything was going his way. His instincts scented success and ultimate victory. They had never failed him. The biggest gamble of his business life was coming to the final throw, and all the signs told him that luck was on his side.

"Billy," Evelyn Western said firmly. "You've got to stop driving yourself. You're awake half the night, and you're so on edge, you can't relax, even on the weekend."

"How can I?" he demanded. "When nothing's happening? Nothing. There's a bloody feature coming out about the vulnerability of politicians to blackmail in their private lives and nothing about King in the pipeline. I told her, I want the slot in December. So far she's done nothing!" he repeated, banging his hand on the tabletop. The cut-glass goblet jumped. He wiped the drops of wine off the polished surface.

"Ever since that woman's murder they've ground to a halt on the whole thing. And now this."

He had told Evelyn the news as they changed for dinner. He was so upset by it, he canceled a theater engagement with friends and said he wanted a quiet evening at home with her. Evelyn didn't hesitate. She made the excuses over the telephone herself, pleading a cold and a temperature. When he was wrought up like this, she humored him. But she lectured him too. Yes, she agreed, forcing herself to appear calm. It was very disturbing news about King's alliance with Field. But he'd known King was in the States raising money. "But not that sort of sum," he protested. "Backed by a huge amount from his own private funds. He's gearing up to strike at me, and I won't be able to stop him. The next step is the rumor mongering. We're in financial trouble. I'm losing control. . . . Good God, Evie, we've seen the technique used on other people. I know how the rot starts. He's got two financial journalists in his pocket; they'll print anything he tells them to—you just wait. As soon as Christmas is over and the decks are cleared for news, it'll start. I'm sorry, I can't eat any more of this."

Evelyn said quietly, "Come on, let's go and have our coffee in the drawing room. I'll pour you a brandy and you settle down. I've got an idea and I'd like to see what you think of it."

William Western had benefited from his wife's ideas before. She was a very intelligent woman, with a mind untrammeled by the minutiae of his daily business problems. Sometimes she saw things more clearly than he did.

"Good idea," he said. "Sorry I've been such a bloody bore this evening. Making you cancel the theater. I know you were looking forward to it."

She smiled at him and took his arm for a moment.

"I'd much rather get a good night's sleep without you tossing and turning beside me," she said gently. "I don't care about the theater. We can go later, it'll run forever after those reviews. All I care about is you getting into a state. It's bad for you, and you know it."

He led her to the sofa. The butler brought their coffee, and Evelyn said, "A large brandy for His Lordship, please, Arthur."

The hapless Filipino was still in the house in Hampshire. Still being bullied by his employer, but tolerated so far because Evelyn Western knew a replacement wouldn't fare any better. The English butler had looked after them in London for twelve years. He had worked in royal service, and Western was in awe of him. He gave the Westerns' establishment prestige.

When they were alone, Evelyn said, "Why don't I talk to Julia?"

"What good would that do?" he demanded. "I've talked to her and I didn't pull any punches."

"I'm sure you didn't, but perhaps that's not the right approach. Have you thought of this, Billy—perhaps she doesn't want the job? That poor woman was murdered. . . . Julia's not the type to come to you and admit that she's too frightened to continue."

After a pause he said, "But she might admit it to you."

"Yes. She trusts me. She thinks I'm on her side. And I am of course, so long as it's not a conflict of interests with you. Let me take her out to lunch and have a heart-to-heart with her. I may even be able to reassure her if she is afraid. A little morale booster." She smiled at him. "Bluster doesn't always work, you know."

William Western looked at his wife. Serene and beautiful, a kindly mentor for a young woman who could be in mortal danger.

"You know," he remarked, "you're more ruthless than I am."

"When something threatens you, I certainly am. Leave Julia to me."

"Did she say why she wanted to meet you?" Ben asked.

"No, she just suggested lunch, and I couldn't exactly say no," Julia answered. "She was always very sweet to me, especially when I started on the *Herald*. Ben, I was wondering—do you think I could ask her about Western? She might confide in me."

He shook his head. For all her flair Julia was still naïve about some people.

"No," he said flatly. "My guess is she's hoping you're going to confide in her. Sweetheart, I know she's a charming lady and she took you around the dress shops and all the rest of it, but she's his wife and you don't live with a prize shit like Western for forty years without some of it rubbing off. You told me they were hand in glove, so just be careful. Don't get conned and don't tell her anything you wouldn't say to him. Promise?"

"All right," Julia agreed. "But you're wrong about her. She's always been a friend to me. Don't be such a cynic."

"Just remember," he insisted. "She's on Western's side, not yours. Don't be too trusting."

He hoped Julia would listen to him, but he wasn't sure.

They met at the Hyde Park Hotel.

Julia was early, and as usual Evelyn Western was late. She came in smiling and apologetic. "My dear—I'm so sorry. I do hope you haven't been waiting long. The traffic was frightful coming through the park. Now, let's have a drink while we look at the menu, shall we?"

She had an ageless beauty; she was as distinguished in appearance as her husband was small and commonplace. People were watching her admiringly as she led the way into the restaurant.

"I asked for a table by the window," she said. "I love this view of the park, don't you? You're looking very pretty as usual. Charming color that deep yellow. Most imaginative with your red hair."

Julia warmed to her, she couldn't help it.

"Thanks to you, Lady Western. One of the first dresses you advised me to buy was a buttercup yellow. I wore it till it fell to bits."

"Good heavens," Evelyn said. "So I did. What a long time ago it was. How many years? And look how well you've done."

"Thanks to Lord Western. He gave me the opportunities."

"He's always promoted young talent. He recognized yours from the very beginning. He really thinks the world of you, you know."

"That's very nice," Julia said. Evelyn Western gave her a confiding look, and said, "He's much maligned. People don't understand what a remarkable man he is, and deep down how genuine and sincere. I've often said to him his manner is so off-putting. He blusters." She smiled indulgently. "I suppose smaller men tend to do that.

"It would be a tragedy if he lost everything he's built up. This wonderful newspaper, all the other businesses. He's given employment to thousands. I don't have to tell you that the pension plans are the most generous in the communications industry. William cares very much for his people. He'd never show it or say so, but of course he does to me."

She leaned a little forward. "That's why he needs your help, Julia. That horrible creature King is out to smash my husband and take everything from him. He's raised a huge sum of money, millions and millions in America, to mount an attack on us and get his hands on the *Herald*. It would kill William if he succeeded. And I wouldn't be able to bear it either."

"Lady Western," Julia said slowly. "I'm trying, I really am."

"It's very brave of you after what happened to Jean Adams."

Julia was unprepared for that. Evelyn Western went on. "My husband talked to me about it. He was worried that you might feel in danger and didn't like to say so. But you must say if that's what's the matter. He wouldn't blame you—nobody would. I'm sure Ben Harris would take over from you."

"Ben would love me to give up on this. He's tried to talk me out of it, he even went to your husband . . . but I'm not giving up. I want to see Harold King in jail and I'm going to put him there. He's a murderer. I cut my teeth as a journalist on those terrible child murders in Rhys. I was very green, very inexperienced. But I stuck it out because I wanted whoever did it caught and punished. That's how I feel about King. Don't worry about me, Lady Western. I'm going on and I think I may just have found a clue. Would you do me a favor?"

"Of course," Evelyn Western said. "If I possibly can. What is it?"

"I'd like a week's leave. Would you suggest it to your husband? Say I need to have a short break away from the office. If I ask him myself, he'll think I'm bailing out, or else he'll want to know why and where and what for. And at this point I can't tell him. Could you do it?"

"I should think so. He knows we're lunching. You can't tell me, I suppose?"

Don't be too trusting, Ben had insisted. *She's on his side, not yours.* . . . For a moment Julia was tempted to confide in her. She looked into the fine blue eyes that were gazing into hers with such intensity.

"I'd rather not," she said.

"Forgive me for asking," Evelyn Western said. "It's

just that I'm so anxious about what may happen. Time is the enemy, my dear. We have so little to spare. Don't fail, will you?"

"No," Julia promised. "I won't. I promise you."

"You were wrong," Julia said. "She wasn't pumping me."

Ben shrugged. Evelyn Western hadn't tried to prize information out of Julia, though she had damned nearly charmed her into elaborating on the clue she had discovered.

What she had done was apply the most powerful pressure on her to continue without regard for her own safety. It was all very subtle, playing on Julia's gratitude for her help in the past. Western—a man who cared about his employees. Genuine and sincere. Ben had kept his temper while Julia repeated the conversation. She couldn't see through it. She liked and trusted Evelyn Western. "He'll give you the leave and pretend he doesn't know it's a put-up job between you. Darling, she'll tell him everything you said. Not that it matters."

"Nothing matters," Julia insisted. "Except that I get to Jersey before Christmas. And that everyone thinks I'm on holiday."

"It would be more convincing if I came with you," he suggested.

"No. I couldn't stay with my cousins. That's all part of it. It's got to look absolutely genuine. You can't hold my hand all the time."

She reached out and squeezed his. "Even though I like it," she added. "Let me do it my way, Ben. If I come up with something, we'll be on course again. And flying."

She changed the subject.

"Any news of Lucy?" He was now in regular touch with his daughter.

"She called this morning. She's feeling sick, but otherwise she's fine. God, I'll be a grandfather by next April. I'm rather looking forward to it."

Julia laughed. "I know you are. You talk about other people conning—you're the biggest fraud of the lot. Grouchy old Harris, hates the world. It was just a big act."

She kissed him lightly. "You're a soft touch."

"If I am," he said, "it's thanks to you. What do you want for Christmas?"

Julia pretended to consider. "Mink coat—no, that's old-fashioned. I don't want to get spat at in the street. Some little number with a few diamonds." She loved teasing him. Then seriously. "A weekend at Fordingbridge after Christmas. To make up for the one that rotten Felix promised me. That's what I'd like."

"That's what you'll have," he promised. "But I don't fish."

"I don't either. We can get lessons. Who's going to look after poor Pussy?"

"I'll ask the porter. If I give him a fiver, he'll feed her while we're away."

They spent a quietly happy evening watching television and talking. Before she went to sleep beside him, Julia thought suddenly, *This is like marriage, this mix of passion and companionship. I've never been bored since the day I went to the pub and had our first drink together. Angered sometimes, frustrated, confused by him, but never bored.* She slid her arm around him and moved closer, then fell asleep.

"He's asked me out to the theater and dinner," Gloria said.

Her father looked up suspiciously. "You're not going? With that creep?"

"He's got seats for the new Branagh production of *Othello*. I'd like to see it. Besides, you told me to chat him up, Daddy."

"That was then," King said abruptly. He thought she looked disappointed. "Do you want to go?"

She hesitated. "Not if you don't want me to. I'd like to see the play, that's all."

Immediately King softened. "Go on, then, darling, if you'll enjoy it. You won't have to go to Mummy's charity gala!"

They laughed.

"I wasn't anyway. That sort of thing bores me as much as it does you, Daddy," Gloria said.

Leo Derwent. She was surprised by the invitation. And intrigued. She had gleaned from her father that he had peculiar sexual tastes. She wondered what they were.

She put on some very expensive jewelry that night. Leo Derwent paid her a nice compliment. "You're looking great, Gloria. Love the dress." He thought she looked like a big cabbage doll hung with diamonds. Grotesque. He wished he hadn't booked at such a smart restaurant for dinner afterward. He was sure to be seen. . . .

The play absorbed Gloria. That was a relief to him. She didn't talk through the performance; they had champagne in the interval, and she surprised him by making intelligent comments on the play and its interpretation. Briefly he forgot how unattractive she was. But dinner was labored. She had no small talk after the subject of the play was exhausted. Mindful of the motive for the evening, Leo prompted her to talk about her trip to the States.

She became animated. "It was fascinating. I'd gone on trips with my father before, but this was special. You know, he's teaching me everything."

Leo smiled at her. "Grooming you for stardom?"

She smiled back, a little color in her pale cheeks. "Yes. One day he wants me to take over."

"Really?" Leo wasn't bored any longer. "What a challenge—think you can do it?"

She was defensive. "Why not? He thinks I can. He says I've got the same kind of business brain."

He said, "You're too attractive to be that clever."

She didn't simper. She didn't blush. She stared at him with King's pale eyes and said, "I'm not attractive to men." He wasn't fazed. He laughed at her. "Come on, Gloria, you know that's not true. You've got a hell of a lot going for you. Why be defensive about it?"

"I've got Daddy's money going for me, I know that," she said.

"I think you've got it wrong," he said. He was enjoying playing this odd creature like a fish. More of a barracuda, he suspected. "Money like yours could be a real turnoff for most men. It'd scare them to death. How to cope with a girl who has everything. . . . How to live up to a father-in-law like Harold King. Have you ever thought of it like that? Have you had a lot of boyfriends?" Then he played it softly. "If you mind me asking . . . just say so . . . "

She considered for a moment. Other men had dated her, but seldom more than once or twice. She'd been bored and so had they. Manifestly. This foxy-faced man with his sharp mind was a challenge. He wasn't talking to her as if she was a rich dumbo.

"I'm not attracted by men," she said, and stared at him. She wondered how he would field that. He allowed a little smile to appear on his lips. They were thin lips over sharp, narrow teeth that were very white.

"I'd say that was because you've never met a man who knew how to cope with you," he said. "You're very like your father. Strong personality, quite a challenge to a man. Do you like girls?"

"Everyone knows you like them," she said. She was rewarded by a change of expression. Just a flash of antagonism. She wondered why.

"Some girls," he said. He smiled at the bitch, probing

the remark for hidden malice. She hadn't answered his question about her own sexual preferences. She had avoided that one. He decided it was time to change direction. He had found out one interesting piece of information. King was grooming her as his successor. Taking her on trips to the States. Letting her in on some of his business activities. He would like to know what those activities were and pass on the information.

If King had set out to destroy him, he was going to hit back at King where it would hurt him most. Through his daughter, with the help of Julia Hamilton. They ordered a last course, and Gloria chose the richest pudding on the menu. He was careful with his figure. He made do with sorbet, which he didn't even like, just to keep her company. She didn't speak, absorbed in eating. Then she said, "Don't you like food? I love it."

"I'm as greedy as the next man, but I have to watch my weight. Fat politicians aren't a good example in our health-conscious society."

She looked at him in faint contempt. "Do you care about things like that? I wouldn't."

"I care about making the right impression," he said. "I'm an ambitious bastard. Everyone knows that too. I want to get to the top of the ladder. If it means watching my waistline, so be it."

Gloria looked at him with interest. "You want to be prime minister?"

"Doesn't every politician? Of course they do. They start the caring bit when they know they're not going to get any farther. You know, I wouldn't talk to most people like this. You have a man's mind, that's why. I like girls, but I can't talk to them. They're too stupid. Have some coffee. I'm going to have a brandy. Will you join me?"

Gloria said, "Yes. I often have a brandy with Daddy after dinner. We sit and talk when my mother's gone to bed." She gave him a sudden smile. "She's terribly stupid. Daddy never discusses anything with her."

"But she's beautiful," Leo countered. "You can't have everything."

"*She's* into the caring bit," Gloria said, "in a big way. She's on every charity committee, fund-raising and running after royalty. She'll love it when Daddy gets his peerage."

He sipped the fine brandy and said lightly, "I didn't know about that. In the New Year's Honors List?" Bile rose in his throat at the thought of it.

"No, maybe the Birthday Honors. He'll get it, he always gets what he wants. He's set his heart on this. I think it's because people like Western got titles and Daddy didn't. He hates being outdone." She giggled. "I tease him about it sometimes."

"And you'll be the Honorable," Leo remarked. "The Honorable Gloria King. Sounds very grand." He smiled. "It'll suit you. You know, I've really enjoyed this evening. I love the theater, and none of my girlfriends would have appreciated that play we saw tonight. You know why I asked you?" Gloria shook her head. The diamond earrings flashed fire. "Because when I was down for the weekend, you told me you liked the theater."

She said casually, "I like opera too. I'm very musical."

"I'm not," he admitted. "I prefer ballet. Do you like ballet?"

"No," she said flatly. "All those gays prancing about. I love Italian opera. They're doing Verdi at Covent Garden next week."

He said, "Then, why don't we go, and see if you can convert me?"

"We wouldn't get seats; they've been sold out for weeks. It's Pavarotti."

Leo Derwent summoned the waiter for his bill. "If I get tickets, will you come?"

Gloria showed her large, even teeth in a mocking smile that was not unfriendly. "If you get tickets, I'll come. I won't tell Daddy." She giggled again. "He tried and he couldn't get any."

Leo said, "That's a deal." He drove her home. He didn't touch her. The idea repelled him anyway, and it would have been a mistake. She wasn't ready for anything like that. Yet. He came to the front door of the house in Green Street and solemnly shook hands.

"Good night, Gloria. It's been fun tonight. I'll call you about the opera."

"You won't get seats," Gloria said.

"I always get what I want," he retorted. "Like your father. Good night."

She opened the door and went inside. She didn't thank him. She was reluctant to thank people; her father never did. It was a sign of weakness. He wouldn't get tickets for the Verdi opera. Not when her father had failed.

"Damn," Julia exclaimed. "They're away. They've gone to France for ten days. I spoke to the daily." She frowned at Ben Harris. "I hoped to get over early next week." Her cousins, the Petersons, were Jersey residents, and she'd intended inviting herself for a week's stay.

The holiday had to seem bona fide. They could make the contact she needed. There was no help for it; she would have to wait till they returned and then fix a date to visit them.

"Stop worrying," he advised her. "Nothing's going to happen in the next two weeks. And besides, you've got Leo Derwent and Gloria King up and running."

"Yes," she agreed. "He's seeing her again this week. God knows what they have in common. . . . But he's clever. I have to give him that."

"And he hates King's guts," Ben said. "So we know King's putting a deal together in the States, bringing the lovely Gloria in on the act, and working toward a peerage. Which ties in with his takeover of the *Herald*. He'll be the biggest single publishing and communications boss in the whole of the UK. Nobody in politics will want to get on the wrong side of him. Even the royals wouldn't be safe from someone with that much clout. Jesus. It makes the flesh creep."

"Which is why every day's delay does matter," Julia pointed out. "Why do the bloody Petersons have to go to France, just at this time?"

He shrugged. She was pacing up and down. He hadn't seen her so uptight since Jean Adams was murdered. That was the goad driving her, and nothing he could say relieved her sense of guilt. "I talked to Lucy today," he said. Julia didn't connect for a moment. "Lucy—yes of course. How is she?"

"Still sick," he said. "But she's told her mother. She took the news about the baby better than Lucy expected, but she wasn't too pleased about me coming into the picture. I'd like you to meet Lucy. Why don't we go up to Birmingham this weekend . . . she's always asking about you."

Julia pushed her hair back; she felt tired and slightly irritable. Frustration was fraying her nerves. She should have been in Jersey instead of going up to the Midlands to meet her lover's pregnant daughter.

"Ben darling," she said, "I'd rather wait. I've got this bloody trip on my mind. I'd be a drag on both of you. Why don't you go?"

"And leave you chewing your nails on your own here? No way. We'll do it another time."

"We could drive down and have lunch with my parents," she said on an impulse. "They're always asking about you. I did neglect them for quite a time. I was so wrapped up in my work, and they didn't like Felix. And they were wrapped up in my brother and the grandchildren. . . . I was jealous of that. But we've grown very close now, and I want to see them before Christmas. Next time we'll go up and see Lucy?"

"Okay," he said. "Why not? I'd like to see where the genes come from . . . either of them redheaded?"

"No." Julia smiled at him. "Daddy's father was. I suppose I get it from him. You're sure you don't mind about Lucy—just till I've got this trip to Jersey over?" She sighed. "It's so bloody crucial to the whole thing. God, I wish I could go there tomorrow!"

"Well, you can't, so relax," he advised. "Call your family and make a date. See if they can have us on Sunday. I hate Sundays in London. It's so dead. Everything's asleep."

"I never knew that," Julia said. "Why didn't you say so before? We could have done something different."

"Because I liked spending my day with you," he said quietly. "Our mornings in bed were rather special."

"Aren't they still?" she asked him.

"Oh, no," he said, mocking her. "You turn me off these days. Haven't you noticed?"

"Not really," Julia said, "if last night was anything to go on. Why do you always manage to wind me up? Why do I fall for it?"

"Because you're so crazy about me," he said solemnly. "Don't chuck that cushion at me . . . go and call your mother."

Listening to the telephone call, he watched Julia and realized how much she had changed his life. Sundays had been his worst day of the week. There was nothing to do, no work unless some crisis broke, just his own company in the empty flat. Quite often he opened a bottle of whiskey and settled down to drink his way through it till he fell asleep. Now he thought of the country on a Sunday morning. As a child he had woken to a world that was green. His father loved birds, and for a time he had managed to interest Ben in watching them. They were country people with simple values and hobbies that weren't dependent upon money. They had been blessed with a clever and ambitious son. Sometimes Ben wondered how much of a blessing he had really been to them. A foreign wife, a broken marriage, grandchildren that they seldom saw. They were both dead, and in those few minutes, listening to Julia talking to her mother, Ben Harris admitted how much he regretted the past. It was too late for them, but he had a second chance. A chance with a woman he loved and a chance with his daughter, Lucy. His son, Frank, had sent him a friendly message through his sister. He had been the more hostile to Ben of the two children when they divorced. It could all come right, he thought.

Julia hung up and turned to him. She looked happier, less strained.

"They're thrilled," she said. "Sunday will be fine. I warn you, Mum's a terrific cook and she believes in feeding everyone to bursting point. One thing . . . " She hesitated, and then said, "They're dying to see me settled. I could hear the wedding bells in her voice. Don't be put off by that, will you?"

He gave nothing away. "Don't worry, J, I won't. Why don't we go and catch that new Harrison Ford film at the Odeon?"

"Some men," Julia said sweetly, "just never grow up. Harrison Ford . . . I'll get my coat."

"Gloria's going out with that Leo again," Marilyn King remarked. King looked up and scowled. "It's becoming a bloody habit. What's he up to? I'll talk to her."

"Why do you have to interfere, darling? She's never had a steady boyfriend. I think she likes him." Gloria's mother couldn't imagine any man wanting her daughter, but the slim chance of getting rid of her made her take Gloria's part.

"Balls," King snapped. "She wouldn't like a turd like that. Anyway, if I want to talk to her, I'll talk to her." He went back to his newspaper. After a time he looked up and said, "Where's she going with him, then?" Marilyn said in her soft voice, "She didn't say. They went to the opera last week. Pavarotti. You couldn't get tickets, remember?"

That irritated him. His face reddened. He glared at her. "I didn't try," he said. "You wanted to see it." Leo Derwent dating his daughter. He shouldn't have let her go out with him in the first instance. He'd put a stop to it right now. He threw the newspaper aside. "Where is she?" he demanded. His wife knew that tone of voice. "Upstairs," she said. "Getting ready." Her hopes were dashed. King wouldn't let any man take his daughter. She sighed and resigned herself, as she had done all through her married life. Fortunately her expectations of happiness were limited to money, clothes, and social activities. She had given King what he wanted sexually until he obviously tired of her. She had borne the one child and been surprised that he had not insisted on more in the hopes of a son. He had been content with his daughter and left her to her own devices. They had never included lovers. She wasn't that interested in sex; it had been a means to an end with her as soon as she recognized the market value of her own beauty and appeal. It was a great relief not to go through the charade of pretending to enjoy it. All that thrashing about and moaning, she remembered with distaste. So boring. Life was better than it had ever been, with her circle of smart friends, her charity work, and the magical contacts with royalty. When she was Lady King, her cup would overflow.

She stopped thinking about Gloria and her short-lived romance.

Harold King didn't knock on his daughter's bedroom door. He banged it open and walked in. Gloria was putting on a smart velvet coat lined with fox.

"I want to talk to you," he said. She smiled at him placatingly.

"Daddy darling, I'll be late. . . . Is it very important?"

"You're meeting that shit Leo, aren't you?"

She looked surprised at his tone. "Yes, I am."

King sat on her bed. He looked at her and said, "Put him off."

"Daddy—why? What's wrong?"

"What's all this interest in you all of a sudden? He's got some ulterior motive."

A slight color crept up into her face.

"He enjoys my company, that's all. There's nothing in it. We like the theater and the opera. Daddy, there's nothing ulterior about it. There's no sex, if that's what you're worried about. He says I've got a man's mind and he can talk to me. . . . We're just friends—"

"Balls," King said angrily. "All he wants with women is to tie them up and cane their bottoms. He's trying to pull something." He didn't notice that she had flushed bright red. He had never seen her angry with him. "Call him and say you can't make it."

"It's the first night of the new Lloyd Webber," she said. "I can't just let him down at the last minute."

"Lloyd Webber? Very cultural." The sneer wounded her.

"Please, Daddy," her eyes were filling with tears. "Please. I'll go tonight and I won't see him again. I'll tell him, I promise." And then, in the first independent gesture of her adult life, she picked up her evening bag and brushed past him.

"I'll tell him," she repeated, and went out, leaving him there.

Leo had booked a table at Annabel's for dinner after the theater. He was advancing very slowly and carefully on his prey and he felt she was sufficiently off guard to go to the smartest nightclub in London; perhaps even to dance. She was good company, he was forced to admit that. She was sharp, with a cynical cast of mind that he enjoyed. She could even be witty in a mordant way. And she was flattered. She liked the attention he paid her, and she felt safe because there were no sexual overtones. Those, he thought coolly, could come later. Lesbians were said to be better in bed with a man than their heterosexual sisters. More practiced in the skills of arousal.

She was ugly and coarse, but she had her father's aura of power about her. He didn't find it attractive, but he found it challenging. And most important of all in his scenario was to hit Harold King right in the balls. He knew all about Leo's fun and games. He'd seen and heard the evidence. He wouldn't find it so amusing if the partner in the playacting was his own daughter.

Gloria sipped her champagne. She hadn't enjoyed the musical. She couldn't concentrate and relax because of what she had promised her father. And she was hurt. Once or twice during the performance she had blinked back angry tears. Her father had been brutal. He had dismissed the idea that she might have anything to offer anyone. The implication was clear. No one, not even someone he despised as much as Leo, would bother with her for herself.

There must be another motive. She had never felt a stirring of sexual interest in her companion. She liked his quick mind and shared his penchant for the arts. She liked going to good restaurants and first nights. That's all there had been in it until now. Hurt pride was accompanied by a childish desire to have her own way. And by something else. Her father's angry words whispered in her mind. *All he wants with women is to tie them up and cane their bottoms.* Curiosity uncurled inside her like a worm. What would it feel like? The worm became a pang of sensuality, and on an impulse she pushed her leg against him in the darkness. Leo felt the pressure and pressed back. Christ, he said to himself, pretending to concentrate on the spectacle on stage. *She's jumping the gun.* . . .

In the intimate gloom of Annabel's he turned to her and said, "You don't seem on form, Gloria. Anything the matter?" She put down her champagne glass. It was empty, and he signaled the waiter to refill it.

"You mean I've been boring?" It was so quick and defensive that it caught him off guard.

"God, no, don't be silly. You're never boring. I always enjoy myself so much when I'm with you it makes other women boring. What's the matter? Here . . . drink that up. Tell me. . . ."

Unlike King, whose teetotalism was famous, Gloria guzzled her wine as greedily as her food. She looked down and then up at him.

"My father wants me to stop seeing you."

Leo kept his head. "I'm sorry to hear that. Did he say why?"

She would never admit the reason. She said stubbornly, "He didn't say. He doesn't give explanations. He just expects people to do what he says."

"Even you?" he questioned. "I thought you were his favorite."

"Oh, I am," she said quickly. "He adores me. I adore him. He's wonderful."

Leo said gently, "Can't you make him change his mind? I don't want to stop seeing you, Gloria. I mean it."

"I don't want to stop either," she admitted. "I've had fun. We like the same things. . . ."

He said, "What's he got against me—did he say anything to you?"

There was a slight glaze over the very pale blue eyes as they considered him. It shocked him for a moment. He had seen that look in women's eyes before. He waited and moved his knee a little till it brushed against hers under the table. She didn't shift away.

"He said you liked bondage," she said, and her voice lowered to a breathy whisper. Leo risked everything on his instinct.

"And if I did," he said equally low, "would that matter to you? I'd never ask you to do anything. Unless you liked the idea . . . "

"I don't know," Gloria went on. She was staring ahead of her into the dimly lit reaches of the room, where couples gyrated to a throbbing disco rhythm. "I don't know," she repeated. "I've only done it with girls. I might like it, but I don't know."

"Well," Leo said, "you don't have to make any decisions. I'm happy as we are, if that's what you want. . . ." He placed his hand on hers for a moment. She didn't respond, but she didn't pull away. "Can't you talk your father around?"

"I don't think so," Gloria said. "He doesn't expect me to argue."

"Just do as you're told," he prompted. "That's the trouble, they go on thinking you're still a child. My old Dad was the same. I had quite a hassle, even after I was elected . . . he was still telling me what to do." He laughed, indulgent of parental foibles. "I don't blame your father, Gloria. I'd be the same if I had a daughter. One thing . . . how are you going to make decisions in business if you're not allowed to make them in your private life?"

"I *can* make my own decisions," she protested. "If I do see you—he doesn't have to know."

"I don't think that's the way to tackle this," he disagreed. "I don't want you deceiving your old man because of me. I've too much respect for him. Talk to him, Glory. Don't lie about us. Lies always get found out." She amazed him by laughing.

"Not if they're clever lies," she said. "Don't pretend to be moral, Leo. It doesn't suit you. What did you call me just now?"

"Glory," he said. "Sort of pet name. I always give pet names to people I like. Do you mind?"

"Do you have pet names for your girlfriends?" she asked.

Leo smiled. "No," he said. "I told you, only for people I like. Let's have another bottle, shall we? And how about a dance?"

"I hate dancing," she said flatly. "I haven't any sense of rhythm."

"I hated opera," he pointed out. "But I tried it and liked it with you. Come on."

She was clumsy. And she was right, she had no sense of rhythm, which was odd because she was genuinely musical. She had no confidence in her big body, that was the trouble. She looked awkward and uncomfortable.

He pulled her up against him. She went rigid. Then he took her wrists and held them firmly behind her back as they moved. He felt her relax and he tightened the grip. She started to move with him instead of resisting. Over her shoulder he smiled. Then after a few minutes he brought her back to the table.

"Well, that wasn't too bad, was it?" he said. "You've got a very good sense of rhythm." She took her place and looked at him.

"It was all right at the end," she said.

He drove her home and pulled up outside the Green Street house. "How are we going to play this, Glory? I can't call you at home."

"I could call you," she said. "I don't know. I'll think about it. . . ."

"I don't want to cause a row with you and your father."

"I'm not worried about that," Gloria answered. "I don't like going behind his back. He wouldn't take it out on me, but you might be in for trouble."

"He's not a man to cross, I know that much. But I'll chance it, if you will."

"I'll think about," she repeated.

She opened the car door and got out. She sounded very matter-of-fact.

"We could meet next week," he suggested. "Call me."

She nodded and turned away. He didn't linger either. He was used to her abrupt departures. She traded on her grace-less manner, copied from her father. As he drove home, Leo had a private bet with himself that, without knowing it, King had given him a key to Gloria. Perversion intrigued her. Imprisoning her arms on the dance floor had turned her on. Oddly enough, he admitted, it had done the same to him. He felt distinctly horny at the thought of that big, arrogant bitch lying helpless. He'd read somewhere that women with fixations on Daddy could only get satis-faction from sex by submitting to punishment. It eased the guilt of their subconscious incest. He grinned and switched on the radio. Time would tell.

Julia's mother loved a postmortem after a party. Julia's father wanted to go to sleep, but he indulged her. Besides, he was interested as much as she was. "He's obviously in love with her," May Hamilton said. "And I liked him."

"But?" he added when she paused.

"He's divorced and he's got grown-up children, and he's quite a bit older . . ."

"My dear, you can't have everything. One marriage in

three goes down the drain these days. Julia's not likely to find a bachelor unless there's something pretty odd about him. I liked Harris, he's intelligent. You've been hoping she'd settle down with someone for ages, and I think he might just be the one."

"Yes, I think so too. It's just that with a daughter I hoped for a nice wedding, you know, darling, all the trimmings. Like we had."

"I know." He smiled in the dark. His wife was a hopeless romantic. She dreamed of Julia floating down the aisle of the local church in a white dress and a virginal veil, with the grandchildren as page and bridesmaid trotting after her. It wouldn't happen like that.

In his way he was sorry too. "Julia's not twenty-one," he pointed out gently. "She's lived her life and she's an independent woman. She was always like that, even as a child. Went her own way, did her own thing. You used to fight with her about it, don't forget. You said it was such a relief dealing with Tom, he was so easygoing. Nothing was ever easy with Julia, and it's not going to change. I only hope she does marry this chap. Most of her generation don't bother—they live together and that's it."

"They're afraid of commitment, that's why," his wife said. She settled down beside him. "We weren't," she added.

"I know, May, we were all perfect. . . . Come on, let's hope it turns out for the best. I think it will. I think he'll cope with her. Not many men would be able to. Now, go to sleep, it's late."

"It was a lovely day, though" his wife had the last word. "I was so pleased they stayed on to supper instead of going after lunch. They must have enjoyed themselves. Why don't we ask them to come and spend Christmas with us? Darling, don't go to sleep . . . Wouldn't that be a nice idea?"

"We're going to your sister's," he mumbled. "You promised, you can't put her off."

May didn't answer. Her spirits were high with the anticipation. A big family gathering would be like the days when their two children were young, before there were other in-laws to be considered. She could ask her sister and her husband to join them instead. . . . She drifted off happily to sleep.

CHAPTER
8

"JANEY? HELLO THERE . . . IT'S ME—JULIA.
How are you?"

"Julia, what a lovely surprise. We're fine, how are
you? How's the job? May said you were a big noise on
the *Herald* now."

"Don't take any notice of Mum, she exaggerates," Julia
said. "Listen, I've got a week's holiday due, and I wondered
if you could stand having me to stay. I'm tired—actually
I've been working flat out—and a breath of sea air and a
few days with you and David would be heaven. . . ." She
paused, praying that her cousins weren't going on another
trip or coming to London to shop before Christmas.

Janey sounded delighted. "What a good idea—darling
Julia, we'd be thrilled to have you. When do you want to
come?"

Julia sighed with relief; her stomach had knotted with tension as she made the call. As she had said to Ben, this trip was crucial . . . and it had to seem completely unconnected with her work. An innocent holiday with relatives. That's why a hotel wouldn't do. King had used surveillance before, with fatal results for Jean Adams. She and Ben were sure they were still being followed. "Would Monday be too soon? I'm desperate for a break."

"You sound it," Janey Peterson remarked. "Monday would be lovely. Let us know what time your flight gets in and we'll meet you. David will be thrilled. . . . you're such a favorite of his. Do you want to have a quiet time, or shall I organize some jollity? It's up to you."

"Whatever you like—so long as there aren't any journalists!"

"Nobody in your league over here," her cousin said. "I've boasted about you to all my friends for ages . . . now I can show you off. See you on Monday. 'Bye, Julia. 'Bye."

They had retired to live in Jersey when David Peterson's mother died, leaving him her house. They had been there for two years, and Julia had seen them on trips to London. They declared themselves blissfully happy on the lovely island. David Peterson had been a consultant at one of the big teaching hospitals and had a thriving practice in Harley Street. He had abandoned what he described as the rat race of the National Health and private medicine in England for a similar job in Jersey. His mother was May Hamilton's sister. He was fifteen years older than Julia, and his wife, Janey, was a bouncy forty-year-old who was mad about tennis and sailing. They were a warm and friendly couple, and Julia had always got on very well with them. She pushed her hair back, making a mental note to get it cut before she left.

The Petersons knew everyone in Jersey. They were hospitable and popular. Their circle was not confined to the multimillionaires who settled there for tax reasons. David's mother had been a longtime resident, and her legacy entitled them to move to the island without the stringent financial conditions applied to the super rich. They could get her the introduction she needed. She called through to Ben at his office.

"I've fixed up to go on Monday," she said. "I'm going up to see Western."

On the other line Ben said, "Don't be surprised when he makes it easy for you. She'll have told him you're on to something."

"I don't think so," Julia bristled in Evelyn's defense. "She wouldn't do that. . . ."

Ben didn't answer. He just said, "I'm glad you've fixed it, but I wish you'd let me come with you."

Julia said, "No, darling. My mother called this morning. She thinks you're great. So do I." She hung up and dialed through to Western's private number and arranged to go up to see him in an hour.

"I can't see why you need to take time off," William Western said. "All you've done is help Stevens put together a feature on blackmail among MPs that anybody could have written." He stared at her accusingly.

"The feature's explosive," Julia protested. "Everyone says so."

"I'm the one that matters, and I don't think so," he snapped. "If you hadn't hooked Leo Derwent, there'd be no excuse at all."

"He's already given us valuable information," she countered.

"Nothing I didn't know already," Western remarked. "I knew about the deal King's putting together in the States. Whether he's bringing in that ghastly daughter to take over from him is irrelevant to me. So is the life peerage. He's out for my head, and so far nothing's been dug up to stop him. Now you come and ask for a holiday. . . . My wife said you were tired and needed a break. I said it was bloody nonsense."

He waited. Evelyn had primed him carefully. "You're supposed to think it's genuine, Billy. I said I'd persuade you she would benefit from a few days away. Don't let her see you know there's a reason behind it. Be nasty. She'll expect that." Evelyn was his right arm, he thought. Shrewd, invaluable in situations where feminine judgment was so superior to his own. And ruthless, as he said. She liked Julia, that was genuine. But she would sacrifice her without a qualm on his behalf.

Evelyn Western hadn't betrayed her trust, Julia decided. She had kept her word, in spite of Ben's suspicions. "Lord Western," she said. "I do need just a few days to clear my head. Then I promise you." She emphasized the word. "I promise you I'll get a breakthrough before Christmas. If I don't"—she faced him calmly—"then I'll put my resignation on your desk on the first of January."

"And I'll accept it," he said briskly. "Oh, all right, then, take a week if it's so essential to you. I'd get into trouble with my wife if I didn't say yes. Pity she took such a liking to you. When do you want to go?"

"From Monday?"

She hadn't confided fully in Evelyn, so he tried on his own account. "Where are you off to? Sunshine, I suppose. . . ."

"No, I'm going to stay with some cousins, that's all. Thank you, Lord Western."

"Don't thank me," he grumbled, "thank Evelyn. But I'll hold you to that promise. Before Christmas."

"I know you will," Julia answered. "And I'll deliver."

She went down in the private elevator to her own floor.

Inside her office she sank down in one of the big armchairs.

"What a bastard," she said aloud. "If I'm right, he'll eat his words. That'll be some consolation. He said I could name my price, and, by God, I'm going to! And for Ben too. . . ."

Harold King had called a special board meeting in his private penthouse. On occasions like this he used his sitting room instead of the massive boardroom on the floor below. His sitting room was the chosen venue whenever he pushed through something of dubious legality. It overawed his company secretary and his finance director. They sank or swam with Harold King and they wouldn't give him any arguments, whatever he suggested. Gloria was there too. She had been admitted to the board of his pension fund. When that formality had been completed, the real work would begin. The transfer of millions of stocks and bonds held on behalf of King's thousands of employees into an investment company of which he had dual control with his daughter. Then he could fly back to New York and wind up the financing deal with Field. After that, Christmas at Gstaad as usual. He had a house there; Marilyn skied and so did Gloria, who showed nerve and unexpected athleticism on the slopes. He had given up some years earlier. One fall where he pulled thigh muscles and was out of action for weeks had taught him to be his age. He read biographies and travel books in the sunshine and planned for the coming year. He loved Switzerland.

It reminded him of home. Gloria was quiet that morning. He had asked her briefly if she'd given Leo Derwent his marching orders the day after their argument, and she'd nodded rather sheepishly and said, yes, she wouldn't be seeing him anymore.

King didn't think about it again. She had never deceived him or disobeyed his wishes. He thought she seemed subdued that morning, when she should have been excited. While they waited for the secretary and the other director, King said suddenly, "What's wrong with you, sweetheart? You don't seem yourself. Got the curse?"

Gloria hesitated. She was miserable instead of happy. She had lied to him and she hated it. But she was torn between guilt and a growing obsession. She loved him, he was her world. But seeing Leo wasn't a disloyalty. It didn't change her feelings for her father. It was harmless. Nothing had happened between them. They met once or twice a week, went to the cinema or the theater. Sometimes they had dinner together in a discreet restaurant where they were unlikely to meet anyone they knew. It was completely harmless because Leo had made no sexual advance. The idea of a sexual encounter with a man had always disgusted her. But what she imagined would happen with him at first tantalized her and then obsessed her. It spoiled her lovemaking with an older woman she had met.

She was restless and dissatisfied, and the lesbian lady soon went looking for another lover. She took in a deep breath. "Daddy," she said. "Daddy, don't be angry, but there's something I want to tell you."

King stopped thinking about his own question. Women were often funny at the menstrual cycle. He wasn't listening properly when she spoke. "Been running up bills?" he joked with her. "Your mother was complaining about it yesterday. She says you're always buying clothes. . . . 'Why not?' I said. 'Why shouldn't she? She can have everything she wants and more.'" His secretary buzzed through that the two men were in the outer hall. "Ah, here they are. Remember, always insist on your employees being punctual to the second. It's good for them. And always make a point of keeping them waiting. That's good for them too. But not this morning. We've got a lot of business to get through."

"Send them in, send them in," King said. He slipped his arm around Gloria for a moment. "Naughty girl," he said. "Spending so much money. You're going to start earning it now. . . ." Gloria said nothing. The moment had passed. She wouldn't get up the nerve to try again.

The flight to Jersey was bumpy; Julia was never airsick, and she loved flying. It was a blustery day, with rain clouds gathering above the island, but as always the temperature was mild. Janey came hurrying to meet her at the airport.

"Julia darling," she exclaimed. "How lovely to see you. David couldn't get here—he had an emergency at the hospital. How was your flight?"

"A bit rough, but it didn't bother me. You're looking great, Janey. I haven't got much luggage. I always look as if I've come to stay for a year when I go away . . . I tried to cut down on it this time."

"You can stay as long as you like," Janey said enthusiastically. "All our friends are dying to meet you." On the drive down to Trinity she chatted at top speed.

Life was uneventful, the usual round of parties gathering momentum for Christmas, their trip to France had been great fun, but she got a tummy bug, which rather spoiled the last few days. David was happier than ever, enjoying his work and finding plenty of time for golf or sailing. It had been such a hassle living in England; nothing on earth would persuade them to go back now. Julia let it flow over her, making appropriate comments. The Petersons had a charming house, legacy of his mother, with the lush garden for which Jersey was famous. The rain had started, and they hurried inside. "Damn," Janey said. "It was glorious yesterday, blazing sunshine and quite warm. I hope it's not going to be like this for your visit."

"I shan't mind," Julia told her. "It's such a treat to get away."

They were sitting with a prelunch drink in the comfortable sitting room. It had French windows and a view of the beautiful garden. The rain lashed down against the view.

"You do look a bit tired," Janey remarked. "Have a nice rest while you're here. Nothing wrong, is there?"

"No." Julia smiled at her. "Nothing. Just a lot of work and pressure. Nothing a few days with you and David won't put right. How are the boys?"

They had two sons in their late teens, one up at Cambridge, the other traveling through Australia before starting medical school. Julia hadn't seen them for over a year. The schoolboy seemed nice enough, the undergraduate was rather arrogant and offhand. He had reminded her of Felix at the time. Felix. She hadn't thought about him since Ben told her how readily he had cooperated in contacting Harold King's sidekick, Joe Patrick. She was surprised that Ben, who had always been so scathing about Felix, spoke rather well of him. He wasn't jealous, that was why. Felix was part of her past. She looked up quickly when her cousin said, "How's the boyfriend?"

"Which one?"

"Oh, my goodness . . . like that, is it? Lucky you." Janey laughed. "Felix, I met him with you last time we were over. Who else have you got in tow?"

"Felix and I broke up quite a while ago," she explained. "I've met someone else. He's pretty special."

"I'm glad," Janey said. "Felix wasn't for you, darling. David couldn't stand him, I can tell you that now. I thought he was rather a dish, but a bit brash. What's the new one like?"

"Older than me this time," Julia admitted. "Very bright indeed. We're living together to see how it works out. He's divorced, but a long time ago. It was a bad experience. We aren't going to rush anything. But he's lovely. You'd like him. So would David."

"You should have brought him over," Janey said. "What's he do?"

"He's on the *Herald*," Julia answered. "He was my boss until I got this new job heading up 'Exposure.' Next time you come to London, we'll fix dinner together."

After lunch Julia unpacked and asked Janey if she'd mind if she went for a walk. A large red setter wagged its tail at the word, and Julia offered to take him with her. It had stopped raining. The sun was forcing shafts of light through the retreating clouds; the air smelled sweet and warm after the rain. Janey didn't offer to go with her. She had things to do, because a couple of friends were coming to dinner. Not a party, she assured Julia, not on her first evening, but two very close friends. . . .

Julia set off with the sleek dog on a lead. There was a path leading down to the shingle beach and she took it. Once off the road, she unleashed the setter, who bounded happily up and down.

He was on the island. His photograph was imprinted on her mind, like a transposed negative. Nearly fifty years ago, young, smiling, confident that he would live out the conflict that was claiming so many lives. And with him was another figure, less well defined but clear enough. She stopped and paused to throw a piece of driftwood for the setter. It raced into the surf to bring it back.

If King's bloodhounds had tracked her to the island, then she had very little time to waste before they picked her up.

Tomorrow, she decided. She would go back now and help Janey in the kitchen and suggest it.

Janey was taken by surprise. "Richard Watson? Yes, we

know him. He's very nice, lived here for years. He was a friend of David's mother. Why do you want to meet him especially?"

"I read a book he wrote," Julia said. "Actually it was my boyfriend who read it and passed it on. He said it was very interesting and well written. About his time in the army and being a prisoner of war. I think it was privately printed. It said he'd retired to live here in a footnote. I'd rather like to meet him if you can arrange it."

Janey said, "I never knew he wrote anything. He was rather a successful businessman. ICI, I think. I'll ask him to dinner. What a good idea. He'll be flattered at you wanting to meet him. We've told him all about you."

Julia smiled. "I hope he won't be disappointed."

"Don't you believe it," her cousin said. "He loves attractive women. I'll call him now."

Julia finished setting the table. She could hear Janey's voice and then her cheerful laugh. She came in and said, "It's all fixed. He's asked us to dinner. Tomorrow. He had arranged a small party and he was thrilled at the idea of meeting you. Says he's read all your stuff in the newspaper. He's making it black tie in your honor!"

"How very sweet of him. Thanks, Janey," she said. "I brought a silk shirt and a long black skirt, will that do?"

"Of course . . . we're not that smart over here. You'll look terrific. You always do."

The evening was relaxed. David Peterson made a fuss of Julia, opening champagne to celebrate her arrival. The couple who came to dinner in the spacious kitchen were a retired diplomat who was a native Jerseyman and his English wife. They were full of amusing stories about his last posting in Rio de Janeiro. Janey told them about Richard Watson's invitation. They assured Julia that she would like her host and find him an interesting man with a lot of personal charm. "He's all of that," David agreed. "I always thought he and my mother might get together. But they never did. She was very fond of him."

"He's been a widower for years," the diplomat's wife said. "People get set in their ways. Quite a number of ladies have had their eye on Richard, but he's never fallen for anyone. I think all those years as a POW had an effect on him. It was an experience that marked a lot of people. My brother for one. But he was with those bloody awful Japanese. Came home and went into the Church. He's a parson in Norfolk. High Anglican, never married. Loves bells and smells. Extraordinary . . . But he seems happy enough."

"Which is surely all that matters," David said tartly, Julia noticed. Then she remembered that, unlike the rest of the family, he was a regular churchgoer. The more they talked about Richard Watson, the more intrigued she became. There was nothing in the slight volume of his wartime reminiscences that marked him as different from thousands of other young middle-class men who became officers in the forties. But forewarned is fore-armed. Watson was obviously no elderly waffler who would part with information freely. She would have to tread carefully. Before they went to bed, Ben telephoned her. Janey took the call and said, smiling slyly at Julia, "I think it's the boyfriend, darling. You can take it upstairs if you like."

"Thanks," Julia said. "I'll do that."

His voice was reassuring. She felt a pang when she heard it.

"How are you? How's it going?"

"I'm fine. Everything's going better than I hoped. I'm seeing our man tomorrow night. Janey fixed it up for me. They're being so sweet, I feel lousy to make use of them like this. I miss you, Ben. I really do."

"Me too," he said. "The flat's like a bloody morgue.

Pussy won't settle down either. We're both just too fond of you. Get this interview over and get back as soon as you can. I don't like you being out in the big world on your own. No sign of any followers at the airport?"

"No, but I wouldn't see them if there were," Julia pointed out. "If King's still got tabs on us, someone is probably on the island looking for me by now. So long as I connect with Watson before they pick me up, it won't matter. Then I'll think of an excuse and come home. Don't worry about me, darling. Take care, won't you."

"You too," Ben said. "I love you. Call me tomorrow night. Doesn't matter what time."

When he had rung off, Ben took the cat on his knee and skimmed through the book with the smiling young officer on the cover. He paused at the group photograph in the middle section. There weren't that many privately printed records of one man's war. A few dozen at the most. Memories of men grown old or dead who had fought in a war the world wanted to forget. But if he had chanced upon it, thanks to his War Office friend's suggestion, why shouldn't someone else with an interest in the subject? Someone with powerful resources at the push of a button, who knew what they were looking for. . . . He shouldn't have let Julia go there alone. His instincts had been against it, and he'd let her overrule them. He swore at himself for giving way. Just twenty-four hours more. Then he would insist she come home, or he would fly out, however much she argued. On that resolution he was able to sleep.

Joe Patrick cursed the detective-agency contact. They met at a pub in the city, and in the seclusion of a corner table Joe Patrick hissed four-letter insults at him. The man sat stolidly, not answering, showing no emotion, though a line of red crept up his neck from under his collar. Patrick leaned toward him, teeth bared, menacing as a rat at bay. "Jersey!" he spat at him. "Fucking Jersey and you lost her at the airport—Jesus H. Christ—"

"We sent a man over on the next flight," the agency man protested. "He checked all the hotels, and she's not registered. Nobody answering our description has booked in anywhere. He even went around the bloody bed and breakfasts, and you know how many of them there are—"

"I don't fucking know, and I don't care," Joe snarled at him. "What else have you tried?"

"Her office. We asked for an appointment. Her secretary said she was on a week's holiday. No contact number. Said she'd give us a provisional for ten days' time but couldn't confirm till Hamilton got back. Look, stop bollocking me for a minute, will you? Maybe she is on holiday. Staying with friends—"

"Then find the friends," Joe said. "Your job is to know where she is and what she's fucking doing twenty-four hours of the day, till I tell you to get off the case. You find her, you hear me? Or no payment. My boss pays for results, not some arsehole who can't get his act together because the cow gets on a plane!" He stood up, buttoned his long cashmere coat. He was white with rage and fear of King's reaction. "You can put the booze down to expenses," he said. "And hope you get paid. . . ." Then he pushed his way out through the evening crowd of drinkers.

He was in a vile mood. Fear made him vicious. He needed to take it out on somebody. He unlocked his car and drove back to his flat, seething at the agency, at King, at the stinking luck that lost Hamilton on a stinking, pissing little island. He dared not tell King. And he dared not keep him in ignorance either. That would be the most dangerous. King wanted daily reports. He conveyed that the immediate threat from Hamilton was over, but he never let up on his precautions. Belt and Braces was King's motto. The bitch had taken a holiday. Just before the launch of the new "Exposure" feature in November. "Very likely," Joe said savagely, cutting through the traffic. Leaving the lover boy behind. The team were still covering him, and he was in his office and flat, without any change in his routine.

Maybe that meant it was a genuine holiday. . . . Joe bit his lower lip, trying to reassure himself. If Harris had gone with her, it might well have been an assignment. He could try that on King. He could try anything, but it wouldn't stave off his rage. And that rage wasn't confined to a flow of insults and abuse. Joe didn't give a toss about that. Words didn't hurt him, but losing money did. That wounded him. King took a lump out of his retainer when he fouled up anything, and that made Joe Patrick bleed.

He parked his car in the underground garage of the apartment block and took the elevator up to the third floor. He opened the front door very quietly. He moved with the stealth of a stalking animal. He'd catch those two bitches whatever they were doing. They wouldn't expect him to be back so early. They'd be sitting on their black arses taking it easy. He'd give them a nice surprise.

"It is a marvelous place to unwind," Julia said. "I slept so well last night."

She didn't look particularly relaxed, in Janey's opinion, but she didn't say so. She was living at a high pitch with that demanding job; it would take more than twenty-four hours of beneficial Jersey air and slow tempo to get through to her. "I'm so glad" was what she said. "The Lejeunes thought you were a star. Madge phoned this morning. They say you must come over for lunch if you stay a bit longer."

"How nice of them," Julia said, feeling guilty at the deception. "I'd love to—but I don't think I can take more than the week."

They were such nice, uncomplicated people. She thought suddenly, walking along the beach with Janey and David and the joyous red setter, that she had forgotten what normal couples were like. The island and the Petersons were light-years away from the brittle, power-hungry circle in which she had moved for so long.

And they weren't dull; their lives were busy and their interests were wide. They traveled, they read voraciously; there wasn't a single new novel they couldn't discuss. They were making plans to come over to London early in the New Year and see the latest plays and go to the ballet. David was a fanatic balletomane. They lived comfortable, useful lives, and they based their lives on a set of simple values that had been derided in Julia's media world for so long that she had been in danger of forgetting them herself. When all this is over, she made a private resolution as they walked together, I'm going to think about changing things. I'm going to talk to Ben and see what he thinks. Then, dressing for this all-important dinner, Julia mocked herself. Opting out wasn't a real option for her. It was an indulgence, a fantasy, engendered by envy of her cousins' easy lifestyle. She'd go mad with boredom after a few months. And so would Ben Harris. No cozy domestic routines for them. Babies in prams and gardening on weekends. What a fool to have imagined it.

She looked very elegant in the long, pencil-slim velvet skirt. The cream silk shirt was simple, too, with the simplicity of haute couture. Her red hair blazed like a bonfire around her head. Richard Watson liked attractive women. She hoped he wouldn't be disappointed. She checked her watch. She was ready. Seven-thirty, and she was down in the hall waiting for Janey and David. Lateness made her very uptight. It was a bad start to what might be a difficult evening. She needed to be at ease with herself. And it might be an advantage to get there independently.

She knew where Watson's house was; they'd driven over there during the morning as part of a shopping and sight-seeing tour of the island before going out to lunch at Longueville Manor. She could drive there in Janey's car. She went up to the landing and called out. "Janey? Look, would it be all right if I went on ahead of you? I'd rather like to get there dead on time, and I don't want to rush you. Could I borrow your car?"

Janey's voice came through the door. "Wait a minute—" then the door opened and she looked around. She hadn't finished making up her face. She was always late, and David wasn't much better. Julia thought he must still be in the shower by the sound coming from the bathroom.

"We won't be more than ten minutes. . . . Don't you want to come with us?"

"I'd rather get there on time," Julia explained. "It's one of my phobias, I'm afraid. I'd really like to set off now . . . sure you don't mind?"

"No, no, not at all. You can find your way, can't you?" Janey raised her brows at her cousin's eccentricity, but she didn't argue. "My car keys are on the hall table. Don't take David's by mistake, will you . . . he goes absolutely ape if anyone touches that precious new Volvo of his. See you there, then."

As she went downstairs, Julia heard her shouting to her husband.

"David! Hurry out of there, darling—Julia's gone. Got a thing about being late. Must be the crazy life she leads . . . " And then, muffled as Julia reached the ground floor, "No she *hasn't* taken your car. . . ."

• • • •

It was a lovely night, quite crisp with bright stars in the cloudless sky and a fresh breeze blowing in from the sea that made her huddle into her velvet coat as she crossed the courtyard to the garage. The drive took twenty minutes, because she couldn't drive fast on the twisting, narrow roads. Rich immigrants with their Rollers and Bentleys were a joke among the islanders. There were few inland roads wide enough for two cars to pass each other.

The house stood on a rocky promontory overlooking the beach and the sea far below. It was illuminated like a beacon in the darkness, and as she crossed the driveway, the exterior lights came on automatically. She parked the car and got out. The sharp, salty air stung her face. Two steps up to a large, white-painted front door. She rang the bell. After what seemed a long pause she rang a second time. Almost as soon as she took her finger off the brass button, the door opened. A tall man was silhouetted against the inner hall light. She said quickly, "Mr. Watson?"

"Yes, I'm Richard Watson. And you must be Julia Hamilton, David's and Janey's cousin. Do come in out of the cold. Quite a wind's come up tonight." He stepped aside and closed the door.

"I came ahead of them," she said. "I hope you don't mind. Am I the first?"

He smiled down at her and held out his hand. "Yes, you are. How very nice. It will give me a chance to talk to you before anyone else arrives. Let me take your coat. You know, Miss Hamilton, I recognized you from your photograph in the *Herald*. But you're even prettier in the flesh." He had a gentle hold of her arm, and he guided her through the hall and up a short flight of stairs. The house was very warm.

Julia looked around and turned to him. "What a fabulous room. Oh, and look at that view!" She walked over to the floor-length plate-glass window that made up almost one wall. He came beside her. Lights from the house swept down the cliff; below them a cluster of houses with a bigger building rising up on the very edge of the dark shoreline gleamed and shimmered with lights. And, far out, the sweep of a lighthouse beam flashed across the inky sky in warning of the rocks.

When she turned around, he was watching her and smiling. He was a handsome man, with deep blue eyes. The hair was thick and gray, and a small well-trimmed mustache was like a relic of the soldier he had been so many years ago. He had the upright, lean figure of a much younger man. "It is even more spectacular in the early evenings," he said. "The sunsets here are unbelievable . . . every color in the rainbow. It's a shame it's dark, but it's still beautiful. That's Saint Brelades down below, with the Cour Rouge Hotel. It used to be marvelous, but it's always full of tourists now. What can I get you to drink? Gin, whiskey, vodka, or white wine?"

"Vodka," she said, "with ice and tonic. That would be lovely." He poured her drink and came back with a whiskey for himself. "I do hope I haven't been a nuisance getting here dead on eight o'clock. I think the dear Petersons thought I was quite mad, but they weren't nearly ready, and I'm paranoid about being late."

"I'm delighted," Richard Watson said. "It's rather unusual, isn't it? Ladies aren't famous for time-keeping. My late wife never managed it. What a charming dress. It is a thrill to meet you, Miss Hamilton. And may I call you Julia?"

"I was going to suggest it," she said. His charm was washing over her, soothing and seductive. He must have been a serious knockout with women only a few years ago.

At that moment the doorbell sounded, and Richard left the room.

Julia turned back to the window. He was right, daylight would be the time to see it at its best. Sunset or dawn. But she wouldn't be staying.

A middle-aged couple came into the room, led toward her by their host.

"Julia Hamilton, Bob and Fiona Thomas." The man had a hearty handshake and a hearty voice. "You're Janey's and David's famous cousin, aren't you? We've heard all about you, haven't we, Fi?" He also had a hearty laugh. His wife was small, very thin, and spoke in a very quiet voice. "Yes, we have. Aren't they here?" She looked around.

"I was early," Julia explained. She saw the woman's quick scrutiny of her clothes. Satisfied, she smiled at Julia. "I expect David was held up at the hospital, he works so hard. They've been telling everyone about your visit. You're quite a celebrity before we've even met you." Small and thin, with that reedy voice, she was rather a bitch, Julia decided. There was only one way to deal with that. She smiled sweetly at her and turned to talk to her husband.

"This is my first visit to Jersey," she said. "It's such a lovely island. I'm already determined to come again in the spring." He beamed appreciatively.

"I should hope you will. Come and see us next time. This is all in your honor, you know. Dick was just having us to play bridge and have supper till he heard you were here."

"I told you," his wife murmured, "you're a celebrity. . . . It's Janey. . . . I can always tell when she's a mile off. One of those wonderful voices that carry."

"Well, nobody can say that about you, Fi, can they . . . can't hear a bloody word she says half the time." Bob Thomas guffawed at Julia. She laughed. She said to his wife, "One thing about Janey, she always says nice things about people, so it doesn't matter if they do hear what she's saying."

The drinks before dinner lasted half an hour. Watson was generous and knew how to get a party going. Soon they were all mingling, including Julia as the only stranger in their midst who needed looking after. Even the Waspish Fiona Thomas came up and tried to make amends. "You're right about Janey," she whispered. "She is kind to everyone. I didn't mean to say she had a loud voice. It's just that Bob shouts all the time, and I feel nobody ever listens to me."

Julia softened. "I'm sure they do."

Richard Watson came up and led Julia aside. "I hope Fiona's been behaving herself," he said quietly. "I saw you being nice to her. She can be a bit sharp, but she's had rather a difficult life. Bob's been a great swordsman in his time, and she had a lot to put up with from pretty women. Dinner's ready. I can see Maria signaling. What would I do without her? The Portuguese are such lovely people. Shall we go in?"

They went in to dinner, in a glass-fronted room that seemed to be suspended over the cliff. Watson placed her on his right. The table was elegant, with candles and silver; the food compared favorably with the best London restaurants. Julia began to enjoy herself; the atmosphere was relaxed, so civilized and friendly that her tough, competitive world seemed a moonshot away. It was seductive, but she resisted. It wasn't a social occasion. It was the culmination of a careful plan, undertaken at risk to herself if it misfired.

"The definition of age," Richard Watson was saying, "is a desire to talk about the past. I find myself doing it more and more. I spent a few nights in London with my nephew . . . the solicitor. You met him, Janey, he came over for a sailing holiday last summer—"

"Yes, I remember him, charming young man," Janey said brightly.

Richard Watson grinned. "Not particularly, he's rather bumptious and pleased with himself, but at least he's kin, so I keep in touch. He took me out to dinner at his smart club—excellent food, much better than restaurants—I found myself talking about the time I spent as a prisoner of war. I don't think I'd thought about it, let alone talked about it, for years! But there I was in full flood, banging on about being captured and spending three years in a camp in Germany. I suddenly realized he was bored stiff, poor chap. So I cut it short and changed the subject. I felt what a boring old fool I'd become."

"That's the trouble," Bob Thomas snorted. "The young think they know it all."

Richard Watson said gently, "Didn't we? I know I never listened to a word my father said after the age of eighteen. Sad thing was, you know when I did come back from the POW camp, we couldn't communicate at all. Of course they were delighted to see me—my mother cried and rushed off to make tea; my old father managed to put his arm around me and then hurried upstairs with my bag. He just didn't know what to say."

Julia judged the moment had come. "Did it affect you badly? It must have been awful trying to adjust."

"It wasn't easy," he admitted. "I'd come back home a stranger. To myself as much as to them. I didn't realize what the loss of freedom had done to me. I couldn't make my mind up about anything. I'd lost the habit of taking decisions. If someone had told me what socks to put on in the morning, I'd have done it."

"How long did that last?" Julia leaned close, engaging his full attention.

"Couple of years. I tried several jobs, couldn't settle into anything; it was quite a common manifestation of

POW fatigue. Then I was taken on by ICI as a trainee, and I got interested. Absorbed actually. And it all started to come right after that."

Julia took a breath. *Now.*

"I read your book," she said. "I have a friend who's mad on the last war and he gave it to me to read. I really enjoyed it. Did you map it out while you were in the prison camp?"

"Yes," Richard Watson said, "I did. It was so desperately boring and miserable, and so damned cold in the winter. . . . We were always hungry too. Most of the chaps spent their time talking about escape or playing chess or bridge. I worked on my insignificant wartime memoirs. I can't believe you found them interesting, but I must admit I'm flattered."

He smiled at her.

Bob Thomas boomed out, "Book? What's all this, Dick— been keeping secrets from us?"

"It was years ago—long before I came over here," Richard Watson protested. "I had some copies privately printed. I didn't know there were any circulating anywhere. I just wanted to get it off my chest, I suppose."

"Hidden talents." Bob Thomas had their attention. "Better watch out, Julia, or you'll have a rival in Dick here. . . . I'd like to read it sometime. I bet you've got a copy of the great work stashed away. The army was the best time of my life. I often regretted not making a career of it. Too young to get into the actual war, but I enjoyed my national service."

He looked around for approbation.

Julia said quietly, "Did you feel like that, Richard? Your book didn't read like that."

He turned to look at her, and then, suddenly, he turned away.

"I hated the army," he said. "I hated everything about it.

And I wasn't a good soldier. The idea of killing someone absolutely appalled me. I had no blood lust."

"Did you ever kill anyone?"

He hesitated for a moment. Then he said, "No. But I did save a man's life."

"One of ours?" David Peterson spoke up.

"No. It was a German."

Julia said quickly, "How? How did you save him?"

"I stopped my sergeant from murdering him," he said.

"Good God—" Bob Thomas was leaning across the table. "Go on, tell us about it."

His wife said, "How riveting," but nobody noticed.

"It was in the Western Desert. We were on the run from Rommel's Afrika Corps—before Monty took over—and we'd got separated from our unit. We were trying to get back to Tripoli. There were seven of us. My captain Tim Phillips, me, the sergeant, and four privates. The desert was crawling with desert patrols, mopping up after the battle. We picked up this German on the way. He had a slight leg wound, and he'd no weapon. I'd say he'd deserted. We took him prisoner because it was safer than leaving him and have him warn one of his own patrols we were in the area. . . . I knew the sergeant wanted to shoot him. He was that sort of man.

"We struggled on, hoping to get clear before nightfall, but the German lagged behind, he'd lost quite a lot of blood, and he was a miserable specimen anyway—couldn't have been more than eighteen, if that. . . .

"The sergeant started chivying him along with a bayonet, but he couldn't keep up. We saw a dust cloud in the distance. That meant a German armored patrol was coming our way. We clambered down into the wadi and dragged the boy down with us. My captain took out his revolver and held it to his head. He told the German he'd blow his brains out if he made a sound."

Richard Watson filled up his glass with wine. "He didn't mean it. His hand was shaking like a leaf, and he was scared stiff. I was watching our sergeant. He had his bayonet at the ready. He said, 'We can't risk a shot, sir. And he's slowing us down. You put that away and I'll finish him off with this!'"

Julia said, "You mean he was going to bayonet him?"

"Oh, yes, wouldn't have hesitated. None of the others said anything. He'd had Tim Phillips under his thumb from the start. He actually started to holster his revolver, so I had to do something before the boy was killed."

"And what did you do?" she asked him.

He shrugged. "Nothing heroic, I'm afraid. I just announced loud and clear that I wouldn't be a party to murder. Meaning they would have to kill me, too, to stop me reporting what had happened."

"God," David Peterson said. "That was brave."

"No, it wasn't," Richard Watson insisted. "But it stopped them. So we went on and left the wretched German behind." He offered Julia more wine. She refused.

"Did he understand? Did he know what was going on?"

"Oh, he knew all right. He was shaking with terror. I was sure he understood more English than he let on. He didn't say anything. But he looked at me as we left him. It was very odd, that look. I couldn't make it out. Our sergeant came up to me and said, 'You made a mistake there, sir.'" Watson mimicked the heavy sarcasm in that one word. "'You should have let me kill the little bastard. Mark my words, he'll send a bloody patrol after us.' Which," he said slowly, "is exactly what happened. We were captured within the hour."

"What an extraordinary story," Bob Thomas said. Richard Watson looked around at them. He sighed. "It didn't end there, I'm afraid. Phillips and I were put in a truck and taken back to a POW compound at their base. Preferential treatment for officers. The Germans were like that. The other five were marched off to join a column of British prisoners going to the rear. They came under crossfire; the sergeant was the only one to survive his wounds. The other four poor lads were killed. I only found out about it when the war was over because Phillips kept in touch and he made inquiries about his men." He paused, and Julia saw the muscles tighten in his jaw. "He had some crack-brained theory that they'd been gunned down deliberately. The cross-fire story came from the sergeant, but Phillips said he couldn't find any official record of a skirmish between our patrols and theirs anywhere in the area. He'd got a real bee in his bonnet, but nothing came of it. You know, I've often wondered whether those poor devils would still be alive if I hadn't interfered."

"You can't possibly blame yourself," Bob Thomas insisted. "You did absolutely the right thing. More than a Hun officer would have done for one of ours, I'd say. Though it was quite a clean war—"

"Who would have shot them?" Julia said. "Wouldn't the sergeant have reported an atrocity like that?" She had to clear her throat and swallow, it was suddenly so dry.

"Well, he didn't," Watson answered. "It was just talk, and Phillips tracked him down, but he stuck to his story. . . . You're right, Bob, it was a clean war in the desert. There weren't any war crimes . . . most likely due to Rommel. He was a Prussian of the old school. Well"—he smiled at them—"sorry to have bored you with all this. Comes of getting old, I'm afraid. Now, let's have some coffee. Janey, would you look after Julia and Fiona for me, and we promise not to sit on here too long."

Janey led the way upstairs. "How weird," she said.

"What an awful story. But he was right to save that poor German. He couldn't help it if they got killed in a battle afterward, could he?"

"No," Fiona Thomas whispered. "But I think he blames himself deep down."

It was long past midnight when Julia was able to leave at last. And get to a telephone. Ben, she thought. Oh, Ben, you're not going to believe this. My God. I can hardly believe it myself. . . . As they gathered around the front door to say good-bye, she managed to draw Richard Watson aside. "What happened to Phillips? Is he still around?"

"No, he died back in 'eighty-one. Cancer. His wife wrote to me."

"And the sergeant? Was he the one in the photograph in your book?"

"Yes, same man. Whenever people go on about German atrocities, I think of him. He'd have bayoneted that boy to death and enjoyed doing it."

"And is he alive?" Julia asked, trying to sound casual.

"I've no idea." His tone was suddenly abrupt. He turned away from her and kissed Fiona Thomas good night. It was a very firm dismissal of the subject.

He was smiling, his charming self again, when he said good-bye to Julia.

"Thank you for a wonderful party," she said. "And I really did enjoy your book".

"I'm flattered," he said, but the eyes were wary in spite of the smile. "It was just an exercise in self-indulgence."

Julia stood her ground. "But you never mentioned this amazing incident."

"Perhaps I didn't feel it reflected much credit on anyone," he said coldly. "And Phillips was very much alive. I'm not an investigative journalist, you see. I didn't want to inflict hurt. It has been a pleasure to meet you. I hope you'll come to see us all again."

"I hope so too," she said, and shook his hand. "Thank you again."

At ten-thirty next morning Ben made the call as they'd arranged. Julia went through the charade for Janey's benefit, saying guiltily, "That was the office—I've got to go back early. I'm so sorry to cut it short like this. I've had such a lovely time."

"Oh, damn," Janey exclaimed. "I'd planned a big drinks party so all our friends could meet you. It was going to be a surprise before you left. Damn. . . ." she said again. "David will be so sorry he hasn't seen more of you." Then, because she was good-natured and she saw Julia looking embarrassed, "Oh, never mind, I'm just being selfish, that's all. Of course you've got to go. Sorry I made a fuss. Come in the spring and we'll do it all again. And don't tell your bloody office where you're going!"

"Janey," Julia said, and put her arms around her, "you're sweet to put up with me, messing you around like this. I will come in the spring, and you and David have promised to come to London before that, and I'll fix a gala evening with the parents and my new man. That's a promise. Now I'd better call the airport. I really *am* sorry."

And she truly meant it. But if she could have grown wings, she'd have flown home to Ben Harris at that very moment.

CHAPTER 9

"COME ON," THE WPC SAID. "TELL ME what happened. Who did her over?"

The girl had covered her face with her hand. She was sobbing. Mandy Kent had been on the force for ten years. She was inured to violence and the hideous results of domestic rows. She prided herself on her emotional detachment. It was essential if she was to do the job properly. "How did you ever get her into a taxi in that state? Too scared to call an ambulance, weren't you?"

Most battered women refused to lodge a complaint and the bastards got away with it. A badly beaten prostitute was no exception.

She had never seen a girl so smashed up as Tina's friend Tracey, lying unconscious in the ward next door. She knew them both; she'd worked on the Vice Squad, and she knew the tarts and the pimps in the square mile where drugs, hookers, and every kind of sexual malpractice were on offer at a price. She hadn't seen Tina or her girlfriend on the streets for a long time. She went on, speaking in her calm way.

"She's got fractured ribs, a broken jaw, a smashed right arm—trying to defend herself, wasn't she?—and the doctor thinks whoever did it kicked her so hard, her spleen's ruptured. She could die, Tina. So who did it?"

Slowly Tina touched her own face. It was so bruised, her lip was puffy.

"She can't die . . . she can't . . . " she mumbled. "We've been together since we were kids. We were in the same fucking council home. . . ."

Mandy Kent said firmly, "If her spleen's ruptured, she could. Next time it could be you lying in there."

She waited, instinct sensing a change in the weeping girl. It was said very low. "Joe Patrick. Joe Patrick beat her up."

Mandy Kent stood up. "I'll get us some coffee," she said. She came back with two plastic cups from the dispenser in the corridor and gave one to Tina.

"I put sugar in," she said. "You're in shock. Sugar's good for you. Tell me about this Joe Patrick. Is he your pimp?"

"No," Tina shook her head. Sipping the hot, sweet coffee hurt her mouth. "He doesn't run girls. Doesn't need to. He's a businessman. We picked him up a year ago in the Caribbean Club. He likes blacks. He's got a hang-up about it. We live with him. I dress up like a secretary sometimes. It's not the first time he's laid into us, you expect that. But this time he came in looking for someone to take it out on. He just wanted to punch the shit out of one of us."

She finished the coffee and winced.

"Why did he pick on Tracey and not you? She talk back?"

"Christ, no. Tracey never did, she was too scared of him. She was wearing a bracelet he'd given me. A fucking bracelet, just borrowing 'cos she liked it. . . . He went ape. He was like a crazy, yelling and swearing. He just laid into her. I tried to stop him, but he gave me a backhander and put the boot in, and I just lay there and watched. . . . I thought she was dead. Then he went out. Slammed the door and went out."

"And you got her out to the street and into a cab," Mandy Kent prompted.

"I said it was a hit and run," Tina muttered. "I had to get her to the hospital."

"And just because she was wearing your bracelet," Mandy repeated. "Why, Tina? Was it valuable?"

"No, he never gave us good stuff. Just bits of junk." She wiped her face with the back of her hand. "I've told you," she said. "But I'm not doing more than that. I'm not giving evidence. You charge him, I'll deny I ever said anything. If I ratted on him, he'd kill me. Or get someone else to do it."

Mandy Kent had not expected anything else. Girls like Tina and the helpless assault victim, Tracey, would always be beyond the law's protection. They lived by the rules of the criminal underclass, where the rat was deemed worse than a murderer, and the only law that mattered was survival. "Maybe Tracey will charge him," she suggested. "If she regains consciousness. If she dies, it'll be murder. You won't be able to run away from that, Tina."

Tina said slowly, "She won't rat on him either. I want to go home now. I'll come and see her tomorrow."

"You're not going back there, are you? I wouldn't, if I were you."

"I'll go to a friend's," Tina said. "Just for a day or two.

Give the bastard time to calm down. See how Tracey is. . . . Thanks for the coffee."

"If he kicked you, you should let the doctor in Casualty take a look."

"I'm all right. Just a bit sore. It's not the first time he's done it."

"I'll get the squad car to take you where you want to go. Keep in touch, Tina. I'm on your side."

"Like fuck," Tina said without rancor. "Nobody's on my side except me."

Mandy Kent saw her into the squad car. She felt suddenly tired and angry. They'd run the name Joe Patrick through the central computer. Businessman he might be, but the attack had the hallmark of the petty criminal and former pimp.

Not that she had any hope of bringing him into a court. Neither girl would press charges or give evidence for fear of reprisals. She couldn't blame them, but the frustration of seeing a bastard like that get away with it made her seethe. She went back up to the ward. The doctor on duty came out to meet her.

"Any luck?" she asked him.

"No, still unconscious. Lucky for her the spleen's okay. She'll be a terrible mess, though. We've wired up the jaw, but she'll need plastic surgery. No luck with her friend?"

"She told me who did it, but she won't go into court or swear an affidavit. So there's nothing we can do. Makes me really sick."

"Did she say why he did it? What had the poor little devil done to get a hiding like that?"

"Borrowed the other girl's bracelet. Can you believe it? He was just a thug looking for an excuse to beat up on someone. I know the type. Anywhere I can have a look at her belongings? I might as well see what she got herself half killed for."

"Go and see sister," he suggested. "Her office's through there. She'll have the stuff till it's documented and locked away. Good night."

"Good night," Mandy said.

"Oh, yes." The sister in charge was as familiar with the type of incident as the WPC asking to look at the patient's belongings. "Yes, I've got everything here, in my desk drawer. You have to be so careful, or some of these people will claim things have been stolen. I'll get out what there is."

There was little enough. A chain with a lucky charm, three costume rings with blood dried on them like a dirty-brown film, and a thin chain bracelet with little stones that glittered in the light of the anglepoise lamp.

Mandy Kent picked it up. The sister said, "I haven't seen one of those for years."

"Oh, what's special about it?"

"It's a 'DEAREST' bracelet," she explained. "My father gave one to my mother for their silver wedding. Not as nice as this, though. Hers came from Bravingtons, I think. This has some nice little stones. They spell 'DEAREST.' Diamond, emerald, amythest, ruby, emerald, sapphire . . . what's the last one . . . tourmaline. That's right. They were quite fashionable a long time ago. This is a nice one, even though the stones are very small." She had taken it from Mandy Kent and weighed it in her hand. "I've got my mother's, come to think of it. She died last year."

"Sorry," Mandy Kent said. "If it's not junk, it might be worth running it through the computer for stolen goods. I might just get that bastard on receiving. I don't think it belonged to his mother. I'll sign for it, if that's all right."

"I just hope," the sister said, "you can find something to charge the brute with."

Mandy Kent looked at her. She put the envelope with the

bracelet sealed inside it in her inner pocket. She put on her hat and said, "So do I."

Ben Harris was waiting at the airport. She saw him outside the arrivals and waved. He hurried to meet her and, for a moment, undemonstrative in public as he was, he took her in his arms and held her for a long embrace.

"Good to see you, darling," he said. "God, it's been a long few days."

"Me too," Julia assured him. "I've missed you every minute, but"—and drawing back, she looked up at him in triumph—"but we've cracked it. We've got Western in our pockets and we'll have Harold King for war crimes."

Arms around each other, they made their way to the parking lot. They were only driving on to the motorway toward Central London when Joe Patrick got the call to say Julia had been picked up landing from Jersey and they were on her tail.

At last he could face Harold King. He didn't have to mention that they'd lost her on the island. His spirits had been dour and his mood uneasy when he came home and found his birds had left. There was a mess of vomit and blood on his smart carpet, and no one around to clean it up.

He had gone over the top with that silly black cow. Seeing her with the bracelet he'd given Tina sparked off the blind rage that was seeking an outlet because he was so scared of King. He'd done her over good and proper and given Tina a fistful for trying to interfere.

But they'd be back. He wasn't worried. They knew what would happen to them if they complained or talked to the police. If they never showed their faces again, he didn't care. Plenty more girls where they came from. Might be good to have a change. He made his appointment and set off in his Mercedes to give Harold King a carefully worded report.

"She went on a holiday," he said. "Spent a few days in Jersey, flew back this morning."

Harold King stared at him. He seemed to change color, but Joe Patrick dismissed it as imagination. He had been so shit worried, he was still nervous, that was the trouble. "Jersey," King said. "I see. Doing what?"

"Taking a break," Joe insisted. He decided to invent. "Staying with friends. Harris didn't go with her."

"Friends," King repeated. He got up and walked around his desk to stare at the London skyline with his back to Joe. "Jersey. Staying with friends."

"Yeah," he heard the Irishman say, his voice lighthearted. "She's a busted flush, like you said. And they're using our plant for the November feature." He laughed. "They paid me good money to prove it."

King didn't turn around. "Who did she see in Jersey?"

Joe said, "Nobody. It was just a few days off."

"She never went out, she didn't meet anybody?" The voice was deceptively calm.

"No. Just got on the plane and came back. She's gone into the office with lover boy. He was there to meet her."

Harold King swiveled around. "Those stupid fuckers lost her, didn't they? She slipped them and went to the island and nobody knows what she did or who she saw till they picked her up at Heathrow this morning. Isn't that how it happened, Joe? They lost her!"

Joe bluffed. "Jesus, they never told me." He raised his voice in self-defense. "They gave me the info, just as I've given it to you, Boss. Lookit"—he dropped into Dublin slang in his agitation—"lookit, if they've screwed up and tried lyin' their way out—"

"Get out," King said suddenly. "Get out. You're finished."

Joe stood up. He said in a whine of self-justification,

"It's not my fault. . . . Anything you've asked, I've done for ye. . . . Anythin'. I've risked my bloody neck for ye. You don't mean it; you won't throw me out."

"You've done nothing for me that wouldn't put you away for the rest of your dirty little life, if that's what you're talking about. Or are you trying to threaten me, Joe? Trying to blackmail me?" To Joe's terror he burst into a roar of laughter. "You piece of piss, you try anything like that with me, and you'll be scraped from the pavement. I've got friends who'd like to do me a favor. You know them, Joe. You know how long you'd last if I said one bloody word to them, don't you?"

Joe Patrick bit his lower lip. It was a throwback to his boyhood when he was going to get a strapping from the orphanage principal.

"I'll go," he said. "And I'll be no trouble to ye. No trouble at all. Ye may change your mind. You may need me again. I don't hold no grudge. You've been fair with me."

"Get out," King said. "And keep your mouth shut if you want to stay alive." Then he turned back to the window again. He didn't hear Joe Patrick close the door.

Joe's firm of private detectives had lost Julia Hamilton when she went to Jersey. But islands were small places, places where gossip spread faster than a bushfire. While the London legmen wasted their time on the hotels and public venues, the fact that the well-known surgeon David Peterson had a famous Fleet Street journalist staying with him was all over the island in a few hours. And the guests at Richard Watson's dinner party had been regaling their friends with stories about Julia Hamilton. King's own contact was a radio reporter on the local station. It was his business to pick up news items, local gossip however slight. For ten years he kept a watching brief for Harold King's publications with particular emphasis on a retired ICI executive called Richard Watson. He had reported direct to King. King had been prepared for Joe Patrick's lies. He knew where Hamilton had been. To see the man who had saved the life of an eighteen-year-old German soldier in the Western Desert fifty years ago. She had found Watson, as he had done, through some unlucky chance. Because she hadn't dropped the investigation. Joe Patrick had been deliberately misled. And misled King in turn.

This was not a problem to be solved by a cheap killer like the Irishman, a rapist and murderer of an old woman alone in her house. This needed sophistication and brains to bring it to solution. He paused, thinking about Joe Patrick. The Irish were a treacherous and vengeful breed. He couldn't leave Patrick like a loose cannon with a grievance. Belt and Braces, he said to himself. Patrick would have to go.

He'd deal with him later. He was due in New York at the end of the week. Gloria was flying out with him. He'd make the arrangements then for that red-haired bitch. And then he could deal William Western his death blow. And pay back the debt he had thought paid in full. Until ten years ago.

Gloria shifted against him. They had fallen asleep, exhausted, and when he woke, he sent Gloria to the kitchen to make coffee. She had obeyed meekly. She liked being ordered about, waiting on him was part of their foreplay.

She said, "Leo—what am I going to tell them?"

"I don't know," he answered. "What have you said before when you were out all night?"

"I never stayed away all night, I always came home." She looked at him over the coffee cup. "They never knew I'd been with anyone. I just said I was out with friends."

He flicked her cheek with his finger. "Girlfriends," he mocked. "But it's better with me, isn't it?"

"You know it is." She lay back against the tumbled pillows. "I always hated the idea of doing it with a man. But not with you. I love it with you. Daddy would kill me. . . ."

"How about Mummy?"

"She wouldn't care," Gloria said. "She's dying to get rid of me, so she can have Daddy to herself. She'd love it if I had a boyfriend . . . or I got married and was out of the way. I never will," she added.

Leo didn't say anything. Marriage. The thought had never occurred to him. All that money, all that power at his disposal. She liked to talk in a little-girl voice sometimes. She simpered at him. "Shall I get you more coffee? Anything else you want?"

Leo said, "I want you. Come here. . . ."

"Darling," Ben Harris said. "We can't prove it's King."

"Western can," Julia insisted. "I'm going to face him with it."

"Now?" he asked her. She looked at him. "Now," she said. "Are you coming with me, Ben? I don't understand why you're hesitating? I thought you'd be thrilled, over the moon. What's wrong? What is it?"

"Sit down for a minute," he said. "Look, of course I'm excited. You brought it off, you did a marvelous job. All your instincts were right. But, we've no proof!"

She stared at him. "We have!" she exploded. "And it's on the top floor of this building—I'm going upstairs and see him now!"

"If you do," Ben said quietly, "he'll take you off the job. Just as he did with me. And for the same reason."

"He can't," she retorted. "You didn't know the truth. I do. He can't stop me now."

"He can and he will. Exposing Harold King means exposing him. He'll never let it happen. You haven't thought this through," he went on. "Don't fool yourself. Western is no pussycat. He'll protect himself by any means he can. Think of this—if you're right, then he knew King shot down those prisoners. Why didn't he say anything when you told him? Why did he lie and let you go on looking for proof when *he* was the proof . . . the only witness? J, for Christ's sake, there's something missing in the whole scenario. I don't know what it is, and you don't either. You can't run bullheaded into a situation like this. Western was ready to stick a bayonet into an unarmed prisoner. You're going to face him with that. Okay. And he knew what happened when he and the others were captured and separated from their officers. He said they were killed in crossfire and he was lucky to survive. So he covered up the whole bloody massacre. Why?"

"That's what I'm going to ask him," Julia said angrily.

"Wait a minute. Let's take it step by step. We're *supposing* King came on Richard Watson, just like we did, when he was trying to find some dirt on Western, heard the same story, and blackmailed him. So what's changed?" he asked her. "Something has, or Western wouldn't be out to get Harold King now. He'd lie down and let him walk over him, take everything. But he decided to fight back. He brought you and me in on it. He's encouraged and backed us every inch of the way. Didn't he say he'd fire you if you didn't have a result and put King in the December issue of 'Exposure'?"

"He's gambling," Julia said. "Gambling that I can pin the war crime on King without involving him. It's simple; he's got everything to lose to King and he's not going to let it happen."

"And have King show him up? No, it doesn't add up."

"Well," Julia said, and got to her feet. "There's only one way to find out. And that's ask him. Which I'm going to do right now."

"Lord Western is in Rio de Janeiro on business," the secretary said, conveying disapproval of the way Miss Hamilton had marched into her office without an appointment. "I am in contact with him every day, so perhaps you'd like me to give him a message?"

"No, no, thanks," Julia said. "When is he due back?"

"I couldn't say. He didn't indicate a date to me. Before Christmas, I expect." She favored Julia with a condescending smile.

"I expect too," Julia snapped, and turned away.

Rio de Janeiro. No return date. She felt like bursting into tears. She hadn't realized how wrought up she had become. Fighting Ben Harris hadn't helped. The anticlimax, the frustration, just when she had put the last piece into the jigsaw puzzle . . . only Ben said she hadn't. . . .

She went into her office, gave instructions that she wasn't taking any calls, and tried to calm herself. Think it through. But she had, surely to God she'd got the answers at last. Harold King had murdered the British prisoners, in reprisal for Western's plan to kill him. Western had escaped, somehow, wounded, but not dead. Lied about it to cover his own conduct. Been discovered and blackmailed by the German who'd killed his companions. She raised her head suddenly. No. No, that wasn't right, that didn't hold up. . . . She got up from her desk, began to pace the office. He wouldn't have feared exposure by the man who stood to be accused of cold-blooded murder. . . . Neither one could risk a collision with the other if that was the scenario.

"Oh, God," she said aloud. "God! Ben was right . . . there is something missing. . . . But where do I look for it? Where do I start?"

"Don't lie to me, Gloria. Don't even try to lie to me."

He wasn't shouting at her. He was so calm that she was wrong-footed and she stumbled over her explanation. "You came in at six this morning," King said. "I was up and I heard you. I saw you sneaking up the stairs into your room. You were with that little creep, weren't you?" He came close to her, and Gloria shrank back. He gripped her by the upper arm and put his strength into it. She cried out.

"Don't, Daddy. You're hurting me—"

"Tell me," he said, and squeezed harder. "You spent the night with Leo Derwent, didn't you?"

She burst into tears of pain. "Yes . . . yes, I did."

He let go of her. "You slept with that creep?" he asked her. His voice hadn't been raised. Gloria clasped her arm and wept. "Why shouldn't I? You have women—" He slapped her across the face.

"Sit down," he commanded, and she collapsed onto her bed. He watched her for a moment. He loved her; she was the only person in the world he cared about, and she had betrayed him and lied to him. She heard him sigh heavily and ventured a look at him.

"He's the first," she mumbled. "The first man . . . I like him. He likes me."

King came and sat down beside her. She cringed a little, and then he put his arm around her. "Don't cry," he said. "I shouldn't have hit you."

Gloria melted; pain for him joined her pain for herself. "I deserved it. I shouldn't have said that to you. I shouldn't have lied."

"He's using you," he said.

She stiffened. "Don't say that! Don't say that to me. You think I'm ugly . . . nobody would ever want me . . . just because I'm not like my mother. And what is she? What is she to you, Daddy? All tits and no brains! That's what you say about women. I've heard you. . . . Leo *does* like me, and we get on together."

She knew that her father was wrong about her and Leo. Maybe for the only time in his life, but he was wrong about Leo. She said in a very low voice, her head leaning against King's shoulder, "Don't spoil this for me, Daddy. I'll always love you the best. But don't spoil this for me. Please?" King held her and didn't answer. Leo Derwent. Gloria wanted him. Shared his tastes in sex . . . He shied away from that. He couldn't contemplate it. He ran up a mental shutter on what his daughter did with a man like that.

"You're not ugly, sweetheart," he said. "You're my girl. We're doing everything together. We're going to New York. He's not *good* enough for you. . . . He's a nothing. For Christ's sake, Gloria, you're my daughter. You could have any man you wanted!"

She said, "I want to go to the States with you, Daddy, you know I do. How long will we be gone?"

He was too shrewd not to see the significance of that question. She had never queried the length of a trip before. "About ten days," he said. "Then we go to Gstaad for Christmas." He stood up. Her swollen, tearstained face reproached him. "Come here and kiss me," he said. "We never fight. We're not going to fight now. Let's put this thing on ice, shall we? You see him if you want to."

Her arms went up and clasped him tightly around the neck. "Oh, Daddy, thank you! He doesn't mean anything to me, really. . . . I hated deceiving you. I really hated it. . . ."

But you did, he thought, embracing her. *He meant that much to you*. Again the unthinkable came to mind. Like to like. He swallowed bile at the idea.

"Go wash your face," he said kindly. "And have lunch with your old father today to show him he's forgiven."

"I'd love to," Gloria said, and kissed him warmly on the cheek.

King went to his own room. His wife was at her dressing table, starting the long ritual of making up for the day's engagements. She looked briefly at him. He'd left their room in a fury to confront his daughter. She thought she had heard Gloria cry out. "Is she all right?"

"Yes. I talked with her. I got too heavy, but it's okay now."

"Did she say where she was?" she asked him. He glared at her. "Leave it, Marilyn. We'll sort it out between us." He went off to his dressing room. He'd sort it out. He wasn't having Gloria thrown away on any third-rate little ass licker like Leo Derwent. If she wanted that kind of sex, she could get it with someone in a bigger league. He realized, as he lowered himself into his steaming bath, that he had to accept that his daughter was a woman with her own sexual needs. His girl had grown up. But Leo Derwent wouldn't be difficult to send running. So long as Gloria didn't know he was responsible.

"They've gone to the States," Leo said. He met Julia in his office at the House of Commons.

"For how long?"

"Ten days. Then they're taking off for Gstaad for Christmas." He glanced at Julia. "She wants me to fly out there so we can meet."

"You have made an impression, haven't you?"

Julia disliked him so much, she found it difficult to look him in the eye.

He was aware of her feelings and he wasn't bothered. "Yes, I have," he agreed. "We're growing very close." He grinned. "Daddy's not been too pleased about it, but she's talked him around."

Julia watched him sharply. Something was up. She could sense a smugness that made her uneasy. "The purpose of the trip to New York?" she reminded him. She wasn't sitting there with him to listen to him boasting about his prowess with King's daughter. No doubt they made a lovely couple.

"To tie up the big financial deal. Then he fires the first shots at Western International when he gets back in January. She was very excited. She tells me everything. I don't even have to ask."

"Did she tell you any details?"

"Oh, yes. First there'll be some well-placed rumors in the financial press. Rumors about Western and some pending financial crisis due to overexpansion in South America. He's got big interests over there, hasn't he? And he's bought a Spanish-language publishing company, with two newspapers in Brazil. All authentic stuff. But what won't be authentic will be the implications that he's mortgaged his U.K. interests to support the new ventures. And once that sort of thing starts—one or two bent journalists letting hints drop—there'll be a run on the shares. People are panicky; so are the institutions. They were caught with their pants down by Maxwell, and they're not taking any chances. So King starts heavy buying. With the money he's got, Western won't be able to fight him off. So"—he grinned his foxy grin at Julia—"you'll be out of a job. Unless you can dig up this dirt you told me about and stop him in time. How's your end going?"

"We're very close," she admitted.

His eyes gleamed. "That bastard," he said softly. "The way he set me up. Any other way I can help?"

"Not unless you can get him drunk," Julia said bitterly.

"He's a teetotaler, lifelong, everyone knows that." Leo said. "Why, why do you say that?"

"Because he got drunk once," Julia answered. "Everyone

who knew what he said has died since. Except me," she added.

He stared at her. "You're not serious?"

"I'm very serious. I mentioned a criminal charge the first time we met, didn't I?"

He nodded.

"It's murder," Julia said quietly. "The murder of unarmed British prisoners in 1942 in the Western Desert. So you see what we're dealing with. I'd be a bit careful with that daughter if I were you. Get ready to back off. If he wasn't happy about you in the first place, he's not going to change his mind, whatever he tells her."

"Thanks," he said briefly. "You shouldn't be giving me advice like that."

"I've got enough on my conscience," Julia told him. "There isn't room for you." She got up. "I'd better go. You'll be seeing her when she gets back from the States?"

"The same evening," Leo answered. "I've planned a cozy reunion. If this is true . . . what you've said . . . shouldn't you have a minder?"

"He thinks I've given up," she said. "And my flat is as secure as Fort Knox. Don't worry about me."

"I'll be in touch as soon as I've seen her."

"I'll go, then," Julia said. On an impulse she started to walk toward Saint James Park. It was a crisp winter afternoon, with a pre-Christmas buzz in the air. The shops were festive, and people were walking with the purposeful stride of the shopper. Christmas. Her mother wanted her to come down and bring Ben with her. She couldn't think of Christmas. She couldn't think of presents and turkey and family gatherings while Harold King walked the earth as a free man. William Western was in Brazil. She was expected to launch the attack on King in December. She had the whole format in her mind. Every headline, every paragraph was already written and burned in her brain.

But she could do nothing without the vital piece of evidence that identified Harold King as the German prisoner whose life had been saved by Richard Watson. And who had exacted a terrible revenge upon his former captors. The only man who could provide that proof was William Western. It was too cold to sit in the park by the lake, so Julia walked toward Whitehall. The roofs and central turret of the old palace gleamed through the frosty air above the line of trees, like some Oriental backdrop. There had been no record of a German massacre of prisoners in the annals of that Desert War. Not even a rumor circulating. Just the drunken confession of Hans Koenig to his wife and the suspicions of a dead officer called Phillips, who was unhappy about the fate of his men. William Western, the only survivor, wounded and repatriated, had insisted that they had been caught in crossfire during a skirmish between British and German patrols.

Julia paused by the splendid Guards memorial. The clock in the palace across Horseguards chimed the hour. Three o'clock. It had a sweet if ghostly chime in the still air. Traffic heading up Birdcage Walk toward Parliament Square seemed strangely muted to her as she stood there. She looked at the massive bronze figures on the stone plinth. Dead men from both wars. Dead men in the desert sands. A dead woman, outraged in her bed and brutally beaten. Harold King with his neo-Nazi connections to protect him, controlling Western's media empire as well as his own, taking his seat in crimson and ermine in the House of Lords. She said it out loud. "I don't care what Ben says. I'm going down to Hollowood and see Evelyn Western. Tonight."

"Good to see you, Harry. You're looking well. How's business?"

"No complaints," Harold King said. He spooned up pasta and muttered between mouthfuls. "Mario, this is the best . . . mmm . . . what a sauce. . . ."

The New York garment manufacturer smiled in gratification at the compliment. "My favorite restaurant. So good I bought a piece of it. Pity you don't drink wine, Harry. You miss out on a great Chianti."

King said, "My only regret. I don't have the stomach. I have all the other vices, so why should I be greedy?"

He looked at the man sitting opposite him, napkin tucked into his collar, washing the rich Italian food down with drafts of red wine and sopping up the creamy sauce with hunks of bread. He was very fat, with a bulging belly and heavy chins. King had left Gloria to amuse herself that evening and asked his Mafia contact if they could share a meal together. And maybe a few problems.

They didn't talk about the problems till they had finished eating.

Over tiny cups of espresso, the host fortifying himself with a glass of oily Strega, he asked Harold King about those problems.

"I've got media trouble," King said. The coffee was so strong, it made his heart race.

"What kind of media?" the Italian asked him. "The media's shit. They've been on my back this last year, so I know how it feels. What's the problem?"

"It's a smart-ass woman," King said. "Making a big name for herself. She's digging dirt on me, Mario. And she's good. I don't know where it might end up." He left the mafioso to work out that conclusion for himself. Money had passed between them on its way from Colombia via the Cayman Islands and then to its destination in a Swiss account. Drug money, with a sweet percentage from vice in New York City.

"In London?" he asked King.

"London," King agreed. "I need an outside contract."

"So what happened to that Mick who worked for you? Can't he find someone?"

King said, "This won't be an ordinary hit—she's big news. I can't trust a local to do it. I want a contract man that hits and is out of the country in a couple of hours. This bitch is well protected, and she's got brains. If she's killed, our media will go ape. Could you help out with someone?"

"You'd have to pay," Mario said. He picked his teeth with one of the sharpened quills provided by the management. "Prices are high if you want the best. How soon?"

King said, "Sooner than soon. Now."

"You want an accident, a sex crime, or just a straight hit?"

"I don't give a damn, just so long as she's dead," he answered. "Your man can choose. I don't want to know any details. And don't worry about money. I can match any price that's needed."

The Italian leaned toward him and laid a fat, ringed hand on King's arm. "You just give me the name and address, Harry. Then forget about it. Ok? Leave it with me. Some more coffee?"

"I'll be getting back. My daughter's at the hotel. I'm grateful, Mario. You're a friend. And thanks for the dinner."

"Next time," the Italian raised his hand, and a waiter came hurrying, "next time, bring your little girl with you. We'll have a family party."

"How was your evening?" King asked her.

Gloria smiled at him. "It was fine. I read through that draft cost accounting and it's just as good as you said. You're so clever, Daddy. Just brilliant the way you make figures work out the way you want."

"It's not so difficult; it's a trick, sweetheart," he said. "You'll learn it. Never be afraid of figures. Get to know and love them, and they'll be your friends."

He laughed. He was in a good mood, ebullient and confident. Mario would solve his problem before it could become his problem too. Everything was tied up, just the formalities to be gone through, like a big corporate dinner being given by Field in his honor. He thought, I'll take Gloria to Tiffany's tomorrow. Buy her a memento. Something she can wear at the dinner. He looked at her fondly.

It might be his imagination, but she was looking more attractive. She took a lot of trouble with makeup, hair, and clothes. There was a satisfied glow about her that made her seem more mature, as if an overgrown girl had developed into a confident woman. He didn't want to think of the reason.

He said, "How would you like a necklace—something special? I want you to knock the eyes out of them all at the Field Bank dinner. I want them to know who you are and that one day they'll be dealing with you! Tiffany's tomorrow—shall we go there together?"

Gloria had spent half an hour on the telephone to Leo Derwent. She had arranged to pay for the call herself. There was no need to irritate her father. He was mean about private telephone calls.

"Daddy, that would be wonderful. But you don't have to buy me anything. I brought plenty of jewelry with me. You told me to, remember?" Then she added, unable to resist the dig at her old adversary. "You'll have to buy something for Mummy, too, or she'll be jealous."

"Not this time," he said. "I'm going to bed now. Good night, darling."

She came and kissed him. "Good night. Sleep well."

She didn't go to bed for some time. She sat on in her suite and thought about Leo Derwent. They had talked about what she was doing in New York; he was always so interested in the business side of her life and so encouraging. Just like one man to another.

She wanted to know about him, too, what was happening at his ministry, in the House. Most of that long call was devoted to a mutual résumé of their professional lives.

And then he changed the conversation. There was no smut, just innuendo, coded references to the relationship they shared. Hints of ecstasies in store when she returned. He had warned her fiercely once, when she began to say explicit things, that telephones could be bugged. It added spice to the hidden meanings to clothe them in words that couldn't be understood by an outsider. It heightened their mutual titillation.

She was so restless thinking of him that she flung herself into a bath to try to soothe the urges. Only another five days and she would be home and able to see him. *I'm not in love*, she told herself. *I don't love him, I love Daddy. It's just that he makes me feel so good about myself. He knows how I feel and what I like. I never thought a man could get me going like he does. And I can drive him wild.* The thought crept into her mind. *We make a good team. And now that Daddy's being nice about it. . . .* She drifted happily away.

Ben said, yes, put his daughter through, and as soon as he heard Lucy's voice, he knew something was wrong. She was crying as she spoke.

"I'm losing it . . . Daddy, I've been bleeding since ten o'clock this morning—"

Ben Harris interrupted, "Are you in the hospital? Lucy, for God's sake, where are you?"

"I'm at home." She wept. "I went to the surgery, and they said to go to bed and rest, and it'd probably stop. But it hasn't. . . . it's getting worse, and I've got pains. I've just called again, and they said my doctor's out on an emergency but one of the others will be here as soon as they can. Oh, God, I'm so scared."

"Have you called your mother?"

"She's away," Lucy wailed. "They've gone up to his mother's on the Borders. Dad, I don't know what to do. . . . If I lose my baby . . . " She burst into hysterical sobs.

Ben Harris forced himself to be calm. "Lucy, Lucy darling, listen. Calm down, please. Get hold of yourself. Listen. I'll fly up there. Give me the doctor's number. If they send you to the hospital, I'll go directly there. And don't worry, try not to. . . . These things happen. It'll settle down, I promise you."

"I've even felt it move." She wept. "Oh, hurry up, won't you? Please hurry."

"I'm on my way to the airport. I'll charter a plane if I have to. Hang on, and don't worry. I know you're going to be all right." Then he slammed the phone down. He dialed Julia's direct line . . . no answer. The call was automatically transferred to her secretary.

"Miss Hamilton's gone home," the girl said. "She called through on her mobile phone to say she wouldn't be in till tomorrow morning. Can I get a message to her, Mr. Harris?"

He looked at his watch. Nearly five. He had to get to Heathrow. If there wasn't a shuttle till late evening, then he'd charter. . . . He couldn't waste any more time. "Call through for me and say I've had to go north; my daughter's been taken ill. I don't know when I'll get back. I'll contact her. Thanks, Jenny."

A call to the internal airline established that there was a seven-o'clock shuttle flight to Birmingham; he was lucky—there was a single seat available. Ten minutes later he was speeding out of London on the M4.

• • •

"My dear Julia," Evelyn Western said firmly, "I can't possibly see you this evening. I'm going out to dinner."

"Then I'll wait till you get back," Julia said. "I'm on my way now."

"I insist that you tell me why this is so urgent," Evelyn said. "I'm sure you wouldn't force yourself on me like this if William was here."

"No," Julia admitted. "I wouldn't have to; Lady Western, I don't like behaving like this, but I haven't any choice. You asked me to help your husband. That's why I've got to see you and talk to you. I'll be there in the next hour." She disconnected. Evelyn Western had tried being charming, and then coldly disapproving when the charm didn't work. If the door was slammed in her face, she'd sit outside and shame her into seeing her. But that wouldn't happen. Evelyn Western was a strong and determined woman who loved her husband and would do anything to protect him. She would see Julia, and when Julia had finished, William Western would cut short his Brazilian trip. She drove faster than usual; she felt exhilarated, strung up with the prospect of the battle to be fought and the truth at the end of it. Old lies, old cruelties had enmeshed her like a web of lies. The time had come to tear the strands apart and free herself. She slowed at the turning to Hollowood and started down the long gravel drive to the entrance. She could see lights shining in front of the house through the trees.

Ben Harris caught the shuttle to Birmingham. A last-minute call on his mobile phone had established that Lucy was taken by ambulance to Reidhaven Hospital. The airport teemed with travelers; businessmen, families with chil-

dren, the skiing contingent with their equipment, pas-
sengers from every part of the globe in transit, departing
or arriving. The bars and cafés and duty-free shops were
full; the lounges had their usual complement of exhausted
sleepers curled up on the seats; babies cried, toddlers
wandered off, and package tours assembled around their
coordinators. Life rushed to and fro. Death came in on the
Pan Am flight from New York, arriving at six forty-eight
at Terminal 3.

He had sixteen murders to his credit. He was thirty-three
years old, a married man with two young children. He
lived in Queens, New York, with his wife and mother-in-
law, who was an invalid. He was a respectable businessman
who traveled for a firm of software manufacturers. He
lived modestly, and he had never had a criminal record.
He had learned his skills from a Vietnam veteran when
he was very young and had been persuaded by his uncle
to branch out in private business. He carried out his first
contract on a debt defaulter in New Jersey, shooting him
at point-blank range through the head as he got into his
car to go to work. That murder earned him a retainer and
led to other contracts. He was called Mike, because he had
an Irish mother. He had been a good son, who stayed clear
of trouble in a rough neighborhood, did his schoolwork
diligently, and went on to be a good husband and father.
And kind to his wife's crippled mother. Killing made no
impression on him. Taking a human life didn't excite
him, or trouble his imagination afterward. It was a job,
and it was very well paid, depending upon the complexity of the target and the risk involved. He could command
the top price after the car bomb that killed a Head of
Family in Los Angeles. Right outside his massively guarded
house. Mike was a rich man with a long business life ahead
of him. He didn't drink or smoke, and he worked out three
times a week to keep himself in top condition.

He had taken the job in London. The sex of his victim didn't concern him. Nor did the method he chose; details were left to his discretion unless otherwise specified. Some contracts had to be accidents, others the result of violent crime, robbery, or sex murders. Some, like the target in Los Angeles, were plain executions, designed to scare off opposition. He had never lost an hour's sleep over what he did.

He had the name, address—private and business—and a description of the woman he was going to murder. How he did it had been left up to him. He preferred to choose his own method. It didn't tie him down. He liked exercising his own judgment and ingenuity. He prided himself on his professionalism. He took the Underground from the airport and booked into a small hotel on the Bayswater Road. He had made several trips to London. He liked the city and planned to bring his family over one year for a holiday. His two boys would love the changing of the Guard outside Buckingham Palace.

He had been given no contacts for this job. He always worked alone. He booked into the hotel and went out to get something to eat. By Underground again to Sloane Square, and then on foot to the apartment block in Chelsea Green.

As he expected, it was a secure block, but to someone familiar with the fortress mentality of wealthy Americans, with closed-circuit TV, armed guards, and trained dogs, it presented him with little problem. He walked the perimeter, noting the position of the outside fire escape visible at the rear of the building. It was four stories high. Her flat number indicated the top floor. That was no problem either. He'd carried out a killing twenty-two floors up and walked out of the building unchallenged. He checked the entry system by pressing a number at random. They would have internal TV screens to monitor the caller at the front; he always wore a soft fedora-type hat; the brim shaded his face.

A man's voice answered. "Hello?"

Mike emphasized his midwestern accent. "Sam? It's me . . . Pete."

The voice was sharp. "There's no Sam here. You've got the wrong flat."

"Sorry—shit, I buzzed the wrong bell. Sorry . . . " he said again, but the irritated man in the apartment didn't answer. Then he buzzed Julia Hamilton's number. There were no names, only numbers on the index beside the panel of buttons. He waited. No answer. He buzzed again. Nothing. She was out. He checked his watch. Nine-forty. Not working that late. On a date, at a movie with the live-in boyfriend. His brief was one killing, not two. He'd have to wait till he could catch her alone. He went back to his hotel and watched TV for a couple of hours. He called his wife before he went to bed. He'd had a good flight, he said; he was missing her and the kids already, but he'd get her some of that English cashmere she liked and a souvenir for the boys.

"Love you," he said. "I'll be home in a couple of days, if I get the business done quick." He fell asleep and didn't even dream.

Evelyn Western was watching by the library window as the headlights of Julia's car beamed up the drive. She had canceled her dinner engagement with neighbors. She had put through a call to her husband in Rio de Janeiro as soon as Julia rang off. He had been in a meeting in the city center. She left an urgent message, and the hotel promised to contact him and get him to call her immediately. This was no ordinary visit by Julia Hamilton. Her attitude was forceful, even aggressive, and Evelyn was instantly on her guard. Whatever she had discovered, it must be to Billy's disadvantage. There was no friendliness, let alone her customary deference to a much older woman who was her employer's wife. Then, to her relief, the call came through from Brazil. She didn't waste time.

"I've had Julia on the line," she said. "She's got hold of something. I'm afraid it doesn't sound good. She's insisted on coming here, I couldn't stop her. . . . Darling, I'm not being alarmist. If it's what I think, you'd better be ready to fly back. . . . Yes, yes of course I'll call you when she's gone. . . . All right, don't worry. I'll cope. Take care of yourself. . . ." *I'll cope.* Her own promise mocked her.

She had always coped, ever since they were married and living on her meager earnings as a librarian while William started out in business. She had coped with his struggles, his adversities, and his success. She was his rock, his closest ally. And his lover. That had not died in all the years they'd been together. They were indivisible. That girl was coming down with some revelation that could damage William. Yes, Evelyn Western decided, mustering her courage and her will, I'll cope. As she saw the car lights sweep to the front of the house, she stepped back from the window. She rang for the Filipino.

"Miss Hamilton has just arrived," she said. "Show her straight in here, please, and don't worry about offering drinks, we'll help ourselves. I don't want to be disturbed. Thank you, Felipe. No," she added in answer, "she won't be staying the night. So far as I know." She was placed strategically in the big armchair reserved for William Western. The light was behind her, turning the soft white hair into a silver halo. She got up slowly and came toward Julia. She seemed taller than ever.

"Come and sit down, Julia," she said quietly. "You sounded so agitated on the telephone, you quite alarmed me. I'm sure you'd like a drink. . . . Sherry?"

"No, thank you, Lady Western." Julia sat on the sofa facing her. She sensed the cool antagonism, and it distressed her. She liked and admired the older woman and she had trusted her, in spite of Ben's reservations. The message about his daughter was on the answering machine when she went back briefly to her flat. Poor Ben. Poor girl, losing her baby. Then she banished everything from her mind but what had to be said to Evelyn Western. *I won't be put off*, she insisted, watching Evelyn take her seat again and carefully arrange her long skirt as she prepared for a tiresome and unnecessary intrusion into her evening. *Jean Adams died because of the job they gave me. I'm not going to pull any punches.*

"I canceled my dinner engagement," the cool voice said. "It was very awkward for me. I had to make up a story. I hate telling lies and letting people down."

"I'm sorry," Julia said. "But it just can't wait."

"What can't wait? You said it concerned my husband. Surely it's not so earth-shattering that it couldn't wait until tomorrow?"

The sarcasm suddenly infuriated Julia. She blushed with anger. "Lady Western"—she kept her voice level—"at the beginning of this year I came down here at your husband's invitation, and he offered me an assignment. My own feature. 'Exposure.' It was a top job, the chance of a lifetime to get to the top of my profession. You were in the room; we opened champagne together. I'm sure you remember."

Evelyn Western nodded. "I do. I remember it very well."

"But the bottom line on that job offer, and the editorship to follow—he even threw that in—was to expose Harold King and bring him down."

"Yes." The voice was calm. "Yes, that's absolutely right."

"So I took it on," Julia said. "I persuaded Ben Harris to join me, and we started to investigate together. Because of what we discovered, a woman called Jean Adams was murdered."

"I remember. William told me about it." The beautiful blue eyes were cold and blank as they considered Julia.

"Did he tell you what happened to her and why?" Julia asked slowly. "She was an elderly widow, living alone. She was also the niece of King's first wife. King confessed to shooting British prisoners of war; he told his wife when he was blind drunk, and he tried to murder her afterward. But she'd already told Jean Adams. Perhaps you don't know all this? Perhaps Lord Western didn't bother you with details?"

Evelyn Western didn't answer. She sat absolutely still with her hands clasped in her lap. Julia went on. She was standing now, moving in agitation in that silent room with the silent woman sitting in her big chair, watching her.

"We found Jean Adams and we persuaded her to give an affidavit. We didn't know it, but we were being tagged and her phone was tapped. The night before she was due to sign that document, an intruder broke into her house. He raped her, Lady Western—she must have been close on seventy—then he beat her to death. He stole a few things to make it look like a robbery."

"How dreadful," Evelyn Western said. "I didn't know that."

"Well, your husband did. You asked me out to lunch and said you quite understood if I wanted to back out after what had happened to that poor woman. Your very words, weren't they?"

"If you say so. Yes, I did say that. I didn't want to pressure you."

"Oh, please." Julia gestured in dismissal. "Please stop trying to make a fool of me. You pleaded with me to save Western International and not give up on Harold King.

The irony is, you didn't need to soften me up. I have to live with what happened to Jean Adams, and the only way I can do it is to bring King into the dock. I've just come back from Jersey. I went there to see Richard Watson."

There was no movement, no betrayal, just a tightening of the slim hands in Evelyn Western's lap.

"Watson told me the story of the young German your husband wanted to bayonet in cold blood. That's what King discovered and blackmailed him with ten years ago . . . just when he was coming up for a peerage. It would have ruined him. So he backed off. He told Ben Harris to drop his investigation because he didn't want the world to know he was no better than a murderer himself."

Suddenly Evelyn Western rose to her feet. "Don't you dare say that! Don't you dare accuse my husband!"

"That German was Harold King," Julia went on. "He went berserk and shot those poor devils because he knew your bloody husband had been going to murder him. . . . Jean Adams died for nothing because your husband was *there*. He knew what had happened. He just hoped I'd proved it without getting him involved. You should have bought off Richard Watson. I bet you tried. . . ." She stopped; she realized that she was trembling. "I should be saying this to him instead of you. But he's in Brazil, building up his empire."

Slowly Evelyn Western turned away from her. She moved to a drinks table on the other side of the room. She poured a small measure of brandy. She came back, sipped it, and looked at Julia with her vivid blue eyes.

"You fool," she said. "Full of righteous indignation. Setting yourself up as judge and jury and finding William guilty. Now, you listen to me. You're right about the blackmail. King contacted Watson—that miserable man—God knows how, but he did. He had a tape of Watson's story.

Watson's version, making himself out such a hero. I even sent someone to see him, but it was useless. He was so high-principled, you see. If a newspaper broke that story, he felt honor bound to corroborate it and destroy my husband. So King escaped, and went from strength to strength till he's now in the position to drive us into the ground and take everything. You've been very clever, Julia, and so far you've got it right. Except that the German taken prisoner was *not* Harold King. He was a garage mechanic living in Strasbourg. He died of a heart attack last year."

She finished her drink. "You were so anxious to accuse William, weren't you? If he knew King was guilty of shooting prisoners, he would have been able to destroy him. So much for your theory." She sat down again, crossed one leg over the other, and examined her foot in its black patent slipper. "Of course we have proof of the mechanic's identity and a signed affidavit that he was the soldier taken prisoner at the time and date stated. He denied any suggestion that William was prepared to kill him. I'm sure my husband will let you have sight of it."

"I believe Richard Watson," Julia said slowly. "I'm sorry, but I do. Your husband gambled with other people's lives and held back a piece of vital evidence to protect his own reputation. Nothing alters that. The other officer with Watson was convinced there'd been an atrocity. But he's dead too. Like your mechanic."

"You can believe what you like," Evelyn Western said. "You stand there making judgments. What do you know about war? How dare you presume to judge . . . you weren't even born! William was right. Captain Phillips was right. Their first duty was to their men, to get them back to their own lines and out of a bloody running battle. Watson had his precious principles, but they cost the lives of all those men because that German was left alive. He did exactly what they said he would. He told his patrol where to find them. Nobody murdered the prisoners. They were caught in crossfire when a British armored car opened up on the column. William was so badly wounded—shot three times in the back. They repatriated him because he was likely to be paralyzed." She looked at Julia. "I trusted you," she said. "So did William. Now I'd like you to go, please. Just go." She turned her head away.

"I'm going," Julia said quietly. "But I'm not giving up. From now on I'm working for myself. Good night, Lady Western."

WPC Mandy Kent was going off duty. She and her husband planned to have supper with friends and go down to the pub for a karaoke evening afterward. Her husband had a nice voice and he wasn't shy about getting up in public. Mandy would have died with embarrassment, but she was rather proud of Dave when he performed.

"Mandy?" She turned; her sergeant was bearing down on her.

"I'm just off," she said defensively.

"DCI wants to see you. Won't take a minute."

"Oh, shit," she said, not quite under her breath. It must be trouble. She couldn't think where she'd slipped up.

"Don't worry, it's a pat on the back."

She looked up in surprise. "You're joking?" The sergeant grinned at her. She was popular with her colleagues. A good policewoman who didn't trade on her sex or try to be butch to prove a point. She came into the DCI's office. "Sir? You wanted to see me?"

"Yes. Sit down, will you." He looked down, referring to something on his desk. Then he said. "Couple of weeks ago you were involved in an assault, hospital case, a girl called Tracey Mervyn. She wouldn't press charges, and the friend wouldn't either. Usual story. The boyfriend had beaten her up."

Mandy said, "Yes, sir, I remember. It was a vicious assault. They were two prostitutes, black girls, well known in our area. I made one more effort to talk them into making charges, but it was no good. Anything happened?" Maybe the bastard had found them, or even worse, the silly cow had gone back and he'd done her over again. It often happened.

"You sent a bracelet into Stolen Property on the off chance, didn't you?"

She nodded, remembering the odd name the hospital sister had given it. "Yes, sir. The stones spelled out 'DEAREST.' It's popular for anniversaries, stuff like that."

"Well, for your information, it spells out MURDER," he said. "Our computer picked it up. An identical bracelet was listed among the jewelry stolen from a woman in Midhurst, who was raped and beaten to death by the intruder. It's been positively identified by the local jeweler, who made it specially to order. That was smart thinking on your part. I'll pass that on to the right quarters."

"Thank you, sir. If I can do anything more. . . ."

He shook his head. "It's out of our hands," he said. "It's CID's baby now."

Evelyn Western sat up waiting for the call from Rio de Janeiro. He was in the middle of delicate negotiations with a Brazilian bank. Western had decided to finance a fight back, and the best way of doing that was to issue shares in the new Brazilian publishing and newspaper companies that he had just acquired. He could raise cash, and cash was what he would need as soon as King began his frontal assault on Western International. Evelyn felt very tired as she waited. Emotional scenes exhausted her;

she hated Julia Hamilton for what she had said and done. She felt her age, and she couldn't afford to when William was threatened and needed her. She had weighed up the situation and decided that he mustn't interrupt what he was doing. She had faced out that damned girl, and the next move would have to come from her. She was sure it would be a letter resigning. She thought of her parting words, *I'm not giving up. From now on I'm working for myself.* . . . Not easy without the resources of her job. She might reflect upon that threat and see just how impossible it would be. . . . But she was proud and determined. The qualities Evelyn and William had both admired in Julia made her a dangerous maverick, capable of pulling the roof down in her pursuit of what she deemed to be justice and truth. She started when the telephone rang. She must have dozed in the big chair. She heard his voice, and said quickly, "It's all right, Billy. I've seen her. Yes, I was right; she came out with that bloody man Watson's story. . . . It was very unpleasant, but I didn't let her get away with anything. She had some crazy idea that King was the German prisoner and you knew he'd murdered your men. . . . Darling, please . . . I told her the truth and gave her a piece of my mind at the same time. There's no need for you to come home, I was just panicking when I said that . . . No, absolutely not. I was so angry, so furious at her attitude. No, I'm not upsetting myself, I feel better already because I've said it. How's it going out there? Oh, good, good . . . that's what's important. Yes, I will, I'll go to bed now. Don't fuss about me, Billy. I'm a tough old bird. . . . I'll call you tomorrow if there's any more news. And, whatever happens, I think it's time we stood our ground and stopped that Watson telling lies about you once and for all. . . . Yes, darling, good night. . . ."

William Western heard the line clear. He had left the meeting and made his call in a private office. Don't come home, his wife had insisted. He knew her tenacity and her courage; he also knew that she was too old to suffer sleepless nights and emotional turmoil. He thought of Julia Hamilton. His temper boiled over suddenly. "Bitch . . ." He snarled it aloud. Bullying Evelyn. . . . He knew her home telephone number; he had a photographic memory for figures and never needed an address book. He asked the switchboard to put the call in and he'd wait. He grabbed the phone at the first buzz. He heard her voice, sleepy since it was the middle of the night, say, "Hello . . . ? Ben?"

"It's Western," he shouted. "I've just spoken to my wife. You're fired, Hamilton, and you can tell Ben Harris he's fired too. You give in your keys and your car first thing tomorrow morning. You be out of that office by ten o'clock!"

"I will be," Julia said. "But don't think that's going to stop me or shut me up."

His line went clear.

Ben Harris sat by the bed and held his daughter's hand. He thought how very young and vulnerable she looked; her face was white and drawn, with deep shadows under the eyes. The nurse had briefed him before he went in.

"I'm afraid she's lost the baby," she said. "At this stage in the pregnancy it's very traumatic. She's been sedated, but she's not asleep. She'll be so glad you've come."

Ben came to the bed and said softly, "Lucy? Lucy, it's Dad. . . ."

She opened her eyes and tried to smile at him. A hand came out, and he took it quickly. Tears seeped down her face.

"I lost him," she whispered. Him. It struck Ben like a blow. "It was a little boy. They didn't want to tell me, but I had to know. Oh, Daddy . . ."

There was nothing he could say to comfort her. Instinct

warned him that this was no time to take refuge in male reticence. He cradled her in his arms as she wept, and kissed her. "Let it out," he said. "Grieve, darling. . . . Cry all you want. . . . I'm here and I'm staying."

At last she fell asleep, exhausted, dulled by the sedative. He sat on, holding her hand. The ward sister came and beckoned him away. He followed her unwillingly.

"It's better you leave her to sleep now, Mr. Harris," she said. "Get some sleep yourself. We'll see to the disposal of the fetus; there's nothing to worry about."

"Disposal?" Ben squared up to her. "What's that supposed to mean . . . ?"

"It needn't concern you." Her tone was soothing. "We have facilities here. It's less distressing for the mother."

"My daughter knows it was a boy," he said. "It's not a stillborn puppy, it's her child and my grandson. You do nothing, Sister, you understand me. The baby's going to be buried properly. I know that's what Lucy would want. And I'll make the arrangements, thank you."

He swung away from her and walked toward the elevator. He felt a sense of grief and loss, coupled with outrage at what might have happened. Lucy would need a focus for her grief, not a heap of ash in a hospital incinerator. Five months of expectation, of hope and joy, had ended that night in pain and disappointment, leaving a terrible vacuum.

She'd need time to recuperate and come to terms. Time to realize that life went on and that her very youth was her strength. He would make certain she had that time. He had booked into a hotel near the hospital. He felt drained and sick and he needed Julia badly. It was late, past midnight, but he dialed her number.

There was no reply. She must have gone out with a friend. He'd leave it till the morning. He woke very early; his first call was to the hospital. Yes, his daughter was sleeping, she had passed a quiet night. There were no complications, but the doctor would be in to see her later that morning. "I'll be there," Ben said, and hung up.

When he called Julia, it was the time they normally had breakfast before leaving for the office. She answered so quickly, he knew she was waiting for his call.

"Ben . . . ? Oh, Ben, what's happened?"

"She lost the baby," he said.

"Oh, darling, I'm so sorry. . . . Is she all right?"

"She's fine," he said. "Physically. But the worst is ahead of her. It was a boy."

"I'm so sorry," Julia said again. "Where are you? Can I send her some flowers?"

"No, I don't think so. I want to get her out of the hospital as soon as possible. Darling, I may have to stay with her for a few days, see what she wants to do. Her mother's away, and I don't want Lucy staying on her own after this. I may bring her down with me. I'll let the office know."

"Don't worry." Julia took a quick decision. This was no time to tell him the bad news. He sounded so low. "Don't worry. I'll do it for you. I'll ring tonight—what's the best time?"

"Around eight, I think. She might even be discharged today, I don't know. But try me here at eight. Thanks, darling. I just wish you were here with me. . . . No, I didn't mean that, you know what I mean. . . . How are you?"

"Missing you." Julia evaded any question about their last disagreement.

"You didn't go and see Western, did you?"

"No," she said. "He's in Brazil."

"Good. Do nothing till I get back. I love you."

Julia said gently, "I love you too. I'll talk to you this evening."

He was outside the apartment block when she came out. He was standing with a street map open in his hands, studying, and watching the entrance. The description had been accurate, even without the photograph, copied from the inset picture that appeared in the newspaper under her byline. Red hair, real fiery color, medium height, good figure, legs, pretty face. Tense expression, purposeful way of walking. Black BMW on residents' parking space. He took a note of the car registration number and jotted it down on his street map. She unlocked it, got in, drove off. He checked his watch. Then he crammed the map into his pocket and set out to find a cab and take a look at her office. He needed all possible venues checked out and weighed up before he decided where to hit her. On balance the apartment block looked the best; he liked the outside fire escape as a way out afterward, but an underground garage at her office might be a better option. He had done several jobs in that kind of environment. He dismissed the cab and took out the map again as he studied the entrance to the big glass-and-steel building. Outside lifts were a pain. He glanced up at the antlike figures speeding up the walls of the building. He came to the entrance, and the doors hissed back automatically.

A security guard approached him. "I'm looking for the garage," he said.

"Left and around the corner, you'll see a sign. Can I help?"

Mike grinned disarmingly at the suspicious look. He knew the type. Ex-cops, ex-army, dickheads in uniform. "No, thanks," he said. He walked out without any explanation.

The garage was on two floors with an underground area. There was a man in a cubicle behind an automatic barrier. As he waited, map in hand again, on the opposite side of the street, two cars came in, halted, pushed a card into the machine beside the cubicle, and the barrier lifted. He noticed that the man, also in uniform, leaned out and scrutinized the drivers and saluted them as they drove past him. He didn't like the idea of the garage. It was impossible to slip in from the street, and although there would be an internal entrance in the building, a stranger wouldn't get past the security guard at the entrance without some identification. He wasn't in the business of being recognized by anyone. He gave up on the office. He hailed another cab—he never hired a car on a job; that left traces such as license and insurance certificates. Phony or not, paper was something he avoided. He spent the rest of the day shopping for his wife's cashmere sweater, bought two because the rate for the dollar was so favorable, and spent a couple of hours choosing toys for his sons in the toy department at Harrods. At five o'clock he called Julia's number from a public phone. No answer. He called again at six. Nothing. He called on the hour until eleven P.M. without success. He gave up. She was not home, and his one chance of gaining entry diminished the later at night it became. Tomorrow he would go through the routine again.

"Sorry to burst in on you like this," Julia said. "But I just needed to come home and talk to someone."

"We're so glad you did," her father said. "After all, what are families for?"

"Not all families," Julia said. "I'm lucky."

"But why?" May Hamilton asked. "Why did he sack you? And fancy having to clear your desk and give the car up, just like that, in one morning!"

"In one hour," Julia corrected. "I'll be going back to discuss the termination of my contract of course. . . . They'll have to pay me off, because there's no reason for my dismissal. But it was quite an experience. My staff didn't know what had hit them. Jenny, my secretary, burst into tears. I was very moved."

"I thought they only behaved like that in America," her mother exclaimed angrily.

"Not anymore," Hugh Hamilton said. "It's another of their customs we've adopted. Disgusting way to treat people. You stick out for a damned good payout, Juliette. If you need a good lawyer, I'll ask around."

Julia said gently, "Don't worry, Daddy. I know lawyers if I need one."

"You could sue," her mother suggested. She was up in arms over the way her daughter had been dismissed. She had a fiery sense of injustice; Julia didn't realize how much of her own sense of fairness she owed to her mother.

"Mum, I'm not getting into all that hassle. Western won't cheat me. He'll pay proper severance money, and that'll be the end of it. Now, why don't we have a cup of tea? I've talked it all out, and now I want to hear about what you've been doing."

She hadn't explained the real reason to them; it was too complicated. A policy disagreement was the reason she gave for losing her job. They seemed to accept that. Neither of them had any experience of high-powered journalism and the despotism of the great press lords. Luckily for them, Julia thought. *And Ben has to be told sometime. Maybe tonight, if his daughter's out of the hospital. He doesn't have to hurry back. They can clear his bloody desk and send his things around to the flat. . . . Typical Western to punish him as well. But he needn't sleep easy because he's got rid of me. I meant every word I said. I'll show the world what Harold King really is, and now I don't have to protect William Chancellor Western or cover up for him.*

"They want you to go around ahead of them and soften the girls up. They know you, it might help."

Mandy Kent said, yes, both girls did know her, but she didn't hold out much hope they'd be cooperative. She'd go and catch them at home half an hour before the CID arrived. They were staying with another girl and her boyfriend on Brixton Road. It was a heavily black area, and they felt safer there. Mandy changed out of uniform; it made her less threatening. Tracey, with her broken jaw and multiple injuries from that beating, and Tina, her friend, were the only witnesses who could tie in their ex-boyfriend with that bracelet.

She found the place on the busy Brixton Road, a run-down wreck of a mid-Victorian house, cracked walls, windows on the ground floor boarded up, a few curtains hanging drunkenly on the first-floor windows. There was no bell, only an old-fashioned cast-iron knocker. Mandy banged on the front door, and after a long wait and a second series of knocks a young woman with a baby on her hip opened the door. Mandy said in a friendly way, "I've come to see Tina and Tracey—are they in, love?"

"Upstairs, dear," the girl said. The baby smiled enchantingly at Mandy, who smiled back and touched the smooth, fat cheek.

"Sweet kid," she said. "How old?"

"Fourteen months. Always laughin' . . . never cries." The girl had a West Indian lilt in her voice. "First floor," she told Mandy, and stood aside to let her pass.

The bruising and swelling had gone down on Tracey's face. Her jaw was mending, but still painful. She looked haggard and miserable. Tina had always been the stronger personality of the two; she had more self-confidence.

"I thought I'd drop in and see how you were getting on," Mandy said. Both girls were expressionless.

"Taken up social work, then?" Tina asked.

Mandy didn't rise. "No. Just a routine follow-up. On my own time. How's it going, Tracey?"

"All right." It was a mumble. "I'm mending."

"That bastard know where you are?"

"No," Tina answered. "And he's not going to find out. Soon as she gets the nod from the doctor, we're going up to Liverpool. My friend's got a friend there." She looked at the policewoman with suspicion. "What do you want? And don't give me any 'friendly' crap. You're a copper. So why are you bothering us?" She stood with both hands on her hips. She wasn't afraid of the cow. She and Tracey were both clean. No men, no drugs, nothing since it happened. She glared at the symbol of white authority. People like her had been pushing her around since she was a skinny teenager, put into care because she was working the pubs for a few quid to feed and clothe herself after both parents walked out and disappeared, taking her little brother and leaving her behind.

Mandy didn't answer. Or react. Then she opened her bag and took out a pack of cigarettes.

"Mind if I light up? Want one?" She proffered the pack.

"No," Tina snapped. "Why don't you just leave us alone?"

Mandy Kent made a police decision. Nothing would be gained by being nice. No hearts and minds to be won with either of them.

"Because I can't," she said. "There're other police officers on their way here. They want to ask you some questions. Serious questions. You won't talk back to them, Tina. Or you'll find yourself down at the station in real trouble."

Dealing with criminals for the last ten years had hardened Mandy Kent. It had made her the match for any of them when it came to being tough. Tina's dark skin paled. The girl, Tracey, made a frightened sound.

"What trouble?" Tina wasn't cowed yet. "We've done nothing, we're not in any trouble."

Mandy Kent said, "That bracelet, the one that caused the row and got you both beaten up . . . it was stolen. Did you know that?"

"No," Tina sat down suddenly. Theft. They could hang anything they liked on her. She didn't know where it came from, only that Joe gave it to her.

"It was a present. He gave it to me. I told you."

"I know you did," Mandy agreed. "We ran the description through on a computer and it came up. Stolen property. Part of a robbery in Midhurst. And you didn't know?"

She saw Tracey turn in anguish, and Tina got up and slipped an arm around her protectively. She had suspected, and she was sure now, that in their own time the girls were lovers.

"We knew nothing," Tina said fiercely, thinking of Tracey, not herself. "He just gave it to me one day. Said, 'Here's a present for you.' I'd given him a good time the night before. We both had. He was feeling really generous. . . . We never stole anything."

"If you didn't," Mandy suggested, "maybe he did?"

Tina's scorn was genuine. "Him? Steal a crappy thing like that? He was in the money . . . big money. He didn't need to thieve."

"Well, he got it from somewhere, didn't he?"

Tina shrugged, still holding on to her friend. "Must have. Look, what's this all about? You're trying to scare us—"

"I'm not." The answer was very calmly spoken, and the look was hard. Tina had seen its kind before and she bit back an insult. "You wouldn't give evidence against this man Joe Patrick, would you? You let him half kill your girlfriend, but you were too chicken to charge him. Not that I blame you. You were right to be scared, Tina. Shit scared of what he'd do to you. But if you and Tracey want to get back at him and be in the clear yourselves, now's your chance."

Tina sneered. "On thieving a bracelet . . . ?"

"On thieving a bracelet," Mandy agreed. "A bracelet that belonged to a sixty-eight-year-old widow who was burgled, raped, and beaten to death." She pushed back her coat sleeve and checked her watch. "It's murder, Tina. The CID will be here any minute. I hope you two have good memories. They'll be asking you a lot of questions."

She got up and turned her back on them. She drew back the flimsy curtain on its sagging wire and looked down into the street below. The squad car came into view, its blue light flashing; the thin wail of the siren came through the badly warped window frame. Joe Patrick. They'd learned a lot about him since that first check—a onetime pimp, a petty crook who had gone on to bigger and better things in the criminal world, posing as a businessman. But, elusive as an eel, never convicted for lack of evidence. He might live to regret losing his temper with his girlfriends. But she had done her part. The rest was the responsibility of the Murder Squad. She turned back to them. The girls were sitting side by side, staring at her. They could hear the loud rattle of the iron doorknocker from below.

"I'll be off now," she said, and walked out of the door as the first steps echoed on the bare stairs up to the landing.

"You can't stay here on your own," Ben insisted. His daughter looked up at him. She was pale and hollow-eyed, but in control.

"Biddy's here," she said. "She'll look after me." The student she shared with had been kind and anxious to help, but she couldn't stay away from her classes to keep Lucy company.

"I know she is," Ben agreed gently. "And she's a sweet kid, but she can't be here in the day. Listen, Lucy, you're going to feel shaky for a week or so. The impact hasn't sunk in yet. You're still in shock. Let me take care of you. Just for a little while. Please."

She had made a good recovery, and the medical staff felt she would benefit from living in her own environment. The sad little funeral was over, and Ben refused to go down to London and leave her to grief and loneliness. Her mother had been contacted; Ben felt she was secretly relieved at the resolution of Lucy's problem, but he didn't say so. His ex-wife was openly relieved when he assured her that it wasn't necessary to interrupt her stay with her parents-in-law. He would remain with Lucy and look after her. He had spoken to her husband for the first time.

His mother was in her eighties, and far from well . . . He didn't really feel they ought to hurry back if he, Ben, was coping with the situation. He was very sorry to hear what had happened, of course, and please give his best to Lucy. Thank God she was all right, that was the main thing. . . .

It's my responsibility, Ben decided, and prepared to do tactful battle with his daughter for her own good. He'd let that responsibility slip all those years ago when he made the job his first priority. He was not going to fail his child a second time.

Julia was out of London, taking time off to be with her parents in Surrey. He didn't have to worry about her, and it eased his mind to think of her staying with them. She had sounded unworried about being away from the office; it was out of character, but he didn't question it. She knew what she was doing; he had never tried to direct her life except when he felt she was in danger, and it had the opposite effect. And he was relieved she wasn't on her own. He didn't feel pressured. He didn't have to hurry Lucy into going back with him. Speaking to Julia, he poured out his anxieties for his daughter and even admitted to a pang of personal grief for the little stillborn child. So Julia didn't burden him with the news that they were both out of a job. That could wait. He needed time to sort out his personal difficulties, and, she realized, expunge a sense of guilt for that marriage breakup all those years ago. She realized it made her love him even more.

"Darling," she told him, "Lucy can stay with us. We've an extra bedroom, and we might even take her away for a few days. Do you good as well." And when he protested that he actually had to go back to the office before too long, she said disarmingly that he could worry about that when he was back in London.

"All right, Dad." Lucy had surprised him by giving in sooner than he expected. "All right, I'll come south with you. I can't stand seeing you doing the cooking and washing up another minute." She'd managed to smile at him when she said it. "If you're sure there's room . . . and your girlfriend doesn't mind. I don't want to get in your space. . . ."

"She wants you," he said firmly. "She's been asking to meet you for God knows how long. And you'll like each other. I guarantee it. How about we go tomorrow?"

"Day after?" Lucy asked him. "I want to sort things out and get myself organized. I want to go and see my principal and make sure they'll keep my place open."

"Day after tomorrow would be fine," Ben said. "I'll ring Julia tonight and tell her. Thanks, sweetheart. I would have missed you like crazy."

"I must go home," Julia said. "I've been dodging the issue long enough. It's been lovely unburdening everything, but it's really time to go and sort myself out. And see a lawyer. Before I go and talk to my ex-employer's contract department."

"You do that, darling," May Hamilton said. "Don't you let them cheat you out of a penny that's due you!"

Julia laughed. "Don't worry, Mum. I'm not your daughter for nothing. I won't! And thanks for being so supportive. You and Dad have been angels."

"Nonsense," both parents insisted. "And you and Ben are coming for Christmas, don't forget. And if his daughter's still with you, bring her too. We'd love it."

Julia drove back to London in a glow of gratitude and thankfulness for both of them.

When her telephone rang at six o'clock, she put down the ginger cat who had dug herself into her lap, delighted to have company, and rushed to answer. It might be Ben . . .

"Hello, Julia Hamilton . . . " It buzzed in her ear before the words were out. Wrong number or misdial, she thought, and picked up Pussy, who was sulking at having been put down. The porter had fed her daily as instructed, but she missed her human friends and had relieved her feelings by scratching vigorously at the upholstered sofa.

She lifted her back onto her lap and stroked the silky fur. Funny how fond she had grown of Ben's cat. It gave her a feeling of calm and domesticity to fuss over her. Dogs were her parents' passion, but they lived in the country. London flats were no place for dogs. Maybe one day, if she and Ben moved . . .

She caught herself by surprise. Jumping the gun, as her father would say. Going far into the future. It wasn't like her to think impractically. Three days removed from the mainstream in sleepy Surrey and she'd gone soft. It made her smile. Those musings were for much later in her life. When she had finished what she had set out to do. *Harold King.*

No doubt Evelyn Western was telling the truth. There *was* an affidavit signed by a dead German mechanic exonerating William Western of the intention to murder an unarmed prisoner. Whether it was genuine was something else. But who was to disprove it? Very clever, she thought bitterly. They'd got a fail-safe, by bribery or God knew how. Then why hadn't they felt secure enough to dismiss King's first blackmail attempt and shut Richard Watson's mouth? She sat up sharply.

Of course they couldn't, because the stooge in Strasbourg was still alive! Western couldn't risk a confrontation or have his witness brought into court. Now, with its signature beyond cross-examination, that affidavit would hold up in court. Harold King was going for the jugular, and William Western had weighed the risk and decided to strike first. He'd fired her in a fit of fury, frustrated that she had opened the closet on his skeleton and failed to incriminate King. Maybe he regretted it. But she didn't. She had been careful with her salary; she had enough saved to go ahead alone.

And to look after Ben if he'd been less provident. There'd be offers pouring in for both of them. They could name their price anywhere in the media world. That was no cause for worry.

The telephone shrilled again. "Julia? Hi, it's me, Felix."

"Felix? Well, hello. How are you?" She hadn't thought of him for so long, his voice was quite a shock. Antagonism rose in her; the same cocky, casual tones grated on her, reminding her of a relationship that shamed and irritated her.

"I'm fine. I've been trying to get you for a couple of days, but you forgot to switch on your machine."

"I didn't forget," she said tersely. "It's an invitation to break in if you're away. I was staying with my parents."

"Good on you." He chuckled down the line. "You weren't the loving daughter when I knew you."

"What do you want?" Julia asked.

He had a skin like a rhino. He said, "I heard on the office grapevine that you'd been given the shove. Sorry to hear it."

"Thanks," she said. "I'm not worried. I'm relieved."

"All that lovely money—" She had a mental picture of him grinning in disbelief, and just stopped herself from hanging up. "What happened? You were the old man's 'blue-eyed baby.'. . . Fall out with him?"

"Felix, why do you want to know? Why should you care? It's not your province. There's no mileage in it for you."

"God, you do think I'm a shit," he protested. "I was just sorry to hear it, that's all. I was even going to ask if you and Ben would like to meet me for a drink."

"Ben's not here," she said. She felt guilty because she'd been so hostile. He was brash and tactless, and she'd overreacted. "He's up in Birmingham, family business."

"Didn't know he had a family," Felix said. "Why don't you come out, then?"

"I don't think so," Julia said. "I've got a lot to sort out."

"Oh, come on," Felix urged. "Just for old times' sake. I might even buy you dinner if you stop biting my head off. Look, I'll come and pick you up in half an hour. I'm in a pub now. It's that lovely lad Joe Patrick's watering hole. Full of gorgeous tarts. See you. 'Bye!"

She didn't want to go. But it was typical of Felix to steamroller when he wanted something. A drink with him wouldn't hurt. Joe Patrick . . . King's contact man. The photographs and tapes supplied to ruin Leo Derwent. Yes, she'd meet Felix. It might clear her own mind to talk to someone who wasn't so closely involved. She bribed the cat with a dish of milk, changed out of her leggings and sloppy sweater into trousers and a top, and brushed vigorously at the fiery, untamed hair.

Then she recorded a message for Ben in case he phoned while she was out. "Gone for a drink with Felix. I hope you're jealous. Back around nine. I'll call you then. Love, darling."

Felix, inevitably, was twenty minutes late. When he buzzed from the street, she said, "I'll come down," and hurried out, double-locking the front door. The man with the street map idling by the corner turned his head and watched her leave.

CHAPTER 10

"HE JUST SAID HE WAS GOING OUT?"
Detective Chief Inspector Roy Bingham was being calm and patient. The girl who'd been beaten up was cowed and compliant. The other dyke was a much tougher proposition. Intelligent and wary, still trying to protect the girlfriend and herself at the expense of bringing a murderer to justice. Roy Bingham considered both of them to be the scum of the earth, but he went on with careful questioning, leading, not bullying. Everything was going down on tape, and his detective sergeant and a CID woman police officer were present. They'd given the two women coffee and ordered sandwiches. He went on, "He was going out. That's all he said?"

"That's right," Tina agreed sullenly. "'I'm going out.'" She remembered the glib insult that went with it: "You

· 305 ·

two tar babies wait up for me. . . . I'll want something special tonight." And Tracey's apprehensive whisper as he left them: "What's up? Where's he off to. . . ?" And her answer: "Some poor bugger's going to get done over. . . . Joe always gets a hard-on afterward." The widow at Midhurst had been done over good and proper. And raped.

"And when he came back," Roy Bingham prompted, "then what happened?"

Tina glared at him. "I told you. We went into our double act. You want to know the dirty details?"

"No," he said. "I'm not interested. What I'm asking is did he say where he'd been, give any indication what he was doing while he was out?"

"Nothing," Tracey muttered. "He never did."

"And you never asked?" That was the detective sergeant, taking the lead for a moment.

She looked at him. "You must be joking. He'd have knocked the shit out of us. He didn't like questions."

"He often beat you up, then?" He was concentrating on the weaker one, leaving his boss to wear down Tina.

"Not often," Tracey admitted. "If he felt like it."

"Didn't you resent it?"

She shrugged slightly. "He was good to us in other ways. He fancied Tina more than me. That's what got up his nose, her lending me the bracelet."

"And when did he give you the bracelet?" It was the boss, taking it up with Tina.

"I told you. Next day. We'd given him a good time."

"When you were with him the night before, did you notice any marks . . . bruising, skinned knuckles . . . anything at all?"

"No." Tracey turned her head. "If he did a job, he always wore gloves. He never marked himself."

Tina glared at her in warning, but it was too late.

"What do you mean by a job?"

Roy Bingham sensed a breakthrough. He abandoned Tina. He moved his chair a little closer to Tracey. It seemed to her as if they had all moved in on her, crowding her. She stared from one to the other and around to the policewoman sitting in silent witness of the scene.

"When he did someone over. He used a knife on the girls. He never cut us. He only used his fists."

"And his feet," Roy reminded her. "He kicked you, didn't he? Kicked you in the ribs so hard, he fractured three of them. Kicked you in the back. The old lady who owned that bracelet was kicked too. And punched. I've got some photographs. I'd like to show you what was done to her."

"I don't want to see," Tracey said, and started to cry.

Tina got up and came over to her. "You bastards!" she snarled. "Leave her alone."

"If you'll sign a statement," the sergeant suggested, "you can both go home."

"Yeah?" Tina turned on him. "And wait for a visit from his mates when he finds out we've been talking to you? Get lost. We're not signing anything."

The detective chief inspector got up. He addressed the tape recorder. "Termination of interview at seventeen-twenty hours, Thursday, ninth of December." He snapped the machine off. His tone changed. "Right," he said. "Let's separate these two. Joan, take Oswald to another interview room. Mervyn stays here." He barked at Tina, "Come on, Oswald. Move your ass."

"I'm not going," she said loudly. "I'm not leaving Tracey. I won't, and you can't make me!"

Her voice rose. He heard the panic in it and he mocked her.

"You want to bet? Joan, call up another WPC and get this one out of here. I want a few quiet words with her friend."

Tina stood rigid. She heard the mutter from the police-woman into her mike: "Send someone up to Interview Room Five, will you? We've got a recalcitrant."

They'd manhandle her out, and Tracey would be left to fend off that ugly white bastard on her own. She was still weak and shaky from the ordeal. Her jaw was set, but it was a mess and it would have to be rebroken and done again. Then surgery on her nose and cheekbones. She slept badly and panicked if Tina went out for long. She was scared to be alone. Joe Patrick hadn't killed her, but he'd marked her inside and outside for life.

Tracey clinched it. "Tina," she wailed. "Tina . . . don't leave me. . . ."

Roy Bingham knew he had won when the body language changed. Tina slumped as the fight went out of her.

She said, "All right, all right. I'll make a statement. Just don't get heavy, will you?"

Bingham nodded to the policewoman, who canceled her request. He switched on the tape recorder and started the interview again.

"Interview recommenced at seventeen twenty-eight, ninth of December. Detective Sergeant Fitch and Detective Constable Joan Lewis present, interviewees Tina Oswald and Tracey Mervyn, conducted by DCI Roy Bingham. Now, Tina, let's get the story right from the beginning, shall we? The bracelet identified as the property of Mrs. Jean Adams, who was murdered in the course of a rob-bery at her home address. . . ."

The monotonous tone went on, repeating the details. Then the real questions began.

"You can positively identify this bracelet as the one given you by Joe Patrick on the twenty-seventh of September?"

Tina said, "Yes."

"And the night before, Joe Patrick left you both in his apartment at approximately what time?"

"Around nine," Tina said. There was no turning back.

"Did he say where he was going?"

She hesitated. Then she took a breath. "He said he was going on a job."

Bingham stared at her. "He said that? He said he was going on a job?"

She was lying, and he knew it. He spoke to the other girl. "Did he say that to you too?"

"No, he didn't."

Tina interrupted. "He said it to me. She didn't hear him."

Bingham nodded. "I see." He switched off the recorder. "You've decided to nail him, have you?"

Tina looked at him. "That's what you want, isn't it?"

He didn't answer for a moment. He took out a pack of cigarettes and lit one. He'd tried and failed to give up smoking. He couldn't afford frazzled nerves in his job.

"Right, then," he said briskly. "Let's have some more coffee and get down to business."

They dropped Tina and Tracey back in an unmarked police car. The flat was empty. The friend and her man spent a lot of time out picking up punters and pushing drugs. Tracey looked at her. "You've done it now," she muttered.

"We'll be all right," Tina told her. "We'll be moved out of here tomorrow and we'll have protection. I'm glad I did it, Trace. After what that piece of dirt did to you, I'm glad. I always said I'd pay him back one day. Come on, let's get to bed. We'll be fine. So long as we've got each other."

Felix took Julia to a wine bar on Jermyn Street. It was discreet and expensive. They settled into a corner banquette. "This is like old times," he said.

"Except that I'd be paying." Julia cut that approach off

at the start. "You must be doing well if you come to places like this."

Unabashed, Felix grinned. "I told you, I like the good life. And I am doing well, as it happens. I'm the Warbler's assistant now. You wouldn't believe how many important politicians I know."

Julia said, "Go on, impress me, then."

It was silly to rise to him; nothing would change Felix. He had always rather enjoyed needling her. She might as well relax and enjoy her drink. He named several MPs, including one ambitious cabinet minister. "I get asked to lunch and taken aside for off-the-record chats. . . . It's fascinating. They all talk such a load of crap, really—doesn't matter which side they're on." He drank his gin and tonic and ordered another. "What are you going to do now?" In sheer mischief he added, "Some people'd change sides. Trot along to King and offer to work for him. Bringing a few tidbits about the noble lord along with you—"

Julia said angrily, "Don't be so bloody stupid, Felix. As if I would!"

"I only said 'some people,' not you," he pointed out. "You've got too many principles, that's your trouble."

"And you've got none," she countered.

"Never pretended I had," he said. "Have another vodka, and let's stop scoring off each other. What *are* you going to do? You'll have to drop the King investigation for a start."

"I'm not going to," she said.

He glanced sideways at her. "That's a bit rash," he said. "Without backup? What does Harris think?"

"I haven't told him, he's had to go to look after his daughter. He's got enough to worry about. But he'll go along with me. Felix, can I try a few things on you? Would you mind? It might help me to see my way clearer."

"Mind? I'm flattered. Go on, try me."

Julia didn't notice the time. At the end Felix said, "That's quite a story. A riddle inside an enigma. If Western's wife was telling the truth, you're back to square one. An unsubstantiated allegation that King shot British prisoners, somewhere in the Western Desert. Did you believe her?"

"I believed her, but not what she was saying," Julia answered slowly. "I know that four men were killed and Western was wounded, and I know Harold King was responsible. But how do I prove it? What have I missed?"

"God knows." He shrugged. "Unless you can get King drunk!" She stared at him.

"Felix . . . Felix," Julia said slowly. "Can you drop me home?"

"Why don't I buy you dinner?" he suggested. "Pizza on the Park's great. . . . What's the matter? You look funny."

"Nothing's the matter," she said. She picked up her bag. "I won't eat, thanks anyway. Can you drop me back?"

"Yeah. I'm not doing anything else. I'll get the bill. You're a Liberal Democrat, by the way. Goes on expenses."

They came out into the crisp winter night, and Julia shivered. Not with cold but with a growing sense of excitement. Felix, flippant as always, had said something more momentous than he would ever realize. She saw a cruising taxi, its orange light gleaming up front, and on an impulse she turned to Felix.

"Don't worry, I'll take this cab. Thanks for the drinks. Thanks for letting me talk it out."

"Okay." Felix didn't mind not driving out of his way back to Chelsea Green. There'd been a dishy little redhead in Joe Patrick's favorite pub who'd been eyeing him earlier. She might still be hanging around there. Being with Julia had turned his thoughts to more than pizza. "Sorry I couldn't help," he said.

"I think you have." To his surprise Julia reached up and kissed him lightly on the cheek. The cab had drawn to the curb, and she got inside. Felix stood looking after her for a moment. Definitely the little redhead, he decided. She wasn't Julia, but she'd do.

He dialed the number from a public phone. He listened to Julia's message for Ben Harris.

"Gone for a drink with Felix. I hope you're jealous. Back around nine. I'll call you then. Love, darling."

The time was just past seven. He went into a pâtisserie in the shopping center nearby and had some cakes and two cups of coffee. He never drank on a job, but he loved sweet pastries. Then he went back to Chelsea Green and slumped down in the darkness of a doorway. It was just across the street from the apartment block. The entrance was well lit, part of the security system. That suited him well. One or two pedestrians passed by, but didn't bother to look twice at the figure huddled in a doorway for shelter. London was full of homeless drifters, begging by day and sleeping rough. He had seen a number of them for himself. He wore dark clothes and trainers; the overcoat made him look respectable, as did the fur hat, earflaps pulled down. The footwear was light and made running easy. If he had to run. He didn't expect to; he expected to walk away from the job and simply disappear into the London murk. Then the first flight home in the morning. He had an open-ended ticket. The killing wouldn't be discovered till he was well en route across the skies. A single man and then a couple, followed later by another, came to the apartment block and went inside, but he didn't move. Then he saw what he was hoping for. Three young kids, teenagers, converged on the front door. He had noticed girls and boys coming and going while he was on watch during the day. He moved very quickly, up from his seat on the step and across the street, catching up with them just as the front door opened. One of the girls had a key; as she pulled it out of the lock, he pushed in past her. He said, "Thanks," over his shoulder, and he was past the TV camera in the entrance hall as they followed. He heard them laughing and talking behind him as he hurried to the stairs and began taking the first flight two steps at a time. They'd been too busy to notice him. He'd counted on that. Kids, he thought dispassionately. His would have been just as careless. Hamilton's apartment was on the fourth floor. Top of the building. He slowed his pace and listened for sounds coming from above.

He paused, watching the red eye of the elevator. It stopped on the third floor. He heard teenage voices floating down the stairwell, and stayed out of sight. Then he climbed the last two flights of stairs. An arrow pointed right for two flat numbers. Another arrow indicated one number only, Hamilton's number, on the left. Through glass doors and around a corner. It made an isolated little cul-de-sac on that top floor. The front door of the flat was at the end of a short passage. 403, in gilt bronze figures on a heavy mahogany door. He moved without sound on the thick pile carpet. He noticed the TV eye sunk in the wall above head height. Anyone ringing the bell would be instantly viewed on a double screen inside. One screen for the street entrance, another for the passageway outside the flat. He stood and listened. She had said around nine. It was near that time now. He went back down the passageway. From his observation from outside the building in daylight he knew the fire escape must be close by. And there it was. Clearly marked with a red arrow and the warning This Exit Must Be Kept Clear at All Times. It was a simple push-lever model, easy for a young or old escapee to open. He shifted it with one hand and stood for a moment on the narrow iron platform outside. Heights didn't worry him. The wind was biting up here, and he shrugged deeper into his coat. Then he went back inside. He pushed the glass door and let it swing back. It made a definite click as it came to rest. He'd hear that. And he could watch through a crack in the door to the fire escape and see Hamilton come in. If she was alone, the hit was on. If she wasn't . . . He never carried out more than one contract at a time. He didn't believe in two for the price of one. He'd seen her meet a man outside. If she brought him back to her apartment, then he would slip downstairs and go to his hotel and try the next day. He was calm; postponement wouldn't bother him. He had no nerves, just a dislike of any kind of risk, however minimal. He stepped back onto the narrow fire escape, the door just an inch ajar, and looked up at the stars in the clear, dark skies above him. And waited.

Julia paid off the cab, opened the front door, and took the lift up to the fourth floor. It was later than she had intended, long past nine o'clock. She let the glass door swing back behind her and hurried to her door.

She didn't even glance near the fire exit. Pussy came into the hallway and mewed. She stroked her and went quickly to the telephone to see if Ben had tired of waiting and phoned her. The machine winked at her. She pressed Play and heard his voice. "I'm taking Lucy out for supper. It'll cheer her up. I'll ring if we're not too late. Otherwise tomorrow morning. Then home on Friday. No more drinks with other men for you . . . 'Bye, sweetheart." "Damn," Julia said out loud. Damn . . . just when she needed to talk to him. She wasn't hungry; her stomach was tight with tension. She poured herself a drink and ran a hot bath. She opened a new tin of food and gave the cat an extra feed to make up for being absent. Ben said she was getting fat. Julia was always giving her tidbits. He'd said to her once, half teasing, "God knows what you'll be like with a child. . . . You'll spoil it to death." She stripped off her clothes, took the drink into the bathroom, and sank into the hot water. A riddle inside an enigma. And it seemed that now there was only one way to prize open that enigma and solve the riddle. King couldn't control himself with alcohol.

Which was why, since the fatal night with his wife, Phyllis Lowe, he had never touched even a glass of wine in forty years. *Get him drunk.* Felix had tossed in the flippant suggestion. She was going back now, her memory in full recall. The bathwater chilled her without noticing, the drink was unfinished on the side. He'd told Phyllis that he had murdered the prisoners. In the wild confession that spilled out under the influence of alcohol, he had put himself in thrall to her. There were people who lost all control, who couldn't tolerate even one drink. Not alcoholics, but people suffering from a kind of mental allergy. The inhibitions common to normal behavior were suspended. They were at the mercy of a drug that robbed them of self-will. They were rare cases, very rare, but they existed. Harold King was such a man. The evil was in him; the alcohol made him proclaim it without fear of the consequences. She got out, dried herself, changed into pajamas. She tipped the unfinished vodka down the sink and heated some hot milk. It might help her to sleep. Ben hadn't called. It was midnight; he wouldn't ring now. She got into bed, the cat curled up by her feet, and lay awake, thinking. How? How to trick King into breaking that embargo. . . . And then, suddenly, the answer came to her.

· · ·

He had come into the passage; he was getting too cold outside. He checked his watch. Ten to twelve. He went to the glass door around the corner and opened it, watching the lift panel to see if anyone was coming up. The red eye didn't change to green. The block was very quiet. He went to the top of the stairs and leaned over the stairwell, listening. Sound traveled upward. There was nothing. No voices, no movement. He stayed where he was, making sure that no one was coming in late. Nobody did.

At twenty-five minutes past twelve he went back around the corner, through the glass door, and came up to the entrance to Apartment 403. He wore tight leather gloves. He muffled his mouth with his left hand and struck a heavy blow on the mahogany panel. Then another. And another. And he shouted.

"Fire! Fire! The block's on fire! Everybody out!"

Julia was half asleep when she heard the hammering on her door. She woke fully and sprang up. She heard the voice yelling, "Fire . . . Fire. . . "

Fire! She felt a rush of terror. Four floors up . . . Oh, God . . . She paused to grab the coat she'd tossed on a chair. The cat . . . Where was the cat? She couldn't leave it. She was still on the foot of her bed. She grabbed her, breathless with fear, and ran barefoot to her front door. She wrenched the safety chain out of its socket and fumbled with the latch. He heard the movement inside and he drew himself up; a knife with a thin blade was in his right hand. As Julia opened the door, he crouched to spring.

She saw the figure, saw in one second that it was poised to attack her. She gave a piercing scream of terror, and blindly, instinctively, she threw the cat at him. The cat was wild with fear—Julia's fear, communicated in that rush for safety.

It half sprang of its own accord, hissing, teeth bared and claws extended. It struck him full on and it clung to his face, ripping and snarling before he wrenched it off him. He had dropped the knife, and, in the same few seconds, Julia slammed her door shut.

She didn't think; she was so shocked, she could hardly breathe. She had slipped and fallen to her knees. She managed to crawl to the door, and it took both hands to slide the heavy chain into place. She began to shake, and she felt for a moment that she was going to be sick. He was out there. Outside the door, waiting. He couldn't get in. He couldn't. . . . She couldn't hear anything. No sound. Just that terrible, menacing silence, with the man who had tricked her into coming out still there.

She found the keys on the hall table, and, trembling, fitted them into the interior locks and turned them both. The locks and the chain. Nobody could break that door down without a sledgehammer. She stumbled to the sitting room. Her legs were giving way. She calmed herself, or believed she did. There was no fire. There was an alarm system throughout the building, smoke detectors, signals relayed to every flat. There was no danger, except in the passageway outside. The police . . . She lifted the telephone and dialed.

His face was bleeding. It was on fire from the deep scratches, and blood stung his lip. He didn't waste time. He picked up his knife. He'd failed, and he wasn't going to push his luck. He turned and sprinted down the passage, through the glass door, and raced down the stairs, into the entrance hall, and out the front door into the street.

He was gone before Julia had finished locking herself in from the inside. He wiped his face; the handkerchief was stained.

Jesus Christ. A cat . . . He made for the Underground. A few taxis cruised the streets; one of them might recall picking up a man in the area around the time of the attack. He had asked for a key, explaining that he might be late picking up his luggage. He had paid his bill, and they had left his suitcase behind the reception desk.

He had stayed there on two previous trips to London, one of them connected to his genuine business, and he was known and trusted by the proprietor. A nice, quiet American businessman, a prompt payer and no trouble. A lot of foreigners tried to slip women in past reception. Nothing like that about him.

He looked at himself in the hallway mirror. His nose was swollen and oozing blood from the cat bites. His cheeks were ripped by scratches. He was scarred and thereby recognizable. . . .

He opened the case and took out his wash bag. He always carried a small first-aid pack. Bandages, antiseptic ointment, pain killer. He covered the deep scratch and bite mark across his nose with a bandage, pulled up his coat collar, and drew the earflaps over his burning cheeks.

It was safe to hail a taxi and, after a little while he spotted one on the Bayswater Road. Suitcase in hand and keeping his face in shadow, he said, "Heathrow," and jumped inside. He tossed a double fare to the driver and hurried into Terminal 3. He spent the night in the departure lounge, the cap pulled down over his face.

He boarded the eight-o'clock flight to New York, refused breakfast and said he wanted to sleep. He hunched himself in his pillow and dozed.

It was around ten A.M. New York time, when they landed. He collected his car from the terminal garage and drove home. A cat. Nobody would believe it. He could hardly believe it himself. He had reason to, when the bites on his face turned septic a few hours later.

· · ·

"Now," the WPC said, "is there anyone you can stay with tonight?"

Julia was drinking hot, sweet tea. She had made her statement to the police, who arrived after the emergency call. The building had been searched, the caretaker roused from his bed, and the immediate neighbors woken and asked if they had seen or heard anything. Nobody had. They suggested it was more likely to be a burglar who'd been prepared to turn very nasty once inside, and Julia found herself agreeing. They would dismiss any suggestion of a more sinister motive as hysteria on her part. She was much calmer now. The woman police officer was good at her job, quiet and reassuring.

"You don't want to be here on your own," she said. "You've had a nasty experience. And a lucky escape, if you look at it. We'll be going soon, now the building's been searched. An officer from the Crime Squad will be down to see you tomorrow morning, and we'll test for fingerprints. Isn't there a woman friend you could call on? We'll drive you wherever, don't worry about that."

"I'm all right," Julia insisted. She wouldn't call Ben. She wouldn't panic him in the middle of the night. And she wouldn't call anyone else. She had to keep the incident quiet.

"I could try a man friend," she said. "He's just a friend, but we were having a drink earlier this evening. He might come around."

"Good idea. I'll dial the number for you."

Julia didn't mean to do it, but when Felix arrived, she burst into tears. He was around at the flat within twenty minutes. He looked tousled and disheveled. He had only just sent the redhead home in a cab an hour before the telephone call. He had been "sleeping the sleep of the just," as he liked to say, laboring the joke. The "just after". . . .

The police left them. Julia sat and cried and tried to tell him what had happened. He put a brotherly arm around her and let her go over it again and again, reliving the few nightmare seconds when the man loomed up at her, arm upraised.

"He had a knife, I'm sure of it," she whispered. "I'm sure I saw something in his hand. . . ."

"Did you tell the police?"

"I tried to, but I could see they thought I'd probably imagined it. Oh, God, it was so terrifying. . . . The worst thing is, they can't find Pussy!"

"That," Felix said, "is the least of your worries. It's probably hiding somewhere, terrified out of its life. You really think he was going to kill you?"

"Yes," she said slowly. "I'm sure of it. That was no burglar. He'd planned it all, waiting till the middle of the night, shouting 'Fire' to panic me into opening my door. It's Jean Adams all over again." She shuddered. "It could be the same man. . . ."

"Look," he said. "You put this on the back burner for tonight. Do you have a sleeping pill? No—okay. Then go to bed and try to sleep. I'll doss down here on the sofa and we'll call Harris first thing in the morning. My guess is he'll move you out of here. I haven't got room, or you could stay at my place. It's just a bachelor pad."

Julia looked at him. "Thanks," she said. "Thanks, Felix. Thanks for coming over. I didn't know what to do, or where to turn. . . ."

"No problem." He grinned at her. "What's an ex-boyfriend for, when you nearly get yourself murdered? Now, off to bed. And don't worry about the cat, you silly female, it'll be found tomorrow."

• • •

Joe Patrick was not at his address. The office was closed, and there was no one in his luxury flat. He hadn't been seen for nearly a fortnight. Nobody knew where he had gone. Inquiries were circulated among the shady denizens of the half world where Joe Patrick had his early contacts. The word was out. Find Patrick and there was money or favors in kind. No public statement was issued; Jean Adams's killing was still unsolved, and interest had soon died down. Murder, even with such a vicious element in it, was too commonplace. A pre-Christmas child abduction made the tabloid front pages and filled the TV screens. The search for Joe Patrick was kept under wraps for fear of alerting him. Tina and Tracey were living in a safe house under round-the-clock police protection. But so far nobody had come forward with information.

"I'll never forgive myself," Ben Harris kept saying to her. "I shouldn't have left you."

"Darling, don't be silly, I wouldn't let you come home. You had to look after Lucy . . . I was just shocked. I'm all right now."

"No, you're not," he said. "You look a wreck. We're packing up here and you're coming to a hotel with me and Lucy, and that's the end of it. This place belongs to that bastard Western, anyway. He can have it back. I called the office, and he's due home tomorrow. I've got an appointment. He won't like what I've got to say to him."

She let him hold her close. It wasn't time to argue. He was too upset by what had happened to her, too guilty about his absence. The news that he had been sacked didn't give him a moment's concern. His only thought was for her. She knew that he would insist on her giving up. Publicly withdrawing from the campaign against

Harold King. Stepping out of the firing line. And she knew that, in spite of nearly losing her life, she wasn't going to do it. But it wasn't time to tell him. Yet. She changed the subject gently. "Thank God we found Pussy. Do you know, darling, I was so upset about losing her."

She had been discovered the next day crouched down under the vacuum cleaner and cleaning materials in the caretaker's broom cupboard. No one could think how she got there, except that she'd slipped in during the police search when the door was open.

"She saved your life," Ben said slowly. "That makes me feel even worse."

No, Julia decided, changing roles and trying to reassure him, it was not the time to argue about Harold King. She had made up her mind what had to be done, and she had to do it alone. Afterward she could explain it to Ben Harris and persuade him that she hadn't had any choice.

"I feel bad about it, Harry. Real bad. He's never fouled up on a business contract before." Mario was apologetic. He had called King in the country on a weekend, just a few days after he got back from his trip.

"These things happen." King was dismissive. "I understand."

"I didn't!" the voice was an angry snarl. "Just didn't believe it. I sent a guy down to verify. And it was true. Cat attacked him; he's just out of the hospital. Yeah . . . blood poisoning. Incredible, eh? Never keep a cat." Then, after a pause, "You want we should send another contract expert to take a look at the proposition, find a bottom-line solution?"

"No need," King said. "It's solved itself. Thanks, anyway. There's no fee for your expert, then." It wasn't a question.

"We pay on results" was the answer. "No fee. He can

meet his own goddamned medical bills. How's the family? Getting ready for Christmas? We've got my wife's mother, my sister and her kids, my uncle and their kids. But it's Christmas. It's good to have the family all together. How about you?"

"We go to Switzerland, to my place in Gstaad. Just Marilyn and Gloria and me."

And Leo Derwent, but he didn't mention that. Gloria had booked Leo into the Regent. He wouldn't be at all surprised if she was paying the bill. A junior minister couldn't afford a week's stay at the Regent around Christmastime. If he'd even been able to get a room in the attic. The name of King had secured a vacancy.

"You ski?" Mario was making conversation. King knew he was embarrassed by the failure of his man to get Julia. It didn't matter now. Her departure from the *Sunday Herald* was in every newspaper and rated a mention on BBC and ITV news. Western had fired Harris too. It was made to sound like an amicable parting, with a lot of unctuous horseshit from Western himself saying how sorry he was to lose such a talented young journalist. "Exposure" would be headed up by a new star in the newspaper's stable. The December issue would expose a national scandal, and so on and so forth. Western had lost his nerve. And Harold King knew it. Hamilton had gone to Jersey looking for something to incriminate King and had come back with Richard Watson's well-told tale about a sergeant, name of William Western. And nothing else.

He answered the question about skiing. "Not me, not now. I used to be good, but one accident was enough. I haven't time to lie up with a broken leg." He laughed. "Like you, I'm a busy man. Have a good holiday. My best to all the family."

He hung up. It was a cold, gray day. Western's feature was due out that Sunday. He wasn't worried. Hamilton would get another job, but she wouldn't be taking any story with her. And when Western went down, he'd exercise a little influence with her new employer. She wouldn't hold on to any job for long. If she was lucky, she could write another book—if she could find a publisher prepared to make an enemy of Harold King. He chuckled to himself. He went to the window and looked out at the gray landscape, the leafless trees and the mist rising from a lake that he could glimpse from his study window. It was cheerless, bleak. He thought of the crisp snow and sun, the bright skies of Switzerland. The mountain air, the majestic Alps rearing their heads into the clouds. . . . The scenery spoke to him of his origins. He would never go to Germany now. Switzerland was as near as he would come to his roots. He had no roots, he reminded himself, impatient with the brief twinge of nostalgia. Nostalgia was for the senile. He had years ahead of him. He thought of his daughter and her infatuation. Let it run for the moment. He wouldn't buy Leo Derwent off with money. His price was political office. Soon King would be powerful enough to obtain it for him. On condition that he give up Gloria. She'd get over it. She'd go on to a better man, a man worthy to be her consort.

He felt contented, happy. He turned away from the dreary view of an English landscape in December. They'd go to Gstaad early, he decided suddenly. Marilyn could spend his money Christmas shopping there just as well as in London.

"William," his wife said, "you can't win." He had never expected her to say that. If ever his spirits flagged, Evelyn rallied them with her own courage. They were out walking in the chill, damp afternoon, muffled in tweeds and heavy scarves, two elderly people braving the miserable weather to take exercise in their own parkland. Two golden Labradors ran on ahead of them. Western didn't like dogs, but they were part of a country gentleman's equipment, like Purdey guns and a keeper. Evelyn made pets of them, so they were not good gun dogs. He didn't care. He used his shoot to impress his guests, not for his own enjoyment.

"I can try," he said. "I've got a lot of money. I can fight back."

"You can't fight on his terms," she answered. "Rumors, share fixing, bought financial journalists. You can't win, darling. Not without Julia Hamilton."

"I can't win with her," he said. "After what happened at her flat I had to buy Harris off with public statements and a hefty contract settlement. It could have been a burglar, it could have been something else. Harris was convinced it was a contract killer. Like Jean Adams. It's no good, Evie— I tried to get Harold King exposed for what we know he is. A crook, and probably a murderer. But I failed, so all I can do now is fight him in the open and take my chance. It's getting really cold. I think we should go back in." They turned, calling the dogs, who trotted back to them obediently. They walked in silence until the house came into view.

"She wasn't telling the truth, was she, Billy?" The question caught him unprepared.

"What do you mean? Truth about what?"

"Those other men weren't shot down, were they? It was crossfire?"

He stopped and turned her to look at him. A wisp of white hair had escaped her hat and drifted across her cheek. It filled him with tenderness to see it. She was so beautiful, he often forgot how old she really was. "I've never lied to you, Evie. Never."

"I know you haven't," she said gently. "I shouldn't have asked that. I'm sorry."

He hooked his hand through her arm and guided her toward the house. "We'll have tea together by the fire," he said. "I'm not going to do any paperwork tonight. We'll have a nice evening, just the two of us."

He hoped she didn't notice he hadn't answered her question.

"When are you leaving?" Julia asked.

Leo said, "On the Tuesday after Christmas. She wants me to stay for ten days. She's making it a Christmas present." He thought she looked thin and very pale. "You know it's a crazy idea, don't you?"

"You don't have to do it," Julia said. "If you want to play footsie with his daughter and let him get away with trying to ruin you, it's up to you."

"I never forget a bad turn," he said.

"How about a good one?"

He glanced up at her sharply.

"I persuaded Western not to run that story," she reminded him. "I don't expect you to be grateful, Leo. I don't think it's your style. But this is your one chance to get back at King. Don't think he'll let it run on between you and his daughter; he'll find a way to finish that too. It's a gamble, that's true, but if it comes off, it's the Old Bailey for him."

"If it doesn't," he mused, "we haven't lost anything."

No, only my job, and Ben's job, and nearly getting knifed. . . . She didn't say it; she hadn't told anyone about the terrifying incident. She said, "Are you on?"

He played with his watch. "Yes," he answered. "Yes, I'll give it a go. Where can I reach you?"

"I'm going to my parents, in about two hours. Staying for Christmas. I'll contact you at the Regent when you get there."

"Merry Christmas," he said.

"Thanks, same to you."

Julia had parked her car at a meter; a warden was loitering nearby, hoping to catch an overdue shopper. Julia checked the time. She and Ben and Lucy were driving down to Surrey that afternoon. With the cat in a basket. She had gone through the motions, bought presents for everyone, wrapped and tagged them and piled them up in the trunk of the car. She was sorry for Lucy; she was subdued and shy with Julia, and she clung a shade too closely to Ben. All she knew was there had been an attempted break-in at Julia's flat and they were moving to a hotel. Then on to Julia's parents' for Christmas. Lucy had shown no desire to go back and spend the holiday with her mother and stepfather. Some mornings she met them at breakfast with red eyes, obviously downcast. Julia tried hard to get close to her, but there was a quiet resistance that she hadn't overcome. She reasoned that Lucy was still mourning, still trying to readjust physically, as well as emotionally, to the loss of her child. Julia was sympathetic and rational about it, but there were times when she felt left out. Ben was protective, dividing himself equally between the two women who needed him. He paid their hotel bill, reacting with a display of male pride that surprised Julia when she offered to pay her share. When they traveled down together, the cat howled in protest at being confined in her new basket, and Lucy finally took it on her knee.

"She's so furry," she said. "I wish I had a kitten. . . ."

Ben said quickly, "I'll get you one. Cats aren't like dogs; they're very happy in flats. We'll look for one tomorrow."

Later he said to Julia when they were washing up in the kitchen after dinner, "That's a good idea. She needs something to look after. Poor kid. You've been wonderful, darling. She thinks the world of you, she told me. . . . And your mum and dad have made us both so welcome." He turned Julia toward him and kissed her. "I love you so much, J. I want to put everything behind us now and make a new start. I'm glad we're out of the whole bloody mess. Coming down here, being in a normal family, makes me realize what life's about. Why don't you go and sit down and watch telly with them? I'll finish this."

"I'd rather be with you," she said. "Darling, you've let the drying cloth fall in the sink. . . . Here, let me do it. I love you, too, but you're not domesticated."

"I could be," he protested. "The new Ben Harris. Wouldn't you like me to be a New Age man and do the housework?"

She laughed. "I wouldn't. I'd hate it. I like the old model. Grouchy, tough as old boots, and the best editor in the business!"

They shared the big double guest room, and he made love to her that night, and when they rested in each other's arms, he said suddenly, "Will you marry me, J?"

She turned to look at him. "Do you want to get married? We don't have to."

"I know we don't," he said. "But it would stop you having drinks with Felix. I hated that, you know. It really churned me up to think of you with anyone else. Even him. That's when I knew I wanted a full commitment. I'm ready for it, and I won't make the same mistakes as last time. What do you say?"

Julia didn't answer. She held him closer for a moment. It was the wrong time. She couldn't give an answer and do what she was planning. In two days it would be Christmas. The house was decorated, the tree was up, and the presents stacked beneath it. Even Pussy had a few parcels. Her parents were so happy, so ready to give to them all. Her brother and sister-in-law and their children were coming over on Boxing Day. It was all planned, and it was going to be idyllic. A healing process for Lucy. A family gathering to celebrate the family. She wished with all her heart that he had waited until it was over.

He touched her tenderly. "What do you say? Can you take me on?"

"Ben," she said very gently, "we've just made love and all I want to say is yes and not think it through. . . . That wouldn't be fair to either of us. Will you give me a little more time?"

"As long as you need," he said. "I'm not about to ask anyone else. Good night, sweetheart."

He slept very deeply; Julia didn't. She saw the dawn creep through the edges of the curtains. The air ticket to Gstaad was in her purse. It was dated the twenty-eighth of December, the Swissair flight leaving Gatwick at eleven in the morning.

Joe Patrick was in Dublin. He had lost his sinecure with Harold King, but he had plenty of money stacked away, and he didn't owe anybody except his bookmaker. And that wasn't much. But he had decided to go into a different kind of business. He'd run girls, he'd come up through pimping and protection, he'd fixed a few nasty problems himself, such as the old biddy at Midhurst, and traveled as King's troubleshooter to the States and the Caribbean. He had dabbled in drugs, and he had a keen understanding and love of money. And in this new business the money would be as big as King's retainer and bonuses. He had felt his way carefully in his native city, throwing hints to known sympathizers. He had baited his hook, and the fish had struck.

The IRA could use a front man in London, a man with

a business exporting leather goods to Europe. He could launder money through to centers in Amsterdam and Bruges, where they had units whose mission was to strike at military personnel in Germany and on NATO bases. He had a lot of criminal contacts in the city itself who would assist with safe houses and target surveillance. Joe Patrick had a lot to offer, and because he was a man with money, he wasn't expected to come cheap. He had done the deal in Dublin City itself with a man whose name he didn't know and didn't ask. He had a cash deposit in his briefcase when he flew home. Home was London now. He found Ireland too provincial, its rackets too seedy. He liked the high life. He hated Christmas. It reminded him of the grim celebrations in the orphanage that never varied year after year. He came back to his smart flat. No girls to greet him and wash the travel dust off him in the Jacuzzi. He'd find others. He had some correspondence . . . a few bills . . . some Christmas cards. He threw them away. He showered and changed and went out, making first for his favorite pub and then, if he found a pickup he fancied, he'd take her on to Soho to his favorite restaurant and then home. He never went to a tart's place. He was fastidious about clean sheets and general hygiene. He got slightly drunk that night and had to kick the girl out when he woke in the morning. . . . Usually he sent them home with a taxi fare on top of the fee, whatever time of night. But he was in a good mood. He'd enjoyed himself, been welcomed back by cronies anxious to curry favor with him. God never shuts one door but he slams the other. He laughed. Life was looking good. . . . It was Christmas Day, and he'd bought himself a present. He was sitting with a Scotch in his hand watching a television sitcom about three girls sharing a flat when his front door buzzed. Joe wasn't expecting anybody. He turned the sound down and went into the front hall. He had closed-circuit security TV. Two men showed up on the screen. The bell buzzed again, and then there was the powerful knock.

"Mr. Patrick! Open up! Police!"

"It's been such a lovely Christmas," May Hamilton said. She smiled at her husband in contentment. "Everyone got on so well, and the children were so funny opening their presents. . . . Patsy said, "Granny, it's like Christmas Day come twice!""

"I know," Hugh said. "She's a dear little thing. And did you notice Tom and Julia didn't cross swords once?"

"That's because she's so happy," his wife said. "Ben's such a nice man and he's so in love with her. . . . That poor child, Lucy . . . it was pathetic to see her fussing over that kitten."

"Clever thing to give her," Hugh agreed. "She's young, she'll get over it. It's been a great success and it's all thanks to you, darling. You worked so hard to make it a happy time for all of us. Thank you." He reached over and squeezed her hand.

Hugh Hamilton hesitated, but he never kept his thoughts on anything important from his wife. "Maybe it was my imagination," he said, "but I felt Julia wasn't quite herself. She made a big effort, but she was strained . . . not quite herself. . . ."

May nodded. "I did notice something," she admitted. "I thought I was imagining it, but since you say so, she wasn't relaxed, not really. I just wonder whether it isn't time for that girl to go home to her own mother?"

"You think she's jealous?"

"I think they're both a bit jealous of each other and they can't admit it. Ben doesn't see it, of course. Men never do."

"Why should they? They only want a quiet life and everyone getting on," he countered.

"You're probably right. That's what was wrong with her. . . . I think that's Ben and Lucy coming in now. I'd better get the lunch."

"What time will Julia be back, then?" Hugh asked.

"Not till teatime. She's gone to buy shoes and get her hair done. Oh, Ben—there you are. Had a nice walk?" She turned to him, smiling. "Lunch won't be long, you must be starving. . . ." She hurried out to the kitchen. Ben didn't find the letter Julia had written him till he went up to their bedroom later that afternoon.

Julia had booked into a small pension on the outskirts of Gstaad. It was a modest little chalet, scrupulously clean, the bedroom functional and sparsely furnished.

"You're not here for the skiing?" the proprietress asked her, helping carry her one case upstairs.

"No," Julia said. "I don't ski. I'm here to see a friend."

She closed the door and looked around the rather bleak room. She unpacked her clothes. It might happen in the first twenty-four hours. It might take a week. She was prepared. The flight had been uneventful. She felt tired, but too tense to rest, so she went for a walk instead, wrapped in a thick coat and with a fur hat pulled down against a cold, crisp wind that carried flurries of snow with it. Harold King owned a luxury chalet in the smartest residential area. The Regent Hotel was close to the slopes, exclusive and expensive, a playground for the super rich and the parasites of both sexes who lived off them. She thought of Leo Derwent and King's daughter, Gloria. She was so hooked on him that she was paying for him to be near her during the holiday. And Harold King himself, probably adding the last refinement to his plan to seize

Western's media outlets and make himself the single most powerful figure in mass communication in the country. Power was his lifeblood.

She had lost her job and her power base. He knew he was safe because Western had sacked her. He wouldn't bother sending any more nocturnal messengers armed with a knife. Soon King would be so powerful, he could ruin her professionally by dropping a word. Her career was finished, and Ben's equally destroyed. She had come here to confront him, and she wasn't afraid. She was risking everything on one last challenge. Her future and, above all, her future with Ben Harris. He must have read her letter explaining what she had done and why, even as she ended her walk and sat in a café drinking coffee to warm herself.

He would see it as a betrayal—she realized that. He would be deeply hurt at her deception and very angry. He was a man who nursed anger, goaded by his own self-doubt. He might never forgive her, whatever the outcome. King didn't frighten her, but that did. She sat on for a time while the lights went on and the town began to vibrate with disco music and the onset of the *après-ski* as the gilded young and the darlings of the gossip columns prepared to enjoy themselves after a day on the slopes. She ate at the pension; the food was heavy and too rich. The atmosphere oppressed her. She had called the hotel and left a message for Leo. He knew where to reach her. But though she waited up till nearly midnight, there was no call.

It came in the morning, while she was having breakfast. There were two couples staying and a single woman, well into middle age, who left for the slopes before the others came down. There was a German husband and wife—keen skiers, who made no effort when they found out she wasn't a devotee—and a French boy and girl, who seemed to be either quarreling or fondling each other regardless of an audience. Julia hurried from the dining room into the hall.

"I got your message," his nasal voice said. A less than Oxbridge accent came out when he talked on the telephone. "I'm going to try to fix it for tomorrow. I'm having lunch with them today."

"You think he'll fall for it?"

She heard a snigger. "He will if golden girl asks him to; and she'll do anything I tell her. She loves it!"

"When will you know?" Julia cut in.

"Give me till this evening," he suggested. "We're having some time together, and she can go back and work on him. I'm pretty confident he'll say yes. And then we put your theory to the test." He lowered his voice slightly. "What do we do if he gets violent?"

"I'm sure you'll deal with it," Julia said. "You're a man, after all. When will you know?"

"This evening," he said. "They're all going out to dinner—I'm not included. I'll come over to you."

"All right," Julia agreed. "I'll be here."

Then she hung up. She hated him, but she had to trust him. Not because of his loyalty or his obligation to her but because of his malice and desire for revenge. Whatever she felt about him, he was her only ally.

Gloria had gone off skiing, and Marilyn had decided to have a full beauty treatment instead. She had come back to lunch, and she was pleased with the result. She didn't look a day over thirty-eight . . . well, maybe just forty, and she decided to be nice to her husband. He'd given her a set of crocodile luggage and half a dozen sets of Janet Reger underclothes that were mouthwatering. He was working as usual, and he grunted when she came up and kissed him.

"You smell good," he remarked.

"I ought to, at a hundred and eighty francs an ounce." She giggled slightly. "I've been very naughty. I had everything done this morning. Does it look all right?"

She stepped back and posed for him, one hand on a slim hip. She was beautiful. King nodded. He was proud of her, proud of the way even the glitzy glamour queens of the resort stared at her. Not to mention their men. But she didn't arouse him anymore. He enjoyed her as he would a piece of lovely Dresden china.

"It looks very good," he said. "That little shit Leo has asked me to come over this evening."

"Oh?" Marilyn was wary. She knew how much he hated Gloria's lover. And lover he obviously was. She was so libidinous when he was near, it made Marilyn squirm. And he was playing his part very cleverly. Deferential to King, charming to her, and attentive to Gloria. Marilyn didn't claim to be clever. She had got where she was without brains, but she was acutely streetwise. Leo Derwent was in the game for big stakes. And Harold King knew it.

"Hasn't he asked both of us? That's surprising. He's had a lot of hospitality. It's about time he returned it."

She sat down and crossed her fine legs and wiggled her foot. It was a habit he found irritating.

"For Christ's sake, stop doing that," he snarled at her. "I told you, he wants to see me. He called up while Gloria was here." He scowled. "She went on and on at me to go."

"And you said yes in the end," Marilyn prompted. "You always do. She's crazy in love with him, you know." She couldn't resist needling him, just a little.

"She doesn't know what she's doing," he said, scowling at her now. "This is the first man she's ever had. . . . what do you expect?"

"Well, what did he say? What reason did he give?"

"He said he wanted to discuss something with me. It was very important. I suggested he come here, but he wouldn't do that. And there was Gloria standing beside me, listening and saying, 'Oh, please, Daddy; please, Daddy, he does want to talk to you.' So I said yes, I'd go. If he thinks he's got a proposition with my daughter, he can bloody well think again."

His wife looked at him. He was jealous of Leo Derwent. He hated the idea of his daughter shacking up with anyone. Personally she couldn't imagine how anyone would want to; she was so big, so brutal, with her clumsy body and mannish ways. Drooling like a lovesick girl over the mean-faced, foxy man. If only King was right and he wanted to marry her . . . what a relief it would be to get her out of the house and leave Marilyn some space. . . . She said softly, "Don't be too hard on them. You could lose Gloria over this. If she's really in love, she'll never forgive you if you scare him off."

King looked at her with contempt. He understood her motives, and maternal concern wasn't one of them.

"You think I'm a fool? I'm not going to get heavy. I don't want to alienate my daughter. I'll buy him off. And he'll be bought."

"I'll go and tell Monique we're ready for lunch," his wife said. She permitted herself a rare oath of disappointment when she was out of his hearing.

"I don't understand," Hugh Hamilton said. "What do you mean she's gone?"

It had been a difficult scene, which became distressing when Julia's mother burst into tears. Ben had come down with the letter and said brutally, goaded by his own feelings, "You needn't expect Julia for dinner. Or for anything else either. She's gone to Switzerland."

He was torn between anger and pain; he had no time
for social niceties. She had deceived them all, planned it
well ahead and simply taken off, leaving with lies to her
parents and that letter for him. He dismissed what she
had written about loving him. He rejected out of hand
her plea for understanding of why she had to go without
telling him. . . .

*You would have tried to stop me or come with me, and I couldn't
have stood the pressure. It's taken all my courage as it is. . . .*

Courage. He had exploded when he read that. Obsti-
nacy, foolhardiness. And, above all, upside-down priori-
ties. Never mind about her family, never mind about
him. She has to go on and try to win. . . . Seeing May
Hamilton in tears calmed him down. He apologized.
There was no use alarming them. It wasn't fair. They
didn't know what had happened at the flat; it wasn't the
time to tell them now.

So he lied to them. It was a job offer, he said. She knew
he didn't want her to take it, so she went off without
telling him. He was hurt and angry, but he had no right
to take it out on them. They'd been so kind to him and
Lucy. It might be better if they packed up and went back
to London. . . . They wouldn't hear of it. May Hamilton
recovered quickly; she made light of her tears and said
she was just a foolish old woman. "Please stay, and don't
upset Lucy." When did he think Julia would be back? He
couldn't answer.

*I don't know how long this will take, but I've got to see it through
to the end. I wish I could tell you about it, but I will when I get back.
Promise me you'll listen.*

"I don't know," Ben had to tell them. "It may take
some days. She didn't give an indication. If you're sure . . .
of course we'll stay. It's done Lucy so much good. Thanks."

The rest of the day and the evening had been a strain,
of which his daughter was unaware. Forced bonhomie

on all their parts for her benefit, and Ben was glad to excuse himself early. He felt like getting drunk. But he couldn't. He wanted to be alone, but the bed where they'd made love and she'd sidestepped his idea of marriage was no place for him to sleep. Marriage, commitment— they weren't for her. He had been building a fantasy world for both of them. No cozy domestic future with a child of their own instead of a cat. . . . Her career came first. It had always come first, and he had refused to face that. She was going to confront Harold King. She had said it in those words and then added something that turned his stomach with jealousy. *I won't be in any danger. There'll be someone with me.* Someone. Not him. Who? Whom could she ask to go on such an assignment? Felix Sutton. Sutton had been the one she'd called on after the attempt to kill her. She'd been out drinking with Sutton that same evening. Sutton, the ex-boxer, must be the "someone" she'd taken with her. He was too cautious, too bound up with Lucy. . . . He wouldn't be up to the challenge. He was too old.

He slipped downstairs in the small hours and helped himself to Hugh Hamilton's whiskey. Then he dialed Felix Sutton's home number. Officially the holiday was over, all newspapers were working, but not necessarily the political staff. The House was in Christmas recess. He swallowed the neat spirit and tipped more into the glass as he let the phone ring. He wanted to yell, "Answer . . . answer, you bastard. . . ." But there was no reply, and no taped message. Sutton wasn't home.

He went back upstairs and fell asleep on top of the bed without getting into it. When he woke in the morning, he realized he couldn't spend another night in the Hamiltons' house. He said to Hugh, "I'm afraid I raided your Scotch last night. I couldn't sleep. I must buy you a bottle."

"Don't talk rubbish. I raided it myself." He lowered

his voice slightly so that his wife wouldn't hear him in the adjoining kitchen. "All this upset, it's so bad for May. I'm sorry to say this, but what Julia's done was very self-ish. We thought she'd changed in the last few months. For a long time she thought of nothing but getting on and getting to the top. We hardly saw her. . . . I'm going to say something when she does come back. Lying and walking out like that. Especially on you. It's just not good enough. I hope she'll think this damned job is worth it."

"If she brings it off," Ben said bitterly, "I don't think she'll care. I have to tell you, I think this is the end of the road for us anyway. And I'd better get back to London. I lost my job too. People forget about you if you're away from the action. I'll go and get Lucy up and organized. See you and May later."

When they had gone, Hugh came and slipped an arm around his wife's shoulders.

"He was so hurt," she said. "He looked dreadful, as if he hadn't slept. I just can't understand my own daughter."

"Well, we're not going to try," he said firmly. "All I can say is that she'll regret it. He's a good man and he'd have made her happy. No, darling, you're not cooking lunch. I rang up Tom, and they've asked us over. We can spend the day with our grandchildren. That'll cheer us both up."

"This is grim," Leo Derwent remarked, looking around the small residents' lounge. "Are you the only one here?"

"No," Julia answered. "Two couples and one woman. She's English, but she spends all day skiing and goes to bed early, I think she said good morning once. Anyway I didn't come here to have fun."

His condescension irritated her. She recognized it as a sign of nervous tension. When she was uptight, she snapped for very little reason. Ben teased her about a red-headed temper. She dared not think of Ben. Leo had asked for whisky and soda. She had ordered wine for herself.

"He didn't want to come to me," Leo said. "Tried to get me to go over there. But Gloria talked him into it. She thinks I'm going to ask for her hand in marriage."

He had a sneering laugh that grated on Julia. She stared at him. "You haven't asked her?"

"No, but I might. Depends how this turns out. And she's shown me how to make his favorite drink. He mixes it himself at home. It has to be just right." He looked at her; he had pale, flint-colored eyes. "Grenadine, Perrier, and freshly squeezed lemon juice."

She said slowly, "And he won't taste anything else?"

He shook his head. "No. I tried it out—with alcohol and without. He likes so much lemon juice and it's so strong, it masks the taste of the vodka. He's coming around at six-thirty. So you'd better arrive at about seven. I can keep him talking and get two drinks into him. He swallows the stuff like water. I've noticed when I've been at the chalet. I must admit," he said suddenly, "it could be very interesting when you walk through that door. Aren't you just the teeniest bit nervous?" He mocked her to disguise his own apprehension.

"No, not nervous. Scared witless," Julia answered. "And so are you. I've brought the tape for you. Here."

It was so small, it fit into her purse, a narrow oblong box less than six inches across.

"It's simple; you just set it and it's voice-activated. The range is thirty feet minimum. Just put it on a table out of sight. It'll record up to two hours."

He weighed it in his hand. "It's small enough."

"They come much smaller," Julia pointed out. "But they're not so accurate and the range is less. We want every word clear."

"What a dirty business journalism is," he remarked. "Almost as dirty as politics."

"I'm glad you said that instead of me. I'll be there just before seven. But what happens if by any chance he hasn't drunk the stuff?"

"They'll ring through from reception when you arrive," he answered. "If anything's gone wrong, I'll tell them I'm busy and will meet you in the bar. Don't worry, I've thought of everything. My head's on the block, too, don't forget."

Julia stood up. She held out her hand. "It'll be worth the risk. He's an evil man, Leo. It's time someone stopped him. Good luck."

He shook her hand briefly. He still had that limp clasp she remembered from all those years ago when she met him with William Western. Somewhere, buried in a box file, was the unpublished profile she had done on him. It was ironic that they should have come together in common enterprise. "Good luck to you too," he said. "We're both going to need it."

Then he was gone, and as he left, the young French couple poked their heads around the door, saw Julia sitting alone, smiled at her briefly, and retreated. It was the last evening she wanted to spend alone.

CHAPTER 11

"DADDY," GLORIA SAID, "YOU WILL BE NICE to him, won't you?"

Harold King was in a bad mood. He didn't want to leave his own home and drive to the Regent Hotel. It disturbed his evening. The meeting with Leo Derwent hung over his day like a cloud. Gloria's pleading annoyed him. "She's crazy in love with him," Marilyn had said. She was certainly behaving as if she was, and that enraged him. He didn't soften when she clung to his arm and smiled up at him.

"Depends what he wants," he snapped. "If it's some political screw-up and he thinks he can make use of me . . . I won't be nice!"

She looked away from him. "I'm sure it's not anything

like that," she said defensively. "He'd never try to take advantage of you."

"He knows he wouldn't get away with it, that's why."

Gloria stepped back from him. "Supposing he wants to talk about me?"

He glared. "Why should he? What about you?"

"About our relationship," she said. She felt close to tears. He had a bruising way with other people; she wasn't used to it, and it hurt.

"Your relationship is no business of mine. What are you, for Christ's sake, a child? You're sleeping with him, and that's nothing to do with me. You know what I think of him, and I haven't changed my mind. I'm going, and it had better be something important, or I'll have his balls!" He swung away from her.

Gloria blinked back tears. She started to get angry. He was being deliberately brutish and difficult. She didn't know for certain why Leo wanted to see him in private, but there had been hints: "If you ever do decide to get married," he'd mused one day, "your father would have to agree first."

She had allowed herself to think of something more permanent than the episodic lovemaking, the evenings spent together at the theater and the opera, and the days they had to spend apart. When she did spend a full night with him, which was not too often because her father didn't like it, she enjoyed making him breakfast and pandering to his little whims. It satisfied her need to feel enslaved instead of guilty.

She found her mother watching television. King had satellites and could tune in anywhere. Marilyn loved Sky TV. She had never had a serious interest in her life, Gloria thought.

"Has your father gone?" She glanced up and then said, "You look upset—anything the matter?"

Gloria had never confided in her mother. She had never shared anything with her. They had been incompatible from the start. She had never, ever criticized her father to her. Gloria said sharply, "No—nothing! Do we *have* to watch this crap?"

Marilyn was used to her rudeness. She shrugged, "You don't. There's a set in the library; there are sets all over the house. But I'm watching this one. And I'm not changing channels." She heard her daughter slam the door as she went out.

Leo hadn't felt so nervous since he stood up in the House and made his maiden speech. His stomach was churning, and it heaved when reception phoned through to say Mr. King was in the lobby.

"Ask someone to bring him up," he said.

Good manners required him to go down and greet Gloria's father, but he dared not risk a suggestion to go to the bar. He was in the corridor when King emerged from the elevator, following a page boy.

"Good evening, Harold," he said, coming forward. He slipped a few francs to the boy and guided King to his room. "Sorry I couldn't come down when you arrived, but I was in the middle of a call from London. Official business. They never leave you alone. . . ."

King grunted. Call from London. . . . Self-important little sod, trying to impress him. He looked around the room aggressively. "This is nice," he said. "Must be costing Gloria a bucket."

"Please sit down." Leo's freckled skin tinged with pink at the jibe, but he smiled at King and added, "It's very nice of you to come; I do appreciate it. And I have your special all ready for you." He turned to the table with the jug of rosy grenadine and lemon juice. Ice cubes bobbed on the surface. He had poured half a bottle of 80-proof vodka into the mixture and stirred it vigorously to distribute the spirit. He had sipped some himself. No taste; just the bitter-sweet mix of lemon and grenadine. That was the advantage of vodka—it was flavorless and didn't smell on the breath. His hand shook slightly as he poured out a glass and then added Perrier. He stirred once more with a long cocktail spoon and handed the drink to Harold King. "I've been coached by Gloria," he said. "I hope that's how you like it?"

King took it and set it down beside him. "What's this all about, Leo? Why do you want to see me?"

Leo took a deep breath. "I'll get myself a glass of wine," he said. And added, "Dutch courage." He poured some Chablis for himself and came and sat down opposite Harold King. He couldn't take his eyes away from that untouched drink. He swigged it down in a few swallows when he was at home. But not this time. He sat and glared at Leo, emanating hostility.

"Well?" He raised his voice.

Leo lifted his glass of wine. "To your very good health," he said, and waited.

King didn't respond.

"I asked you to meet me in private because I've got something rather . . . well, personal to talk over with you. See how you feel about it. Is that drink all right?"

"How do I know when I haven't tried it!" King snapped. "Get to the point, can't you? Stop waffling." It was Gloria, he knew that now. The little creep was going to sound him out about Gloria. He felt a rush of anger. His pulse rate began to rise.

"I've been seeing Gloria for some time," Leo began. His throat felt so dry, he sipped more wine before he could continue. The ice was melting in that untouched drink by King's elbow.

"I know that," King interrupted. "I can't say I'm impressed by her choice, but that's her business."

"I know you aren't happy about it." Leo was losing hope. He'd been there long enough and hadn't touched the drink. It wasn't going to work. At any moment he might just lose his temper if Leo got it wrong, and walk out. Julia mustn't come up. The whole bloody plan was going wrong. He said, "She told me how you feel about me. I don't blame you. If I had a daughter like Glory, I'd be protective too. That's why I wanted to reassure you."

King looked at him. "I don't need reassurance from you. I don't know what the hell you're talking about." He shifted forward in his chair. It was the attitude of someone about to get up.

Leo risked everything. "I'm in love with her," he said. "I've never been in love with anyone before. I've never met a woman like her. She's got everything—brains, poise, personality. . . ."

King sat back in his chair. He said in a flat voice, "She's ugly." Then he reached out and took the glass and drank very deeply from it as if he was thirsty.

"Not to me, she isn't," Leo said. He tried not to look, but a second's glance showed King had drunk half of the lethal mixture in one swallow.

"She's not ugly. She's different, she's not a bimbo."

He got up, he felt excited, all his nervousness had disappeared. He said, "Let me refresh that for you," and taking King's glass, he refilled it to the brim and handed it to him.

"She's rich," he said. "She could give you everything you want, that's what you mean. She's my daughter, and you could ride to the top with me behind you. Isn't that what you really mean, you little bastard?"

Leo couldn't be sure he detected a change. He went on, "I've told you, I love Gloria. She's in love with me. I haven't talked to her about marriage. I wouldn't, till I'd had a chance to discuss it with you."

King leaned forward. "Well, you've discussed it," he said, "and the answer is no. Not in a million years will I let my girl marry a fucker like you."

His voice had grown louder, the German accent more pronounced. Leo stayed calm. He said in a pleasant way, "You don't have to insult me, Harold. I've told you, I understand how you feel. She's your only daughter; you're very close in every way. You don't want to lose her. But you've nothing to fear from me. I'm not a possessive type."

He got up again, and as he passed the table on the other side of King's chair, he switched on the little tape recorder hidden behind a pile of magazines. He filled his glass with wine and turned to Harold King. "I'm glad you like my mixture," he said. "One more refill?"

And then the phone rang. Leo answered it. He smiled, and said, "Yes, up to my room, please." He came over with the jug this time. The glass was empty. King had drained it while he was speaking. He looked different, Leo realized; his features were suffused with red, his nose seemed enlarged, and his mouth had slackened.

The eyes were bright and glowing with a demonic rage. For a moment Leo's elation waned. He felt afraid. Then there was a knock at the door. King didn't seem to hear it. "Another," he snarled at Leo, holding out his glass. "Fill me up, dummkopf! Marry my daughter. . . ." He started to laugh. "She likes her bottom smacked, that's all you mean to her!"

Leo had gone to open the door. He said quietly, "Come in, Julia." He glanced back at Harold King and nodded to her. "He's pissed," he murmured, and then stood aside to let her pass. Julia hadn't seen him since that night in the restaurant when he was showing off by bullying the manager. He had looked so powerful, so bestial, almost, then. Now he was *louche*, sprawling, his limbs at an angle, his face red and bloated.

She stared at him. Her heart was beating so hard, she felt it in her throat. Leo was right. King was drunk. Drunk and dangerous, his eyes traveling over her, resting on her face. She said, "Good evening, Mr. King. I'm Julia Hamilton."

"I know you," he said. "I remember that ugly red hair. I won't have anyone with that hair in my building. You stink like foxes. You're Western's bint, aren't you?"

"No," she said. "I'm not anyone's bint. I don't sleep with my employer."

"More bloody fool him, then," King sneered. "If you worked for me, you'd have to dye that mop."

"I wouldn't work for you," Julia answered.

Leo said, "Why don't you sit down, Julia. Like a glass of wine?"

"Try some of my special mixture," King heaved himself up from the chair. "Go on, try it. This little creep that's screwing my daughter made it for me. Trying to curry favor, aren't you? He thinks he can fool me. . . . You know I can't be fooled, don't you? Nobody fools me."

"I'm sure they don't," Julia said. "I'll have some wine, please, Leo. Thanks." As she took the glass, he saw her hand was shaking. But she was composed, very cool; he had to admire her for the way she was handling the brute.

"I've always been curious about you, Mr. King. I've wanted to interview you. But you don't give interviews to Western journalists, do you?"

"The only thing I give to anyone working for that little shit is a kick up the backside," he snarled, suddenly aggressive. His eyes raked her up and down, lingering on her legs. She uncrossed them and pulled down her skirt to cover her knees. He said, "Western fired you, didn't he? Why don't you come and work for me? You've got brains, even if you haven't any tits. Why don't you come and work for me, eh? Why don't you? What did that shit pay you? I'll double it!"

He was swaying on his feet. Julia said, "Why don't you sit down, Mr. King, and we can talk about it."

He shrugged his big shoulders, his mood changing abruptly. "Why not?" He repeated it as he lowered himself back into his chair. "Why not."

"Would you like to talk to me about yourself?" Julia asked. "Now that I'm here, there's such a lot I want to know about you."

King leaned his head back. "Like what? The story of my life and achievements—I'll send you the book. . . . It's very heart-warming." He broke into laughter, coarse and raucous. "But that's not what you're after, is it? You've given me a lot of trouble, snooping. You're good at it, you know that? Better than any of the other hacks. You were getting close, weren't you? But then it all went wrong. You found out about that little shit Western. So he threw you out. You realize that saved your life?"

Leo bit back an exclamation. Julia was very pale. "Yes," she said. "I expect it did. I met a Mr. Richard Watson in Jersey. I asked him a question. We were talking about the last war. I asked him if he'd ever killed anyone."

Harold King cleared his throat. For a moment she thought he was going to spit on the carpet. "Not him," he jeered. "A real English gentleman, a man of principles— an arsehole, in my book."

Julia waited. It was coming close now, the crucial moment. He was drunk, but was he drunk enough . . . ?

"In your book, then," she said quietly, "people do get killed? If I asked you the same question I asked him, what would you answer?"

"Oh, very clever, aren't you! I'll ask you a question: What's so special about dying? Everyone dies in the end. What's it matter when?"

He pulled himself up in the chair; he turned and looked at Leo. "You put something in that drink, didn't you?" Leo said nothing. King hunched his shoulders, gathering his body as if he was going to propel himself out of the chair and launch himself on Leo.

Now, Julia decided, *before he goes out of control* . . .

Her voice cut across the tension. "You call me a bint, Mr. King. That's a wartime expression. It's Arabic, isn't it? You learned it in the Western Desert, didn't you? You were with Rommel's Afrika Corps. What did you do out there, Mr. King, that you've taken so much time and trouble to hide for all these years? Murder unarmed British prisoners?"

He had started by laughing, then he talked and talked, the truth flooding out in a tide neither Julia nor Leo could have stemmed. The vile and brutal truth about what he had done. Suddenly he stopped. He glared at them. Then he lurched at Leo, both fists upraised like hammers to strike at him. He was yelling. "I'm drunk. I'm drunk, and you did it . . . you spiked my drink with something. . . . I'll kill you."

Leo was quick on his feet; he sidestepped him easily, and impelled by his own weight, King crashed into the wall and almost fell. Leo had retreated to a safe distance, safe enough for him to gloat and shout back in defiance, "You bet I did. You've had half a bottle of vodka in that filthy pink muck, and you're pissed out of your skull! And you've opened your big mouth wide."

Hitting the wall had steadied King. He pulled himself upright and leaned against the door. He had told her everything. He'd talked and he couldn't stop himself. He was out of control, just like the night when he confessed to his wife, Phyllis Lowe, and pursued her upstairs to rape and beat her in a fury of rage and lust because he had betrayed himself.

The same with this woman, standing out of reach behind a sofa, that hideous hair flaming in the light. He had been unable to stop the flow of words, the rush of memories. He'd dragged her back with him into the past, back to the heat and sand-filled dust of the North African desert, as if she were a witness born out of her time.

Leo's voice taunted him. "You tried to ruin me, you rotten bastard. You set me up with your paid whore and sold the evidence to Western. But I've been bonking your daughter, and I've got some pretty pictures of my own now!"

"You'll pay for this," King shouted him down. "I'll make you pay—"

"You threaten me . . . " Leo jeered, "you try anything and I'll have the hotel throw you out! You're finished, bust. . . . We've got it all on tape!"

As he said it, Julia reached over and slipped the little tape recorder into her purse. King had blundered about like a maddened bear, and she had heard Leo shout at her, "Look out, Julia . . . " and sprung out of his way.

Just as abruptly, his strength seemed exhausted. He was breathing hard, glaring from one to the other of them. He held on to the door.

"You can't touch me," he said, and he seemed less than drunk. "You can't threaten me, either of you. I made the whole story up. There's nothing you can do to me. . . . I'm too powerful—I'm more powerful than God!" He drew himself upright. Then he wrenched the door open and stumbled out into the passage.

"Oh, my God," Julia said. She sank down onto the sofa. "My God," she repeated. "I feel completely gutted. I'm shaking all over."

"Well, I'm not," Leo exulted. "We got him. Between us we got the bastard. Come on, he's finished. I'll take the tape to the right quarters, and he'll be arrested as a war criminal. Christ, I'm going to order a bottle of champagne."

"Not for me," Julia said. "After that scene I couldn't celebrate anything."

Leo stared at her. "What's wrong with you? You should be dancing on the bloody table. You've got the evidence . . . a full confession. Everything you could have wanted. Let's switch on and run through it. Here, where's it gone?"

He was searching among the magazines on the table, peering down to see if it had fallen to the floor. "Where is it?" He swung around in alarm.

"I've got it," Julia said. "Leo, I'm sorry. I want to listen to it on my own. Then you can have it. We should get copies made as soon as possible. And make sure the original goes to the right people. We'll have to give affidavits swearing to its authenticity and in witness of what happened here. We haven't won yet. When he sobers up, he'll fight."

"Practical lady, aren't you?" he mocked her. "Very cool head. What do you have in your veins, antifreeze? Never mind, you go home and have a listen and I'll come around and pick it up later. Meantime I'm going to celebrate. I've just thought"—he stopped, and then he said—"I wonder if he had his driver tonight? Those roads up to his chalet are pretty tricky. . . . Now, that is a thought." And he laughed.

Julia stood up. "I'd rather he stood trial," she said quietly. "It's owed to all those people." She left without saying good night.

"I'm drunk," King said aloud to himself. "I'm drunk. I shouldn't be driving." They'd brought his car to the hotel entrance, and he'd managed to steer it out and onto the road. His vision wasn't clear and his reactions were muddled. He pulled in. He could wait, even sleep for a while till the booze wore off. He'd talked about himself. He'd lost control. But his God-like vision of himself insisted that he had nothing to fear. He could crush the pygmies with a gesture. He switched off the engine and wriggled down into the seat to get comfortable. Thoughts, wild and disconnected, danced like goblins in his mind when he closed his eyes, so he abandoned the idea of sleeping. He would rest, give his formidable system time to absorb the poison and dispel it. Then he would drive home. He switched on the radio; Swiss popular music assaulted his ears. He pushed the button several times at random till he found the BBC World Service. That was better. Listen to things of importance, events of moment. That was his world, his métier, not unimportant crap from an old war that nobody cared about anymore. Nothing could touch him; no law could reach him. He could buy immunity from anything. World issues were his concern. He opened the window an inch to let in some fresh air, and settled down to listen and sober up.

Julia went straight up to her room. She put the tape recorder on the table. The voices were clear. The opening gambit of her confrontation with him, "What did you do out there, Mr. King . . . ? Murder unarmed British prisoners . . . ?" How confident she sounded, how calm. No sign of the pounding heart, the feeling of apprehension.

"What do you have in your veins, antifreeze . . . ?" Leo Derwent had sneered at her. He wanted to savor his personal triumph. If King had dropped dead in the room, he'd have kicked the corpse. By the end Julia had felt numb. King, voice rising, accent thickening, jeering and insulting them, falling into the trap.

"What did you do out there, Mr. King, that you've taken so much time and trouble to hide for all these years?" And he had told her. The voice didn't sound slurred or the sequences confused. It was a strong voice, full of self-confidence and contempt.

"We were on patrol . . . armored cars. . . . We picked up one of our own men—he'd been taken prisoner and been left behind." Her own voice interrupting him. "What do you mean? You were the one they captured!" His brusque denial, "Me? No, I wouldn't have surrendered. I was a German soldier, by Christ! I wouldn't let the enemy piss on me! This was just a boy . . . he'd got a leg wound, no weapons. . . . But I didn't like him for putting his hands up. He told us where to find the British. We came on them, two officers, an NCO, and four men. They didn't even fight, yellow bastards. They put the officers in a truck, and then I laid into the kid, in front of the rest of them. I kicked his arse and told him he was a disgrace to the Corps. Nobody tried to stop me. I was tough. I scared them. They looked the other way. I got so angry with the kid . . . then he told me. He told me they were going to kill him. He knew a bit of English and he heard them talking. Going to stick him with a bayonet. Like a bloody pig." The angry voice filled the bedroom. She felt as if she might look up and see him standing there. Then her own tones, still deceptively calm and unemotional. "So what did you do, Mr. King?"

"I said to the boy, 'Don't you worry, forget I kicked you around a bit. I'll sort them out for you. And just you remember, you're a German soldier! You ever forget that and I'll kill you . . .' It was so hot. I remember, I'd got prickly heat in my crotch and under the arms. The itch was driving me crazy. We had some brandy in the scout car. One of us had pinched it off a dead officer. We made the British form up and marched them back toward our base. We went on ahead with our machine gun trained on them. Any move and that was it. . . . Their sergeant was leading them. And you know who he was, don't you? You found out when you went to Jersey, eh? William Western. Lord Western of Bradenham." His ugly laugh boomed out, "Peer of the realm, upholder of public morals . . . Wanting my hide just to save himself . . . You heard the story, didn't you?"

"Yes." Julia's answer. "I heard it. But I thought you were the prisoner they were going to kill." He wasn't listening to her, caught up in his own flow of words. "I watched them trudging through the sand, all set for a nice base prison camp and then back to Germany and out of the war, while we had to fight on and maybe die." He paused then. The tension had been broken suddenly by Leo Derwent. "So tell us, Harold, what did you do about it?"

"Do?" King sounded like a lion. "Do?" It was a roar, and it ended in a sharp German expletive. "*Scheisse!* I'll tell you what I did. I took over the machine gun and I started to play with it, swinging it from one to the other of them, making them sweat. Like the kid sweated when he was going to be stuck. . . . I had fun with them, real fun." Listening to the disembodied voice, Julia shuddered. "I called the kid, and he came to the back of the scout car and sat with me. I said, 'You know English? You tell them . . . you tell them I'm going to teach them to respect the rules of war. . . . You tell them that . . . ' And he did; I'd given him a few sucks at the bottle, and he was shouting at them. You know what happened? Western turned and ran like a fucking rabbit. Left his men and ran to save his own skin. So I gave him the first burst and dropped him. He hadn't got far. Then"—there had been a deliberate pause for dramatic effect—"Then I shot the rest of them. I just kept my finger on the trigger and went on firing, making them jump about on the ground. . . . Raised so much bloody dust, it got into my throat. . . . Then the stupid kid started to vomit. Perhaps it was the brandy or the corpses. I don't know, but he hung over the side of the car, puking his guts out." There was a breathless "Jesus" from Leo in the background.

King didn't notice. He went on, "But I made a mistake. I didn't stop the car and go and check. That shit was hit, but he was still alive. One of our patrols came along later and picked him up and took him to the hospital. I thought I was safe. I thought I'd killed them all. We were back at base when I heard about it, some talk about British casualties being caught in crossfire and only one survivor. In the very same place on the same day . . . I knew then it could mean trouble for me. When we lost the war, I knew it might mean big trouble. So I deserted, got myself in as a refugee. . . . Faked the whole story. . . . Clever, wasn't I? Poor stateless, homeless victim . . . I was so thin, I even looked the part. We hadn't eaten for days on end, grubbing for roots and berries like bloody animals. . . . Then the nice lady from UNRRA took pity. All she wanted was my hand up her skirt." His laughter rasped in Julia's ears. "Crossfire," he said. "He thought that up to hide his own stinking cowardice. Running off, leaving his own men. . . . I was the crossfire!"

She remembered so vividly, seeing him get to his feet, reaching the climax of his self-imposed performance. His harsh voice rising in exultation. "I killed them all," he shouted. "And you know something? I'm proud of it. . . . Proud. . . . I'd do it all again if I had the chance!"

Then her own voice broke in, a scream of loathing.

"You bloody murderer! You filthy, bloody murderer! You'll go to jail for the rest of your life. . . . You had Jean Adams murdered. . . ." And then she had broken down in a flood of tears. He had answered with surprising calmness, almost indifference.

"She asked for it. She was stupid. Stupid, meddling little bitch . . . " The next sound was a crash as he knocked a side table over and the splinter of glass as it crashed to the floor. She heard her own gasp and Leo's shout of warning "Look out" as he sprang to safety himself. Without warning Harold King had gone berserk. He had lashed out blindly and then launched himself at Leo Derwent, hurling himself into the wall. The tape played it all back to her, the shouting, Leo's taunting voice, the megalomania of that last boast as King was leaving.

"There's nothing you can do. . . . I'm too powerful. . . . I'm more powerful than God. . . ."

Julia switched off the machine. She felt sick and exhausted. The last piece of the jigsaw puzzle was in place, and the hideous story of cowardice, treachery, and evil was complete. She had been duped by William Western. He was a coward who had deserted his comrades and lied about their murder to protect himself. He'd lived with that betrayal, safely buried with the bones of his own men until his enemy and rival, Harold King, unearthed an ex-officer with a tender conscience living in retirement in Jersey.

Both were public figures; neither recognized each other after thirty years. That was the irony. Why should King connect a British infantry sergeant with the millionaire newspaper owner, Lord Western? Why should Western identify the mega-rich King with a drunken German sitting behind a machine gun?

When King went on trial, it would all come up. The two would be each other's Nemesis. Leo might drink champagne in triumph, but for Julia there were too many losers to warrant any celebration. King's description would haunt her for a very long time. Perhaps she would never get it out of her mind. "I just kept my finger on the trigger and went on firing, making them jump about on the ground. . . . So much bloody dust. . . ." Jean Adams, his casual dismissal: "She asked for it. . . . Stupid, meddling little bitch." She had died an obscene death. Poor, deluded Phyllis Lowe, in love for the first time. She had ended in a brain-damaged twilight. No, Julia thought, there was nothing to celebrate except that justice would be done to all of them at last. The shrill sound of the telephone made her jump. It was Leo Derwent. He sounded in high spirits and slightly drunk.

"Julia? Had a listen yet?"

"Yes," she said. "You can pick up the tape anytime you like now. I'm going to bed. I'll leave it downstairs for you."

"We won't be needing it," he said. "Get over here. The bastard's dead."

Gloria had been waiting for her father. She avoided the sitting room, where her mother was immersed in some mindless TV quiz show. The vacuity and banality of her mind amazed Gloria and made her furious with contempt. She read the financial papers in the study and tried not to watch the time and wonder what was happening with Leo.

He had been secretive and teasing with her, refusing to be drawn out when she asked him what it was he wanted to see King about . . . about her? In a way yes. . . . But why, why wouldn't he elaborate? Then the hints, the sly looks, and the hard, probing kiss with the injunction to open her mouth and stop talking. She switched on the big set, ranged through the channels, and found nothing to interest or distract her. If he did want to marry her, would she want to take such a big step? Leave home, commit herself to a man other than her father—leave that stupid woman with a clear sphere of influence? She havered, clinging on to Harold King, yearning for Leo at the same time. How late he was! Her own dilemma had made her forget that it was past their time for dinner together.

Nine o'clock. What were they discussing? What was happening? She reached for the telephone to call the Regent Hotel, when she heard the front door open. Immediately she sprang up and ran out into the hall. He was standing there, still in his heavy overcoat; he was so red in the face, so odd and unlike himself, that she hurried up and caught him by the arm.

"Daddy? Daddy, what's the matter—are you ill?"

He didn't answer. He just looked at her with bloodshot eyes, and put his free arm around her, drawing her close.

"What is it? Daddy, for God's sake . . . "

"I'm all right," he said. He sounded out of breath. "Just don't ask me any questions. Don't take any notice of me. Leave everything till the morning. You're my girl, and I love you."

He lifted her face up and kissed her on the forehead. He seemed unable to let go. She had never been so frightened as she was then. Not of him, but for him. It gave her unexpected strength. "I won't ask anything," she said. "Just come and sit down. You need a doctor. . . . You don't look at all well. Not at all well."

He let her guide him to the study, take off his coat, minister to him as if he were a big, helpless child. He sank into his favorite chair.

"I'll get Dr. Halperin," Gloria said, and moved to the telephone. He must have had a heart attack. She couldn't think what else it might be. That terrible red, purplish color, the labored breathing . . .

"No!" His voice was loud and rough, and it stopped

her. "No! I don't need a doctor. Leave that alone." She put down the telephone. He said slowly, "My darling girl, I didn't mean to shout at you. I'm not ill, believe me. Just get me a glass of water, will you? That's all, ice water."

She opened the cabinet where there was a supply of iced Perrier and soft drinks always on hand for him. She poured a glass, her hand unsteady, and hurried back with it.

"Here you are. Do you want anything else . . . anything to eat? It's so late for you. . . ." She had forgotten Leo Derwent. She thought only of him, in her terror that something was wrong and he wouldn't admit it.

"Nothing." He sounded breathless again. "Nothing to eat. There's nothing to worry about, silly girl. I'm not sick. I'm never sick, you know that. Just do as I say. Switch on the news, will you, and go out and leave me for a while. Leave me alone till I call you. And give me a kiss. I'm proud of you. Never forget that. Now, go on and don't worry about me. . . ."

She did as he told her; she switched on the set and gave him the remote control. She bent over and kissed him and went out, closing the door quietly.

Her mother came into the hallway. "Is he back? What happened? How did it go—?"

"He didn't say." Gloria cut her off. "He doesn't seem well, but he won't let me call Dr. Halperin. He wants to be left alone for a while. Don't go in. He doesn't want you!"

Marilyn shrugged. "No need to shout. I know his moods better than anyone. Look, I've told Monique to serve supper. She can't wait all night. I take it he's not eating with us?"

"No," Gloria snapped. "I asked him."

She looked backward at the closed door. She could just hear the faint murmur of the English television newscaster. Gloria's anxiety always expressed itself in hunger. She devoured potatoes, two omelets, and stuffed herself with the hot fresh rolls and butter. Her mother said to her at last, "You're such a pig, Gloria. You shouldn't eat so much." She gave her a look of malice. "Perhaps your father and Leo have had a row. Maybe you should go and see if he's all right?"

"He'll call me, he said so. Why don't you go? You never take any care of him. All you think about is yourself!"

Marilyn ignored that. "I think I'll have some fresh fruit. Oh, Monique, bring me some grapes and some of those nectarines. . . . they are ready, aren't they? Good. You want anything more, Gloria? . . . Chocolate torte, ice cream?"

"I hate you, Mother," Gloria said when the maid had gone.

"I know." The beautiful, smooth face was quite impassive. "You've never said that to me before. Why now, suddenly?"

"I'm going to see how my father is." Gloria stood up. She turned her back on Marilyn. The door to the study was open. The room was empty. The fire was low. The television set was blank, with the single red eye glowing below the screen.

The envelope with her name on it was propped on top of it where she couldn't fail to see it. Gloria picked it up. She felt a surge of panic standing in the empty room, opening a letter written to her by her father. He had fine handwriting, legacy of a teacher who expected a fine German Schrift and got it by the use of a sharpened ruler across his pupils' knuckles. The page was covered with his writing, but it sprawled, as if his hand was unsteady and the pen slipped between his fingers. She read it, mouthing the words.

My darling Daughter. Something has happened and you have got to be very brave. I employed a man called Joe Patrick. You may have seen him, he came to the house once or twice. He took care of problems for me. When you are Harold King, you need people like that. He has been arrested and charged with murder. I heard it on the car radio tonight. It's just been on the TV news. I gave him a special job to do, and he bungled it. He will implicate me. I'm not going to stand in a court and let them throw mud at me. My enemies would love it. So many people want to see me brought down. I won't give them that satisfaction. And you wouldn't want me to. I know that. So I write this letter to you because when it's written, I am going out and I won't be coming back. Everything is in order; you will want for nothing; your mother is well provided for. I saw Leo Derwent tonight. He tried to blackmail me with photographs of what you did together. You know what he is worth; you will know what to do when he comes back. He will, once I am gone. I have left you great power and all the money you can imagine. Use them as I would have done. You are part of me—I shall go on living through you. No one but you must read this letter. Destroy it. Always remember two things: You are my daughter, and I am your loving Daddy to the end.

Gloria knelt by the fire, poked at the smoldering logs until a little flame spurted, and then fed the letter to it till it blazed up briefly and then fell into ash.

She went on kneeling by the fire, not moving, not even able to weep. The world had come to an end. He had gone and he was never coming back. She was so chill and numb, she felt as if she had died with him. She didn't move till she heard the doorbell ringing, and then, after an interval, men's voices and her mother screaming. Slowly she raised herself, smoothed her dress, lifted her head, and went out to take control.

She packed her mother off to bed and summoned the

doctor, who gave her an injection. She was interviewed by the police officers in the sitting room. They were sympathetic and very tactful. Harold King's car had been found wrecked on the road to the valley below. He had driven straight into a tree and died instantly. Privately they remarked on her extreme composure. She didn't shed a tear. She turned her pale eyes on them and just nodded and said, "It must have been a heart attack." And dared them to question that solution.

There would be an inquest, all very unfortunate and distressing for her and her mother, but of course the Swiss authorities would make the ordeal as easy for them as possible. She thanked them gravely, and ended the interview by standing up and walking to the door with them. Then she summoned the staff. They gathered around her in the hall, headed by the housekeeper. She was an upright, austere German Swiss who had been with them for ten years. Gloria addressed them.

They looked shocked and subdued; they had felt secure in King's tyranny. Without it they were uneasy. Gloria said, "You must know by now that my father died in a motor accident tonight. When this is known, the media will come here, and we will be under siege. They will turn my father's death into a circus. If anyone of you, or any member of your families, is induced to speak to anyone about this, you will be instantly dismissed without a reference. And I will make certain that no one else in Gstaad ever employs you. My mother is in shock. I won't be taking any calls or receiving any visitors. Without exception. Nobody is to be allowed in. Is that understood?"

The housekeeper took a step forward. "It's understood, Fräulein Gloria. You can be certain of our loyalty to you and to Frau King. We are all very shocked by this terrible thing that has happened."

"Thank you," Gloria said. "You will be glad to know that it was instantaneous. My father didn't suffer. Good night."

One by one they filed past her and went through the service door to their own quarters. She put the lights out and locked the doors herself. Then she went upstairs to her own room. She was alone. She would always be alone from now on. The tears began to stream down her face.

Ben had taken Lucy to Euston. On the platform she hugged him. "Thanks for everything. You've been great to me. Everyone has. And you will come up and see me, won't you?"

"Don't worry," he assured her. "I'm not losing you a second time. Give my best to your mother. Call me in a day or two. I'll be at the hotel till I get myself a rented flat."

Lucy held on to his arm. "Dad . . . don't lose Julia, will you? She's pretty special. Don't make the same mistake again. . . . Like you did with Mum."

That surprised him. He said, "What do you mean?"

"Being too proud to make up. Mum would have gone back if only you'd got in touch. She's happy enough now, but she was miserable for a long time. Don't mind me saying it, will you?"

Ben put his arms around her. "I don't mind. I'm just sorry I screwed up on all of you. You'd better go, sweetheart— find yourself a decent seat. And don't forget to call."

"I won't." She smiled at him and paused on the step of the carriage to wave. "'Bye, Dad. Don't screw up a second time!"

He turned and walked down the platform and into the body of the station. A muffled announcement about a train departure boomed out over the loudspeakers. He thought it might as well have been Swahili, it was so indistinct. As he came out into the street, he saw the huge headlines on the *Evening Standard* billboard: HAROLD KING DEAD. He stopped, stared, then rushed to buy the newspaper. More headlines, splashed across the front page: MYSTERY OF TYCOON'S DEATH. FATAL CAR CRASH AT SWISS HOLIDAY RESORT. Ben read it through at speed, only too familiar with the news format. It was unbelievable. King was dead, killed in his car in an unexplained drive from his chalet down twisting roads at night. The information was still sketchy, so speculation was passed on as news. A probable heart attack. His wife and daughter were flying back to England. They were refusing to make any statement. He got into his car and listened to a newsflash. It had a slightly more slanted angle than the newspaper story.

It was reported that the financier and publishing magnate had been seen leaving the Regent Hotel shortly after eight o'clock in a distressed state. Distressed, Harold King. . . . It was newspeak for a variety of conditions. He couldn't imagine which one it could be. When he got back to his hotel room, there was a message for him.

A Miss Julia Hamilton had called from a Swiss telephone number. What had she done? She and Felix. . . . What part had they played in this incredible development? Or had fate intervened to settle it for them? He felt sick with jealousy. He banished Lucy's parting words in angry denial. Julia had broken faith with him, turned for support to another man, put her crusade above their relationship. . . . He wasn't going to call that number. Or take a call from her if she tried again. He dialed reception and said, "I'm not accepting any calls from Switzerland," and the girl said, "There's a call on the line for you now, Mr. Harris. A Mr. Sutton . . . Shall I have the switchboard put him through?"

"Yes," Ben said quickly. "I'll talk to him. . . ."

He heard Felix's cheerful voice. "Are you opening a bottle?"

"Aren't you?" Ben demanded aggressively.

"Bloody amazing, isn't it?" Felix went on blithely. "Bet Julia's over the moon."

"You tell me," Ben snapped at him.

There was a pause, and then Felix said, "What's that supposed to mean? What's going on? I just rang up to share the glad tidings. . . ."

"She's out in Gstaad," Ben said slowly. "I thought you were with her."

"Me? I'm in bloody London, in the office. . . . Are you off your trolley?"

Ben took a breath and said, "Not now, but I was. . . . Sorry, Felix. What's the word in the office? Was it an accident? What was all that about him being distressed when he left the hotel?"

"About as distressed as a bull elephant," Felix retorted. "Rumor going around is he was pissed . . . staggering."

"He was a teetotaler . . . never touched booze. . . ."

"Well, it sounds like he broke the golden rule last night," Felix answered. "Maybe the arrest of that little sleaze bag Joe Patrick had something to do with it. . . . He's been charged with murder—that old widow Julia was so worked up about. All happened within hours: His legman gets picked up, he gets boozed and runs into a tree. Why aren't you at the hot spot? What's Julia doing out there on her own? And why the hell did you think I was with her?"

Ben said, "Why don't we open that bottle together? If you don't mind drinking with a bloody fool."

Felix Sutton laughed. "I'll drink with anyone so long as they're paying. See you around seven." He hung up.

Joe Patrick had been arrested for Jean Adams's murder.

Ben had been occupied with taking Lucy out to a film and giving her dinner on their last evening together. He hadn't switched on a TV set or opened a newspaper that morning because she was catching an early train. He had missed out on it all till he saw those flaring headlines outside the station.

He switched on the set in time for the twelve forty-five news bulletin on ITV. It was the lead item. There were clips of Harold King, comments by media experts, and then, staring at him from the screen, William Western.

"A remarkable figure in the world of publishing and communication," the precise voice intoned, the expression suitably grave. "We had differences of opinion about a great many issues, but his energy and abilities earned the respect of everyone in the media. His contribution to our industry will be greatly missed."

"Christ Almighty," Ben exploded. He snapped the control to Off, fading that calculating, lying image into darkness.

Then he picked up the telephone and asked for a call to Switzerland.

"I didn't think you'd forgive me," Julia said. "I didn't expect you to. . . ."

"I didn't think I would either. When does your flight get in?"

"Six o'clock, your time. Ben, I can't wait to get away from here and get home. Are you sure you want to come and meet me? I've got so much to tell you. . . . I've got a tape of the whole thing. I wish I felt happy about it, but somehow it's left such a filthy taste. . . . I had to do it. I had to follow it through. Please try to understand. . . . I tried to explain in my letter."

"I know," he said. "We'll talk about that later. I'm glad about one thing. Jean Adams."

"That's the best part," Julia said slowly. "It helps to make sense of the whole dreadful nightmare. Oh, Ben—I do want to talk to you . . . tell you . . . "

Ben Harris said, "We've got a lot to talk over, Julia. I'll see you at six."

"You came over beautifully, Billy," Evelyn Western said. "Just the right balance. Dignified, generous . . . Oh, what a wonderful relief!"

He held her hand under the table. They were lunching at the Connaught. She looked so animated and beautiful, he was proud to show her off.

He felt twenty years younger. He kept smiling all the time. "Word is," he told her, "he committed suicide. There's a lot of rumors flying about. . . . He seemed to be drunk when he left the hotel. There was a time lag unaccounted for when he came home and then went out again. And that Irishman being charged with Jean Adams's murder on the very same night. . . . I think he realized the game was up, and he killed himself. Well, my darling, here's to him. I only hope hell's hot enough!"

They lifted their glasses of champagne and drank the toast together. Evelyn Western said gently, "You've nothing to worry about anymore. It's all over."

William Western looked at her. "If you wanted a quiet life, Evie, you shouldn't have married me. Hasn't it occurred to you that there's nobody there to pick up the pieces? He only had that daughter. I think the whole thing will be up for grabs. And I'm going to take the first handful."

"Knowing you," his wife said calmly, "you'll take it all."

• • •

"Julia—I thought you were in Switzerland?"

"Felix . . . how are you?"

"Pissed off; Harris asked me around to the hotel for a drink and never turned up. I had to pay for my own. What the hell happened?"

"He came to the airport to fetch me and forgot," she said. "He's here. Do you want to talk to him?"

"No, I don't want to disturb the reunion. Just tell him he owes me."

"I will," she promised. "And, Felix . . . we're getting married. You'll have to come." She looked across at Ben Harris. "He says the cat went on hunger strike when I left, that's why he asked me."

She heard Felix laugh. "Sooner you than me. But good luck, anyway. You won't be asking for your old job back?"

"I'm quitting journalism. I've got a book to write and a man with a cat to look after. I'll let you know the time and the place."

Ben Harris came and took the telephone away from her. She reached up to him and said, "I'm so happy."

He said before he kissed her, "So am I."

It was strange, they admitted, how well she filled her father's chair at the head of the boardroom table. Nothing had been changed in his office except that the portrait of him that used to hang in that same boardroom now hung on the wall opposite his desk, where Gloria King could see it. There were six men sitting there, grouped at one end. The finance director, the deputy chairman of a major London merchant bank, and a director of Field who had flown in from New York. The company secretary had been Harold King's employee for twenty years. King had trusted him, and bound him to loyalty with share options. There were two other directors present, both seasoned King employees. The principal board meeting would follow in a week's time, followed by an Extraordinary General Meeting of the shareholders. This had been postponed till after the funeral as a mark of respect. The inquest had revealed that Harold King had a high alcohol content in his blood, and the verdict was accidental death. Over two million pounds in life insurance had been claimed for his estate.

Gloria sipped from the same carafe of ice water he had used, and spoke to them. "I'm grateful to all of you for your support," she said. "It's been a sad and difficult time for my mother and me. But it's over, and my father is at rest. He's left me a daunting legacy—everything he built up and achieved, his plans for the future of one of the biggest and most powerful communications networks in Europe. And he had already involved me in his plans for that future.

"I want you all to know that I am Harold King's daughter, and I shall do what he would have done if he were still alive. We have the money and the means. We will proceed with the bid for Western International and the *Sunday Herald*. That will be announced at the Extraordinary General Meeting.

"Thank you, gentlemen."

She got up, and one by one they shook hands and left. She said quietly to the company secretary, "A word with you, Ken," and he stayed behind. She said, "I want a top-class defense lawyer for Joe Patrick. I owe it out of loyalty for work he did for my father. On condition that my father's name is not mentioned during the trial and anything he may have said in his statement to the police is withdrawn."

"That can be arranged, Miss King. I know just the QC for the job."

"Good," Gloria said bleakly. "And one more thing.

There's a junior minister called Leo Derwent, Department of Trade and Industry. My father didn't trust him. We should bear that in mind when it comes to political editorials."

He said blandly, "I'll make sure that message gets across. Anything else?"

"No," she said. "Nothing else. You can go now."

"Good afternoon, Miss King."

He paused, but she didn't answer. When a meeting was over, Harold King had never bothered with good-byes.